T

"You must want a kiss," Harriet said.

Benedict did not move and Harriet's smile began to fade.

"Mr. Bradbourne?"

"Benedict." His attention dropped at the movement of her tongue and he took a step toward her.

Harriet was certain her heart had stopped. She could not move her limbs, could not convince herself that she really wanted to move away. "Benedict?"

"Yes," he said, "I do want a kiss."

He was so close she could feel his breath against her lips, but he moved no further. His gaze held hers, almost black and stark with an emotion she could not remember ever being directed toward her before. Harriet's hands trembled as they lifted and she reached for Benedict's shoulders. His jaw flexed and she could make out a shadow around the lower half of his face where his morning beard was coming in.

Harriet closed her eyes and kissed him . . .

BOOK YOUR PLACE ON OUR WEBSITE AND MAKE THE READING CONNECTION!

We've created a customized website just for our very special readers, where you can get the inside scoop on everything that's going on with Zebra, Pinnacle and Kensington books.

When you come online, you'll have the exciting opportunity to:

- View covers of upcoming books
- Read sample chapters
- Learn about our future publishing schedule (listed by publication month *and author*)
- Find out when your favorite authors will be visiting a city near you
- Search for and order backlist books from our online catalog
- Check out author bios and background information
- Send e-mail to your favorite authors
- Meet the Kensington staff online
- Join us in weekly chats with authors, readers and other guests
- Get writing guidelines
- AND MUCH MORE!

Visit our website at
http://www.kensingtonbooks.com

DARK WHISPERS

Samantha Garver

ZEBRA BOOKS
Kensington Publishing Corp.
www.kensingtonbooks.com

ZEBRA BOOKS are published by

Kensington Publishing Corp.
850 Third Avenue
New York, NY 10022

All Kensington titles, imprints, and distributed lines are available
at special quantity discounts for bulk purchases for sales promo-
tion, premiums, fund-raising, educational, or institutional use.

Special book excerpts or customized printings can also be created to fit specific needs. For details, write or phone the office
of the Kensington Special Sales Manager: Attn. Special Sales
Department. Kensington Publishing Corp., 850 Third Avenue,
New York, NY 10022. Phone: 1-800-221-2647.

Zebra and the Z logo Reg. U.S. Pat. & TM Off.

First Printing: December 2006
10 9 8 7 6 5 4 3 2 1

Printed in the United States of America

Prologue

The pirate saw it evident in the delicate curves of her face, those ink-black eyes, and knew the precise moment he broke her heart. Despite the fury that gripped his insides in an icy fist, tightening as she blatantly refused to deny his accusations, her anguish hit Rochester with the force of a physical blow. She remained motionless; not even a whisper of sound came from her skirts. The dark ringlets of her hair lay silently against her shoulders. It was enough to fuel the fires of his wrath further.

"How could you think such a thing of me?" She finally spoke, her onyx gaze fixed on her husband only a step above.

"Deny it then." He reached for her wrist, the fine bones meager in his large hand, and he knew his grip was painful. "Damn it all, Annabelle. The entire village is laughing at me as you carry on behind my back. Tell me what you have been doing roving about in the shadows with that man!"

Her eyes betrayed despair behind a shimmering wall of tears before she dropped her gaze to the wooden stairs between them. "You cannot let it be, can you?" Her whisper bore a sorrow that made the dark of the stairwell desolate. "Your suspicion has consumed your soul and you refuse to trust anyone." She looked up at him through her lashes, great tears rolling down her cheeks. "Not even the one who loves you more than anything in this world."

"I had you followed, Annabelle," Rochester said through his teeth. "I was told you spent more than one afternoon in his company. Always after telling me you were going elsewhere."

The sound that erupted from her throat was a bitter semblance of laughter. She tugged on her wrist. "Let me go."

"You are my wife."

"I'll not tolerate your treating me this way. You've been made an easy mark for those resentful villagers who manipulate you with their embellished tales, if not flagrant lies." She put all her weight into pulling at his grip. "Let me go."

It was unexpected. His hold was firm, but she fisted her hand and gave her arm a twist. The moment she broke free, the sudden chill of awareness washed over Rochester. He felt the slap of dreadful premonition at the same time he met her eye and saw the understanding reflected in her gaze.

Her fall was graceful. Her feet never touched a stair. Silken skirts rustling melodically against the backs of her legs, her hair lifted as she plummeted toward the ground. Her arms spread out, one hand reaching for the rail but never making contact with the wood.

"Warren." His name parted her lips without question, with no particular tone. As if she were only breathing it to do so.

"No!" He was already moving down the stairs, running at a haste that put his own life in danger.

Even as he followed Annabelle down, he knew he was too late.

She hit the small table at the foot of the stairs, the half-burned taper atop it toppling to the floor. The candle flame caught the thick Persian rug, the same on which Annabelle landed with a hollow thud. There was a faint snap as the fragile bones of her neck broke.

Warren landed on his knees beside her, drawing his wife's limp body into his arms. Her eyes, vacant and wide, were at odds with the warmth that still clung to her body. Flames rose around them; Warren could feel them closing in and catching his shirt. He ignored the pain, the scent of burning flesh. Holding her to his chest, the pirate waited for the fire to consume them both.

1

The apartment was filled with the muted sounds of sobbing, the air thick with grim awareness. Disbelief had departed only a short while before, leaving behind quiet shock and sorrow.

The door opened without a knock and with no surprise the family in the front room looked at the man who entered. He was one of them, if not by birth, then by the friendship that bordered on that of a father and son with the man behind the closed door down the hall.

Wilhemina Ferguson managed a small smile as she disentangled herself from the two grandchildren clinging to her skirts. She used one hand to brush back the tangled gray hair that had come undone from its knot and held out the other to the newcomer.

"Benedict."

Horror unlike any he had ever felt burned inside Benedict Bradbourne. It had begun pounding at his insides since Wilhemina's oldest son had come for him. He refused to look at the others in the room, loathed seeing the faces of the children and grandchildren so haggard with loss. He did not take Wilhemina's hand when she touched the back of his. Her fingertips were so cold he chose to ignore them as he did her children's grief.

"Where is he?"

"Our bedchamber. It shan't be long." Her eyes suddenly filled with tears and she pressed a closed fist to her mouth. In a moment she composed herself to say, "I think he's been waiting for you."

Benedict had to control the workings of his throat as he strode down the hall that seemed longer than it had ever been before. He paused outside the closed door and squeezed his eyes tightly closed. Images of Garfield Ferguson played across his mind's eye: those of him as a middle-aged man welcoming young Benedict and his siblings into his home, laughing through a mouthful of fish and chips, and cupping Benedict's shoulder with a rough palm as the adolescent told of his mother's death and recounted the trials of keeping what was left of his family together despite an unstable and often jailed father. As the man's fiery hair became tinged with gray and Benedict developed the strong shoulders and independence of manhood, the images contorted to those of the two men crouching down behind an overturned wheelbarrow, Benedict keeping a band of thieves occupied with erratic bursts from his pistol as his mentor crept through the back door of the jeweler's shop and then charged at the three like a rampaging bull—taking the crooks down just that easy. When those exciting memories gave way to thoughts of the pride in the old man's eye when Benedict had his first commendation pinned to the front of his uniform, the earnestness as he insisted the younger man take part of his wages to care for his sisters— money the young man knew Ferguson could use for his own family—the man in the hall let his eyes open immediately to make the memories disappear.

The door opened into a silent room. Only one candle was lit, sending off brief flickers of light from the table near an opened window. Ferguson was a great mountain beneath the bedclothes, mostly in shadows. Benedict's gaze focused immediately on the man's large chest, and it took so long for it to rise and fall that the younger man began to worry he was too late.

Then Garfield said, his voice uncharacteristically weak, "Donna' beat all, lad?" His brogue was worse than usual and Benedict doubted a man not from his home country would even understand the other. "All these years a tackling crooks and playing with me pistol an' I git done-in by a footpad."

Benedict approached the bed, sat stiffly in the chair still warm from Ferguson's wife. The old man was pale, his skin the same color as the thick mustache and beard covering a good portion of his face. Benedict scanned his longtime friend, starting at his balding head and moving downward. A muscle in his jaw went taut when he saw the dark stain spreading across the blankets over the lower part of Ferguson's belly.

"Knife wot got me." Being at death's door did not dampen the man's ability to read the other's mind. "A dagger or sheave mayhap."

"Where?"

"Not far from the office. I didna' even see 'im comin'."

Benedict saw Ferguson frown, his heavy brows drawing together. His eyes darted across the ceiling as if searching for something.

The younger man looked at the floor between his

feet then lifted his gaze to the hand lying limp atop the bedclothes. He reached for it.

"Thank you," he said. "For everything you've done for my family."

Ferguson coughed and laughed at the same time. "Ye did well by yer sisters, especially considering what ye come from. Ye would have done it even without an old codger like me in yer life." The old man sighed. "I am proud to have known ye."

Benedict met the other man's eye. "You are my best friend."

"An' yer mine." Benedict watched with a clenched jaw as a tear streamed down from the corner of Ferguson's eye and into the pillow beneath him. When the younger man looked up again, his eyes were closed.

Benedict sat for a long moment with his teeth pressed tightly together before he removed his specs and brushed angrily at his eyelids with the heel of his hand. He was rising from the chair to tell Wilhemina her husband was gone when a fiercely strong hand reached out and grabbed his coat.

Benedict's gaze flew to Ferguson's face and he saw with surprised wonder that the old man's eyes were opened wide and brilliantly cognizant. It was a familiar expression. The same Ferguson wore every time he understood the working of a crime, the sudden realization that brought a series of events together.

His head turned and he said to Benedict, "The watch. The bastard was after me watch."

2

It was late, almost closing time, when the stranger entered the shop. He was tall, had a good two feet on the man standing behind the counter, counting up his sales for the day. He blended almost entirely with the dark outside until the door swung closed behind him—clad in black breeches and stockings, a long black coat, with a heavy scarf draped across the lower half of his face. A tricorn hat was pulled low over his brow and the newcomer made no move to remove it indoors, though he did touch its brim when passing the woman who had been perusing the books of poetry stacked on a far table. The heavy metal braces that encased the woman's legs made a nerve-wracking creak as she turned to inspect another set of books.

The man behind the counter winced impatiently at the sound before saying, "Good evening, sir." Green-brown eyes shifted in his direction. "The name is Christian. Welcome to my store."

The stranger said nothing, but walked on quiet heels toward the counter. He had a stiff gait, keeping his shoulders square and his arms straight at his sides.

"I don't believe we've done business before." Christian

tilted his head upward, squinting in an effort to make out anything besides the other man's pale cheeks and straight nose.

The stranger shook his head and cleared his throat. "I'm looking for a book."

"You've come to the right place, my good man."

"I shall be the judge of that." The stranger's voice was low in his throat, nearly inaudible behind the wool of his scarf. His gaze roamed the walls lined with books, the lids of one eye drawn slightly together. "It is a volume by a Madame Winifred Lacey."

"Ah . . ." Christian grinned. "The notorious *Book for Lovers*."

"You have it, then."

"Oh, yes. One copy left in the back. I keep it hidden so as not to alarm those with fragile faculties." He nodded in the direction of the woman who had opened a volume of poems. Christian leaned over the counter and whispered, "Man to man, I've read Madame Lacey's book and sorely wish my own wife was capable of perusing a few pages without having a fit of the vapors. She could learn a thing or two about doing more than laying stiff between the sheets." Christian laughed.

The stranger did not and the bookseller sobered quickly.

"I'll get the book then."

"Do."

When the proprietor of the bookstore disappeared into the back room, the woman who had been looking at the poetry books without really seeing any of them lifted her gaze. The stranger at the counter turned to meet her eye.

The woman with the poetry books couldn't help it.

She forced her attention toward the table and lifted a palm to stifle a laugh.

"Would you believe a woman was in here earlier today," Christian huffed as he reappeared at the counter, "with the audacity to try to buy this book?"

"Is that so?" The stranger accepted the book with slim fingers encased in black leather gloves.

"Mrs. Emily Paxton, if you can believe that." Christian had no eyebrows, so it was the pink skin of his forehead that bobbed up and down. "The Queen of Ice herself." He did not see the stranger's hand falter in removing a purse, nor the drawing together of tawny brows. "I did not give her the book, of course. I don't give a bloody damn about her reputation as a ball-breaker or how much money she had to offer. A book like this is not meant for the eyes of a woman."

The stranger ran a gloved finger over the elegant script engraved into the book cover, the name of the author. The fact she was a woman had somehow escaped the book vendor's notice.

"It just isn't suitable for women's eyes. Their constitutions are too weak, you know."

The stranger only stared at Christian.

The woman who had been at the poetry table moved slowly, fluidly despite the braces encumbering her legs, toward the exit.

The stranger in dark clothes almost made it to the door where the woman was tugging on her gloves before the silence was broken.

Christian watched the man come to a halt, saw the woman at the door glance backward with a worried little frown. Then the stranger's head turned toward Christian. His eyelids were drawn together as he stared at the shopkeeper.

"Your wife may be the one to benefit, Mr. Christian."

"I beg your pardon?"

"From your perusal of Madame Lacey's infamous book. Perhaps it is not her fault, you see, she is so lack-luster beneath your sheets." The stranger's eyes crinkled at their corners, as if he were smiling.

The two women sat in companionable silence as darkness crept up to the open terrace. The outside nook of the elegant café would have been crowded were it not so close to winter. As it were, there was a distinctive chill in the air and a slight breeze that played about the hems of the women's skirts, as if toying with the idea of creeping underneath.

The two offered the oncoming stranger a brief glance, both noting his dark attire and the scarf that fluttered about his neck and over the lower half of his face. They might have dismissed the individual in the black stockings and breeches at that single look were it not for the large book he carried against one thigh.

Emily Paxton and Isabel Scott were struck with incredulity at the same moment, though Isabel showed hers in a shocked gasp and the other woman in only a slight lift to one sable brow.

"What's a pair of beautiful ladies like yourselves doing out alone at night?" Familiar eyes sparked with mirth above the scarf.

"Harriet!" Isabel hissed, eyes wide as she took in the trousers that fit snug to the other woman's legs.

Harriet removed her hat as she dipped into a bow. "At your service."

Isabel rushed to her feet, pushing her spectacles up higher on her nose as she scanned their surroundings. Theirs was the only outside table occupied, but the inner clientele of the restaurant was visible. With an emotion akin to horror, she eyed the aging dowagers in their layered pearls and the plump gentlemen that accompanied them.

"What on earth are you about?" She did not look at Harriet as she lectured through her teeth. "You will be ruined if anyone sees you like this."

Harriet felt the edges of her mouth curl even higher. She was touched that her friend thought that a woman who barely had enough funds to survive was so significant to London society.

"I should think no one will even bother looking this way," Emily said between calm sips of tea, "unless you continue making a scene, Isabel."

The other woman flushed and shifted back toward her chair.

Harriet gallantly pulled it toward her.

Isabel, appearing utterly nonplussed, swallowed deeply from her glass of lemonade.

Emily turned toward the woman dressed as a man as she took her own seat. "We took the liberty of ordering you a tea with a dollop of cream."

"And brandy?" Harriet reached for the delicate cup.

"And brandy." Emily nodded once.

"Thank you."

Isabel carefully set her glass atop the pale linen tablecloth. She peered at the woman in the tricorn hat over the rims of her specs. "Harriet."

"Isabel."

"Would you kindly explain why you are walking about London in men's breeches?"

"I'd have thought you knew." Harriet noticed the plate of scones at the middle of the table. "Emily said she was certain Mr. Christian would not deal with a woman on a matter of business, especially not concerning a novel reported to go into details of sexual acts. I knew I had to do something extraordinary to obtain the book Lady deVane so kindly prepaid us to obtain for her. Especially if the piggish man would not give over to Emily, a force to be reckoned with."

"Thank you," Emily said. Though her lips moved only to form the words and her features were impenetrable, her eyes glimmered. She pushed the plate of scones nearer to Harriet.

"So you dressed like a man," Isabel was saying, "pretended to *be* a man to deal with Christian?"

"Exactly."

Isabel gaped at Harriet and then Emily. She shook her head when she realized neither woman grasped the oddness of their situation.

"You acquired the book," Emily said.

Harriet, still chewing a sweet date scone, dropped the pastry onto her plate and lifted the book from her lap.

"Well-done, Harriet." Emily removed a square of white cloth from her reticule and proceeded to wrap the book carefully in it. When passing on a book of sexual tales to an aging duchess, a little decorum was to be expected.

"Not to be a prude"—Isabel was frowning now, well aware she was a prude and unconcerned over the matter—"but I cannot imagine what might have happened had you been found out."

"I'd like as not be thought a lunatic." Harriet rolled her eyes in an imitation of madness.

"Do not make me laugh, Harriet." Isabel smoothly changed her giggle into a muffled cough. "I am upset."

Emily's brows drew together. "Isabel is right. It was dangerous for you to go alone."

"I wasn't alone," Harriet explained. "Abigail accompanied me."

"Excellent." Emily was appeased.

Isabel, still wide-eyed, downed the last of her lemonade in one swallow. It was the closest she ever came to hard drinking.

Harriet, who had already finished her tea, set her cup aside and forced herself to push away the last of the scones. "I thought you were to meet with the duchess in Hyde Park. Why did your note say to come here?"

"A man was attacked a few days ago while walking the park."

Isabel sputtered, lifting a napkin to her mouth to stifle the sound as her eyes watered.

Emily was removing another book from a bag that had been sitting beneath the table. "It was a bungled robbery, I'm sure. Still, I did not want anyone going near the place at night."

Harriet watched Emily as she flipped through the pages of the book then set it atop the table. She wondered if Mr. Christian or anyone else who dared to call her the Queen of Ice behind her back knew how she watched over her friends. Emily looked up and caught her stare.

"Happy birthday, Harriet."

The other woman blinked in the shadows of her hat brim. Her gaze dropped to the book being pushed her way. It was the latest novel by Randal C. Shoop, her favorite author of tales of unhappy spirits and their desperate pursuits of revenge from beyond the grave.

"My birthday was yesterday." She reached for the book, eager already to read the third story in a series about a dashing ghost hunter who solved the crimes of those dead and buried.

"We regret we couldn't have been with you and

Augusta to celebrate." Isabel momentarily forgot the fact her friend was wearing trousers.

"We had a wonderful time by ourselves." Harriet spoke fondly of the woman with whom she had lived for the last four years. "We went to a play, though I think her Mr. Darcy purchased our tickets. Abigail was at the town house on our return. She gave me a lovely valise and Augusta had wrapped together a very nice journal and a set of quills." Harriet accepted both gifts with delight, though she never traveled and had nothing so interesting in her life occur that she felt the need to record it in a diary.

"All that and a book assured to be a good read." Harriet grinned, lifting the book off the table. "What more could I ask for?"

A small envelope fell from between the pages and into her lap.

When her brows drew together in puzzlement, Emily spoke, looking as if she were holding back a smile. "There is more, Harriet. We were to have given it to you with the valise and quills, but it hadn't yet arrived."

"I can imagine"—Isabel giggled—"Abby and Augusta were quite worried that you would not understand their gifts."

Setting the book aside, Harriet opened the envelope and removed from it parchment as thin as onion peel. The writing across the paper was in great swirls and elegant curves.

"It is a letter welcoming you to the estate of the widow Lady Dorthea Cruchely."

"It took," Emily said as Harriet skimmed the letter, "quite an investigation to find for you the best sort of haunt.

"After much consideration we decided this would be the best place to enjoy your holiday. If the spirits rumored to visit the place do not make an appearance, at least you will have a chance to enjoy the countryside. I personally made certain those individuals also partaking in Lady Cruchely's peculiar brand of entertainment would be as respectable as yourself."

"Thank you very much." Harriet smiled politely.

"You've no idea what we're talking about, do you?" Emily asked.

"You're sending me away?"

The corner of Emily's normally straight mouth twitched again. She signaled the server for more drinks before speaking. "Dorthea Cruchely allows visitors to her estate on a semi-annual basis. It is more than rumored that those permitted to be present to see them are engaged in the company of specters, spirits, and the like. At, of course, a minimal fee."

Isabel smiled politely as the server took away their empty glasses and cups before leaning in close to whisper, "The estate is said to be the most haunted in all of England. Apparently many souls have yet to be laid to rest about the manor."

"The gift is from all of us, Harriet," Emily said. "Even Isabel contributed."

"In truth," Isabel admitted gravely, "I've always worried about your interest in those awful tales of murder and mayhem and spirits from beyond the grave." She brightened. "But that is only my opinion."

"Well, that means a lot." Harriet was forced to press her lips together to keep from laughing out loud. "So this explains the valise and journal."

"We did not think you had a bag and it was Augusta's idea that you might like to record your adventures on paper."

Harriet looked from her friends to the paper still open in her lap and felt her heart flutter strangely in her chest. How different her life would have been if she had never met the other owners of the Precious Volumes Book Shoppe. Her voice was uncharacteristically solemn as she said, "This is the nicest gift anyone has ever given me."

"Then it is fitting," Emily said, "because you are one of the nicest women I've ever known." She did not smile as she reached for her cup.

Harriet, who once held in her possession a naked statuette of a woman and riffled through men's undergarments without hesitation, flushed bright pink at the compliment.

3

"Benedict!"

It had been a long time since he'd heard his name shouted in such a manner. On the occasions before, it had most often been to call him in for dinner or to enlist his support in extracting the children from some sort of mischief their mother could not handle. Though that had been more than ten years before, he knew as he paused stepping into the carriage it was Wilhemina Ferguson calling to him.

He peered down the lane and saw her running, a large basket bouncing against her middle and one of her youngest grandchildren clinging to the back of her skirts. Whereas the aged woman had sweat-dampened features, the tot wore some sort of chocolate ooze down her chin and across her cheeks.

"I was afraid"—Wilhemina came to a breathless stop—"I would not make it in time."

"Is something wrong?" Benedict stepped down from the carriage steps.

"No. I only wanted to bring you a few provisions for your journey."

Provisions, Benedict knew, to the Ferguson family

included great amounts of sugar and spices and other delicacies reserved for special occasions. It was perhaps one of the reasons he could chase down a thief in the time it had taken Garfield to run less than a dozen steps and have to stop, gripping his knees and wheezing.

"I had some." The child had released her grandmother's skirts, leaving behind brown handprints that matched the smudges on her dress.

"I didn't know you were leaving town until this morning," Wilhemina continued, "so I didn't have much time to bake. There's a meat pie or two, some fruit, and chocolate scones."

"I had some of those!" The child beamed, exposing teeth and tongue coated in a thick layer of goop.

"I can see that, Phoebe," Benedict said.

"Phoebe"—Wilhemina pointed to a hedge in front of Benedict's town house—"is that a particularly green and slimy frog over there?"

The girl's blue eyes went wide with joy and she dashed over to the shrubbery, dropping to her knees with as little concern for decorum as she had for keeping tidy.

"Now, then." Wilhemina lowered her voice, pressing the basket into Benedict's hands. "Are you certain this is what you must do?"

Benedict nearly dropped the basket, not expecting it to weigh almost as much as the woman who had carried it from her home to his. "I have nothing else," he said.

She looked at him, thin pink lips pursed. "I worry about you going alone. What if you do find something that pertains to Garfield's death?"

"Don't worry." He said the words he had heard Garfield say to his wife a hundred times before.

She made a face then shook her head. "Benedict, I sincerely hope you do not find anything at that estate. I hope you spend the next week or so lounging in bed until well past dawn and staying up late playing cards with a gent or two." She reached up with a weathered hand and touched his cheek. "Garfield would want you to be happy, not spend all your free time searching for whomever took him from us."

"This is the last link I have to that bloody watch." He spoke through his teeth, though his anger was not directed at the woman who was like a mother to him. "I cannot ignore it and let a killer get away."

"I know," Wilhemina whispered, and dropped her chin to stare at the ground. "I so wish you had better things than murder to occupy your mind." She looked up at him through her lashes. "A wife perhaps, and one could always use a few little ones."

Benedict restrained a groan. It was amazing how the woman could even now turn the conversation to marriage and family, or lack thereof.

"Grammy"—Phoebe bounded over, hands now caked in chocolate and dirt—"I couldn't find no frog. But I did get this!" She opened a palm to proudly expose a fat, wriggling worm.

Benedict lifted a brow at Wilhemina.

"Very nice, love. He is a handsome little fellow." She ruffled the girl's amber curls. "What shall we name him?"

Phoebe looked at Benedict and he winced as she declared, "Benedict!"

"Good choice," Wilhemina said.

"I have to go." Benedict hefted the basket into the carriage and allowed Wilhemina to press a quick kiss to his cheek. "Do not worry," he said again, and she nodded.

As the conveyance drew away, he could hear Phoebe and her grandmother talking.

"Do you think Uncle Benedict is mad I ate a scone?"

"No, Phoebe. Very little makes him mad, and he was never opposed to sharing."

"Good." Benedict looked out the window in time to see the girl give her worm a loud kiss. "I ate two."

It was a hulking structure that loomed over the surrounding countryside on a shelf of land meager in comparison. The façade was brutally scarred where the great manor faced the weathered road, as if to challenge the world head-on with its haunting beauty and stark wound. Most of the stone structure was perfect, pale in color and surrounded by lush greenery and thick layers of grass. A quarter of it, however, was black with soot, as dark as the sky above, though it had no stars to dot its bleakness. One of the windows in the uppermost row that stretched across the front of the house was void of glass and light. It peered out at the oncoming carriage like a blind eye.

Harriet loved the battered manor upon first sight. She gazed at Rochester Hall steadily as their carriage, buffeted by storm winds and rain, lumbered its way up the rocky drive.

The sound was muffled so she couldn't be certain, but could have sworn it was a moan of dismay that flittered across her ears. Harriet looked back over her shoulder at her companion and caught the woman quickly dropping a fist from her mouth. Her forced smile was almost painful to behold.

"Interesting, is it not?"

Harriet eased back into her seat. "Indeed."

Silence stretched between them as she waited. They

were coming upon the iron gates of the estate when Isabel spoke again.

"Harriet"—she removed a handkerchief from her reticule and began to polish her spectacles—"if things do not turn out as well as you expected, do send word and I shall dispatch a carriage for you right away."

"I would rather not easily dismiss the gift my friends have given me."

"If it grows too frightening . . ."

"Ghost stories, Isabel. We'll like as not sit in a gloomy room and listen to ghost stories. I cannot imagine I'll see anything more peculiar than the structure of Rochester Hall itself."

"You truly believe it is all rubbish?"

Harriet looked out the window again as the carriage began to draw to a halt. To her companion she said, "I have always enjoyed a good ghost story."

"Then"—Isabel took a breath—"I am certain you shall have a wonderful time."

Harriet lifted a brow at the other's false gusto.

Isabel offered a wobbly smile. "I am trying, Harriet."

Harriet reached out to squeeze the gloved hands Isabel had folded in her lap. "I know you are."

They both jumped when the driver pounded on the wall behind Isabel's head.

"This be it!"

"Goodness"—Isabel frowned—"Emily's driver would have opened the door and helped with your bags."

"Not all drivers are as wonderful as Hildegard." Harriet swung open the door and winced into the pouring rain.

"Lord," Isabel whispered, and jerked at the sudden crash of thunder.

Harriet's bags began to tumble from the roof of the conveyance.

"I had best get along before I'm tossed out."

Harriet stepped down from the carriage and narrowly missed being hit in the shoulder with the last of her bags. She stumbled to the side to avoid the valise, slippers sliding in the muddy earth. As she fell to her knees, mud oozing into the material of her only well-fitting coat, she wished it were more commonplace for women to wear trousers and sturdy shoes of the likes she had worn a fortnight before.

She struggled back to her feet, Isabel helping with a surprisingly strong hold on her wrists. She was shouting to be heard above the wind, not at Harriet but the man hunkered behind the reins of the hackney.

"Look here, sir!" Her tone was stern and demanding, "You're the poorest driver—no! The poorest pretence of a gentleman I've ever seen!" She turned back to her friend. "Oh, Harriet, what shall we do? You're a mess."

The other woman was laughing, amused Isabel's tone could shift from scolding to carefully concerned so quickly. "My only hope is that we are so late that most of the house is already abed."

"Were it not for that scoundrel of a—"

"It's all right, Isabel." She pushed her back into the conveyance. "You'd best get in before you're made a mess."

The other woman plopped back into her seat and Harriet's grin faltered when she saw the worry etched in Isabel's features. It began to drizzle steadily and Harriet could feel cold mud creeping into her slippers. "I'll be fine," she insisted.

"I know you will." Isabel's voice was clear and certain. She forced herself to smile.

Harriet moved forward and did not hesitate to go up the set of stairs leading to the front doors of the house. Without thinking about it, she lifted her already-chilled knuckles to rap at the wood.

When the mournful howl of some woodland beast rang through the night, she peered thoughtfully over her shoulder into the darkness.

There were no sounds of locks sliding out of place, not even the creak of the door handle, before the door slowly swung inward. Harriet frowned into the foyer filled with a soft light. Her chin lowered when the man who had opened the door cleared his throat.

He was almost a full head shorter than she, most of his features hidden behind a cloud of facial hair. The fine garments he wore—a maroon jacket, dark stockings, and shined shoes—had Harriet doubting he was a servant.

He beamed at her as if he had been waiting for Harriet all evening. "Hello, hello!"

"Hello." It was hard, despite the downward spiral of her evening, not to return the large smile.

"Come in, dear lady. Get out of the rain and cold." He had a soft touch as he reached out to cup her elbow and guide Harriet inside. "My goodness!" Every word he said came out an excited whisper. "What happened to you?"

Harriet's nose wrinkled as she attempted to wipe away the last remnants of rain from her cheeks and brow. "The carriage was slowgoing. I'm terribly late."

The small round man made a tsking sound as he shook his head. He abruptly pressed the lamp into her hands, shifting the bags she'd been carrying to the floor. "We can build a warm fire in the parlor to the right. I'll just inform one of the servants we have another guest."

"I do not wish to be of trouble . . ." Harriet's words died off as the man disappeared into the darkness beyond the light of her lantern. "All right, then." Her lips pursed as she peered into the darkness, then let herself move forward down the hall.

Harriet could make out little of her surroundings even with the light and almost passed the first door to the right before she realized it was there. It was opened slightly and gave in with a little shove from her open palm. Her feet were silent on the thick rugs below as she lifted her lantern high. The first she saw was a large globe. The round ball of the earth was bound in engraved leather, each continent, island, and stretch of water painted an amazingly brilliant color. When her gaze lifted she found an aged map—faded and stained in some places—framed on a nearby wall. Beneath the glass pane there were tiny X's marked on various spots. She walked along the map, recognizing places ranging from the Americas to Greenland, releasing a soft cry of pain when her hip encountered a sharp edge.

She rubbed the sore area through her skirts as she frowned over the piece of furniture she had collided with. The desk was enormous.

Harriet's brows drew together as she whispered thoughtfully, "This is not the parlor."

"No, it is not."

Later she would take pride in the fact she did not scream. She gasped and spun around. Harriet had a brief glimpse of the large figure that had come up behind her before the lantern slipped out of her grasp and fell to the floor. The flame died before the lamp hit the carpet.

Silence filled the room, nearly as oppressive as the

dark that closed in around Harriet. Her hands shook as she reached to grip the desk behind her.

"Stay where you are." The man who had frightened her spoke again and Harriet bit her bottom lip when she realized how close he was. His voice was deep and bore a hint of accent she couldn't quite place. "I will find the lantern."

Harriet's breath trembled in her chest when fingertips brushed her ankle. She jerked her foot back.

"Pardon."

Her eyes squeezed shut as she wondered briefly what she had gotten herself into. What manner of household scurried about in the dark with only a few lanterns to light the way? What sort of man crept up on unsuspecting women and scared the life out of them? Harriet's much-too-imaginative mind went to work on the possibilities. She had painted a rather vivid picture of a figure with dragging arms, hairy knuckles, and teeth pointing at odd angles from his mouth when she heard the strike of a flint.

She wasn't certain if it was because of the dark that came before it, but the lantern seemed to give off a hundred times more light than when she had been holding it. It illuminated the space about her completely, including the stranger with gray lips, drool curling down their corners.

4

As he straightened, lantern in hand, Benedict let his gaze travel the length of the latest arrival to Rochester Hall. As his attention moved upward from her mud-caked slippers to her soiled skirts, he could understand why Randolph thought she had suffered some sort of accident. Benedict was unsure as to what had occurred to make her gown and jacket sit so unevenly upon her frame. The hemline on her skirts was rather high and a full inch separated the ends of her coat sleeves from the delicate bones of her wrists. He wondered if her attire had shrunk in the rain as his focus lifted.

His brows drew together as he took his first look at the woman's face, or what he could see of it. She had lifted a closed fist to her mouth and was silently staring at him.

Benedict cleared his throat. "It was not my intent to frighten you."

"It was not mine to invade your privacy."

The woman's voice was not breathless with apprehension or trembling with fright. When she spoke, the corners of her mouth became visible and, in fact, it appeared as if she were smiling behind her hand. There was something very peculiar about this woman, Benedict decided as he eyed her mussed hair and then the dark smudge of dirt that adorned one of her cheeks.

He could easily imagine it was her unkempt appearance that stirred an odd sensation of interest within him or, even more so, the fact she was taller than any woman he had ever encountered before—almost his height. More often than it moved to her dirtied gown, however, Benedict's focus was on her eyes. Clearly illuminated in the light of the lantern he still held, her gaze was an unusual shade. It reminded him of wheat fields in the moment the green stalks of grain begin to change to brown. It never wavered coyly to his cravat, was never disturbed by the fluttering of thick lashes, but met his stare evenly.

He counted off at least forty-five ticks of the grandfather clock before realizing that the steady cadence was the only sound in the room.

"I am Benedict Bradbourne," he said for wont of anything else.

"Harriet Mosley." She held out her hand.

As another stretch of uncomfortable silence filled the study, Benedict realized that he had finally met his equal in matters of social niceties. It appeared neither one of them knew what to do with the situation. He accepted Harriet Mosley's handshake.

He could not be certain what the substance was, but it transferred easily from the palm of his uninvited guest to his own. It oozed, cold and slightly damp, between his fingers.

Harriet winced, looking between his hand and face as if she expected him to become irate over the matter. "I'm sorry. Mud," she explained. "I'm afraid I took a fall in the rain." Then she reached into the opening of her coat for a clean layer of her gown and proceeded to use the material to wipe the palm of Benedict's hand. Her fingers were long and slim and nearly fit around his wrist as she steadied his hand.

"Is that what happened?"

Benedict released a breath he hadn't known he was holding, relieved that the older man had returned.

Randolph entered the room surrounded by the glow of the taper he carried along with a blanket.

"Landed directly in a puddle." Harriet nodded and made a face as she looked down at her coat.

Randolph did not hesitate to set his taper in Benedict's free hand. He ignored the younger man's look when he smiled at the woman in the muddied coat. "How terrible for you, Miss . . . ?"

"Mosley," Benedict said as he transferred the beeswax taper to a table near the door.

"Harriet," she said at the same time. "You may call me Harriet."

"Sir Oscar Randolph at your service, madam."

Benedict turned back into the room, rolling his eyes as the old man snapped his heels together and dipped into a low bow. His attention focused on the woman as she slipped into a rather awkward curtsy; Benedict's interest was not on her unpracticed movements, but on the smile that curved her lips as she managed them. The tilt of her mouth was vaguely interesting when not hidden behind her hand, and he wasn't positive it was a trick of shadows that created the tiny space between her two front teeth.

"I must insist that you remove that wet coat and put this warm blanket about your shoulders," Randolph was saying. "One of the servants will be present shortly. Let us adjourn to the parlor where my friend, Mr. Bradbourne, will build us a nice fire."

One of Benedict's brows lifted.

Harriet must have read something she did not like in his expression because after one glance his way she made no move to remove her coat. "I don't wish to make myself a bother, Sir Randolph."

"Oscar."

"Oscar." Harriet glanced at the room's only window, the night beyond hidden by heavy curtains. "I will do fine to find what is to be my room and take care of myself."

"Don't be silly, young lady." Randolph began the process of helping her out of her coat. "You must dry off before the fire, or else you'll be sick for our excursion into Rochester Hall."

Her features were really quite expressive. A small furrow appeared between her brows as Randolph tugged the snug coat from her arms. Her gown, Benedict saw, fit her about as well as the coat. The sleeves were rather tight and her full breasts pressed at the material of the bodice. Scraps of silk had been sewn into the décolletage as if to hide the amount of skin visible above it. Gazing at her, Benedict recalled being commissioned to guard a transport of sculptures directed to the London Museum. Harriet Mosley was built not unlike the lithe, yet voluptuous sculptures of women.

She clutched the edges of the blanket together about her as she turned to face Benedict.

Hell, he thought, it would not hurt her to dry off before retiring to her bed.

"I had best start the fire."

"I hope the gloominess of the house does not offend," Sir Randolph said as he lit the last of the tapers. "I believe Lady Cruchely keeps us enshrouded in shadows, all the better to capture ghostly apparitions. There is a lot less fear in the world of light than that of darkness. Though young Bradbourne here has yet to prove intimidated by any out-of-the-ordinary occurrence. He is of the bravest sort, I imagine."

The young man in question, who—to Harriet—looked as if he was in his late thirties at least, shot the other man a quelling scowl. She held back a grin as Randolph smiled at Benedict, completely oblivious of the daggers being aimed his way.

"Perhaps she is trying to save money on tapers."

Harriet said, "It can be difficult to practice prudence in spending."

She was conscious of both men's gazes suddenly upon her.

Randolph spoke. "So you once had to practice frugality, Miss Harriet?"

"Yes." She looked toward the fire in the hearth. "Once." Harriet did not add that she had yet to free herself of the task. She was not certain, as it were, if either of the gentlemen present scorned a lack of wealth.

"It's a difficult path to tread, to be certain." Sir Randolph nodded as he carried Harriet's coat to the hearth and shook it out before the flames. "I have noticed that those who must endure financial difficulty are the better for having gone through it. . . .

"And now you are so independent in wealth you may travel alone on adventures, eh?"

"All right," Harriet said.

As Randolph continued with his philosophy of the poor, Harriet shifted in the leather chair in which she had been seated and let her gaze drift back to where Benedict Bradbourne stood, back rigid, a slightly bland expression upon his face. He did not look as if he had ever been without adequate funds and, as Randolph said, appeared as if little could daunt him.

She lifted the glass of brandy she'd been given.

His clothes fit him as if they had been made with him in mind, the attire a hundred times more suited to his body than Harriet's gown was to hers. His fawn-colored breeches stretched across his long legs and down into the tops of his shined boots. The dark coat he wore, reaching smoothly along his shoulders, the sleeves fitting neatly over his wrists and the backs of his palms, was unadorned with fancy emblems or swirling ribbon and his silken cravat was tied neatly beneath his neck without a fanlike wave or cascading rivulets. Bradbourne's style was a comparison in contrast to the pale silks and jeweled attire currently taking the wealthier men of London by storm.

As her gaze shifted upward from the man's cravat, Harriet amusedly admonished herself. Alone in the dark with Bradbourne she had imagined him all sorts of a ghoul, and when the room had been illuminated by the glow of the lamp, she had realized never would her wild imaginings be so wrong again. Harriet smiled against the rim of her glass.

Benedict Bradbourne was no handsome young dandy, but neither was he a sharp-toothed fiend. The man had a kind of face that suggested he'd go many places in his life and not long after people would forget what he looked like. His hair was brown already touched with gray at the temples, brushed back from his clean brow. His sideburns appeared freshly trimmed just to the exact point where his earlobes ended. A shade or two darker than his hair, his eyes remained cool and collected and devoid of emotion even when they met hers from across the room.

Harriet's breath froze heavily in her throat and she

wasn't certain if it was because she had been caught staring at the man or because his gaze moved down to her curled lips.

". . . Bare the accent of one who has dwelled in the country all her life. You are not from this area, I presume?"

Harriet turned toward the man at the hearth. "No, sir. I am from London."

"So am I. Where do you reside?"

On the few occasions Benedict spoke, his voice was deep and tinged with that unusual accent she had noticed in the study.

"My friend Augusta Merryweather and I share a house on Dove Street." She was more than a little disconcerted with the way Bradbourne was still watching her. Harriet was accustomed to sudden stares when she entered a ballroom or while walking through Hyde Park, as she was accustomed to their redirection after her watchers realized there was nothing interesting about her beyond her unusual height.

"Dove Street . . ." Randolph mused as he gave her coat a fierce shake to release the muddied folds. "Is that near St. James Place, by any chance?"

"Not really." Harriet felt her nose wrinkle. Her humble town house could easily fit into one of the loftier homes on St. James.

A heavy thud rang out through the room. Harriet moved quickly out of her chair to retrieve the book that had tumbled to the floor before the hearth.

"Is that your book, dear?" Sir Randolph looked from the battered tome to Harriet's face.

"What might have given it away, Randolph?" Benedict lifted a brow. "The fact it fell out of her own coat pocket?"

Harriet hurried to press the front of the book to her

gown, hiding the cover from view. It was, however, much too late for the older man to have missed the title.

"It's just not the usual sort of book one tends to see young women read, is all." The ends of Randolph's mustache pointed to the ceiling as he smiled. "One expects tales of knights in shining armor and enduring love, not stories of vengeful spirits and the souls of those who've met an untimely demise."

Benedict stepped nearer to the two at the hearth. "What book is it?"

"A horrid tale revolving around a ghost and the young ladylove he left behind. Tell me, Harriet. What does make a young woman turn away from the popular poems of Byron and Keats for such peculiar books?"

Harriet felt heat roll up her neck to her cheeks. She was reminded of the way her cousin eyed her strangely whenever he caught sight of her reading materials, or the cold glare of the bookseller in London whom she was forced to deal with until another bookshop—whose owners were much more to her liking—came into being.

"I've never been one for love stories" was the best she could explain it.

"I'm pleased to hear it." The old man's smile grew even more until all his even white teeth were exposed and his eyes were nearly hidden by his cheeks. "I cannot express my satisfaction in knowing a young lady, both intelligent and lovely, is my only reader."

Harriet's gaze moved from the newest title in her collection of peculiar favorites to the author's name below it.

"Randal C. Shoop." Randolph continued to beam. "My pseudonym."

"An anagram," Harriet acknowledged aloud.

"Very shrewd of you to notice, Miss Mosley." One of

Bradbourne's brows had lifted, his eyes momentarily showing appreciation.

"An unusual name makes one wonder." Harriet told herself not to be insulted. Perhaps Benedict Bradbourne did not know the same sort of women as she did, those that used their brains for more than retaining gossip and planning dinner parties. She said to Randolph, "I do enjoy your books, Sir Randolph."

"Please, I insist that my one and only fan should not be so formal." The old man tossed her coat across a nearby settee and linked his arm through Harriet's. "You must call me Oscar." He peered at her from the corner of his eye with an earnestness that was touching. "You've read both my books?"

Harriet nodded as she was guided to a pair of wing chairs that faced each other. "*The Ghost of Lily Lake* first, and then *The Haunting of Lady Monroe*"—she set the book neatly atop her lap as she sat—"a week after."

Randolph's cheeks turned pink. "It is nice to know that an individual who is not a member of my family has taken an interest in my writing." He made as if to sit until he saw Harriet's empty snifter. He reached for the glass. "Would you like more, or some tea perhaps?"

Harriet glanced toward the still-standing Bradbourne and noted he showed no aggravation at the older man for taking over the conversation. Something about the silence that had stretched between her and Benedict, after they introduced themselves for the first time, suggested he was as unaccustomed to entertaining as she was to being entertained.

"Tea would be nice."

"Where is that bloody servant?" Sir Randolph—Oscar to his devotees—moved to quickly tug one of the bell ropes that hung inconspicuously near the curtains.

Harriet was aware of the man on the other side of

the room shifting. He folded his hands behind his back and regarded her with a slightly interested gaze. "Miss Mosley, may I be so bold as to ask if you believe in the ghosts and whatnot in the tales Randolph writes?"

"Actually"—she ran her thumbs along the spine of her book—"I have never seen proof to convince me in either way. I must admit, I do enjoy the accounts of specters in old castles and other such tales, but I have never seen a ghost. Although I should like to think with all my reading into the matter, I would know how to solve a spiritual mystery if one arose."

"You do not think they exist, Harriet?" Randolph accepted the tray from a young servant who left as silently as she'd come. He set the platter heavy with a teapot and saucers on the table beside them and took the seat across from her.

"Well, just as I have seen no proof to say such things exist, neither has it been proven to me that they do not." Harriet carefully cupped a delicate teacup in both hands, speaking to him through the steam that rose from its contents. "I have never been to a house of spirits, a haunted dwelling if you will. Nor have any of my friends, who would tell me if they had seen such things. I will not say I do not believe, sir." She smiled. "The world, I find, is a much more interesting place when one allows themselves to imagine there is some truth behind great mysteries."

"Indeed, my dear."

Harriet turned from Sir Randolph's return smile to Bradbourne. It was somewhat disconcerting to find his barren features changed, a furrow between his brows and his gaze again on her smile.

5

Had she been accustomed to the quiet workings of servants, the young woman in the crisp white apron might have entered her bedchamber unnoticed. Harriet, however, had never had her own maid. And in the home she shared with Augusta Merryweather, there would be a polite rap on her door before the other woman entered.

Exhausted from her late-night arrival and the conversation she shared with her most favored author, Harriet hardly moved when the chamber door swung open. Slung out across the bed much larger than her own, face pressed into the pillow and hair strewn about in wild disarray, she opened a single eye. She watched in silence as the young woman—a girl really—with golden hair drawn back in a severe knot walked on silent feet into the room. The maid did a quick survey of her surroundings then placed the tray she bore on the bedside table. The scent of tea and baked sweets pulled Harriet further from sleep as she watched the other woman kneel to retrieve the muddied gown and stockings that had been left on a chair.

Beside the bed, nearly nose to nose with Harriet,

the girl saw her single opened eye through the thin veil of sleep-mussed hair.

"Good morning, mademoiselle." The girl's voice was heavy with accent. French, Harriet determined. Not hard to identify like that of Benedict Bradbourne.

She frowned as she sat up on the still-made bed. Odd, she thought, that the near-stranger should sneak up in her mind first thing in the morn.

"I didn't mean to wake you." The girl smiled apologetically as she layered Harriet's dirty clothes over her arm. "I'm sorry, mademoiselle."

The older woman wiped the sleep from her eyes, blinked a few times, then managed a smile. "I'm Harriet."

The girl curtseyed. "It's a pleasure to meet you, mademoiselle Harriet. My name is Jane. I brought you hot tea and bread." Jane reached for the tray and placed it atop Harriet's legs. "Will there be anything else you need?"

"No," Harriet said, slightly flustered by the bedside service.

Waiting until Jane was gone so she wouldn't hurt her feelings, Harriet set her breakfast tray aside and rose. She dressed as she drank her tea and sat before putting on her stockings to take a bite of the dainty loaf of bread. To her surprise the bread was sweet as if a touch of sugar and cinnamon had been stirred in before baking. It was sliced and buttered then slathered with a thin layer of apple jelly.

Finished eating, she washed her teeth and was on her way to the door before remembering the tray left on the bed. Harriet was holding it in the crook of her arm when she opened the door and found a very large and ominous-looking stranger standing directly before her.

Usually she was pleased to meet anyone taller than she, but the man was nearly ridiculous in size. He was a good foot taller than she and his shoulders were of such a breadth, she doubted he could get through doorways without turning sideways.

Before she could find the breath to speak, the man said, "Miss Harriet Mosley?"

"Yes?" She winced like one expecting a blow.

The man had blunt features. Sharp cheekbones jutted outward from the planes of his craggy face. His nose was flat, as if it had been broken a time or two, and he had cold gray eyes with lids drawn into a permanently drowsy look.

"Lady Cruchely would like to see you."

"All right." Harriet waited for him to lead the way.

The man's sleepy gaze moved to the tray she carried.

"I was going to return this to Jane."

His grimed features shifted and for a moment he appeared puzzled. "Leave it. She'll come back."

"Oh." Harriet returned to the man after placing the tray again on the bedside table. She smiled up at him.

The man's thick brows lifted and Harriet began to take pride in being able to make his stony features shift, before he turned to lead her away.

Mr. Latimer, who appeared better suited to a profession in pugilism or another violent enterprise, had asked Benedict to wait in the study. The room in which he sat was otherwise empty, the crackle of flames in the hearth the only sound. Benedict appreciated the silence the room offered, and much as he had the evening before, he used the solitude to think.

At present, everything was going according to plan. None of the other visitors at Rochester Hall thought it strange that they'd never heard of him—a man who lived in London, as most of them, and had enough funds to afford a stay at the house of spirits. Perhaps they thought him eccentric or a recluse. It mattered little to Benedict. He had planned out everything, even the blatant lie of how he came about his wealth— on the off chance anyone was so gauche as to inquire. He was a man without mercy or contrition. He was set on vengeance. Nothing would get in the way.

Although it did so on well-oiled hinges, Benedict was aware of the door opening behind him.

"Wait here." Mr. Latimer spoke the same words he had said only a few minutes before.

Frowning at the click of the door falling closed, Benedict rose to his feet.

Harriet Mosley looked back at the closed door with a rather comical expression of bewilderment. She appeared none the worse for wear after her ordeal the night before, which included not only the long journey from London, but a discussion on books with Oscar Randolph that had lasted until the wee hours of the morn. Her gown was the color of a ripe peach, and though not muddy like that of the night before, it also had a hemline set just above her ankles.

She appeared momentarily surprised to find Benedict present when she turned into the parlor.

Then she lifted a single, tawny brow and pursed her lips. Her eyes—a lighter shade of hazel in the morning— moved unabashed over Benedict. "You again?" she said, and grinned.

"I'm afraid so, Miss Mosley." As it had been the night before, Benedict's gaze was caught by the supple curvature of her lips. "It appears we are to be given a tour of the house together."

"Oh?"

"We missed the first exploration by our late arrivals last night."

"I did not know you and Sir Randolph arrived behind schedule as well."

"I did. I think Randolph has been here for several days. He spoke with great familiarity about the house when I met him yesterday."

"I had thought you and he were well acquainted," Harriet mused aloud. "He spoke to you like a good friend might."

"As he did to you as the night wore on," Benedict pointed out.

Harriet was visibly thoughtful, and then gave a sharp nod. "Indeed."

They stared at each other for a long moment, and as Benedict struggled to come up with polite conversation, he wondered if Harriet was doing the same.

She gave up before he. She smiled at him a moment longer then folded her arms behind her back and began to stroll about the room. Benedict watched her pause over paintings along the wall and a vase full of flowers. She leaned over the latter, nearly touching a rose petal with the tip of her nose as she took in a deep breath. A brief ray of morning sunlight penetrated the gloom beyond the parlor window, turning her hair to dark gold woven with bolts of pale brown.

Again the sound of the hearth was all that filled the room. It was not, much to Benedict's interest, an uncomfortable silence that stretched between the woman and him.

"Do you know the gentleman who brought me here?" She broke the silence without turning to face him.

"Mr. Latimer," he reported absently, gaze moving from her laced fingers to the straight line of her spine and across her shoulders. "He maintains the household staff."

Her voice was very crisp, hiding nothing of her interest. "He is the *butler?*"

For the first time he said what he had been thinking. "He doesn't look suited to be a house employee, does he?"

"No, he does not. A man employed to break others' kneecaps, perhaps."

Benedict's brows lifted above the rims of his specs. "How do you know of such things, Miss Mosley?"

"I do read some very interesting books, Mr. Bradbourne." Harriet looked back over her shoulder and grinned.

When the parlor door opened, her attention shifted in its direction and Benedict felt a moment's relief. He could imagine the woman becoming horrified were she still gazing back at him. His normally controlled features contorted into a dark scowl and something deep inside his gut shifted almost painfully as he realized he was riveted in the woman's smile.

6

Lady Dorthea Cruchely was a petite woman, appearing all the more so with Latimer standing at her heels. Her skin was like ivory and her hair pale, shading into gray at the temples. She had intelligent blue eyes and the practiced smile of one who dealt with the public on a regular basis and might encounter a few individuals she did not particularly care for.

"Good morning, Miss Mosley!" She went to Harriet first, holding out her delicate hands to the younger woman. "It is a pleasure to have you." She looked to the solemn man in the spectacles while still holding Harriet's hands. "Mr. Bradbourne. Welcome to my home."

Benedict inclined his head, his lips curved but not to the full width of a smile. "A pleasure, Lady Cruchely."

With his accent, all the hard sounds rolled together like music. It was a very nice accent, Harriet decided without compunction. It was, in fact, the only thing about the man that made him different. This morn he wore a somber dark gray jacket and his hair combed as neatly as the day before. He appeared

carefully constructed into being boring and bland
and unnoticeable to those around him.

A bit, Harriet thought for the first time, *too*
carefully.

That, in itself, was of interest. There was something
strange about the man—of that she had been certain
since just before falling asleep early that morning. She
was more than a little relieved to finally put a finger
on what exactly it was about Bradbourne . . . It had
been a sensation present since they first met in this
same darkened study. The rising of the fine hair at
Harriet's nape and the odd lift in her stomach had
been caused by her awareness of Benedict Bradbourne as someone not as ordinary as he pretended
to be.

Yes, Harriet thought as Bradbourne turned to face
her with a single brow lifted, that explained it.

She blinked when she realized Benedict was not the
only one watching her expectantly.

Lady Cruchely was good enough to repeat herself
without being asked. "I was saying, Miss Mosley, you
must be extremely weary after your harrowing journey here."

Harriet shook her head, wondering at the sort of
stuff they thought her made of to be out of sorts by a
storm. "It was not so bad as one might imagine, just a
few extra bumps along the path."

"I see," Dorthea said, as if surprised by the younger
woman's reply. "Well, allow me to show you around
the estate a bit. Hopefully we will be finished in time
for you to meet the other guests for luncheon." As she
led the way to the door and the fellow that still hulked
there, she smiled and lightly touched his elbow. "I
think I'll be fine, Latimer, if you have other work that
needs your attention."

He said nothing, but smiled in a way that made his hard features gentle.

Harriet's eyelids drew together as she peeked from the soft look in Latimer's eyes, to Lady Dorthea's smile, then back again. She glanced at Bradbourne from the corner of her eye, but found his features devoid of any emotion or telltale sign that he was thinking the same as she. She couldn't tell what the man was thinking at all, she realized, and suddenly a shiver stole down her spine.

"The fire occurred before I was born, while the house was under the care of Warren Rochester and his wife. They were my grandparents."

"Did they survive the blaze?" Benedict said.

"They were the only ones who did not."

Harriet's brows drew together as she turned from the two who spoke and focused on the charred evidence of the fire. The late-morning breeze tugged at her hair as her eyes were drawn to the upstairs window in the corner, void of glass and backed with darkness.

"One of my grandmother's servants grabbed what little she could of their belongings, mementos that might prove important to the rest of the family. Rochester's footman wrapped my father in his coat and carried the bundle to safety."

"Then your father had something to remember them by," Harriet said. She squinted when she caught a brief flash of red cloth beyond the darkened window, a fluttering curtain perhaps.

Dorthea's voice remained calm and quite dignified as she said, "Not bloody likely."

Harriet looked from the curtain to her hostess.

"All my grandfather's possessions went into the care of his younger brother. The wastrel sold all he could of that which belonged to the family and sent my father away to school."

Benedict slowly faced Dorthea as well. "Do you have any idea what sort of things were saved from the fire?"

Lady Cruchely was thoughtful. "Family trinkets, I believe, personal letters, and items easily carried."

"You may very well be able to find those effects," Benedict said. "If your great-uncle kept records of sale, it would not be difficult to track down individuals with your family heirlooms in their possession."

"There were no records. He cared about as much for those things as this estate." Dorthea's tone became softer, saddened. "My father spent his life rebuilding the family assets. It was only when I came here, after my husband died, that repairs have begun on the fire-damaged parts of the house. The workers come when guests are not present."

Harriet, who had little family to speak of, could easily imagine what it was like to live without due to the choices of others. It was much easier, however, for men to earn a place for themselves in the world.

Harriet was managing by the skin of her teeth.

She said to Dorthea, "How good of you to save the place."

The older woman blinked first at Harriet and then Benedict, as if surprised she had said so much. Harriet wondered if the family tale was not a part of her normal tour. She looked at Benedict and was curious as to whether or not she had the same quiet stillness in listening as he. The man who spoke little but appeared to hear every word one said, would be easy to talk to.

Benedict was scowling and had folded his hands on

his lean hips. He gazed steadily at the grass between his feet as if deep in thought. It had been, Harriet knew, a pose he had taken shortly after Lady Cruchely spoke of the lack of hope in finding her family heirlooms.

He must, Harriet thought, have great concern for those who have suffered loss. Not unlike herself.

Benedict's gaze snapped upward and caught Harriet's examination. She looked quickly toward the house. Only then did she see the gentleman striding toward them. His elegant coat, the color of a ripe red grape, fluttered in the breeze as did his stylishly tied cravat.

"Ah"—Dorthea followed Harriet's gaze—"Mr. Elliot."

"Good morning, Lady Cruchely." He beamed beneath the wide brim of his hat, a great white smile that went well with his jewel-green eyes. "I see the last of your guests arrived safely."

He was the sort of man, Harriet thought, her friend Rosabelle Desire would have described as *"delicious with a cherry on top."* Inspecting his waistcoat, embroidered in an elaborate floral pattern, and his cream-colored shoes, which matched his stockings, which matched his breeches, Harriet decided this single suit was finer than any gown she owned. Perhaps he would loan her the stockings, she thought, and grinned.

The man caught Harriet's smile and met her gaze.

"Allow me to introduce you," Dorthea was saying. "Miss Harriet Mosley and Mr. Benedict Bradbourne. Mr. Elliot is from London as well."

"Byron," he said as he reached for Harriet's hand. He bowed, pressed a gentle kiss to her gloved fingertips. He looked up at her through his lashes. "Like the poet."

"All right," Harriet said, for lack of a better response.

Elliot straightened to hold out a hand to Benedict. "Did you arrive with Miss Mosley?"

"No," Benedict returned in a dry tone. He shook the other man's hand briefly, his gaze shifting to Harriet.

"Well, then!" Dorthea broke into that bright smile of a professional hostess. "I'm certain you are eager to hear of the many ghosts that have been seen at Rochester Hall."

"May I be so bold as to invite myself along for a second tour?" Elliot asked. He winked at Harriet. "I very much enjoy the lady's ghost stories."

Dorthea nodded. "Of course, Mr. Elliot." She turned back to the doors. "Several spirits of ancient monks have been witnessed roaming the halls. Some have seen specters in chains and armor-clad knights that can walk through walls."

"I hope my bedchamber is haunted by the monks more so than the knights and specters," Harriet said. "The clang of armor and chains can really disturb a good night's rest."

Benedict did not laugh as Dorthea and Elliot did. He was scowling at the house.

7

He felt invisible, watching from an upstairs window as Lady Cruchely led the newcomers back inside the house. The oblivious woman wore what appeared to be a new gown of carefully embroidered muslin and kidskin slippers, bound and trimmed with silk ribbon that matched her dress. He imagined it had cost her a pretty penny to have such a dress arranged to perfectly fit her body and then shoes to match.

He could not identify the gems, but dark stones danced around her neck as if the sunlight chose specifically to highlight their beauty. Even from far away, he could not miss the ring she wore. It was a wonder her hand was not weighed down by the weight of the diamonds.

He smirked, vaguely amused by the woman flaunting a wealth that was not hers alone.

The door behind him opened, but he did not turn, not even when the other man spoke.

"Time's up. The bloody crone hasn't paid again."

"Is that so?" Lady Cruchely and her guests had disappeared into the house and out of sight. He lifted his gaze to the crisp blue sky.

"What do ye want to do?"

"We'll have to make an effort to show the lady there will be repercussions if she does not do as she is told. She cannot ignore us for long."

"Want me to arrange for another carriage mishap?"

The man at the window rolled his eyes. "How tedious you are, sir. It is dangerous, never mind boring, to repeat ourselves in that manner. Have you been doing the work upstairs as I asked?"

"Aye. It's just about done, I'd say." The smile was evident in the other's voice.

"Finish it while everyone is in the garden tonight and let's see if Lady Cruchely will continue casting our demands aside." He folded his hands behind his back and, when he did not hear retreating footsteps, said, "That is all." He glanced over one shoulder, making sure the other had finally gone.

He sorely wished he did not have to go to such lengths to get what he wanted . . . what he deserved. It was bad enough, the tactics he used, but being forced to conspire with another man so void of wit and personality was almost too much to bear. None of this, of course, need happen were it not for Lady Cruchely stealing what was his by birth. He reminded himself of the fact every time he was obliged to speak to his cohort and whenever plotting the manner in which he would put the witch in her place.

8

From the Journal of Harriet R. Mosley

   It has come to my understanding that members of the upper class tend to vary in dress for daily activities, a different costume for each. Every woman present has dressed in a separate gown for luncheon, a walking dress for mundane tasks—reading in the parlor, strolls in the garden—another gown for drinks and dinner, and I can only assume everyone will be in yet another new ensemble for our evening of tea and brandy on the lawn. The women here, on average, have in their possession more than twenty gowns. I have brought five.

   I do not even own twenty gowns.

It was a nervous habit of sorts, one Harriet had acquired as she entered adolescence standing a full head taller than other girls her age and as tall as most boys. She had grown to control the unconscious habit as she accepted the fact she would never be the petite and delicate flower poets crooned about. On only a few occasions the nervous tick would reappear, those being when she was reminded how little she was like others and too tired to remember it did not matter.

As a cool evening breeze tickled her ankles, making the candles illuminating the garden flicker, Harriet tugged absently on the bell-shaped sleeves of her gown. Their laced ends reached a point unfashionably close to her shoulders.

She sighed into the night, scanned the guests spaced out around the lush greenery and scented blooms, and felt a pang of loneliness. It surprised her that she should feel so isolated after only one night away from her best friends and the warm comfort of her town house. A deep part of Harriet, however, nagged her to admit she was searching for someone in particular whom—though she knew the man hardly at all—she felt strangely comfortable with.

Her eyes alighted upon Oscar Randolph, talking animatedly with the much older Lord and Lady Chesterfield, and she smiled. As if sensing her gaze, Randolph looked at Harriet askance and waved. Her smile drifted away and her brows drew slightly together when she recognized it was not the company of her favored author she was searching for. Byron Elliot, clad in a vibrant teal waistcoat and jacket, stood with Lady Cruchely. He smiled and lifted his glass to her. Harriet's lips pursed. Whatever it was governing her insides was not seeking the poet lookalike either.

"I'd liked to have covered your eyes and demand you guess who I am."

Harriet recognized the other woman's voice and turned to face her.

Eliza Pruett, who had asked during dinner that Harriet call her Lizzie, smiled up at her. "But I could not reach."

"Eliza, really!" At her side, as she had been during

luncheon and at dinner, was the young woman's mother. Much as it had been on the other occasions, the woman's features were pinched, her brows close together as if she smelled a particularly noxious odor. "A lady does not speak to others in such a manner." Beatrice Pruett scowled down her nose at her daughter, and then rolled her eyes toward Harriet as if to prove she was above such unladylike behavior.

"You should have told me, Lizzie." Harriet ignored the older woman's look to smile at her daughter. "I'd have covered my eyes for you."

The younger woman, nineteen if that, erupted into giggles. When she laughed, Harriet had noticed during their first meal together, Lizzie always covered her mouth. She had started to wonder if the other had a nervous habit much like hers, but instead of hiding ill-fitting clothes, she sought to cover her prominent upper teeth.

Harriet had felt a pang of pity for the girl when, at dinner, she had been bluntly scolded for lifting her empty glass as a servant paused at her elbow with wine. A sudden silence fell over the table as Eliza lowered her glass and affixed her gaze to her dessert plate. With the skill of a professional entertainer, Lady Cruchely continued from where her conversation had been interrupted and the other guests pretended not to notice the young woman's embarrassment.

Everyone save for Harriet, who continued to gaze at Lizzie until her head lifted. Believing if it could work on Isabel, it could work on anyone, she drew her eyes together to focus on the point of her nose.

Eliza's abrupt cough sounded not unlike a muffled laugh and she had lifted her hand to hide her smile.

"I had thought you did not wish to venture from

your room after dark, Mrs. Pruett," Harriet said, drawing her arms together to cup her elbows.

"I have always wondered at the sort of woman who goes out late at night, Miss Mosley." Beatrice sniffed. "It is in the dark that most women forget themselves and behave in an unsuitable manner."

"Indeed? Several friends and myself enjoy a bit of entertainment after dark—soirées and what have you. I cannot speak for myself, but I assure you my friends have impeccable manners."

Beatrice looked her up and down. "I'm sure," she said.

"I should love to go to a soirée," Lizzie breathed with a kind of wistfulness that touched Harriet's heart.

She could have told the younger woman she had never been to a particularly interesting late-night gathering—save for the most recent she attended to witness a very interesting form of dance between Lady Abigail Garrett and the man who at that time had been her lover and, oddly enough, her butler. Harriet did not have the heart to mention how tedious such gatherings tend to be for women who stand taller than most of the men present. She could not blame the males, however. Asking someone to dance was surely nerve-wracking enough without having said person looming over you.

"Don't be absurd, Eliza," Beatrice was saying. She was busy scanning the others and missed the wounded expression on her daughter's face. "You have no fortune and no prospects for a lucrative marriage. Only women of remarkable beauty are welcome when penniless and unwed. Why ever would your presence be needed at a social gathering? At least Miss Mosley has financial independence to assist her."

Harriet flushed, vaguely certain she had been insulted.

"If you both will excuse me, I shall bid Lady Cruchely a good evening. Then I assume we will be free to retire for the night without appearing rude."

Harriet imagined it would take a lot more than that for the older woman to appear civil.

"My apologies, madam," Lizzie said, her mother gone in a whisper of her stiff gray gown. She looked at Harriet with cheeks pink from embarrassment. "My mother . . ."

When the other could not finish, Harriet said, "She is an interesting woman, your mother."

"She's a dismal old crone," Eliza said with blunt sincerity.

"Lizzie!"

She snatched two glasses of wine from a passing servant's tray, held one out for Harriet. "Forgive me again. My mother never lets me forget I am not the lovely and graceful daughter she always hoped for in order to bring her up a peg or two socially. I'm afraid being around her all day has made me quite irritable and bold. I cannot help but speak my mind."

Harriet slowly grinned. "I knew I would like you."

"I like you too, Miss Harriet. You are witty in a way most women wouldn't dare to be."

Harriet lifted a brow.

"What I mean to say"—Lizzie downed her wine in a smooth, unblinking swallow—"is that you are very confident and unafraid of being yourself. How I wish I could be so fortunate as to have enough wealth to live independently and speak my mind so freely."

"Yes," Harriet said carefully, and sipped from her own glass, letting her eyes drift.

She saw Benedict standing in the opening to the terrace, the brilliant glow of the house behind him. His head was tilted slightly and in the dimness of the candlelight Harriet could just make out his golden brown eyes behind his spectacles, moving with an almost uncanny alertness over the people outside. Harriet's gaze dropped to his feet and moved up over his trousers to where his coat fit snug to his waist. Like her, he wore the same attire he had been wearing throughout the day.

It was immediate, the disappearance of her loneliness.

She smiled.

When Harriet's gaze lifted higher, she saw Benedict had fixed his unyielding eyes on her. She met his stare evenly and, like one might a comrade in a foreign land, Harriet winked at him.

It was not helping his investigation, the presence of this woman who showed no hesitation in meeting his steady stare. Benedict had noticed her the moment he walked onto the terrace, and told himself it was only because his gaze followed the light from the room behind him. The same grin she had offered him in the parlor curved her lips as she listened to the words of Eliza Pruett. As a flash of emotion akin to jealousy came to life inside him, Benedict quickly diverted his gaze elsewhere.

Though his best friend had died four months before, the cut was still fresh enough to bleed. Benedict need only remind himself he was searching for Garfield's killer to hone in upon his instincts and the craft he had learned from the old man himself. His hard gaze fell across and quickly dismissed the figures of Lord and Lady Chesterfield, much too old and stiff to have sunk a dagger into an unsuspecting man's stomach. He inclined his head when Sir Randolph lifted his hand. He scanned Dorthea Cruchely as she feigned interest in whatever Mrs. Beatrice Pruett was saying to her. He did not miss the presence of the butler, Latimer, standing silent as the garden wall no more than three feet from Lady Cruchely's side.

He believed the lady of the manor when she said her grandparents' possessions had disappeared. She had no reason to lie and could do little to help the events that had occurred so many years before her birth. Benedict could hardly contain his disappointment-fueled fury as the woman shared her family history with Harriet and himself. The path to finding Garfield's killer was becoming increasingly difficult to follow. He was beginning to think he had come so far from London to spend a fortnight with strangers for no bloody reason.

Crisp fallen leaves scattered about his booted feet at a chilled wind. The fine hairs on Benedict's scalp lifted as his gaze drew back to Harriet Mosley. She stood with her arms folded and bare against the October wind, her gaze fixed on the center of his chest. Benedict felt his heart give a sudden, unexpected thud against his sternum where eyes the color of wheat were fixed. Harriet smiled.

Benedict's back teeth pressed against each other. He would have to make an effort to keep clear of the woman. He'd learned when first entering his profession that distractions of any sort were detrimental to investigations. He was finding Harriet's presence, when accompanying him on the tour of the estate or seated one chair down at the dinner table, more thought consuming than he cared to admit. Benedict felt like a traitor, letting her focus his attention in a direction opposite his investigation. He would have to make an effort to steer clear of her. She was different,

Miss Mosley, bordering upon unusual. She was, in fact, most unlike any female he had ever known.

As if she read his thoughts, her eyes lifted to meet his. She inclined her head slightly then one row of thick lashes slipped closed in a wink.

Harriet showed no surprise when Benedict began toward her and, in truth, he felt no surprise as he started to move.

"Good evening." She spoke before he could part his lips, and not for the first time her tone was like that one might employ with an old friend.

Benedict wondered if she spoke in such a manner to everyone she encountered in haunted estates.

"Miss Mosley." He inclined his head, looking briefly toward the younger woman at Harriet's side. "Miss Pruett."

"Mr. Bradbourne." Eliza eased into a curtsy.

Silence fell between Benedict and the women. Eliza tapped her finger rhythmically against the side of her glass, pursing her lips thoughtfully. Harriet tugged at the ends of her sleeves.

It was another gown that did not suit her frame, Benedict saw. He could clearly see above Harriet's ankles as he approached, and as she shifted her bodice, he could not help but observe how the front of the dress appeared too tight over her breasts. Another section of material had been sewn from the shoulders and into the edges of the bodice, but it was thin, almost translucent. Instead of adding a measure of decorum to the ill-fitting gown, Benedict thought, it only served to heighten a man's interest in what lay beneath.

"Lovely evening, is it not, sir?"

Benedict scowled at Eliza Pruett, not realizing he was doing so until he saw the expression that crossed her face. The silence that stretched between he and Harriet was not an uncomfortable one. Just in the same way when they toured the house, he felt no urge to prattle on to fill the time. As he had never been skilled with such incessant talk, he appreciated the pleasant quietness of the woman more than he could say.

He carefully concealed his distaste in the fact that young Eliza was ruining their relaxed silence. He cleared his throat, glancing at Harriet who was watching him expectantly. "Yes," he said.

"We were just reflecting upon the scandalous nature of women who enjoy the hours after dark," Harriet said, looking to Eliza, who grinned. They were sharing a private joke, but when Harriet turned her smile to Benedict, he saw she had no intention of leaving him out. "I, for instance, and most of my friends are such outrageous creatures."

"That is nonsense," he said, well aware he had done things in the hours close to midnight that Harriet couldn't even imagine. It was, more often than not, the best time for him to do his work.

"It's true, I'm afraid." The skin at the corner of Harriet's lids crinkled and an amused spark flashed in her eyes. "You are speaking to a woman of poor virtue."

He was transfixed by the glow of candlelight and laughter in her eyes. The corners of his mouth, which had been tempted to curl upward a moment before, went tight. His brows snapped together and he demanded, "Who said this of you?"

Harriet blinked, as if surprised by his earnestness. Her smile faded and her expression turned thoughtful.

"Oddly enough," Eliza was saying with a derisive edge to her voice, "she is coming this way." She managed to drop her glass onto a passing tray before Beatrice

Pruett joined their small group. She held loosely to one of Oscar Randolph's elbows.

"Well," she announced, "I have just been informed that this is not our only evening to be up and about past decent hours."

Harriet coughed into a gloved palm, "Is that so, Mrs. Pruett?"

Benedict recognized her hidden smile, before he turned from Harriet to the older woman.

"It is so, Miss Mosley." Beatrice's features were pinched, and her nose red as if she were suffering from congestion. "Lady Cruchely has seen fit to schedule several activities well beyond the hours of respectability."

"You told her nothing of the threat of night to a woman's virtue?"

Mrs. Pruett peered at Harriet closely and the other woman managed to hold a straight face. "I considered doing just that," Beatrice informed her tightly. "However, one must consider if one is being crude herself when discussing such matters. It is not my place to tell the lady how to carry out her gathering."

"I have rather enjoyed myself tonight, Mother." Eliza lowered her chin in speaking. "I cannot imagine I'd have had another chance to make a new friend. In fact, I look forward to other such nights."

"Absolutely not, young lady," Beatrice scolded. "I have all of tomorrow to decide upon the best way to politely extract ourselves from the proceedings."

Eliza sighed with quiet weariness, her smile gone.

"What does Lady Cruchely have planned for these nights?" Benedict asked. The question took the scrutiny off Eliza and abated some of Harriet's scowl over the younger woman's abrupt change of mood.

"It sounds fascinating, really." Randolph answered

and ignored Beatrice Pruett's disagreeing huff. "The evening after next, there is to be a visit from a woman who lives in a nearby village. A gypsy who Lady Cruchely has dealt with on more than one occasion."

"It is nothing more than witchcraft the woman performs," Beatrice snapped.

Randolph's bushy brows lifted. "She is said to have powers to speak with the dead."

"Oh?" Harriet's curiosity was piqued.

Benedict watched her. "You have departed friends you'd like to communicate with, Miss Mosley?"

Without blinking an eye, she leaned in toward him to say conspiratorially, "No, but I hear Caesar was a handsome man."

Benedict felt the corners of his mouth twitch again.

"On another night," Randolph said between chuckles, "we are to have a cemetery walk. Apparently there is a graveyard close by that is particularly interesting while perused under the light of the full moon."

"We are to converse with the dead," Beatrice said, "then walk upon their graves. Sounds delightful."

Benedict let his attention shift from the growing look of fascination spreading across Harriet's features to the other woman, whose features were far less captivating. "Mrs. Pruett," he said bluntly, "were you not aware of the nature of Lady Cruchely's gatherings before you came here?"

"No"—Beatrice glowered at her daughter, who had found something vastly interesting in the tips of her slippers—"I was not."

9

Harriet awoke to voices raised in anger. She sat up abruptly, surprised that she had fallen asleep at the small writing table, her cheek cushioned against the pages of her new journal. She brushed her warm cheeks with the backs of her hands and blinked sleepily. The taper at the corner of the table had melted into a stub in a pool of wax. Only a glimmer of light illuminated the space around her seat.

The voices increased in volume and only then did Harriet realize it was the arguing that had woken her. She shifted in her chair and squinted in the general direction of the chamber door.

The voices were those of a man and woman, but beyond that Harriet could tell little. Though the man's voice was so deep it seemed to reverberate against the stone walls, and the woman's tone was heightened in nearly hysterical furor, Harriet could make out none of their words.

She rose from her chair and on silent feet moved toward the door, hands leading the way so she would not collide with unfamiliar furnishings. Harriet reached the door, palms laying flat against the cool wood, when good manners got the better of her. She was in the act of turning away from the door and making a conscious effort not to contemplate the heated words being exchanged, when the sudden coldness hit her. It was like an icy fog seeping in from beneath the door and through the cracks around it. The frigid air assaulted her bare toes first and clawed like the hands of a corpse up to her ankles and beneath her sleeping gown.

A violent shiver wracked her frame and with it came a rush of peculiar emotions that were frightening in their intensity. All at once she was afraid and angry and desperate for hope, and Harriet, who had last shed tears over her father's grave some five years before, had the sudden urge to cry. The assault of vivid cold disappeared as fast as it had come, only to be replaced by a nearly oppressive heat. Were it not dark and silent beneath her door, Harriet would have been certain the hallway beyond her room had erupted into flames.

The sound of arguing ceased abruptly.

Hands clutched into fists, Harriet turned back to the door. Her brow furrowed low and her nerve endings alive with discomfort, she watched an orange glow fill the space between her door and the floor and then spread out across her feet. She heard booming footsteps go past in the hall before the light disappeared.

Her senses drawn taut, the fine hairs in her ears twitching to catch any hint of sound, Harriet's heart stopped when the terrified scream pierced the night.

"No! Get away from me!"

It was Eliza Pruett. Harriet recognized her voice a heartbeat before throwing open the door and running into the hall.

* * *

Benedict sat near the fire, fingertips pressed together, elbows resting on the arms of the supple leather chair. His spectacles lay on a table nearby with a bottle that an inconspicuous servant had retrieved for him. He hated the times in a given case when he knew few facts about what was going on and had even fewer leads. This instance, however, was far worse than the others, because he sought vengeance.

In the evening, while working on particularly difficult cases, he would sit back and contemplate his facts, all he had researched and knew to be true. This night, however, he could only make a mental list of that which he did not know.

He had no witness to describe the murderer.

He did not know why the watch was so important a man was killed for it. A man who had only come into possession of the watch via a last minute purchase three days prior to his death.

Bloody hell, he did not even know what the damned watch looked like.

With every passing day, Benedict grew angrier and only hoped to find the murderer still alive himself, for he would gladly enjoy the task of tearing him apart. It was at this thought that a terrified scream echoed down the hall outside his room.

He moved fluidly from the chair to the door, pulling it open a second before the individual inhabiting the chamber across from his would have collided with the unforgiving wood. He caught a brief flash of wide, alarmed eyes a shade of dark wheat in this late hour, before bracing his feet and opening his arms.

Harriet's body collided with his silently. As Benedict wrapped his arms tightly about her middle, holding her steady against his solid frame, she let out a silent rush of air against his bare neck. Her cheek fit like a puzzle piece between his jaw and shoulder and, at her damp breath against his skin, Benedict felt an unusual heat sizzle through his veins.

Though it could have barely been a second or two, it felt like forever that he stood there, clutching Harriet to him. Her heart pounded against his, her hips were warm beneath the thin material of her nightgown, and Benedict could feel their softness through his breeches. Her feminine heat affected him in a fierce primal way that made his heart and other portions of his anatomy begin to pound.

Harriet shifted, removing her cheek from his shoulder and lifting her head. Her hair was loose and flowing down her shoulders, thick, tawny stuff in frizzy tangles that tickled his bare forearms. Harriet parted her lips as her gaze met his and Benedict felt his eyelids grow heavy. When she moved, it was not to pull away, but to rest her shaking palms against his shoulder blades. Benedict realized she had righted her feet and he was no longer supporting her. He was holding her.

His head lowered so he might cover her mouth with his.

Eliza Pruett shrieked. This was followed by the sound of heels scrambling and the slamming shut of a door.

Harriet pulled away before his lips touched hers. The tumult of emotions crossing her features quickly fixed upon determined concern. She released Benedict's shoulders, turned out of his arms, and ran in the direction of the young woman's screams.

He blinked, momentarily affected by the emptiness in his arms. Then Benedict scowled, catching up with Harriet in a few brisk strides. He captured her bare arm in a fierce grip and not only pulled her to a halt, but held her there as he moved to step before her.

For a moment, her gaze was not filled with the worry of a heartbeat before. Instead, Benedict caught a glimpse of blatant indignation.

He ignored it. "Stay behind me where it is safe."

He moved on down the corridor and after a moment heard the soft fall of bare feet follow.

A door to their right opened a crack as they passed, and the watery eye of Lord Chesterfield appeared.

"What's this about, eh?"

"I have no idea," Benedict said. "Stay inside."

Lord Chesterfield was only considering following Benedict's orders when his wife hissed behind him, "You heard the man. Close the bloody door!"

The duke blinked wearily and let the door fall shut.

"That is Miss Pruett's door, is it not?" Benedict nodded in the direction of the last in the corridor.

"It is." The fine hair on Benedict's scalp twitched when Harriet spoke so close behind him her words brushed his nape.

He turned from the door, just outside the light of the wall sconces, and faced the woman. "Stay here until I make sure everything is all right."

Harriet sighed, as if vastly dissatisfied with him, and walked past Benedict, into the shadows. He was stunned into stillness until she rapped on the door of the mother-daughter travelers. Benedict was at Harriet's side when the silence following her first knock spurned her to knock harder a second time.

"Lizzie, it is Harriet. Please, open the door."

Unlike the elderly duke, Eliza Pruett opened her chamber door wide. She glanced at Benedict with little interest, before focusing her desperate gaze on Harriet.

"You must come inside at once, Harriet." Eliza was breathless, her eyes wide as she scanned the hall behind them. "Before it comes back."

Though Eliza reached out and tugged on her wrist, Harriet held back. "It? Lizzie, what has you rattled so?"

"By all that is holy, Harriet, I am not a madwoman, but I know what I saw. It came after me as I returned to my bedchamber, twisting at odd angles and reaching out for me with the palest arms I had ever seen." Eliza appeared on the verge of tears as she focused with all sincerity on the woman standing before her. "The rumors are true. Monsters lurk in the halls of this burned palace and one has just come after me."

One of Benedict's brows lifted. This was perhaps the second item of interest that occurred since his journey to Rochester Hall. His attention moved from the Pruett girl to the first thing that had caught his interest at the quiet country estate. The emotion of fascination, Benedict thought as his gaze roamed across Harriet's pale shoulders to the elegant curve of her jaw, had taken on a new meaning with this woman.

She did not appeared horrified as one might imagine of a woman who had just been told dark spirits frequented the halls beyond her bedchamber. Harriet was searching the corridor anew, and when she turned in Benedict's direction, he saw her eyes were alive with excitement.

He frowned, certain he had misjudged the emotion lighting up her gaze.

Then Harriet turned back to Eliza and spoke, almost breathless. "Which way did it go?"

Eliza's fingers trembled as she pointed to the bend in the hall past her chamber, where the light of the sconces did not make a dent in the darkness.

Harriet turned in the direction Eliza indicated and Benedict did not miss the way her shoulders squared and her chin lifted much the same way as when she had rushed to help her friend in distress. He stood behind for a moment, watching her as she disappeared into the darkness. Tall and well shaped like a goddess, her slip of a nightgown the only light in the gloom, her bare feet were silent like that of a ghost.

"Damnation," Benedict breathed.

10

Harriet expected Benedict to stop her. When he arrived at her side, however, matching every two of her determined strides with a single of his, he said nothing and made no move to bring her to a halt.

The turn in the hall was sudden, dark, dank, and colder against her bare ankles than Harriet liked to admit. She stopped, able to see little beyond the faint light cast behind them. There was no furniture in this part of the corridor, and where pictures might have once hung the walls were stained black and yellow. The fire had occurred many years before, but Harriet could have sworn the faint odor of smoke was not a figment of her imagination.

"This must be where the fire did the worst damage," Benedict said at her side. His voice was calm, his accent suited to the darkness.

"How can you be certain?" Harriet whispered for a reason she could not name, slightly unnerved by their shared thoughts. "I can hardly see a hand before my face."

"I can smell it."

Harriet was not scared of ghosts or the monster

Eliza had described, but a shiver stole down her spine. The hall seemed to grow even darker. "We should have brought a taper." Harriet swallowed and looked back toward the light of the hall where there was no stain of fire or cloying blackness.

"It would not have hurt," Benedict said. "I'd suggest we wait until morning, but there doesn't appear to be any windows here."

Harriet reached out and tested her surroundings, lightly brushing the blistered wall. Using it as her guide, she cautiously stepped forward and gasped when her bare heel did not make contact with the floor. All at once she saw herself standing on the edge of an abyss where the floor had burned into oblivion, about to tumble down into the skeletal remains of a once-great castle.

An arm wrapped about her middle and Harriet was drawn so hard against Benedict's chest she lost her breath. She felt his heartbeat against her back, a strong and even cadence.

"Staircase," he said.

Another shiver wracked her frame.

Like a sudden burst of lightning, light flooded the corridor. At once Harriet saw the remaining few ledges of the staircase and the charred bones of a banister. She squinted and looked toward the wall at her right, where out of nowhere a rectangular glow pierced the gloom. Benedict shifted, still holding Harriet against him.

It was a doorway of sorts, set undetectably in the scorched wall. Harriet had read of such things before and she did not doubt it was a secret passageway. The sudden appearance of the hidden door did not interest Harriet as much as the towering form at its center.

Painfully white beneath the too-bright glow of the

lantern, the thing was much as Eliza had described it. The form garbed in layers of singed cloth wobbled side to side in an almost drunken manner. What appeared to be shoulders protruded from where a normal person's head would lay. Above this the form continued upward for another three feet.

While Harriet stared up at Lizzie's ghost, she was surprisingly unafraid. Even the greatest fan of horror novels should have been put on edge by this strange thing with gaping holes for eyes and powder-white arms, but Harriet felt not the least bit fearful. She wondered if it might be because she still had a steady arm wrapped about her waist.

The thing took one lumbering step toward them, its upper half swaying forward and back.

"Be off with ye, visitors to this house of the damned." The entity's voice was loud in the small space of the corridor. It pointed an ivory finger at Harriet and Benedict. *"Run while ye can!"*

Harriet did not move, nor did the man pressed to her side.

Both they and the shrouded figure stood there for a full minute. Then the ghost spoke again. *"Be off, I say! Lest ye face the wrath of Rochester Hall."*

Benedict's arm left her side and he stepped away from her, closer to the self-proclaimed haunt.

"Get away from me." The ghoul's voice became urgent and more than a little surprised.

Harriet pursed her lips and watched Benedict. The man continued toward the figure. He reached out, wrapped a fist into the yellowing shroud of the monster, and pulled.

"Bugger!" the monster cried, and at the same time it uttered a feminine scream.

It swayed precariously and, a moment after Benedict

stepped out of the way, toppled to the floor. The ghost dissolved into two separate forms, that of a man and a woman struggling beneath the layers of sheets.

Benedict looked at her and lifted a brow.

She scowled at the two as they continued to battle the carefully burned fabric.

"It was you who frightened poor Eliza," she declared. "What sort of game is this where you accost strangers with ugly threats?" She nudged a lump that might have been a shoulder or large knee with her bare toes. "Who are you?"

The woman disentangled herself first from the sheets, her hair falling out of its knot as she drew herself up to her knees. "It is Jane, mademoiselle," a familiar voice mumbled sheepishly. She peered up at Harriet before helping her cohort from their handmade shroud. "This is Jeffrey Hogg. He works in the stables."

The man rose to his feet. He shot Harriet a disagreeable scowl, and then turned as if to give Benedict the same look. Glancing at the other man's broad shoulders and impenetrable features, he rethought himself and focused his dirty look on Harriet anew. "Ye could've killed us."

Harriet's puzzlement at the sight of the maid returned to anger. She said to the stableman, "As I recall, it was you scaring the life out of innocent people, dressed like some sort of nightmarish specter."

Jeffrey sneered, giving Harriet the once-over. "At least we ain't in our skivvies."

She gasped, heat rushing across her cheeks and the skin exposed by her nightgown.

By the time the stableman had got to his feet, Benedict had closed the space between them. Jeffrey blinked up at the other man, surprised by his silent and immediate approach as well as visibly alarmed with the frigidness of his gaze.

"You'll watch your tongue."

"I'm sorry, Mademoiselle Harriet, truly I am." Jane remained on her knees until Harriet stepped forward and reached for her hands. They were, Harriet saw, covered with flour.

"Why ever would you do such a thing? Has Lizzie been unkind to you? Have I?"

"*Non, mademoiselle.*" Jane shook her head quickly, lovely gaze earnest. "I do not even know Miss Pruett, and you've been more than kind."

"Harriet," Benedict said. He squatted to reach for the yellow-and-scorched cloth that had shrouded the pair of haunters.

"Yes?"

"I believe the girl when she says they meant no one any harm." He looked up at her, dark eyes alive with keen intelligence. "They were just doing their job."

Harriet's brow creased. "Their job, sir?"

"I think Lady Cruchely pays them not only to look after the stables and house, but they also serve to provide entertainment to her guests." He straightened fluidly, eyes still fixed on Harriet as he tilted his head slightly. "Is that not so, Mr. Latimer?"

The creak of the floorboards pulled Harriet's attention from Benedict to the opened hidden door. The large man's frame filled the doorway as he looked from the servants, to Harriet, and then Benedict.

"Lady Cruchely would like to meet with you in her study."

Harriet considered putting on a gown before they adjoined to Lady Cruchely's private study, but then that would give her one less to work with when others were present. She had donned her robe, a great and billowy concoction given to her on her last birthday, and a pair of slippers and followed Benedict to the lady's quarters, which took up most of the third floor of the estate.

Latimer was there and Harriet noticed he wore only breeches and an untucked shirt. Dorthea Cruchely was clad much the same as Harriet—to the younger woman's relief—though her hair was not sleep mussed but neatly pinned beneath a sleeping bonnet. In the darkness only a little deadened by the fire burning in the hearth, the woman looked tired and the lines around her eyes and mouth were visible. She smiled apologetically as she went to Harriet, reaching for the younger woman's hands as she had when they first met.

"So you both know my terrible secret."

"We cannot be the first who found you out?" Benedict said from where he approached Latimer and a table laden with crystal decanters.

"You are," Latimer said. When he reached for the glasses, Benedict waved him away, not impolitely.

The latter man removed two snifters from the rest and poured brandy into each.

"Usually, guests do not come in contact with my ghosts in the manner of you and Miss Mosley. Most run *from* the ghouls, not at them." Dorthea grinned at Harriet. "I must say we've never had guests as brave."

"They frightened poor Lizzie terribly," Harriet said.

"Yes," the duchess said sadly. She released Harriet and moved to the chair behind her desk. Latimer stood at the corner of the table like a watchdog. "It is not often the case that guests run headlong into a ghost. My staff makes noise from empty hallways and through hidden openings in the walls. They wear disguises lest someone should catch a glimpse of their passing. It is unfortunate Miss Pruett had retired so late for the evening."

"It is not often the case that a woman of your rank needs to resort to parlor tricks to obtain visitors." Benedict put a snifter in Harriet's hand. His voice was void of caution, as well as judgment. "You do it for entertainment? It cannot be the money."

"Wrong on both counts, Mr. Bradbourne." Lady Cruchely's sad smile remained. "I am not amused by frightening others, but I do enjoy giving them a good tale to share with a friend or two when they depart. And, I must admit, I very much do need the funds I receive from my guests." She and Latimer exchanged a silent look while Harriet watched, sipping her brandy with a small wince. "Perhaps you should both sit. As you are the first to find out the truth about the spirits of this house, you should hear the entire sordid tale."

Harriet, interest piqued beyond anything from one of her horrid novels, felt her way to a chair. She did not want to take her eyes off the woman who, it was certain, had a most excellent story to tell. Benedict remained on his feet. She caught the flicker of firelight on his spectacles from the corner of her eye.

"You will recall my mentioning the transfer of my family's possessions into the hands of a great-uncle? Warren Rochester's brother?"

Harriet nodded.

"My family received nothing from the man. My father had only his name and married my mother who had no name but a good deal in the way of a dowry. I, unfortunately, formed a bond with a man who sought the same financial stability as the men of my family. I was young and naive and imagined him to be the love of my life. I married him despite all the warnings from my family and the fact he had shown no proof that he could support me."

Sometimes, Harriet thought, it was beneficial to be of little wealth or importance. Especially when there were others in the world that thought to use their spouses as a means to a better way of life. It had very little to do with the love and adoration that filled the books her best friend loved.

She drank the last of the brandy from her glass as she looked toward the man standing between her and the fireplace. Harriet wondered, holding the glass against her lips, if Bradbourne was the sort of man who looked for wealth and social standing in women.

As if he sensed her stare, he turned in Harriet's direction. His gaze met hers and then dropped to where the rim of her snifter pressed to her damp lips. His eyes again lifted to hers before he focused on the woman speaking. Harriet thought she saw the muscles in his neck go taut.

"And how did that turn out for you?" Benedict asked bluntly.

"Not well at all." Dorthea's laugh was resigned, mirthless. "Pierce squandered away our funds until we had hardly enough to live. Then he died."

Harriet said no words of condolence. She had never been good at such things and the duchess didn't appear to be in need. Instead she nodded. "So you are using this house to reestablish your accounts."

"Yes. I have always loved this house. My father brought me here as a child when it was in much worse condition than now and I thought it was a mysterious and sad place. I even imagined I saw ghosts here." She chuckled. "Needless to say, I spent most of my nights sharing my governess's bed.

"But that is neither here nor there. The fact is I've wished to rebuild the place to the grandeur it once was and could not do that with the meager funds I had left following my husband's passing."

Benedict lifted a brow. "So you concocted this scheme to help in your restoration efforts."

Dorthea winced. "'Concocted' sounds rather devious. I like to think I provide harmless entertainment at a small fee."

"It is entertainment," Harriet said. She smiled sheepishly. "I was excited to come here and a little, irrational part of me wanted to be surprised by a ghost or two, though my sensible side knew it was quite unlikely. Your guests want to hear strange sounds in the night and catch glimpses of phantoms. That is why you've never had anyone chase your ghosts down before. They want them to be real and don't want to ruin the excitement of it all."

Dorthea smiled at Harriet with genuine warmth. "Thank you, Harriet. I'm glad you understand."

"Can we assume Lady Cruchely's secret is safe?"

Harriet had forgotten Latimer was present until he spoke. His tone was a mixture of concern and warning.

"It is." She nodded.

"Mr. Bradbourne?"

He looked from Latimer to Harriet. He spoke as his gaze focused on her smile. "It appears that way."

The duchess entertained them for perhaps an hour or even more with tales of her ghostly schemes. Harriet could feel the woman's mood lighten as she shared a comical tale of her cook in chains and then one of Jane getting locked in a closet when the bedchamber's occupants retired for the night. Harriet could not be sure if it was Dorthea's hint that Jane was forced to eavesdrop on an intimate encounter or the third glass of brandy she sipped that made her cheeks go warm.

When the clock struck two, Lady Cruchely looked toward its hands and then the two seated across from her. "How terrible of me to keep you up so late."

"It's nothing." Harriet shook her head and frowned a little when the room swayed. She pushed to her feet and bid everyone good night before leaving the chamber for the carpeted staircase.

She frowned again when she peered down the steps to the second floor and wobbled.

"Miss Mosley."

Benedict was at her side, holding out his arm almost awkwardly.

"Thank you." She looked in the opposite direction to hide her blush as she rested her palm on his sleeve. Harriet managed to hold her tongue when she was tempted to inquire if the man participated in some kind of fieldwork. The arm beneath his shirtsleeve was hard. Well muscled—not like the other gentlemen present, save Mr. Latimer.

"I should apologize," he said as they moved down the stairs. "It was forward of me to refill your glass without asking."

"You think me smashed?" Harriet laughed after she thought about it because, in fact, she supposed she was. "My friends and I do enjoy wine and I will admit Gus and I have spent a night or two finishing off the occasional bottle. I do not think the punch we share is quite as potent as Lady Cruchely's brandy." She came to an abrupt halt at the landing leading into their hall, looked up at Benedict. "I did not embarrass myself, did I?"

"No," he said. And when they began toward their rooms, he asked, "This Gus, he is your husband?"

Harriet shook her head. "My best friend, Augusta Merryweather. We share our home." She smiled, thinking of the other. When she looked again at Benedict, he was gazing at her smile.

Her brows snapped together and she pursed her lips. "Benedict—may I call you Benedict?"

"Yes." They drew to a halt in the space that separated their rooms.

"Be honest."

"I will."

"Do I have something in my teeth? A leftover bit of parsley from dinner perhaps?"

"What?" He peered at her as if she'd lost her mind, which made Harriet grin.

"I was wondering if that was the reason you kept looking at my mouth. I thought there might be a little something . . ." She presented her teeth and tapped the front two with her index finger. "Either that"—she shook her head, her smile becoming lopsided—"or I thought you might want to kiss me."

Despite her effort at the joke, Benedict's features remained unreadable. He did not smile, though his brown eyes went darker in the dim light of the wall sconces. "You do not have anything in your teeth, Harriet." When he spoke his voice was tense, odd compared to his normal tone.

"Well, then"—Harriet nodded succinctly—"you must want a kiss."

Benedict did not move and Harriet's smile began to fade.

She licked her lips. "Mr. Bradbourne?"

"Benedict." His attention dropped at the movement of her tongue and he took a step toward her.

Harriet was certain her heart had stopped, though a steady pounding settled in her ears. She could not move her limbs to step back, could not convince herself that she really wanted to move away. "Benedict?"

"Yes," he said, "I do want a kiss."

He was so close she could feel his breath against the flesh of her lips, but he moved no farther. His gaze held hers; it was almost black and stark with an emotion she could not remember ever being directed toward her before. Harriet's hands trembled as they lifted, and she reached for Benedict's shoulders. She sensed movement; it was his hands clenching into fists on either side of him. His earlobes moved as his jaw flexed and she could make out a shadow around the lower half of his face where his morning beard was coming in.

Harriet closed her eyes and kissed him.

11

From the Journal of Harriet R. Mosley
  I should make a note that a woman must never,
ever *decide to take upon herself a forward manner like
that which she uses with her close lady friends when
dealing with a gentleman. Not even to make a joke.*

Her kiss had surprised him as much as his own blatant abuse of her sense of humor. He had known she was making a joke and pretended to think Harriet serious. Forcing her, actually, to follow through with actions that she'd only intended as words in jest.

The soft touch of her mouth to his had been like the brush of a baby bird's wing. He felt her breath mingle with his, tremble against his skin. The dampness of her bottom lip, the way it clung to that sensitive place at the base of his upper lip, had kept him awake and uncomfortable most of the night. Several times as he tossed and turned in the darkness, Benedict found himself eager for another encounter with Harriet Mosley.

When the dining room door opened, he shifted in

his chair to look over his shoulder. He scowled when the newcomer proved to be Mrs. Pruett, and he turned back to his empty plate and fourth cup of tea.

He felt like he had been at the table for hours and the tea was weighing down heavily in his bladder, but he couldn't remove himself from the table until he saw the woman who had left him aching and awake until the early hours of the morning and then sent him into the sort of dream some men only wished they could have.

Harriet hadn't risked a good night after she pulled away from him. They stared at each other for a good minute before the sound of footsteps on the stairs sent her to her room. He had stared at the closed door, his mouth still warm from hers, and restrained the urge to follow.

A heavy thud, like a body hitting wood, preceded her entrance to the dining room. He had made no effort in stealth every time he looked toward the opening door. This time as the door swung open, everyone at the table went silent and stared as Harriet came toppling through. She fell on hands and knees to the hard floor, but before many at the table rose from their chairs, Harriet was on her feet.

Benedict had already risen and was walking toward her when she came to her full height. He stopped then and watched. Her cheeks were flushed, as was the exposed skin of her neck, her eyes wide as she looked back at the near-strangers sharing this embarrassing moment with her.

Her chest expanded as she took a deep breath and grinned, shifting her shoulders for emphasis. "I *love* breakfast!"

Benedict grinned back.

Harriet's audience laughed. Eliza Pruett, Benedict

saw, clutched a hand to her mouth. Harriet looked at the younger woman and chuckled.

When she moved toward an empty chair at the end of the table beside Byron Elliot, the farthest point from him, Benedict drew the chair beside his.

Harriet stopped and made brief eye contact, murmuring her thanks before sitting.

Benedict did not miss the way Elliot's perfect features went dark a heartbeat before he lifted his teacup to Benedict, as if to acknowledge a well-played game.

"Are you all right, Miss Mosley?" Lady Cruchely, at the head of the table, asked once able to control her laughter.

"Yes," Harriet said as she opened a napkin on her lap, nodding in appreciation at the servant who filled her teacup. "I'm not sure if I tripped over my own feet or a fold in the rug. I prefer the latter."

Oscar Randolph leaned over his plate and spoke thoughtfully. "You know, I do believe I saw a rise in the rug. Very dangerous looking. A death trap, really."

"Kind of you to say so, sir." When Harriet drank of her tea, her eyes shimmered over the rim.

Benedict, who would have liked those eyes shimmering on his behalf, scowled.

"Well, did anyone experience anything ghostly last night?" Lady Dorthea inquired with practiced ease.

This brought on an onslaught of voices. Apparently he and Harriet hadn't been the only ones to see the liveryman and maid in their finery. As the guests began to speak, attention was quickly deflected from Harriet. Benedict could feel her relax beside him, but her hand trembled when she reached for her fork.

"Benedict," she said quietly, so others would not hear.

"Yes." His brows lifted because he thought she had been purposely ignoring him.

When Harriet met his gaze, there was no hint of shame or embarrassment. There was, however, an odd gleam to her eye and dark shadows beneath her lids. She was pale and her hand still shook as she reached again for her tea.

Benedict restrained the urge to pointedly ask what was wrong.

"I am afraid that I've grown accustomed to the comfort of my friends." She spoke like a woman choosing her words carefully. "That is to say, I can and usually do anything I wish when I'm with them. I think I took the comfort I feel when in your company too far, sir. I hope you don't think me the sort of woman who . . ." She picked at her napkin before meeting his eye. "I apologize for my unladylike behavior."

She turned away as he felt the impact of her words, and before he could say anything, Lord Chesterfield was pointing at him with the tines of his fork and the piece of sausage speared by them.

"Whatever become of it, eh?"

"What?" The word came out an irritated demand more so than a question.

"The spirit, young man," Lady Chesterfield said. Sunlight gleamed across the spectacles set on the tip of her nose and the streaks of silver in her otherwise white hair. "My husband said he saw you and Miss Mosley follow it down the hall."

"I did indeed." Chesterfield nodded several times, his heavy jowls quivering. "You're either commendably brave or terribly stupid."

Oscar Randolph choked on his toast, sputtering to hold back laughter.

Benedict lifted a brow, considering it.

"What happened?"

Benedict could feel Lady Cruchely's gaze affix to him, but did not look at her. "Nothing," he said.

"Nothing at all?" Lady Chesterfield was clearly disappointed.

"We did follow it, madam." Harriet spoke up. She folded her hands in her lap as she nodded. "Mr. Bradbourne was very brave as he wanted to investigate if Liz—Miss Pruett—was in danger. Yet all we found was the burned-out remains of a staircase and another corridor." Only Benedict heard the slight tremble in her voice as she mentioned the charred remains. "It was as if it, whatever *it* was, disappeared into the walls."

"Oh," Lady Chesterfield breathed with wonder.

"Speaking of disappearing"—Randolph brushed crumbs from his mustache and rose—"I hope you will excuse me for my morning stroll. Join me, Bradbourne?"

He could not stay to speak to the woman sitting next to him without appearing rude. He followed the old man to the door, but paused and looked back at a mass of multihued curls.

"Harriet," he said.

Her spine stiffened and she looked over her shoulder.

"As to the matter we spoke of before," he began cautiously, realizing several others at the table had focused on him, "do not apologize."

Harriet stood close to the staircase. Alone and silent she gazed steadily, if not wearily, toward the end of the corridor. She looked as if she was waiting for, at any minute, someone to come around the corner that she and Benedict had investigated the night before. The corner that led to a staircase that no longer existed and walls charred from the past, a dark chasm she would have fallen into were it not for her companion.

She shivered, as thoughts of what lay below in the darkness flitted through her imagination.

From the time she had awoken late for breakfast and still sleepy, Harriet had been trying to convince herself it had all been a terrible dream brought about by Lady Cruchely's fine brandy and too many thoughts of ghosts and spirits. She could remember it all too clearly, however—the heavy thud of footsteps that woke her where she lay beneath the bedclothes. She rose, bumping into a nightstand and knocking over a small vase there, with an unusual lack of concern, feeling the cool floorboards underfoot and hazy tendrils of sleep clinging to her.

She was like a woman in a trance, who was very much aware of being in a trance, as she opened her bedchamber door and peered out into the hall. Empty save for the meager light of the wall sconces, of which several had flickered out in the night. Footsteps again, she could make them out plainly, coming from the end of the hall.

Filled with the kind of reckless curiosity only dulled senses can bring, Harriet went to the turn in the hall. Perhaps, in some part of her consciousness, she imagined Benedict would be there. Waiting for another kiss.

The burned space beyond the turn, unstable until the lady of the house could profit from a few more visitors, was empty. From where the staircase once stood, however, the hollow thud of footsteps continued.

Only then did Harriet come fully awake, fully aware of her situation, and by then it was too late.

His head crested the bleak darkness. As Harriet watched in horrified wonder, the figure of a man emerged as if the steps were still present and he were climbing them. She saw first his cold eyes, not looking at her, and then his misshapen nose and blunt mouth. There was a scar on his cheek, and another bisecting one dark eyebrow. Even in the inadequate light she could see the smaller scar on his chin.

He was neither translucent nor pale as alabaster, Harriet's ghost. The skin stretched taut across sharp features was dusky and lined like that of a man who spent a great deal of time in the sun. He wore an out-of-date, loose white shirt, unbuttoned comfortably at the neck, loose breeches cinched at the knees, and high leather boots. The vest that ran from his shoulders and over his waist was dark blue, the intricate pattern embroidered upon it done in the same hue and nearly invisible.

Harriet could have touched him by barely lifting a hand—he was so close—but she did not move. She did not breathe as he moved past, though the stranger did not look her way. His gaze remained forward as if in search of someone. Harriet, if one were to look only at the man's reaction, might very well not even have been there.

She watched him with lips parted and breath frozen in her lungs until he strode with purpose in the direction she had come and out of sight. It took a moment for her to compose herself enough to shift, peeking back around the corner, but not long enough for the man to reach the new staircase and go below. When Harriet looked, however, the apparition was gone.

Harriet—her breathing ragged and fingers trembling—had returned to her room then, locking the door behind her and drawing back the blankets only long enough to lie down. Tightly closing her eyes, she pulled the blankets over her head and there she remained until she woke.

It was as she was reminiscing over the odd dream, pushing out of bed and hurrying to wash her face, that she felt a sharp sting in the heel of her right foot. Harriet gave a sharp intake of breath, looking down, and then she couldn't breathe at all.

Harriet had been unable to pick up the broken pieces of the vase that had nicked her foot. Hours later, standing at her door and staring down the hall, she could not make herself go farther down, too afraid she would find more evidence of her encounter.

She turned to her room, praying Jane had cleaned up the mess she had left, the broken porcelain that betrayed her dream for what it was—not a dream at all.

12

She carried the latest Shoop novel, her shawl thrown over one arm. Harriet reached the end of the stairs and had her fingers on the front door handle.

"Miss Mosley!"

Harriet nearly jumped. She pressed her book to her pounding heart and turned toward Byron Elliot. He stood at the foot of the stairs smiling and Harriet wondered if he had been behind her all along, a silent shadow.

His handsome smile faltered. "Is everything all right?"

Harriet shook her head, careful to clear her features of doubt. Perhaps the ghost stories and restless nights were getting to her.

"I'm fine," she said, mostly for her own benefit.

"Excellent." Elliot moved closer, tapping his hat against his leg as he looked at her shawl and then the book she clutched to her breast.

She thought his gaze may have lingered over the skin above her bodice, and then shook off the idea.

"I'm going for a walk," she explained. "I thought I might find a nice, quiet place to read for a bit."

Elliot's brows lifted. "I happen to know an excellent place to bask in the glory of nature and enjoy the written word." His brow crinkled as he again looked at Harriet's book. "Is that a horror novel?"

It had been a while since she'd had anyone react in distaste at her reading material. She lifted her chin. "Indeed it is. Actually, I've grown even fonder of the author Randal C. Shoop since coming here."

"Ah. No matter." His jade-green eyes met hers again. "As I was saying, I know a perfect place for you." Elliot inclined his head. "Would you allow me the honor of escorting you, Miss Mosley?"

Harriet heard him only absently. Her attention was fixed on the movement of his glossy black hair. At his bow, the locks carefully curled over his brow shifted to expose a great deal of forehead. She wondered if he so expertly styled his hair to be fashionable *and* hide his approaching baldness.

"Miss Mosley?" Elliot straightened and fingered his curls back into place.

"I would appreciate your company, Mr. Elliot," Harriet said politely, though she had been looking forward to time alone.

Elliot set his hat atop his head with practiced ease and held out his arm. He pushed open the door ahead and when they came to stand in the sunlight beyond, he halted to smile at Harriet.

He was obliged to tilt his chin upward.

"You are quite tall, Miss Mosley."

"I've been told as much."

"As a matter of fact, I've never met a woman before as tall as you."

Harriet smiled. "Long legs have their advantage," she said, thinking of the help she was to her friends in positioning pictures on walls and placing books on high shelves.

"I'm sure they do." Elliot's chuckle suggested his thoughts were elsewhere.

He and Randolph were coming in through the garden and might not have seen the pair had they stepped ahead a moment sooner. Before he reached the French doors that led inside and the cold gray stones of the house blocked his view, Benedict caught movement on the west lawn. He might have ignored the pair strolling arm in arm away from the house were it not for the fact the woman stood a full foot above the man.

Benedict came to an abrupt halt, turning to stare at the pair. He could feel his brow furrowing in a scowl and a dark emotion kicked at his lungs.

The faint breeze carried to him the scent of flowers and lush greenery, and the sound of Harriet's laughter.

He could not recall ever being jealous before. Certainly not over a woman he had known only a few days. The emotion, so close to his heart, disturbed him.

"What do you think men like Byron Elliot get out of it?"

"What?" Benedict said with a bluntness he could not control.

Randolph moved to stand beside him, hands in pockets and the stub of a cigar in the corner of his mouth. He spoke around it. "Dressing like a dandy and memorizing other men's poems."

Benedict looked at the older man askance. "He memorizes poetry?"

"I heard him in the parlor quoting some verse from Shelley and Keats to Mrs. Pruett."

Benedict felt his scowl darken. Elliot and Harriet had come to a halt, only so the man could wrap a pale shawl about her shoulders.

"He kept making errors," Randolph was saying. "Instead of calling one poem *Ode to a Nightingale* he said it was *Ode to a Rooster.*"

Beneath the old man's plain expression, his eyes glittered with humor.

Benedict chuckled.

"I imagine," Randolph went on, "the fellow spends more time in front of a mirror than you and I combined. Perhaps more than you and I and Harriet combined."

"I do not like him and I don't like how he is always staring at Harriet."

"You are always staring at Harriet." Reading the younger man's hard expression, he sighed. "Harriet is not a green girl, no Eliza Pruett. I suspect she has encountered men like Mr. Elliot before. She strikes me as the sort who knows a thing or two about the world and . . . she will choose the better man in the end."

"Better man?" Benedict looked at the writer.

He grinned. "You, Bradbourne." His bushy brows lifted with surprise and he nodded back to the lawn.

Harriet had come to a halt, was facing the two men at the edge of the garden. She lifted her arm to give a great wave.

Benedict and Randolph lifted their hands in return. Randolph chuckled.

13

The old man looked at the card she had laid upon the table and then at Harriet through his heavy brows. She worried her bottom lip until she saw his grin of appreciation.

"I think I've been had," Randolph said. "Well done, young lady."

Harriet gave an uncharacteristically bashful smile as she reached out to sweep the playing cards into a single pile. "I am a woman of few talents," she said. She made a fan of the cards atop the table, and then used one to make the cards shift back and forth like dominoes. "And I'm afraid most of those talents are quite odd."

Randolph leaned across the table, brows lifting and thick mustache moving fluidly with his whisper. "Now you've captured my interest, madam. What other odd talents have you? Tell me in detail."

Harriet, who had been pressing her index finger into the stack of cards she held, sending them flying over the table and into her free hand, paused. She looked at her favorite author and leaned over the table toward him.

"I've been told while in trousers I make an excellent male figure."

Randolph threw back his head and roared with laughter. Eliza Pruett, who sat in a nearby settee with her mother—the older woman forcing her daughter to leave the card table for the more respectable task of stitching—looked up and sighed.

Movement caught the corner of Randolph's eye— someone entering the parlor—and he quickly sobered. He reached out to cover Harriet's hands where she was dancing one card over her knuckles. He winked at her, clearing his throat.

"Bradbourne!" He waved the man over from where he stood, inspecting the room from the doorway.

The younger man, Harriet thought, looked about to beg off, until his gaze shifted from Randolph to where she sat across from him. Behind the lenses of his spectacles, she thought she saw his eyes go darker. He moved toward their table.

"Won't you join our lovely Miss Mosley in a few hands?" Randolph made a face full of suffering. "I grow weary of besting the poor thing with my talents." He smiled innocently at Harriet.

"That depends." Benedict's gaze was almost brooding as it dropped momentarily to her smile. "Does the lovely Miss Mosley wish to engage herself with a new man?"

Harriet felt her neck go warm. She was vaguely aware Benedict's words had nothing to do with cards.

"Yes, yes." Randolph answered for her, rising from his chair and leaving it drawn for Bradbourne. "She most certainly does."

Harriet wondered, as she watched the older man walk toward where the Pruett family sat, if the writer had not captured her thoughts exactly.

She looked across the table as Benedict sat. He reached for the cards, his fingers lean and nails clipped neatly.

"Cribbage?"

Harriet held back an expression of disgust. She could not think of a more boring game. "Sir Randolph and I have already removed cards from the deck to play Ecarte," she said.

Benedict's brows lifted and he looked at where Randolph sat next to the elder Pruett woman. "I'd imagined Randolph more a gentleman than to gamble with an innocent."

Innocent? Harriet thought.

"Bah." Randolph waved the younger man off. "Play her. Make a bet. It's all in good fun." He ignored the disgruntled murmur of the woman beside him.

Benedict met Harriet's eye. "I would feel ashamed to bet against a lady," he said to her in a very reassuring manner.

Harriet's blood had heated to a simmer. He could certainly see she was no child. Did Benedict think her a fool?

"Let's find," he was saying, "the rest of the cards."

"What is your bet, sir?" Harriet asked through her teeth.

A strangled cough erupted from the settee. It sounded suspiciously like an old man's muffled laugh.

Benedict blinked. "Pardon?"

"I do not have my reticule," Harriet said, "so we must wager without money." Not that she had any funds to waste on wagers, were her reticule in her lap.

She wouldn't have minded playing a game with Benedict without betraying her rather dirty secret. A nice game that hinted not at her lineage. His annoying lack of faith in her abilities, however, had made his head on a platter seem tempting indeed.

"Randolph and I wagered our evening drinks. The loser serves the winner. What would you gamble for?"

"I've no idea." Benedict appeared slightly amused.

"Do you ride, Benedict? Can you manage well upon a horse?"

"Yes."

"I myself have never ridden before. I was raised in the city and had no use for the skill. If I win, then I would like you to take me riding about Lady Cruchely's estate and the surrounding countryside."

"All right," Benedict said, pressing his back comfortably in his chair. His eyelids drew together as if he had a sense of her scheming.

"And what about you, sir? Is there any skill I have that you desire, or should you like me to bring your evening port to you?"

"Yes." The muscles in his throat worked.

Harriet nodded, the wager set. She did not tell Benedict that it was Sir Randolph who would be serving her wine that evening. "Deal," she said, then quickly realized her commanding tone and smiled. "If you would."

Benedict simply watched her for a moment, eyebrows drawing slightly together. Harriet felt the hair at her nape lift and an involuntary shiver skipped down her spine before he began to deal.

The game, such that it was, lasted for five minutes at the most. She had allowed Randolph the pleasure of winning their first hand, but continued to trump his every attempt for the next three games. Harriet offered the man who thought her too much the innocent to focus on a card game no such pleasure. She bested him quickly, and when she put down her last card—looking up at Benedict through her lashes—he carefully put down his hand.

From where he was nearly asleep in the settee, Randolph realized the game was over and peered at the table. He howled then, clapping appreciatively.

"Too bad the lady has no shame in besting you, Bradbourne."

Benedict did not look at the older man, but continued to watch Harriet. He did not laugh with appreciation as her previous opponent had.

Harriet swallowed, some of her pride diminishing. She forced herself to smile at Benedict. "It seems I shall have to serve neither Sir Randolph nor you."

Benedict smiled then and the curve of his lips hinted at a secret. He leaned forward and said in low tones, "But, Harriet, it was a skill I would have had you serve. Not drink."

"A skill, sir?" Her brow furrowed.

Benedict's eyes gleamed like brown gems as they shifted down to her mouth and then up again.

Her lips parted, though she could not speak. Benedict's brows lifted as he leaned back in his chair, and Harriet began to wonder who bested who.

Benedict looked about to speak again when Latimer cleared his throat. Harriet hadn't realized the large man had entered the room, and only looked in his direction when he was almost at their table.

"Miss Mosley, Mr. Bradbourne, Lady Cruchely would like to see you in her private quarters."

She had a sudden, almost frightening feeling of intimacy when she looked at Benedict and he at her. It was much the same look she and her best friend, Augusta, would often share. Benedict rose then and she silently followed, ushered ahead of the men as they left the room. Harriet was thoughtful, struggling to understand how she had come to share such a kinship, as that she shared with her best friend of some ten years, with a man she'd known only two days.

When Harriet peeked back over her shoulder at Benedict, his eyes were ready to meet hers. As if he sensed her inner turmoil, he smiled gently and Harriet felt her confusion intensify.

They followed Latimer up the stairs, past the second floor where their quarters lay, to the third-floor corridor Lady Cruchely had sectioned off as her personal rooms. Standing at the beginning of the hall, Harriet felt an appreciation for her surroundings she hadn't noticed on her first occasion there. Of course, her last visit had occurred past midnight and shortly after, she and Benedict confronted a great white ghoul.

A few hours past noon, the corridor was bisected with rays of sunlight spilling in from opened doors. Harriet peeked into the rooms with polite curiosity.

"How long have you been employed here, Mr. Latimer?" Benedict was asking.

"Twelve years," the man responded in a voice better suited to one of his lady's monsters. "I worked for Lord Cruchely before he died."

Harriet wanted Benedict to ask if he had been employed to encourage tenants to pay rent, but he did not. She did not miss the fact that Latimer seemed less than overcome with sadness at the mention of his deceased employer.

A door at the end of the hall opened and Dorthea appeared in, Harriet saw, a different gown than the one she wore that morning.

Harriet sighed.

A moment later the floor collapsed beneath her.

She hadn't the time to scream, her loss of footing was so abrupt. She heard no wood shatter or crumple beneath the carpet underfoot. One minute it was there and less than a second later gone.

Lady Cruchely cried out as Harriet fell into the floor. The younger woman threw out her arms. She released a pained gasp as her elbows made contact with, then scratched over the edges of the opening. Harriet's heart rose to her throat and remained there as she gripped the edge of a second layer of wood, broken and bent and swaying with her weight.

"Harriet!" Benedict peered down at her from the edge of the hole, appearing as alarmed as she felt. He outstretched an arm. "Take my hand."

She would have to push off from the meager scrap of wood to which she clung and throw her body upward to catch the man's hand. She looked away from the offered appendage to glare at him.

Lady Cruchely was on her knees as well, looking as if she might cry. "Hold on, Harriet."

As if to taunt the woman, the wood to which Harriet clung gave a disturbing cracking sound.

Harriet squeezed her eyes tightly shut and prayed she would wake at any moment and no longer find herself hanging down from a hole in the floor, but snuggled deeply in her bed.

The wood splinted a half inch and the sound tore through her ears.

Harriet cried out.

"What is downstairs?" Benedict demanded of the other two. "Directly below here?"

"Not the second floor," Dorthea said in a terrified voice. "The hallway below is cut short to allow for the ballroom."

"She will fall two stories," Latimer said bluntly.

As if Harriet could not figure that out.

Her skirts fluttered against her dangling legs. One of her slippers dislodged from her heel and then her foot entirely. It seemed to take a long time before she heard the slipper make contact with anything below.

She opened her eyes to see Benedict's booted feet running away.

"Hold on, Harriet," Lady Cruchely said again. "Don't look down."

Harriet looked down. She whimpered. The ballroom floor was very far away. It was awful that her trip would come to such an untimely end. She sincerely hoped the breaking of her neck would be painless before she left this world for the next.

Harriet closed her eyes again, but when her fingers began to slip, her eyes opened wide.

Down below, where only her slipper had been a heartbeat before, there stood a woman. She stared up at Harriet with a worried furrow between her brows. Her long hair was unbound around her shoulders and she wore a flowing crimson gown that made her skin look pale as snow.

The stranger's lips parted to speak but what emerged was a puff of thick gray smoke. Harriet felt her heart stop, the scent of burning timber tickling her nostrils, and then her hands slipped.

Lady Cruchely screamed. The woman in the dark gown disappeared. Benedict ran beneath the spot she had vacated and opened his arms. Harriet felt Benedict beneath her, registered one arm below her knees and another at her back before they both collapsed to the marble floor.

Harriet lay on top of Benedict's chest for a long

moment, staring up at the hole through which Lady Cruchely and Latimer stared down at her.

"Did you see that woman?" she asked almost conversationally.

Benedict was breathing heavily from his run down the stairs. "What woman?"

Harriet was afraid he would say that.

14

Harriet bit her bottom lip—hard—and squeezed her eyes closed against the pain.

Benedict, waiting until she prepared herself for the last of the ministrations, found a strange sensation deep in his stomach. Harriet was putting up a good fight against the pain, and though tears swam once or twice in her eyes, none fell down her cheek. It was not surprising that the unusual woman proved so strong; it was that he seemed to feel her every pang of discomfort in the center of his heart.

She jerked as he plucked the last of the splinters from her elbow.

"Easy, Harriet," he said, and put the sliver of wood, more than an inch in length, on the table where more than a dozen others had already been placed. "It's done."

Her lashes lifted and, when her eyes met his, Benedict could have sworn he heard the rustling of a wheat field and felt the brush of sunlight on his cheeks.

"Poor dear," Lady Cruchely worried aloud as she wrung out a clean washcloth and then held the damp rag to the seated man. "Poor dear."

They were in the kitchen, empty save for themselves and Latimer who stood against the far wall. He stood still, staring at his shoes, until Dorthea began a pot of tea.

"I'll be fine." Harriet smiled reassuringly for the other woman, but when Benedict carefully pressed the wet cloth to her scratches, she winced.

After cleaning the wounds on her right elbow, much the same way as he had her left, he wrapped a length of dry cloth around her arm.

"How are you?" she surprised him by asking.

"What?" For a moment he didn't know what she was talking about.

"I am not light as a feather, Benedict." She grinned. "It's a wonder you did not cause yourself serious injury breaking my fall as you did."

He shook his head, focusing on the snug knot he finished off in her bandage. Remembering Harriet's fall, his heart stopping as he saw her come down from the ceiling and then the softness of her body against his . . . He couldn't recall what the floor had felt like.

"I don't know how it happened," Dorthea was saying. She let Latimer carry the tea tray to the table. She poured. "One moment you were there and the next gone. I was quite terrified for you, dear. And what might have happened had Benedict not made it downstairs?"

Harriet's hands trembled as she lifted her teacup, and the tea spilled across her fingertips.

Benedict reached quickly to steady her hands; he cupped her fingers with his as she lifted the cup to her lips. Their gazes met over the rim.

"Poor dear," Dorthea said again, shaking her head.

"Had the floor been rebuilt during your remodeling?" Benedict asked, dragging his gaze from Harriet's damp lips. "I should be sincerely pleased to meet the man who did such shoddy labor."

Lady Cruchely shook her head. "It was the other side of the manor burned in the fire. Another staircase had once been used more than that we presently frequent. It was that stairway and what was once considered the entrance to the house that felt the flames. My chambers were untouched by the blaze."

"Old floorboards," Harriet said.

Benedict was not convinced. There was something suspicious about what had happened upstairs, and he was not going to let it go easily.

Then Harriet said, "It is a bit odd that the spot hidden beneath the rug gave way, rather than any other. I'd say someone was trying to murder me, if it didn't sound crazy."

"You are not crazy," Benedict said, meeting her eye.

Harriet frowned.

Lady Cruchely laughed and Benedict thought the sound too high in pitch to be sincere. "Murder. Now that is a form of entertainment I do not provide for my guests."

"What was it you wanted to speak to us about, Lady Cruchely? Before all this." Harriet nodded to her wrapped elbows.

"Dorthea"—the old woman waved a hand dismissively—"you must call me Dorthea. And I wanted to thank you and Mr. Bradbourne for what you said at breakfast this morning. It was most kind of you to go along with my arrangement and I do appreciate it."

Benedict watched Harriet purse her lips, looking at the older woman in earnest. "Dorthea, you must not have the opportunity to make friends often or it would not be so surprising to have the support of one or two."

The duchess smiled back, though Benedict thought he saw a lingering sadness—guilt perhaps—in the back of her eyes. "Indeed."

From the Journal of Harriet R. Mosley
  Lady C has been kind enough to loan me a cloak to wear for the evening. It is much too elaborate, a blood-red thing with a soft hood and several layers of fabric, but will suit to hide the bindings around my arms.
  I am fortunate only my arms suffered in the accident. Had Benedict not had the foresight to run downstairs to break my fall . . . well, I can only imagine what might have happened. I will have to tell Gus the whole story when I return home. She will like as not romanticize the tale to become one like those wishy-washy love stories she so enjoys.
  I hate admitting it, even here in writing that no one shall ever read, but Gus has shared too many of her stories. I'm afraid it has taken me a considerable amount of willpower not to romanticize the tale myself. No man has ever saved my life before. No lady either, for that matter.

15

"Some of the markers date back nearly a thousand years. We believe that there are more graves than those we can see, unmarked and stacked atop one another. The oldest legible gravestone looks to bear the year 889."

Harriet nodded thoughtfully. "A good year, I remember it well."

Beside her, Lizzie giggled.

All things considered, Harriet decided as she walked a little behind the group—staying with Eliza, who was obliged to accompany her slow and scowling mother—Dorthea could not have picked a better evening for a constitutional through an ancient cemetery. It was not cold to the point of discomfort, but Harriet was glad for her borrowed cloak. The slight nip in the air was chilling the tip of her nose and she could just make out the pale puffs of her breathing. The sky was a nice shade of slate-blue and violet, and although the sun hadn't yet set completely, a full moon had already made its appearance. There was a light fog lurking close to the ground; it curled around the ankles of the man walking only a few feet ahead of Harriet.

"There is a rumor that King Alfred the Great once stood here," Lady Cruchely announced with the professionalism of one who gave tours at museums.

"If he's so great," Harriet murmured, "why haven't I ever met him?"

Lizzie, who very much needed a smile with her mother on her heels, giggled again.

Benedict looked back over his shoulder, his eyes gleaming behind his specs.

"Have you ever met Alfred the King, sir?"

His lips twitched, though his tone was serious. "I have not."

"Well, then," Harriet said.

"He was to have fought off a band of marauders." Dorthea stopped at the center of the burial ground, turning to face them with Latimer at her side. "Vikings, who threatened to burn and plunder the village nearby." When she spoke, her words were visible in wisps of heated breath. "I'll let you have a look around now. If anyone wishes to return to the manor, Latimer will walk you. It will be dark soon and gravestones tend to be scary no matter how old they are."

Mrs. Pruett looked at her daughter. "We should go back then."

Eliza did not hear, or at least pretended not to. She linked her arm through Harriet's and walked quickly away from her mother.

Harriet saw Elliot in the distance and he smiled when he caught her eye. When he began toward them, however, Randolph appeared out of nowhere to stand before him. She could hear his jovial tone as he spoke to Elliot.

Eliza said, "Wouldn't it be fun if everyone still had titles with their names, like Alfred the Great and William the Conqueror?"

"Yes." Harriet smiled. "You could be Lizzie the Escapist." As the younger woman gave a frustrated growl, looking back at her mother, Harriet spotted Benedict standing by himself. He was frowning over a crumbling mass of rock that had once marked a grave. In the dim light, mingled with the fog and quiet conversations, he was a solitary figure. The shadow of his shoulders broad and his waist lean. Again she found herself wondering how he occupied himself when not on holiday.

She wondered if there was someone who loved him waiting at home.

Harriet guided her companion and herself toward Benedict.

"How are you," she said, "Benedict the Hero?"

He lifted a brow.

Lizzie said, "We were discussing names and titles. I am Lizzie the Escapist."

Benedict glanced toward where the elder Pruett woman was speaking in a heated manner to Latimer. "I see."

"I thought you might be Benedict the Fall Breaker," Harriet said, "but that doesn't have a pleasant ring to it."

"And what is your title, madam?" He focused on Harriet, his gaze unreadable.

"Harriet," Lizzie said thoughtfully, "the Original."

Harriet wrinkled her nose. "Simply Harriet will suffice." She felt warmth that had nothing to do with her cloak spread across her skin when Benedict continued to watch her, and shifted farther into her hood.

"Eliza"—Mrs. Pruett was breathless and flushed when she joined them—"this will not do. It is getting darker and colder and I won't stay in this place of death any longer. Come along."

The younger woman sighed, offering Harriet an apologetic grin. "Good evening, Miss Mosley," she said very properly.

Harriet smiled in turn. "Good evening, Miss Pruett." Then, when Lizzie and her mother were out of earshot, "She said 'place of death' like it was a bad thing." She looked at Benedict and then at the somber stones around them. "Why are so many people afraid monsters and ghouls come up from the grave? I've never met a soul who had any sort of trouble with the dead."

"It is those who live and breathe," Benedict said, "who do the damage." He ignored Harriet's look of curiosity. "There are a few more graves hidden in the distance. See?" He nodded to where the trees grew dense and amidst the darkness of the trunks Harriet saw square cuts of stone and a pale cross pressing upward from the earth. As they approached, she realized the stones were newer than the others. She checked the dates of the first grave and the next.

"Not even twenty-five years old," Benedict said.

The cross was inscribed with the words *Annabelle, Beloved Mother & Friend.* The second grave read only *Capt. Warren Rochester.* Both bore the same date of death. The smaller stone bore the name of a child, lost on the same day it was born, three years before her parents' deaths.

"These must be Dorthea's grandparents," Harriet said.

"Yes," Benedict said. "Murdered and burned. I don't know which would be a more terrible way to go."

Harriet looked at him, thoughtful as the moonlight kissed her cheeks. "I'd like to think that how we go doesn't matter. In the end, I hope we go to a place so amazing that we never think about the awful parts of the journey that got us there." When Benedict only continued to watch her, she cleared her throat, embarrassed. She shifted again to hide her face.

"That cloak," Benedict said. "I can hardly see you in it."

"Oh?" Harriet feigned surprise.

"I don't like it."

Her heart shuddered in her chest. Unaccustomed to compliments by those she hardly knew, she had to really think about what Benedict said and decide if he had meant the words as an accolade.

Then his hands, gloved in supple leather, were lifting—slipping inside the hood until it fell back from her head. His palms cupped her cheeks and, Harriet thought, his eyes sparked in the moonlight.

He said nothing, only stepped forward and covered her mouth with his. His lips brushed hers once, lightly, and his head shifted back as if to read her reaction. Harriet's lashes fluttered and she licked lips that felt as if they had been burned by the brief touch of his. A ragged puff of air hit Harriet's face before Benedict again kissed her, his hands shifting to cup her nape as her own hands fluttered upward to catch his bent elbows.

Feelings unlike any she'd ever experienced before coiled down her limbs and danced back up again to settle at three parts. Her heart, her stomach, and a place she dared not identify.

"Harriet," he said when he broke away again.

"Yes." She blinked, though she didn't think he was asking a question.

"There is nothing *simple* about you," Benedict said.

Her neck and the upper curves of her breasts burned, and though she was certain she should be shocked by—if not Benedict's kiss—her reaction to it, Harriet smiled a little.

The arrow was nearly inaudible. The whisper of the blade piercing the air little more than a tickle of butterfly wings in the ear. The sharp point, however, was less subtle. It tore through the soft fabric falling across Harriet's back. The material tore then caught in the quivers. The neck of the cloak came up tight around Harriet's throat—to the point of choking her—as the arrow yanked the material taut and pierced the trunk of the nearest tree.

She could not see the weapon, of course, and thought that someone who decided they didn't like her very much—Eliza Pruett's mother, perhaps—had grabbed the back of her cloak and yanked. Harriet stumbled and would have collided with the tree had Benedict's arms not come around her, one palm settling at the center of her back to hold her steady as fabric split. He reacted more quickly than she, using his free hand to release the frog button pressing into her throat.

Benedict's teeth met in a grimace as he reached behind her, yanking. Harriet's eyes went wide and she could feel the blood drain from her face as she looked at the arrow in his hand. A bright red splash of fabric hung off its pointed tip.

She looked at Benedict and her words left her lips as a trembling white cloud. "I wish I were crazy."

There were, Harriet thought, some perfectly fine individuals who became the brunt of murder attempts. Struggle as she might, as Benedict grabbed her wrist and marched them away from the spot of her almost-certain demise, Harriet could not think of one.

The problem was, she reasoned as she stumbled over a shard of broken tombstone and Benedict lifted his hand to her elbow to steady her, those individuals tended to be wealthy, or important figures in society. At the very least, they had scorned a lover for one more pleasing. Harriet was neither rich nor famous, and the only lover she had known had been dead for some eight years.

She thought long and hard about the books she read, many involving a murder plot of some sort, trying to figure out the link that made her like the heroines who suffered most bravely until the last page.

Benedict had already found the link.

He brought them to where Lady Cruchely and her so-called butler stood, the woman smiling until she saw the expression on Benedict's face. Benedict shoved the arrow against Latimer's chest until the man lifted his great, hairy hands to catch it.

"Someone has tried to kill you again, Lady Cruchely. And again it was the innocent Miss Mosley who suffered on your behalf."

The older woman gasped, as did Harriet.

"The cloak," she said.

"Yes." Benedict looked at her from the corner of his eye, only releasing his fierce grip on her elbow slightly. He focused on Dorthea again, his expression ugly and showing no apprehension for the larger man easing closer to her side. "My concern is whether or not it was some peculiar scheme of yours, giving Harriet your cloak and inviting her to your private chambers to walk the spot you hadn't tested."

"No!" Dorthea cried with an urgency that bespoke the truth. She was pale in the moonlight, her skin almost the color of the hair at her temples.

"See here, Bradbourne," Latimer was saying, taking a step toward the younger man.

"No," Benedict said, pointing at the other and—amazing Harriet—stopping him in his tracks. "I know not what game you people are playing, but you have a new competitor and I am not about to let a perfectly decent and lovely woman die in your place."

For a moment Harriet forgot she had almost been run through with an arrow.

Lovely? she thought.

Dorthea lifted her hands and her gloved fingers trembled slightly. "I understand you are upset, Mr. Bradbourne."

"Lady," Benedict said through his teeth, "I'm mad as hell."

Harriet's eyes went wide. From far away, Benedict might appear a calm man. Standing straight and lean with a hard expression. She could feel, however, the heat of rage coming through his coat sleeves.

"Please let me explain," Dorthea was saying. She looked up at Latimer, who was watching Benedict with an uncustomary expression of alarm. "Darling, please see everyone into the house. I should like our discussion to be private."

He did not look happy about leaving his mistress, but turned away. Dorthea waited until Latimer had her guests moving in the direction of the house, before facing Benedict and Harriet again.

Harriet saw Sir Randolph look back at them. The man appeared disgruntled at having his graveyard walk interrupted.

Dorthea sighed, lifting the tips of her fingers to her temples. "I do not know where to begin."

"Save the dramatics. Just tell us what the hell is going on here," Benedict demanded in a blunt tone that seemed familiar to him. Harriet felt sorry for the older woman and anyone else who was ever forced to meet his wrath.

"First"—Dorthea looked at Harriet and genuine concern aged her features—"are you all right, dear? Do you need any kind of medical attention?"

"I'm a little shaken up, but not injured." When Harriet finally spoke, Benedict's grip on her tightened. He looked over her features, then down her back where she could feel a slight breeze coming in through the hole in her cloak. "Really," she insisted, when he did not look convinced.

"I am being blackmailed," Lady Cruchely said without compunction. She laughed and it was a dry, brittle sound. "Actually, I *was* being blackmailed. A month ago I made the decision to stop meeting the demands of my invisible adversary."

Harriet, unaccustomed to such tales, was even more surprised by Benedict's quiet grasp of the situation. As if he had heard it before.

"The attacks began shortly after you ceased meeting the blackmailer's demands?"

"Yes," Dorthea said. "There was only one incident before you came. My carriage suffered a terrible accident and I might have been killed were it not for Jeffrey Hogg's skill behind the reins. At the time, I had imagined it only a freak accident. In the past few hours, I've suffered many doubts."

Why was the kind lady being blackmailed? Harriet wondered. She couldn't imagine the woman creating any sort of trouble and wished it were not impolite to ask.

"For what reason were you blackmailed, Lady Cruchely?" Benedict said, and Harriet almost smiled. "What is being held over your head?"

Dorthea looked away, up toward the sky that had quickly turned black. "The notes said they had some sort of information that would link me to my husband's untimely death."

"Did you kill him?"

"No," said Latimer, approaching them from behind. "I did."

"Not," Dorthea said quickly, "before I wished him dead on more than one occasion."

"Why?" Harriet breathed. She felt no fear toward the woman or her murderous lover. Only curiosity as to what had led her so far.

"Pierce was a scoundrel by all accounts. I mentioned he pilfered away our savings on gambling. I thought it a trifle impolite to bring up the opium and prostitutes. Mr. Latimer had been hired as a kind of bodyguard, to carry him through the seedier districts of London. I was quite terrified of him"—Dorthea smiled at the memory—"until the evening I was lost in this very wood, a pack of hounds at my heels, and he came to my rescue."

"There were no hounds," Latimer said, not unkindly.

"It certainly felt like it," Dorthea returned, then, looking at Benedict and Harriet, recalled their point of topic. "I love him, you know. Hiring Latimer was the kindest thing Pierce ever did for me."

The man cleared his throat and Harriet thought his cheeks tinted in the moonlight. "Your husband found out about"—she chose her words carefully—"your relationship with his hired-man?"

"In a most unfortunate way." Suddenly the duchess's features went lax with sadness. "Though I had been certain I was much too old for such nonsense, I became with child. There was no way I could explain it to the man with whom I had not shared the marriage bed in years."

"What happened?" Benedict asked, his tone less demanding than before.

"One of Dorthea's maids told him," Latimer said with grim hatred.

Harriet felt a sudden sinking in her stomach. She had seen no children since being in Lady Cruchely's home.

"He came after me with a fire poker. Hit me with it until . . ."

Harriet lifted a closed fist to her mouth.

"He did not know I was the father," Latimer said. His features remained hard, but his eyes were glossy. "I waited until our next outing, when he was making jests—as he often did—at his wife's expense. He was in bed at a brothel when I shot him."

"Were there any witnesses there?" Harriet asked.

Latimer smiled at Benedict and Benedict looked at her.

"People in brothels rarely see anything."

Harriet nodded as if that made all the sense in the world. She quickly shut off all her thoughts of wondering how Benedict should know about brothels.

"To say anything about what happened," he clarified, "would admit to a knowledge of the disreputable place."

"I see," she said, looking away from Benedict and wishing he would just be quiet with his vast knowledge.

She saw the woman standing in the copse where they had been before the trouble with the arrow began. It was the same who had stared worriedly up at Harriet from the ballroom before she had fallen. It was strange, Harriet thought, that she could see the woman from so far away. It was almost as if a soft ray of moonlight had affixed itself to her, making her dark gown and pale skin glow faintly. The woman was looking down at the stones Harriet had investigated earlier. Then, as if sensing the scrutiny, her chin lifted and she slowly turned her head in Harriet's direction.

". . . I received the first demand for money," Lady Cruchely was saying, "when I began to renovate this old place."

"It might look to some that you are wealthy, with the capabilities to rebuild," Benedict said.

Dorthea laughed.

The woman might have been a statue save for her evenly spaced blinking and the rise and fall of her breast.

Harriet frowned.

". . . It is precisely the reason I could no longer answer the blackmailer. I simply do not have enough to pay what was demanded of me. So I made the decision to burn the letters as soon as they arrived and ceased giving away what little I had."

"Two months later," Latimer said, "she was in a strange carriage accident."

Harriet's heart stopped as she realized what had struck her as odd about the woman. The woman's chest moved up and down, but no faint wisps of clouded breath escaped her nostrils or slightly parted lips.

The woman, since Harriet had been watching her, was not really breathing.

"I want to go inside," she said.

16

"Lady Cruchely, have you heard of a group sometimes referred to as Fielding's Men?"

His words halted Latimer halfway up the staircase, where he was guiding the duchess to her rooms. The man turned to the other, standing silently at the foot of the stairs, with more than a little hard apprehension.

"Yes, sir?" Dorthea said.

"Benedict." It was Harriet who spoke then. She had been noticeably uncommunicative upon their return to the house, following her abrupt and earnest desire to do so. Much like her peculiar behavior that morn, she was nervously tugging on the cap sleeves of her gown and peering back over her shoulder as if something might be following them in the darkness. Now, however, he had sufficiently accrued her full attention.

Harriet faced him from where she had been standing at a foyer window, no longer looking out into the night with an expression of discomfort. "You are a Bow Street Runner?"

"Yes." He nodded.

Women affluent enough to afford a holiday in the country were rarely affected by men obliged to find employment. When Harriet smiled at him, it was with genuine appreciation and what looked to be excitement. Something about the expression made his lower body tighten.

Lady Cruchely's pale hands reached out to grip one of her lover's. "You've not come to take away my Latimer?"

"No, madam, I have not." He understood the hiredman's look of apprehension. Men of his sort, accustomed to living the hard way and knowledgeable on the inner workings of brothels and opium dens, rarely had a high opinion of lawmen. Especially not after they had murdered the husband of their wealthy mistress.

Benedict inclined his head. "I think I can be of some help to you."

"Excellent." Harriet grinned.

"It will be difficult, I imagine, as you have burned all of the evidence that might lead to your blackmailer." Lady Cruchely winced. "But when I look long enough, I tend to find what I need."

"You are serious, Mr. Bradbourne?" Dorthea asked. "You will catch the fiend who is sending me those awful letters and making threats?"

"It goes beyond the letters, Lady Cruchely. The bastard might have killed Harriet on more than one occasion. He cannot get away with that." When he looked toward Harriet, he saw she was cupping her bandaged elbows in both palms and appeared embarrassed at the attention. It made him doubt she'd ever had someone so intent upon keeping her from harm.

He wondered if she'd ever had a man do so.

"Mr. Bradbourne, I would be most appreciative of any assistance you could offer." Dorthea's tone was growing quickly devoid of the demons haunting her past. "So would Latimer."

The man at her side grunted.

"I need your house open to me," Benedict said. "I should not like to deal with agitated staff. I do not, however, want them to know my purpose or business."

"Of course."

"I'll likely as not need the use of a good horse."

"Our guests are always free to use the stables." Dorthea nodded.

"We have a pair of mounts"—Latimer spoke grudgingly—"kept a distance from those available for guest use. They are better suited for long distance rides and my bay can run when given reason to do so. Use them."

Benedict inclined his head. "At daybreak, I shall search the grounds for any sign of who it was that shot the arrow tonight."

"Very good, sir." Dorthea was smiling now. "I am so thankful for your help, Mr. Bradbourne. More than I can say."

He waved the words away. "You had best get some rest. I might have questions for you both tomorrow."

When they were gone, Benedict slowly faced Harriet. "Come with me to the parlor and I will fix you a drink to calm your nerves." He had meant the words as a request, but they emerged a demand.

Harriet, unaffected by his tone or the idea that it was drawing close to midnight, led the way to the parlor. She removed her cloak as he poured the drinks, frowning as she tested the hole in the fine velvet material with a fingertip.

As he approached, she did not look up but said, "Benedict?"

"Yes?" He halted before the chair in which she sat.

"Forgive me for intruding in your personal business, but I have read several books whose characters are Runners, and if the depictions are accurate, such an investigator does not have a salary large enough to cover a jaunt to a themed house in the country."

He nearly choked on his brandy. Coughing, he wiped his mouth with the back of his hand. Harriet blinked up at him.

"I might ask the same of you, Miss Mosley. For some reason you do not strike me as one of the wealthy stiff necks who frequent this place."

He thought he might have insulted her, but Harriet only nodded. "It is most likely because of my clothes. My nicest gowns are hand-me-downs and I cannot manage the alterations that might make them fit more properly.

"I have no family to speak of. I am fortunate enough to find employment in a small bookshop my friends and I share." She rose, spreading the cloak over the back of her chair.

"And your salary peddling books is enough to cover an extravagant vacation?"

She pursed her lips, cocked a hip, and batted her lashes at him. In a low voice that made his body tighten again, she said, "Perhaps I have other employment of which I dare not speak to a man of the law."

He stared at her and she kept her look of sultry independence for a long moment before showing a small smile.

"This holiday is a birthday gift," Harriet said, "from the lady friends who share responsibility of the bookshop with me. They are all much more affluent than I." She was thoughtful. "But then, that doesn't mean much."

Benedict had finished his drink, so he downed the one he'd made for her. It did little to abate the fire that burned within him, not at her sultry acting, but her gentle smile with the mention of her friends. He carried the glasses back to the drink table.

"One of my best friend's sons, Angus, is an accountant. He invests my earnings and has, I must admit, created for me a decent account to live with."

"Oh"—Harriet's tone was touched with disappointment—"I had not thought you the sort of man to be interested in entertainment such as this. I imagined you here on some mysterious investigation."

He was surprised with her acute awareness. How could she, in such a short amount of time, know he thought of the whole of Lady Cruchely's haunted manor rubbish? He made Harriet a fresh drink and carried it to where she stood by the fire.

"A few months ago a very close friend was killed in London. I am here to find his murderer."

"I knew it." Harriet took a brief swallow, winced, and cupped the snifter in both palms. She was not smiling as she lowered the glass. "I am sorry you lost your friend."

He shook his head, wanting neither her sympathy nor pity. "The stranger who accosted Ferguson was after his watch. Nothing else was taken from the old man but the damned timepiece."

"How does that factor into your coming here?"

Benedict folded his hands behind his back. "The watch was purchased at a second-hand jewelry shop in London. When I questioned the jeweler, he claimed he saw so many watches he could not remember any given piece. He could only recall the maker was supposedly famous at the turn of the century. Lived not far from here and, as the engraving on the back might suggest, made the watch for Captain Warren Rochester."

"Lady Cruchely's grandfather," Harriet said.

"I haven't yet had the chance to ask about the

watch. When I heard the duchess was attempting to rebuild the manor, I thought she might have hired someone to find the watch. An effort to pull together the mangled remnants of her heritage."

"A good idea"—Harriet nodded—"but I cannot imagine Lady Cruchely doing such a thing."

"Nor can I."

"Now what are you to do?" Harriet's eyes glowed green and brown in the firelight and Benedict felt as if he could lose himself in her gaze.

"I will help the lady solve her problem with the blackmailer, and while I'm searching the house for related facts—"

"You might find out more about the watch?"

"At the very least, I need to know what it looks like. The killer might be flashing the damned thing right under my nose and I'd never know it."

They heard the sound of booted feet coming down the hall and went silent because of it. When Oscar Randolph appeared in the parlor doorway, Harriet and Benedict were looking in his direction.

He lifted a fluffy white brow. "Am I interrupting something?"

"Please join us," Harriet said. "Benedict was just explaining how dangerous it is to be his friend. Only recently a close acquaintance was nearly run through with a dagger-sharp arrow." She looked at Benedict and grinned.

Again her lovely eyes and smile transfixed him.

He did not miss the way Randolph, who had been moving toward a leather chair next to where he stood, made an abrupt turn and sat in the settee nearest Harriet.

"No offense, Bradbourne."

* * *

They were fighting again. Those voices she could not identify, raised in anger and—Harriet began to think—pain, crept under her door, through the keyhole, into the space between the door and the doorjamb. It was a constant, nagging argument that drew Harriet from her sleep like the persistent sound of thunder.

She lay for a long time, cheek pressed into her palm, listening. She could not make out all the words being said, frowned as she tried, but now and then caught a shout or sob clear as day, as if those doing the yelling had come to stand before her door. The fiery words might have been a ball, bouncing slowly up and down the hall, voices growing distant as it bounced away.

There was a strange thud from the staircase. It made the floor tremble and Harriet sat up amidst the bedclothes. She heard footsteps going—running—down the stairs.

Worried to the point of not caring if she was intruding upon someone's private affairs, she climbed from the foot of the bed, padding in bare feet to the door.

When she found the corridor empty, she went to the head of the stairs, peering down into the less-lighted first floor.

She saw nothing and the silence made her ears ring. Harriet turned back down the hall, searching for another opened door besides her own. Her eyes drifted to the chamber of Lord and Lady of Chesterfield, the only married couple present. Their door was closed, and if Harriet listened closely enough, she could hear the slightly damp rattle of snoring come from the room.

The voices raised only moments before did not sound old enough to belong to the Chesterfields.

Wide-awake, the hour much too close to dawn for

Harriet to be able to fall back asleep, she returned to her room only to don her slippers and robe. As she made her way rather cautiously down the stairs, she lifted a hand to her nose, where a faint odor of smoke tugged at her nostrils.

She found the kitchen occupied and paused to knock on the wall before interrupting the sound of pleasant conversation. They were speaking in French.

"Mademoiselle," the familiar maid said with genuine welcome, "you are up and about early."

Jane sat at a heavy table, folding linens. At another table against the wall, an older, rounder servant was chopping pears into cubes with the sure measured snaps of a large knife. There was a snowy volcano of flour beside the pears, a sweet-smelling concoction of cinnamon, sugar, and other spices at its center.

"So you are the one who will make me too fat to fit into the carriage when it is time to go."

The woman's weathered cheeks plumped up further when she smiled.

"Mademoiselle Mosley, this is Millicent."

Harriet was slightly embarrassed when the older woman curtsied.

"She doesn't know English very well."

"Oh," Harriet said. Because she could think of no better greeting, Harriet curtsied for the servant.

Millicent looked embarrassed. She lifted her brows and nodded to the tarnished silver teapot at the center of Jane's table.

"Yes, thank you," Harriet said, and waved Jane away when she made to rise.

They sat in comfortable silence, she and Jane, as Millicent finished with the pears and began to use her sausagelike fingers to coat the pieces in the flour mixture.

"I am glad," Jane said, making a crisp fold in a linen napkin, "you are not too mad at me for frightening your friend."

"I am only upset you were not a real ghost," Harriet said. "That would have given me an excellent story to share with my friends at home." She had a sudden memory of the woman in the woods the night before and the man climbing up from a staircase that was not there. Her laugh was dry. "I suppose the tale of individuals pretending to be ghosts will be just as entertaining."

Jane still looked worried. "If there is anything I can do to make your stay more entertaining, please let me know."

Harriet set her teacup down and looked at the younger woman anew. "Jane, how long have you been here?"

"Feels like forever. As long as Lady Cruchely has lived here."

"Do you know if there is anything that lists items belonging to the house? Maybe some sort of inventory passed down through the years to keep track of things."

Jane gave it some consideration and then shook her head. "None that I know of. Nothing from before Lady Cruchely came. There was a fire a long time ago and it nearly burned the house to the ground."

"I've heard." Harriet nodded.

Jane watched her closely, then asked, "Do you know the whole story of that fire, mademoiselle?"

Her tone, Harriet thought, was that of one who didn't want her to know the story. One eager to share.

"I didn't know there was a story."

"Oh, yes." Jane smiled. "The family of Captain Rochester and his wife would have the world think no different than a simple accident caused the blaze, but the servants have always known that is not the case."

She pushed the folded linen aside, and rested her elbows atop the table. "It seems that Lady Annabelle was having an affair with a man from the village and Warren found out. Though he had given up his past life for respectable society, Captain Rochester had once been a sailor. A pirate, to be exact. He was said to have had a terrible temper. On the night of the blaze, the servants said, he had confronted his wife on the matter of the affair. No one saw it happen, but many believed he reverted back to his old ways of piracy."

"And what was that?"

"Taking what he wanted, killing whomever stood in his way, then burning everything to the ground."

Harriet frowned. "Didn't Warren die in the fire with his wife?"

"Yes. He might very well have been trapped by his own terrible deeds."

Harriet wondered why the Lady Annabelle did not run away with her lover, if her husband was so vicious. "Whom was Annabelle having an affair with?"

"No one ever admitted to it. Of course, back then such things were grounds for imprisonment, if you knew the right people. Rumor was that the man was a crafter from the village. They had been seen sneaking about together." Jane tilted her head, and then shook it. "*Non*, not a craftsman. A watchmaker."

Harriet's teacup froze between the table and her mouth. "A watchmaker?"

"Yes. Famous for his work, supposedly."

Harriet carefully returned her cup to the table. "That is an interesting story, Jane. Would you excuse me?" She was already pushing up from her chair.

As she walked down the hall, returning to the staircase, vague ideas flitted about inside her head. There was something there, she was certain. She just couldn't put it together yet.

"Mademoiselle!"

Jane trotted down the hall after her, bringing Harriet to a halt at the foot of the steps.

"I was just telling Millicent what we were talking about," Jane said breathlessly. "The inventory and all that business. She said she knew of no inventory, but when Lady Cruchely first moved here another woman came calling. She wanted to sell Lady Cruchely a diary that had once belonged to the family. Millicent thinks she said the diary belonged to Annabelle Warren. Perhaps that has the list you are looking for?"

"Does Lady Cruchely have the diary?"

"*Non.* Millicent says the duchess was very upset because she could not afford what the woman was asking for the book."

Harriet smiled, reaching out to squeeze the younger woman's hand. "Thank you, Jane, and thank Millicent for the information."

"Of course." Jane smiled in return.

She watched as Mademoiselle Harriet, the only lady to visit Rochester Hall who sat down with Jane as if they were equals, went quickly up the stairs. When she turned back in the direction of the kitchen to help Millicent prepare breakfast, her smile froze and abruptly left her face.

He stood in the center of the hall, between her and the kitchen, his expression ugly in the gloom. He looked as if he wanted to kill her.

"What is it?"

No sooner had the words parted her lips than his hand lifted. He moved before she could blink and she fell to the floor. Her cheek burned and in her mouth she tasted the bitter tang of blood.

17

Harriet looked up and down the hall, cautious, before lifting a fist to rap lightly on the door.

"Benedict?"

She imagined him asleep and thought she would have to knock again, but only a few moments had passed before she heard the lock click.

Harriet smiled, eager to share the information she learned only moments before, and then the man opened the door and her eyes went wide.

He had been asleep; that much was obvious in his disheveled hair and the absence of spectacles. Benedict looked very charming when caught unawares, his chin shadowed with beard and his lids hanging low over his eyes. Though it was a sight to behold, Harriet couldn't decide if it was his sleep-mussed state, or the fact that he wore no shirt and his breeches were unbuttoned that sent through her a jolt of awareness.

"Harriet?" His voice was gravelly and low, his accent more pronounced. The roll of r's along his tongue sent a shiver down Harriet's spine.

She fixed her eyes on his. "I'm sorry, Benedict. I

should have waited. I had news of your watch. It can wait until breakfast."

When she moved to turn away, his hand captured her arm, just above where the bandages protected her scratched elbows. In the space of time it had taken Harriet to speak, he had snapped awake. His eyes were clear and alert as he drew her into his chamber and closed the door.

"What news?" he said, resting his hands on his lean hips.

Harriet's gaze fixed momentarily on the flat plane of his stomach set between his fingers, then lifted higher. The muscles of his chest were well-defined, his shoulders round with strength, and along his arms sinew stretched his skin taut.

Harriet cleared her throat. "Jane says there is a rumor that Lady Cruchely's grandmother had an affair with a watchmaker from the village. It is what caused the fire so long ago. Her husband found out and set the house ablaze."

"Rochester?"

"Yes." Harriet was aware of the faraway sound of her voice. Her eyes were fixed just beneath Benedict's chin, where his skin was shadowed and tight. It was a neck much too nice to be hidden behind collar and cravat all day. "I asked if she or the cook knew anything of a household inventory dating back to that time and they said all the records were burned. There is, however, a diary."

Benedict turned away and Harriet felt like a woman suddenly released from a spell. She blinked and felt heat rush across her neck and to her ears. She was ashamed of her lack of shame. She had never so much enjoyed looking at another human being.

He was putting on a shirt, tucking it into his

trousers as he spoke. "This diary belonged to a member of the family I presume? A servant?"

Harriet was able to find her focus and smile. "Lady Annabelle herself."

"Does Lady Cruchely have the diary now?" When he turned to face her, Benedict had found his specs. He sat on the edge of the bed to put on his shoes.

"No. When she first arrived at Rochester Hall, a woman came and tried to sell her the diary. Jane says she could not afford the price and the woman left with the book still in her possession."

"I will have to speak to Lady Cruchely, then." He rose, clasped her shoulders in both hands. "You go back to bed."

Harriet was guided out into the hall, just reaching for her own door handle when Benedict was closing his bedchamber door and moving toward the staircase. He was gone before she could even ask him to find her when he obtained more information. She would have loved to hunt down the diary.

She was seated at a table outside, feigning interest as Lizzie explained the rules of chess, three hours later. The sky was filling with large clouds, but the sun was putting up a fight, and if one kept directly within its light, there was no need for a coat. Harriet, who had already mussed one coat with mud on her arrival and was quite certain the cloak Lady Cruchely loaned her was beyond repair, sincerely hoped the sun would win the fight, at least until she was able to wash her garments. She wore the last of her long-sleeved gowns, and though the cuffs did not reach her wrists in an adequate fit, the sleeves did hide the dressing on her elbows.

"Harriet, did you hear me?"

"Mmm?" She looked up from where she was tugging on her dress. "Rook takes knight, you said?"

"No. Rook most certainly does not take knight." Lizzie smiled, and it was a beautiful smile when she did not cover it. "We do not have to play the game if you have no interest. I am sometimes bored with it, myself."

"It's not that it is boring," Harriet said honestly. "I don't think I have the patience with all the maneuvering."

The younger woman leaned over the small table and whispered, "I wish I could ask you to teach me one of the card games you played the other day. But you-know-who would have a fit." She nodded in the direction of the bench on which her mother sat.

As if she sensed her daughter's thoughts of wrongdoing, Mrs. Pruett looked up from her knitting and scowled.

Harriet folded her hands in her lap and leaned forward to reply, "Perhaps one night when you-know-who is asleep . . ."

"I'd love it." Eliza grinned. She sat back and sighed then. "Oh, Harriet, how I wish I could be as independent as you. Free to do what you want with whomever you choose."

"It's not as exciting as it might seem, Lizzie. I spend most of my time reading or working in the bookshop. Everything remotely interesting that happens to me happens because of my friends."

"But you do read what you will, not what someone tells you to read. Like books on proper etiquette and behaving like a lady."

Harriet's nose wrinkled inadvertently.

"Mother insists if I do not follow the protocols to a T, I will never find a husband." Eliza's fine brows lifted. "But you have no husband and seem none the worse for it, Harriet."

"Thank you," Harriet said.

"I believe there is no guidebook for falling in love, and a marriage based on anything but love is a travesty. Have you ever been in love, Harriet?"

Harriet, who had been watching a pair of bees take turns with a plump daffodil, looked at Lizzie from the corner of her eye. "Almost, but I couldn't say for certain and my young man was gone before I could find out."

"Oh, Harriet."

She shook her head, waving off the other's pity. "It was a very long time ago."

Lizzie checked to make sure her mother was fully ensconced in her knitting, then said, "What of Mr. Bradbourne?"

Harriet blinked at the younger woman and felt suddenly, inexplicably uncomfortable. "What of Benedict?"

"I thought you two were close."

"We are friends, as much as we can be after having met only a few days ago."

"Oh? I suspected you longtime acquaintants. You have a special rapport."

Harriet couldn't meet Lizzie's eye.

"I've made you uncomfortable," she said. "I'm sorry. I just thought . . . I don't know what I thought. Forgive me."

Harriet sighed, neatly placing the chess pieces in their wooden box. "Do not apologize, Lizzie. It is a bit odd for me to become friends with a man who is little more than a stranger. Only because you said something do I see that."

"I think he is taken with you," Lizzie said.

A knight set atop a sculpted horse slipped from

Harriet's fingers and rolled off the table. When she leaned over to retrieve the piece, Lizzie continued. "Do you know that the man talks to no one but you and, on occasion, Sir Randolph? He is very secretive and quiet. I watched him last night during the walk. He deliberately slowed his pace until he was closer to us than the others. I never see him smile unless you are at his side."

Harriet straightened, her head colliding with the edge of the table. She grunted as she sat up, rubbing her head. "Now you are making me uncomfortable."

Lizzie grinned. "I must admit, I can understand him being drawn to your high spirits and excellent sense of humor. I believe you quite refreshing in this dreary place. I, however, have never been compelled to sneak you into a wood and kiss you."

"Lizzie!" Harriet closed the polished game box with a snap.

"I did drag my feet a bit on our return to the manor last night," she admitted sheepishly. "Perhaps he is falling in love with you and you him?"

Harriet's eyes were round as she gaped at the woman who had always seemed so timid and quiet. "I am not in love with a man I hardly know."

"How would you know?" Lizzie tilted her head and folded her palms atop the table in a ladylike fashion. "You've never been in love before."

Harriet, mouth agape and struggling to find a response, felt relief wash over her when Jane emerged from the house and called her name.

"There you are." She smiled and lifted a hand as if to shield her face from the meager sunlight. "I've searched the whole house."

Mrs. Pruett spoke up in a callous tone. "One need not provide her every whereabouts to a servant."

The woman spoke with such disdain that Harriet could not help but shoot her a cold glare. The older woman gasped.

"What is it, Jane?"

"Mr. Bradbourne wants you," Jane said.

Lizzie snickered in—Harriet thought—a very unladylike manner.

"He sent me to find you and ask that you meet him at the stables."

"Thank you, Jane," Lizzie said with kindness that belittled her mother's cruelty.

The servant curtsied and turned away. Harriet wondered if it was a trick of the light that made it look as if the other had a dark bruise on her cheek.

18

"My father gambled since before I can remember."

Benedict paused only a moment when she spoke behind him, then continued checking the tightness of the saddle straps.

"He saw no reason to stop after he married my mother or when I was born. It was how he supported us. My mother died when I was an infant and we were not of the income that employs a governess, so he would take me with him to the gaming halls and gambling houses. He dressed me in trousers and a boy's cap and kept me on his knee as he played. I learned to be silent and emotionless. I also learned to play and I like to think I do so as well as my father did. So you see," Harriet admitted, "it was not fair, my wager with you. You are under no obligation to take me riding."

He straightened and peered back at her over one shoulder.

Harriet wore a navy blue gown, and where the material was not too snug—as it was over her shoulders and against her full breasts—the wind pressed it against her. It was hard for Benedict to picture the long legs, soft and full at the thigh, in a pair of men's trousers. The sunlight was meager but it caught the paler tendrils of her hair, layered between tresses of a darker, golden hue. As often was the case, the wild stuff was curling down around her nape and loose around her temples. Her bonnet hung from its ribbon in one of her hands. He doubted that a meager cap could hold the mass in place.

"Benedict?" she said, and he realized he was staring.

"Are you trying to renege on our agreement, madam?"

Something in her features closed off from him sharply. She looked, Benedict thought, as if she had been slapped.

"No, Benedict, I always keep my word. I was only trying to be honest."

He watched her a long moment, trying to figure out what he had said to make her angry. "This is Mr. Latimer's horse," he said when she remained silent. "I was going to saddle Lady Cruchely's for you."

Harriet's attention shifted to the mount behind him. Her hard expression dissolved to be replaced by another. "Oh."

"The horses they have for their guests to borrow are fine animals, but these are even better."

"I see," Harriet said. She walked around him, approaching the horse warily. The closer she drew to the bay-colored gelding, the wider her eyes grew, as if she hadn't expected him to be so large. She lifted a hand to touch the mount, and when the horse turned his great head in her direction, she took a quick step backward.

"Harriet?" Benedict said.

"Yes?" She folded her hands together, but did not look at him. Her gaze remained fixed on the horse.

Her brow crinkled when the gelding tested the earth with a hoof.

"You've never ridden a horse before, have you?"

She finally met his eye and, Benedict saw, she was afraid. Harriet slowly shook her head.

Benedict spotted the stableman walking another horse out of the narrow building that housed the animals. He met the other man's eye. "We will not be needing the mare," he said.

Unaffected, the old man shrugged and turned back the way he had come.

"There really was no need for me to learn how to ride," Harriet was saying conversationally. "In London, nearly everything we need is within walking distance and we hire a hansom for all else. Or borrow a friend's carriage and driver."

"You will ride with me, Harriet." He went to the gelding and swung up into the saddle. He held his hand out to the woman who had taken another step back. "Take my hand."

Harriet took a deep breath and Benedict could see her finding her resolve. Her chin lifted and she crossed the space that he did not. When her hand touched his and his fingers curled around her smaller ones, he was suddenly reminded of their kiss the night before. Her hand fit to him just as well as her lips. As if she had been made for him.

She gasped, startled, when he swung her off the ground and deposited her neatly into the saddle before him.

She gripped the saddle horn with one fist and the fingers of her free hand sank into the flesh of Benedict's thigh. He felt something hot like fire spread out from where she touched him, and when she looked up at him, eyes wide and lips parted, he had to steal himself against a shuddering breath.

She released him then, holding to the saddle with both hands, and he reached around her for the reins. His arms brushed her sides, and when she shifted he could smell the sweet, clean scent of her soap.

His muscles went taut and he began to wonder if this had been a good idea.

"Where are we going?" she asked when he heeled the gelding into motion.

"Not far from here. Where the woman who has Annabelle Rochester's diary lives."

Harriet's head snapped round. "Really?"

He had to force himself to look away from her smile. "Really," he said, and kicked the horse into a quicker gait. The movement shifted her back, making her hip collide with his inner thigh. He set his teeth to hold back a groan and hoped to God their destination would be even closer than he thought.

The Aldercy home was smaller than Rochester Hall. It was, in fact, the size of the stables at the most. Benedict wondered at the lady of the house's ire at having her offer for the diary turned down.

He and Harriet were left in the entryway of the home as a plump woman with a pleasant smile retrieved her mistress. The servant returned, with much huffing and cheeks turning red as she came down the staircase, wearing a slightly exasperated expression.

"Miss Aldercy would like you to wait in the study."

She led them down a narrow hall to a room the size of Benedict's bedchamber. There was a single painting on the wall and the uncovered tables bore the weight of melted candles.

The maid hurried ahead of them to remove a sheet that had been thrown across the settee and another from a low chair opposite it. She looked a little embarrassed by the room as she guided the guests to the settee.

"Would you like something to drink?"

"Do you have scotch?" Benedict asked.

"We have water." The woman smiled apologetically. "Miss Edwina thinks liquor a sin."

"Ah," Benedict said. His gaze shifted to the room's only garnishment, a painting of *The Last Supper*.

"Water would be fine," Harriet said with a smile that seemed to make the maid less uncomfortable. "Thank you."

Benedict looked at the woman seated next to him on the small couch. She lifted a hand and gave the cushion between them a pat. When a great cloud of dust rose into the air, she peeked at him from the corner of her eye.

Benedict chuckled.

The maid returned with water that, Benedict thought, tasted suspiciously like scotch. She gave them a secretive grin before disappearing again.

When they had sat a full minute or two, no one coming or going, Harriet shifted.

"I don't think I like this place," she whispered. "It reminds me of my aunt's home. Father and I would sometimes stay with her when I was small and then I was forced to live with her family. She was religious in an ugly sort of way."

Benedict nodded.

"Let us not mention our wager. I think Mrs. Aldercy might have a mindset about women who gamble in order to obtain a lesson in riding."

There was a certain amount of self-censure in

Harriet's tone that he did not like. He could imagine this aunt of hers making Harriet feel inferior as a part of her father's actions.

When she turned to him, a slightly uncomfortable smile marring her features, he spoke without thought. "And let's certainly not mention how I cannot wait for our lesson home, to have you in my arms again." He normally would have been contrite for his rash words, but the manner in which Harriet's mouth fell open made him laugh instead.

Before either of them could speak, Edwina Aldercy entered the room. She was shaped like a top, heavy in the upper half of her body with spindly ankles at the hem of her skirts. Her features were ruddy, skin red around her nose and at her cheeks, and Benedict thought perhaps she had a reason other than religion for keeping drink from the house.

As Benedict and Harriet rose, her brows lifted and she moved toward the strangers with hands extended.

"Mrs. Aldercy," Benedict said, "thank you for seeing us."

"My pleasure." She offered him and Harriet a hand, and the latter, not quite knowing what to do with the proffered appendage, shook the older woman's plump fingers. "And it is *Miss* Aldercy." She was smiling at him when he straightened from bowing over her hand. "Please sit. Polly said you come from Rochester Hall?"

"Yes, madam. I am Benedict Bradbourne and this is Harriet Mosley. We are visitors at Lady Cruchely's estate."

"Mosley and Bradbourne?" Miss Aldercy sat in the chair opposite the settee, her head moving slowly as she looked between them. "Polly was under the impression you were husband and wife. You are not?"

"No," Harriet said, shaking her head.

"Oh." The other woman's tone became thoughtful as she faced Benedict and smiled brightly.

He shifted uncomfortably and pretended he did not hear Harriet's strangled clearing of the throat.

"You are looking for Lady Rochester's diary?"

Harriet said, "Do you still have it?"

"Of course, darling." Edwina did not look at her. "It's a family heirloom."

Benedict did not point out it was not the woman's family. "How long have you had it in your possession?"

"It's been in this house since I was a child. My father purchased it when a distant relative was selling off portions of the estate."

"That must have been a long time ago," Harriet observed. Thinking of the great-uncle of whom Lady Cruchely spoke, Benedict thought.

"Not that long." Edwina shot the younger woman a cold glare.

Harriet looked at the cup she held in her lap, the corner of her mouth twitching.

"May we see it, Miss Aldercy?" Benedict said.

"Of course." She pushed off from her chair and turned, looking back over her shoulder at him to say, "And you must call me Edwina."

As the woman moved slowly across the room, Benedict could feel Harriet's gaze. She looked from him, to Edwina, and then back again. She lifted her brows up and down suggestively.

Benedict scowled. They both focused on the woman when she removed the painting and exposed the square opening in the wall.

"I hope I can trust you with our hiding place."

The hiding place seemed to hold only a few folded papers, deeds perhaps, and the book bound in yellowing white ribbon. Edwina returned with the latter. She perched on the edge of her chair holding it out on open palms.

When Harriet reached for the book, however, the older woman drew the leather bound journal out of reach. "No, no. I'm afraid we cannot allow it to be overhandled. The pages are falling free and the paper is so thin, it tears at a thought." Edwina dropped the book in her lap, leaning back in her chair. "I made an offer to Lady Cruchely for her to buy her family journal, but the woman did not accept."

"How much?" Benedict said.

She lifted a brow and said a number that was half his yearly salary. Harriet choked on her watered-down scotch and he patted her on the back.

"Do ask Lady Cruchely if she is interested in my offer now that she is better settled in her home."

Harriet cleared her throat. "Have you read the journal?"

"Oh, yes. Many times." The woman's smile hinted that there were delights in the book her visitors could not imagine. "You would be surprised at what life was like back then."

"Did you ever read of a watchmaker Lady Rochester was to have known?"

"Oh, yes," Edwina said again. She leaned forward conspiratorially and whispered, "I would tell you all about it, but then what need would you have to encourage the new lady of the manor to purchase the journal?"

They walked, Benedict holding loosely to the reins of the gelding as they reached the aged burial ground that marked them closer to Rochester Hall than the home of Edwina Aldercy. The cemetery seemed more haunting on this dreary day than it had been when they first visited it the night before. The gray sky and gray stones, the grass turning brown with the change of seasons, made the place of rest look like what one might expect in the books Harriet favored.

She had always thought the scenes exceptionally frightening while curled up in her favorite chair near the window reading, as the rest of the house was silent with sleep. Actually standing amidst the dead, with the clouds hanging low and thunder rumbling on the horizon, she found it not alarming in the least. It was depressing.

She was the first to speak after their departure from the Aldercy home.

"Damnation." The word escaped her before she could remember it was not one of her best friends with whom she shared the companionable silence. She looked at Benedict from the corner of her eye and he didn't appear offended.

"That woman could have told us about the watchmaker. She was being deliberately difficult." Harriet beat her bonnet against her leg by its ribbons. "It infuriates me."

Benedict chuckled low in his throat, and the sound made the fine hair on Harriet's arms rise.

"You are not upset?"

He looked at her, shaking his head. "I am accustomed to it, Harriet. In my line of work it is not unusual to run into dead ends or uncooperative witnesses."

The thought of that depressed Harriet further, because his line of work involved finding thieves and murderers.

She could feel Benedict looking at her as if he could read her mind. "What is it?"

"In being accustomed to dealing with such difficulties," he said, "I have learned a thing or two about working around them." He smiled then.

Harriet felt her own lips start to curve. "What are you about, Benedict? Do you—"

"Quiet." His smile disappeared, suddenly replaced with a scowl. He stopped, lifted a hand, scanning the low fog swirling about the gravestones and the dark shadows of the wood surrounding them. After a long moment, in which Harriet started to eye their gloomy surroundings nervously, he straightened and tugged the gelding into motion again.

"My apologies. I thought I heard something."

Harriet felt a shiver go down her spine as she stepped closer to Benedict's side.

A heartbeat later the gelding came to a halt on its own, head lifting and ears cocked, its nostrils opened wide as it sniffed the gray air.

There was a snap of twigs and crackling leaves behind them. Harriet saw Benedict's free hand clench into a fist. Their gazes met briefly before they both slowly turned.

Two figures on horseback, a half a dozen yards away. Harriet could not make out who or even what they were as the fog swirled around their dark cloaks. She could see black gloves and boots as the figures came farther into the clearing and closer to her and Benedict. Their gelding made a disconcerting sound at the same time Harriet realized why she could not make out the figures. The two wore grain sacks over their heads, holes torn out where eyes would be.

19

"Harriet."

She stepped backward, stumbling on a crumbled piece of stone and bumping into their horse. Her eyes were wide and fixed on the two who brought their mounts to a halt just inside the clearing. Their grain sack hoods moved as they spoke to each other, then one broke away and moved closer to Harriet and Benedict.

The brush of rough fingers, then a warm hand engulfed hers. Benedict gave her hand a hard squeeze.

"Steady, Harriet," he said in a voice so calm it made her want to laugh. Listening to Benedict speak, one might imagine them still on a casual stroll.

"What is this?" she whispered.

"I imagine," Benedict said as the masked rider drew to a halt only a few feet away, "we shall soon see."

"Ye been asking lots of questions. Too many questions."

Harriet looked at Benedict askance. It was impossible to tell whom the man in the hood was addressing. Benedict said nothing, but one of his golden brown brows lifted above the rims of his spectacles.

"What be yer relationship with Lady Cruchely?"

Harriet's lashes drew together as she scrutinized the cloaked stranger. His accent was grumbling English, familiar.

"What is yours?" Benedict said in his rolling Scottish brogue.

The hooded head shifted and Harriet realized the masked man had been speaking to her all along.

"None of your concern, Bradbourne." The man turned back to Harriet, who had begun to search the shape of his cloaked shoulders and gloved hands for another clue as to whom he was. "Ye might like to find somewhere else to take yer holiday, Harriet Mosley. Somewhere ye won't be getting into trouble."

"I'm in trouble?" Harriet said, mostly to herself. She felt like a child about to be spanked with no idea as to why.

"What happened last night was an accident. If ye keep on sharing secrets with Lady Cruchely and snooping around in things that are of no concern to ye, ye might find yerself really hurt."

"Harriet," Benedict said, "hold these." He removed his spectacles and pressed them into her chilled fingers, then loosely wrapped their horse's reins around her arm. He had shifted to stand before her, so when she looked up from the spectacles, she met his deep brown eyes. "If anything happens to me, I want you to get on that horse and ride away as quickly as you can. Do not go back to the estate. Send someone for your things. Get the hell away from this place."

Harriet blinked, dumbfounded. "Benedict, what—? *No.* You mustn't go out there. At least leave your specs on. One hesitates to hit a man with specs!"

He had turned away before she could complete the thought and was walking toward the man on horseback.

"I don't know who you think you are"—Benedict's tone had slipped into a heavily accented timbre—"but you will not make threats to an innocent woman." He stopped only a foot away from the man on horseback. "Why don't you step down and try to make the same threats to me."

Harriet gasped. "Benedict!"

The masked man shifted, but did not come off his horse. Instead, he abruptly heeled the gray into motion. He went around Benedict, behind Harriet, and as she watched she sent out a silent prayer that he would ride away. The hooded man reared back on the horse then and the animal charged.

"Benedict!" Harriet screamed as the horse ran down at him.

He looked as if he was just going to stand there and let himself be trampled, but a heartbeat before that happened, he shifted. Fluidly, as if he was not a hairsbreadth away from destruction, he slipped to one side of the mount. As the beast roared by, Benedict reached up and locked his fists into the hooded man's billowing coat. In one vicious jerk the man was off the horse and hitting the ground hard. Benedict did not release the cloak once he had hold of it, using the material to lift the other man up off the ground in one hand. Benedict brought his free fist down on his attacker's hooded face.

It all happened so quickly; Harriet couldn't quite believe her eyes. One moment she was squeezing her eyelids shut, certain Benedict was going to be crushed under pounding hooves, then her eyes opened at the hooded figure's grunt of surprise. She saw him hit the ground, saw Benedict move in with the grace of a dancer and give the other the blow that knocked him onto his back. Then Benedict was standing over the man, reaching for the hood, and the crack of a pistol filled the gray sky.

Birds Harriet hadn't seen scattered from the recesses of the wood and she remembered the second man.

He remained at the edge of the clearing, holding the pistol aimed at the heavens. Harriet felt her heart stop when he directed the end of the gun toward Benedict.

He used the pistol to wave Benedict away from the prone man. Harriet almost screamed, it took Benedict so long to move. As the hooded man crawled to his knees, cursing Benedict with words Harriet had never heard before, the other cloaked man spoke. "Come away, you idiot, before you get yourself killed."

Harriet waited, stunned, while the two men rode away as casually as if they had been sharing pleasantries in the graveyard, not threats. The one who had encountered Benedict was none too steady in the saddle. Walking to where Benedict still stood, she returned his spectacles.

When their eyes met she said, "Damnation."

They found Jane in the ballroom on hands and knees scrubbing the floor with rhythmic strokes of a brush.

"Who did you tell about Harriet's inquiry?" Benedict said without preamble.

The pretty maid leaned back on her heels, looking between Benedict and Harriet.

"Pardon?"

"When I asked you this morning about the house record keeping," Harriet explained, her tone less brittle than her companion's.

"Non, mademoiselle," Jane said. "I told no one." She shrugged. "Why would I?"

Harriet nodded, but when she turned to Benedict he was scowling. He read the acceptance on her face, it seemed, because he said, "She had to have said something, or those men would not have threatened you."

"Threat?" Jane climbed to her feet, her brows coming together. "Who threatened you, Mademoiselle Harriet?"

Harriet sighed, shaking her head. "They wore sacks on their heads. One of the voices sounded a bit familiar, but I cannot be certain."

"Mademoiselle!" Jane gasped, eyeing the other woman from head to toe. "Are you harmed?"

"Think very hard, madam," Benedict said to the maid. "There is no one you mentioned your conversation with Harriet to? Even briefly in passing?"

Jane shook her head again, her eyes holding Harriet's in a beseeching stare. "I would not have Mademoiselle Harriet harmed in any way. She is very nice to me."

Harriet smiled.

"They carried pistols."

"Benedict!" Harriet sent the man an admonishing glare when Jane gasped. "It was only one pistol," she assured her.

She could feel the heat of Benedict's gaze when he slowly turned his head. "Madam, are you regularly accosted by strangers in disguise?"

Harriet blinked at him, confused by the anger simmering in the back of his eyes. "Not usually, no."

"Then how is it you can handle such things so easily, as if it is of little consequence that your personal safety was endangered?"

Harriet was a little embarrassed, being the center of his and Jane's attention. "I came to no harm."

"Would you have been unharmed had I not been there, Harriet, or would something more frightening have been done to set you off your path?"

Harriet winced at the thought. She had no way of knowing what would have happened had she encountered the cloaked men alone. Without Benedict at her side, however, she was certain to have been terrified.

She looked at Jane. "You are certain you spoke to no one?"

20

From the Journal of Harriet R. Mosley

My friends, including those who gave me this journal, have never hidden their concern over my choice of reading materials and what those materials might be doing to my sensibilities. I'm afraid I now understand their worries.

Upon our return from the very unhelpful Miss Aldercy, after having been accosted by two men in strange costume, and this only a day after seeing an apparition in the wood and nearly breaking my neck in a fall, I put my valise neatly atop the bed. I removed my nightgown from beneath the pillows and stuffed it inside, even hid this journal in the folds, and then stopped. Though common sense urges me to go, I can no more leave Rochester Hall as I can cease reading my favorite Shoop stories without reaching the end.

In fact, my visit here is so much like one of my Shoop tales, I feel like I am the heroine in some amazing ghost story and perhaps a reader is following in my adventures.

How dreadful it would be for me to leave now, when the excitement has only begun. It's as bad as a favorite

*character hearing a bump in the night and not going
to investigate.*

*I also have a responsibility to help poor Lady Cruchely
whom, as I well know, someone is trying to kill.*

*There is also the unusual circumstance with Mr.
Bradbourne. I feel very odd when in his company, and
he has kissed me on more than one occasion, but that
is only a minimal reason for my staying.*

Harriet lifted quill tip from paper and looked up
from her journal. She faced the room's only window
and the darkness beyond—compiled with the candle
atop her desk—made the glass pane into a mirror.
Harriet met her own gaze in the window and sighed.
She dipped her quill and wrote:

*Benedict's kisses are keeping me here more than I
care to admit.*

Harriet closed the journal, too afraid to write anything more. Afraid to think about the implications of
what she had just admitted—if only to herself. She
wiped the excess ink on a handkerchief before setting
the quill atop the journal and rising from her seat.
Well aware sleep was a long way off, with thoughts of
men in grain sack hats and another in spectacles flitting through her mind, she delayed donning her
sleeping gown. Instead, she found her latest Shoop
novel and made herself comfortable against the pillows stacked at the head of her bed.

She was opening the book to the marked page
where she had finished reading last when there was a
tap on her door. So light was the sound that Harriet
thought she was imagining it. Her chin lifted and she

stared silently at the door. Beneath, the glow of the candlelight was separated by a distinct shadow.

"Harriet? Are you awake?" Lizzie.

Harriet pushed off the mattress and padded in stocking feet to the door. When she opened it, she found the younger woman not only dressed, but wearing a coat and bonnet.

Harriet immediately knew Beatrice Pruett had decided she and her daughter leave the estate, no matter the hour.

"Did I wake you?" Lizzie peeked around her shoulders, as if looking for disheveled sheets.

"No. I was reading."

Lizzie nodded. She toyed with the ribbons on her bonnet, checked the buttons of her coat. "I was hoping you'd be awake."

Harriet frowned, puzzled. "You want to play cards?"

Lizzie laughed a little, and then shook her head. "I've been speaking to the maid, Jane, asking if there was anything exciting in the village. A party or event that you and I might enjoy together."

"Oh?" Understanding dawned on the older woman. She smiled. "And what did Jane say?"

"There's nothing for a man or woman to do so late in the village, but farther up the highway there is an establishment that might prove entertaining. It is called the Gypsy King Tavern." Lizzie bit her lip, looked up at Harriet through her lashes. "I'd like to go, but do not think I could manage if you were not with me."

Harriet looked at the French marble clock on the mantel.

"Is it much too late for such adventures?" Lizzie followed her gaze worriedly.

"No, only a little past ten. I'm afraid this area is

unknown to me. The tavern, or even the highway leading to it, could be in a dangerous place. I worry for our safety."

"We would not be alone, Harriet. I thought ahead and found a gentleman who has more knowledge of this part of the country to accompany us. He has even been to the tavern once."

"Who's this?"

Lizzie stepped back into the hall and pointed.

Oscar Randolph leaned negligently against the wall, hat pulled low over his eyes and hands folded over the top of a polished cane. He looked up at Harriet and smiled.

"Do come, Harriet. I cannot imagine we would have as much fun without you."

Harriet grinned. "Let me find my coat."

While Randolph went downstairs to procure a carriage, Harriet made quick work of finding her slippers and donning her coat—very much clean thanks to Jane. She was deciding upon which of her two hats she wanted to wear, when the door across the hall from hers caught her eye.

She chose her wide-brimmed bonnet with delicate yellow roses about the band, and as she tied the yellow ribbon beneath her chin, she wondered if Benedict ever jaunted out in the middle of the night in search of amusements. She recalled that he'd seemed vaguely uncomfortable while in the garden a few nights past, despite the loveliness of the star-studded sky and the scent of flowers in the air. She wondered if the man found any enjoyment when not out late catching criminals or other such work as a Runner.

Harriet looked at Lizzie waiting patiently on the edge of her mattress. The younger woman glanced pointedly at Benedict's door and nodded.

* * *

She rapped on the door as lightly as Lizzie had tapped on hers. Harriet did not have to wait as long as Lizzie for a response.

"Enter."

Benedict seemed as cursed with insomnia as were Harriet and her friends. He sat in a chair near the hearth, legs stretched out comfortably before him. A nearly empty snifter hung from the fingertips of one hand and the other rested atop a notebook in his lap. Also atop the notebook were his spectacles. He squinted at the doorway.

"Harriet?"

"Good evening, sir. I hope I did not interrupt important work."

He straightened in his chair, apparently unconcerned that he wore no cravat and his shirt was partially unbuttoned.

Benedict really, Harriet thought, should have more care for delicate sensibilities. It was quite shameful to parade about with one's shirt undone to expose the taut sinew of his chest and the strong line of his neck. Harriet swallowed.

"Harriet!" Lizzie peeked in from the opened door. Her cheeks were pink with excitement. "Sir Randolph has found a carriage and driver. We are at the ready." She ran on tiptoes down the stairs.

Benedict had slipped on his specs. "Making an escape?"

"Under the cover of darkness, no less." Harriet folded her hands behind her back. "I want you to come, sir."

The notebook fell from his lap to the floor. As he rose to collect it, Harriet explained Lizzie's plans.

"There is certain to be no threats to my personal safety and I can't imagine blackmailers about," she concluded. "So I cannot guarantee you will enjoy yourself."

Benedict had already buttoned his shirt and paused in drawing his coat over his shoulders. "You think me incapable of finding enjoyment in life's small pleasures?"

Harriet considered him thoughtfully. "I suspect pleasures must be larger than average to bring you satisfaction."

He surprised her with a grin that made her fingers numb. "If you only knew, madam."

The Gypsy King Tavern brought an immediate sense of relief for the one who was so wanting Lizzie to enjoy herself. Harriet had a moment of worry that it would be the sort of establishment that catered to men who hadn't bathed in months and women who didn't mind, provided the men had enough to pay for companionship. Had the tavern been such a place, at the risk of being the one to ruin the outing, Harriet would have feigned illness and ask they return to the estate.

Benedict, eyeing the tavern that shone bloodred in the moonlight, lost some of the tenseness in his jaw. Harriet, smiling at him as he helped her down from the cab, thought he too would have insisted they leave an unsavory establishment. Although she was certain he would have been blunt—not feign illness—in doing so.

Theirs was not the only carriage pulling to a stop at the building. It wasn't even the nicest, Harriet realized, when she saw a gilt-edged phaeton turn off the highway.

There were more than a dozen windows in the

tavern and through these passed the glow of candlelight and an even cadence of drum beats. Because
there were ladies entering the tavern alone and not
holding fast to their reticules in a nervous manner,
Harriet felt even better.

"Oh, my," Lizzie whispered, drawing a hand to her
throat. "This is more than I could have hoped for. Is
that not so, Harriet?"

"Indeed it is, Lizzie."

Their carriage drew away to where several were
parked in the brush alongside the tavern and Randolph straightened his hat.

"Shall we?" He held an arm out to Eliza.

"Indeed." Lizzie beamed.

Left behind, Harriet lifted her chin and held out
her arm to Benedict. She said in a very low timbre,
"Shall we?"—and wiggled her nose, as if shifting a
mustache side to side.

Benedict shook his head at her poor imitation and
pressed a hand low on her back to usher her inside.

The Gypsy King was busy, but not so crowded that a
person couldn't breathe or have room to move. A
woman in gauzy top and low-slung skirt that exposed
her belly slipped past them holding a good eight
empty mugs over her head. The jewel in her navel
winked as she made her way to a long counter and
passed the mugs on to a muscled young man wearing
only a red vest and loose-fitting trousers. Atop the
counter, another man brought the flaming tip of a
torch to his lips and swallowed the fire.

Lizzie looked back at Harriet, eyes wide.

"That is a fit of indigestion I wouldn't wish on
anyone," Harriet said.

"Bradbourne," Randolph was saying, his eyes straying
to another serving woman whose bare belly was swollen

with child, "what say you and I get a few drinks? I am quite horrified with the idea that a pregnant woman might serve me."

Benedict looked at Harriet, features serious. "Stay here," he ordered.

She nodded, and as soon as he turned away, she said to Lizzie, "Let's have a look about, shall we?"

Lizzie locked her fingers through Harriet's as they made their way across the room. The building was divided into two spaces, the larger room filled with tables and a stage on which a couple was dancing. The second room, also filled with tables, was a gaming room of sorts. There was a dice table, but most play was devoted to cards. Almost all the chairs were filled with stony-faced gents and young men who giggled nervously. Along the wall was a padded bench where, apparently, their female companions sat. Harriet could feel the stares upon them when they entered. One woman in an indigo gown with a jaunty blue feather in her hair nodded at them and lifted a hand to whisper to her bone-thin friend. The women laughed in an ugly, mean fashion.

"You should play," Lizzie whispered, to keep from disturbing the quiet room.

Harriet grinned.

Unlike some gatherings she and her friends visited—where the men and more than a few women cast her disparaging glances when she asked to play—these strangers were happy to make space at a table for her. The youngest gentleman held out a chair.

"We'll do our best to be nice to the lady." A man who appeared to be a vagrant sat comfortable amongst the wealthier class. He smiled and winked a watery yellow eye at her.

"I hope you can manage," the man who was dealing said. "The game is whist."

"I'll try my best."

They reached their third hand, many of the strangers now watching Harriet with sweaty brows and worried eyes, when she saw Lizzie rise from her seat and move to another spot across the room. She had been sitting next to the whispering pair, and when she moved they tittered nastily.

Harriet knew women like them. They would comment on her height as if it were a disability and would make remarks in mock concern for her ill-fitting wardrobe.

"Thank you for the company, sirs." She rose from her chair and heard more than one man sigh with relief.

Eliza rose quickly to meet her. The younger woman's cheeks were red and her smile, though still in place, was forced.

"Is everything all right, Lizzie?"

"Yes, yes." She broke quickly when Harriet continued to stare at her. "Those women over there"—she nodded—"they were asking about you."

"Ah," Harriet said.

"They were very persistent and rather rude, so I told them to keep their opinions to themselves."

Harriet blinked, surprised. "Thank you, Lizzie."

She made a face. "Then they asked me why my front teeth are as tall as you."

Benedict found them as they exited the card room.

Eliza beamed and held open her reticule. "Look what Harriet did." More than a handful of coins flashed at him. "Her purse is just as full."

Harriet pretended not to notice his irritated expression. Although the tavern was proving pleasant, that did not mean there wasn't any lack of pickpockets or scoundrels lurking about. He restrained the urge to point that out.

"Sir Randolph found a table."

He led the way to their table, in the first row closest to the stage.

"Great view." Randolph had to shout to be heard over the music. He held Eliza's chair as she sat. "There are several contests tonight. This is the last of the dancing couples." He waved to the stage where a woman in a sheer red gown clung to the muscled thighs of her partner.

"He has no shirt on!" Eliza gasped.

Harriet looked from the dancer's chest, glistening with sweat, and then to Eliza. She smiled wickedly and worked her brows up and down.

Lizzie erupted into a fit of giggles.

There was a single candle atop their table and it cast a golden halo around Harriet's lovely smile and the smoky color in her eyes as she focused on the dancers. She began to clap in time with the rhythm and laughed when the man dropped to his knees and his partner bounced her bottom against his cheek. From the corner of her eye, she checked on the other woman at their table.

Looking at Harriet, Benedict wondered if she would have left the comfort of her bed and the next chapter in her Shoop novel, had it not been Lizzie asking her to do so. She met his gaze and tilted her head. Benedict had an irrational idea that she could read his mind. It would explain much in the way she so often touched him with invisible fingertips.

As she had come to the Gypsy King for Lizzie, he had come for Harriet.

The couple finished their dance with the woman jumping into the air then locking her legs around her partner's hips.

"I can do that," Harriet told Lizzie.

Benedict released a sudden shout of laughter. Harriet looked at him, her features suddenly taking on the same expression she wore in their first and only card game.

"I believe you can do anything, Harriet," Lizzie proclaimed faithfully.

Harriet lifted her nose in the air while still holding Benedict's gaze. She joined in the applause as the winner of the contest was announced, the last couple.

"Excellent," Randolph said. He suddenly scowled with discomfort when the pregnant serving woman replaced his empty snifter with a full glass.

"Look at that," Eliza said, her good humor suddenly gone.

They followed her nod toward the woman in the blue gown who was walking across the stage.

"Her name is Vanessa Bluey, if you can believe that," the serving woman muttered.

"Another contest?" Benedict said.

The woman snorted, rubbing absently at her extended belly. "I don't know that you would call it a contest. It is for ladies, song or dance or other talent. She and her friends are so bloody mean; all the people from the villages nearby are too frightened to go up against her. The fact that her father is a wealthy nobleman intimidates a lot of these women who are mostly the wives of farmers and cattlemen."

"Can you not ask them to leave—Lady Bluey and her friends, I mean?" Lizzie said hopefully.

The woman looked at her as if she were mad. "Are you serious? They've money coming out their ears. It's good for business."

Eliza nodded, understanding.

Vanessa Bluey was introduced and met with a round of applause by a group of well-dressed young women and men who took up a fourth of the room. She smiled and it was, Benedict thought, a rather condescending gesture.

Harriet and Eliza shared a frown.

Music started and she began to sing.

Benedict winced.

For the high note she uttered, however, wobbly and out of tune, her cronies sent up a cheer. She sang a sorrowful tune about a long-lost sailor and paused only once, while singing of the woman obliged to become a prostitute following his disappearance, to nonchalantly lift the hem of her skirt. The leg she exposed was pale and thinner than that of a young boy, but that didn't prevent her friends from hooting.

"Will you excuse me a moment?" Harriet pushed up from her chair. "I need a bit of fresh air."

"I'll come with you," Benedict said, moving to rise.

"No." She lightly touched his shoulder. "I prefer to go alone."

"I'll come get you"—Randolph had hunched his shoulders as if to protect his ears—"when this torment is over."

Harriet smiled absently, reaching for her glass. She downed the expensive wine in one gulp before marching from the room.

21

Between the rooms for sitting and cards, Harriet found a door painted the same olive-green as the walls. One might have missed it entirely were it not that the door was partially ajar and through this opening she could hear laughter.

She pushed inside and was immediately self-conscious when the group—the dancers from the previous contest and a group of men who were to go on next—stopped laughing and fixed their gaze on her.

"You lost, lovey?" The dancer in the clinging red dress spoke up.

Harriet cleared her throat and lifted her chin. "To whom do I speak about joining the contest against Lady Bluey?"

"You have talents?"

"Don't need 'em," a man in a lime-green waistcoat said. His considerable belly pressed open the spaces between the buttons. "She could go out and sit on a chair and it would be a better sight than that dragon."

The dancer without his shirt added wryly, "And a better sound."

Harriet realized she was suddenly in on the joke that had been made before she entered the room.

"Are there costumes available for borrowing?" she said, feeling her courage rise.

"Lovey"—the female dancer propped hands on roomy hips—"we'll loan you anything you need to take that harpy down a peg or two."

Harriet took a deep breath as the various dancers, singers, and actors brought out their wardrobes for her to inspect.

"Does anyone have a pair of breeches?" She smiled.

The gentleman making the introductions, set apart from the rest of the male staff due to the shirt he wore under his vest, announced that there was a second competitor in the contest. Lady Vanessa Bluey lost her cold smile when she was asked to step from the stage where she had been waiting to be told she was again a victor.

"It's my pleasure to introduce"—he laughed as he read the small sheet of paper he held—"simply Harriet."

Benedict had a moment to meet Randolph's wide-eyed stare across the table before the pianoforte played a single note. The figure at the back of the stage, nothing more that a shadow really, appeared to be a man. A hat was straightened, a cane tapped lightly on the floor. Then she sang out softly.

Who wants a man who is wealthy beyond compare?

The same note played again on the pianoforte.

Perfect clothes and manicured hair . . .

The note.

A stiff upper lip and nothing more.

One of the serving women who had paused to watch giggled as if she knew something the others did not.

"Nothing more.

"Who wants this man . . . ? Not me . . ."

Abruptly the drums, piano, and a few instruments Benedict did not recognize came alive with a jaunty, fast-paced beat.

Harriet stepped into the light, and a crowd of strangers, a few Benedict thought he had seen on the stage moments before, sent out a cheer from the back of the room. The wide-brimmed man's hat she wore hid most of her features from view, but Benedict did not miss the smile that slowly curved her lips. When she began to sing again, it was in a throaty, not unpleasant voice that made the hair rise up on the back of his neck.

"I want a man with an impressive physique, nothing less than six . . . feet will do."

Other tables began to clap and a man at the table beside theirs pounded on the tabletop.

"I don't care if he's a titled bloke, I've got my own kind of folk. There's got to be something in the way he moves." Harriet spun around, peeked back over one shoulder, and shimmied her derriere. *"And I mean moves."*

Eliza squealed and Randolph joined in on the clapping. Benedict felt the corner of his mouth twitch. He wondered if another woman clad in tan breeches and black coat with sleeves only a little past her wrists would look as attractive. Doubtful. Not even if she showed more flesh than the brief glimpses of plump curves exposed between the opened buttons at the top of Harriet's shirt. As he watched, she gave her toes a tap with the tip of her cane and then twisted the cane until it was spinning through her fingertips with the same ease as a playing card.

"I always prefer a callused hand over a softer man. A poor man over a rich man if his heart is true." She pointed to a woman in the audience. *"How 'bout you?"*

The woman, clad in well-worn slippers and a faded dress, nodded and shook her fists in the air.

The man near their table put his fingers between his teeth and gave a sharp whistle. He pounded on his table again, this time making his companions laugh when he knocked over their cups. Benedict was the only one who noticed the drunkard's questioning grin and his friends' eager nods.

The man rose unsteadily; Benedict came off his chair fluidly.

"Come 'ere, pretty!" the drunk called. "I'll show ye yer man." He managed one step toward the stage before Benedict's elbow made contact with his sternum.

The stranger's eyes went wide, his mouth opening like a fish out of water, and he stumbled back into his chair.

The crowd roared at the stage and Benedict followed the excited stares. His breath stopped in his chest when he saw that Harriet was on her hands, toes pointed in the air.

The music dropped abruptly into a low thrum and Harriet moved fluidly to the ground on hands and knees. Her hat was gone and her thick hair formed a curtain around her face. Her eyes lifted and focused directly on the man standing closest the stage.

"I want a man. Hold me closer." She began to crawl forward in lithe serpentine movements, eyes fixed on Benedict.

He swallowed.

Randolph chortled. "Ho-ho, she's coming after you, Bradbourne!"

Harriet slipped her legs over the edge of the stage,

dropped to her feet. *"I want a man. Hold me closer."* She walked toward Benedict, watching him through thick lashes, expression serious. She sang the line again, circling him, as he remained frozen in place.

He doubted he could move if the building caught fire. The boiling of his blood suggested it had.

"I want a man." She came up behind him, her breasts pressed to his back, her song heated breaths against his ear. *"Hold me closer."* Pale, long fingered hands came up over his shoulders, slipped beneath his coat lapels, and ran down his chest.

More women than men were whistling now.

Benedict could feel the beat of the music in his bones. Harriet's tactile survey reached his breeches before she moved away from his back—now sweating—and pressed her back against his arm. He could smell her clean hair, feel her fingertips brush his thigh as she slid down his side as if she were a cat with an itch only he could scratch.

His hands clenched into fists.

Apparently members of the crowd knew the song and began to sing with her as she gave his hands a brief squeeze and smiled at him in a completely cordial way. Benedict wanted to throw her down on the table.

Harriet ran up to the stage as the song came to a close, bowing to her standing ovation. Someone found a flower and threw it at her feet. Her eyes shone as she picked up the rose and waved it in the air.

When the announcer proclaimed her the contest winner, even a few of Vanessa Bluey's friends cheered.

"You were fantastic, Harriet!" Lizzie wrapped her in a hug the moment she approached the table. "You certainly put Lady Bluey in her place."

Harriet, still in breeches, threw her gown over a chair and began to work her hair into a coil. She felt much less embarrassed than she thought she would following her song. "I must admit, had that woman not riled me so, I think I wouldn't have had the courage to do it." She pinned her hair to her nape and glanced briefly at Benedict whose features were unreadable, no smile at his lips. "She reminded me a great deal of a woman I know back home. Marcella Rueben says terrible things about people she does not know and a few of those unfortunate individuals are my friends."

"I imagine there are woman like that everywhere." Lizzie wrinkled her nose.

"In London, however, I am always prevented from retaliation because I loathe to embarrass my friends and family."

"Here," Randolph said, "hardly a soul knows you."

She looked at Benedict again. "Do you think I went too far in my connecting the two women?"

Benedict said nothing and she began to worry she had gone too far, not in the reason for her performance, but the performance itself.

"No," Lizzie said, and snorted. "*'Teeth as tall as your friend,'* indeed."

"What is your prize, Harriet? Will you be adding more to your card winnings?" Randolph asked.

"I have earned the esteemed approval of the Gypsy King patrons and staff," Harriet announced proudly, "and a guaranteed spot in next week's contest."

"So you get nothing." Benedict finally spoke.

"Exactly." Harriet looked down at herself. "Oh! I was also told I could keep the breeches and jacket."

"Very hard to find a good pair of breeches." Randolph nodded.

"It's late," Benedict said, not looking at his pocket watch.

"We should probably go back before Mother wakes." Lizzie rose with a sigh. "She's quite grouchy when she rises anyway. I cannot imagine the sort of fit she'll have if she finds me gone."

"It's just as well. No performance could prove more entertaining than Harriet's," Randolph said.

Despite the lateness of hour, they had to work their way through the steady stream of people entering the tavern. The night air was cool and crisp on Harriet's warm cheeks and a slight wind lifted the ends of her coat.

"They look very comfortable, those breeches." Lizzie lightly brushed the material with her fingertips, eyeing the pale cotton thoughtfully.

"They are indeed. I know a marchioness who rides in nothing but."

"I've never ridden a horse before."

"Nor had I, until I met Mr. Bradbourne." Harriet risked the man another glance and saw more than a plain mask. His brows drew together above his spectacles as he stared out at the road.

"Watch yourselves," he said, and grasped both Harriet and Lizzie's elbows, pulling them closer to the building.

"What's this?" Randolph fixed his attention on the carriage coming up the highway.

The conveyance turned in toward the tavern in such a manner that the two right wheels lifted up off the ground. Harriet held her breath as the carriage wobbled a moment before the wheels hit earth again. The driver yanked on the reins and, through the horses' irritated cries, she could hear a familiar shrieking.

"Oh, lord," she whispered.

The carriage didn't manage a complete stop before Beatrice Pruett was bounding from the cab. She still wore her sleeping cap and on her nose was a forgotten smudge of face cream. The wind opened her coat to expose her nightgown before she quickly buttoned it closed. She searched the crowd of wide-eyed onlookers for only a moment before honing in on her daughter.

"Eliza Georgette Pruett! Just what do you think you are doing?"

Harriet could feel the humiliation almost radiating off the young woman at her side. She reached out and squeezed her hand.

"Mother, I can explain," she said, and gone from her tone was the exuberant laughter that had been present moments before.

"There is nothing you could possibly say to bring things to rights, young lady. I raised you better than to go traipsing off in the middle of the night to God knows where." Beatrice's fleshy neck had become an unpleasant shade of red and the color was rising into her ears.

Harriet stepped forward. "Mrs. Pruett, this was my idea. I insisted Lizzie join me—"

"No." Lizzie's fingers drew up into miniscule fists. "That is not true. It was I who asked Harriet to come. She and Sir Randolph and Mr. Bradbourne came only to make sure I was safe."

Beatrice's look was glacial. "I'd have thought you better than an insignificant writer and woman"—she eyed Harriet up and down with visible disdain—"with no sort of decorum whatsoever."

Harriet gasped.

Randolph choked out, "Now see here, madam—"

Benedict said, "Eliza, you had best go along with

your mother." His glare was colder than that of the old woman. "Take her from here before she says something even more foolish."

Lizzie looked back at Benedict and nodded. She strode to the carriage and climbed inside without a backward glance or breath of good-bye. Her mother stomped after her, and before she snapped the cabin door closed, Harriet heard Beatrice hissing, "She's in trousers, for heaven's sake."

22

They were still most of the journey home. Harriet fretted audibly for Eliza's happiness and Randolph made a few jokes about being insignificant in the eyes of a woman who read little more than gossip columns in the *Post*. Harriet could see the lights of the estate in the distance when the man beside her spoke.

"Where did you learn that?" Randolph nudged her with a shoulder. "That dance and song, I mean."

"My father frequented a gaming hall that also offered entertainment. One of the women who danced there was always very kind to me. When it got late"— she smiled at the memory—"she would lay down a blanket for me where it was dark and quiet. I saw her do that song many times and did all the dances I could manage. It was amazing what that woman could do in only a corset and feathers."

Randolph chuckled.

"I wish I could remember her name. My father was tossed from so many halls, it was hard to recall where we had been the week before."

She caught Benedict watching her with a solemn

expression as the carriage drew to a halt. Then the man was climbing down, reaching back for her.

"I believe I'll fix myself a drink," he said as they entered the house.

"I believe I'll wish you a good night." Randolph made a show out of climbing the first few stairs. "I'm getting too old for the nightlife."

Harriet turned to follow.

"Harriet," Benedict said. He waited farther down the hall, staring at her without blinking.

Harriet shivered despite the warm house. She suddenly remembered the same tone coming from her aunt on the occasions her cousin blamed her for his misdeeds. With some effort, she managed to not drag her feet or stare at the floor as she followed Benedict to the parlor. By the time she reached the room, lit only by the flames in the fireplace, he was returning a decanter among its brothers and sisters along the back of a table. He turned to Harriet and offered the snifter with less than two times what his own glass held.

She watched as he took a deep swallow and then took a small sip from her own glass.

"You are angry."

"What makes you think that?"

"You haven't spoken hardly a word since we left the Gypsy King. No, since before. After my dance . . ." Her lashes drew together in thought and then Harriet took a deep breath. "My behavior embarrassed you." The idea that this man with whom she had connected so easily would find her indecent made her heart ache.

"No," he answered quickly enough.

With some effort, Harriet managed to hold back a smile.

"I once walked a man in only his drawers and boots from the center of London to the jail. It takes a lot to embarrass me."

She nodded, thinking. Then her brows lifted. "You are angry because I used you in my dance?"

He watched her in silence.

"I'm sorry, Benedict." She sighed. "I know you are a very reserved person, it was not my place to push you so far. I had thought it would make you laugh." She tried a small smile that disappeared as he carefully put down his empty glass and walked toward her.

He took her elbows in a firm grip and turned Harriet so her back was to him. She clutched her snifter to her breast in two hands, suddenly worried.

Benedict stepped up close behind her. Too close. Holding her elbows again, he brought his chest against her back and his thighs brushed the backs of hers.

Harriet had a sudden, peculiar thought that if she hadn't been so tall, they would not fit together as well. Feeling the warmth of Benedict against her, for the first time in her life she truly appreciated her unusual stature.

"Benedict?" she squeaked.

"Shh . . ." His moist breath tickled her ear, caressing the delicate whorls therein.

Harriet's lashes fluttered.

Benedict released her elbows, his fingertips moving lightly up her arms to squeeze her shoulders. Then his hands slipped beneath her coat and across her back and she felt the brief skim of his thumbs on the edges of her breasts before his hands moved onward, down her waist, and over her hipbones.

Harriet held her snifter so tightly it was a wonder the glass did not shatter.

"Does it make you want to laugh, Harriet?" he said in her ear.

Harriet shivered uncontrollably and shook her head.

He was silent for a long moment, hands cupping her hips, and Harriet realized she could see some of their reflection in the gilded mirror over the hearth. Her lips were brilliant red and her eyes sparking with heat. Benedict, she saw, had his teeth clenched together and his eyes tightly shut.

"How does it feel?" His eyes opened and met hers in the mirror.

Harriet swallowed. "Like torture."

Benedict smiled and Harriet lowered her chin, not wanting to see the satisfaction in his eyes.

So light she at first thought she'd imagined it, the brush of his lips against her ear. He shifted and lightly kissed her other ear.

The corners of Harriet's mouth tilted and she unconsciously leaned back into Benedict's warmth.

"It feels like torture," he said against her neck, making goose bumps rise up on her arms, "every time I'm with you."

"I'm sorry," Harriet said for lack of a better reply.

She felt his smile against her skin. "Don't be. Just promise one day the torture will come to an end."

"Oh?" Harriet felt a moment's confusion.

He chuckled low in his throat and he kissed her neck. His hands slid up over her stomach, the heat of his palms burning through her shirt. Then one arm came across her shoulders, holding her tightly against him. His free hand lightly cupped her right breast, as if the orb were the most delicate and edible peach ever found.

Harriet gasped. She had removed her corset to don

her masculine attire, so only the thin lawn material of her shirt separated her from Benedict's bare hand. She felt her nipple—already constricted from his touch—press wantonly to his palm.

He squeezed lightly, a man carefully testing a fruit's ripeness.

"Harriet?" Her name reverberated against her skin roughly, Benedict's tone ragged.

Her lashes lifted and she met his questioning stare in the mirror. His cheekbones were stark with emotion and in his eyes she could see a fire that had nothing to do with the hearth.

"Yes," she whispered.

This time, his kiss on her neck was hard and her arms began to tremble when she felt the nick of his teeth. He released her breast, and not of her own volition she moaned at the disturbance of his touch, pressed back so far into the growing heat of him, he stumbled a step backward and chuckled.

His hand slipped down the slight slope of her stomach as his teeth wreaked havoc with her senses, tugging on her earlobe and scouring the flesh of her neck. When his lips moved to the sensitive spot at her nape, she bit her bottom lip, head falling forward.

It was then that she saw Benedict had worked free the buttons on her breeches. Her snifter slipped from her fingers and shattered on the floor at their feet when she felt a callused finger touch the bare skin low on her belly.

"It's all right, Harriet," Benedict said, making her head lift so she could meet his unrelenting gaze reflected before them. "I would not hurt you."

"I know you wouldn't." She nodded and managed a small smile, then sucked in a great breath as his fingers slipped through the soft thatch of curls beneath her breeches.

Her mouth fell open but no air would leave her as his fingers moved lower still and then found this most unimaginable place. He worked a single finger in a long, slow stroke.

Harriet's hands dropped to Benedict's thighs, nails digging into the taut muscled flesh there.

Her body trembled violently as Benedict worked measured circles around that delicate place, and Harriet was afraid her legs might give out. Her breathing shuddered in her lungs, leaving her gasping unevenly.

Still making small agonizing circles, he applied his thumb to that most sensitive place and pressed.

Harriet screamed and her legs did go out on her. Were it not for Benedict's arm wrapped so tightly around her, she would have collapsed to the glass-studded rug beneath them. And, she thought as waves of pleasure rolled through her, resonating from that place were Benedict cupped her in his palm, she didn't think she would have even felt the glass stinging her skin.

"Miss Mosley?"

"Damn." Benedict righted Harriet on her feet as the sound of footsteps drew closer. He spun her around and she wobbled like a drunk for a moment as he made quick work of buttoning her breeches. He cupped her jaw, inspecting her features.

"How do I look?" she whispered.

"Beautiful. Go sit on the settee."

She nodded with surprising obedience and walked quickly to the low-backed couch. She winced as she sat. "My breeches are wet," she whispered.

"Terribly sorry, Miss Mosley." Benedict lifted a brow.

"Shall we make sure to cease all pleasures to save your wardrobe?"

"No need," she said primly, making him laugh.

A moment later, Byron Elliot appeared in the doorway.

"I thought I heard glass breaking," he said, his gaze fixed on Harriet as he stepped farther into the room, "and Miss Mosley scream."

She was glad the darkness of the room hid her blush.

"I dropped the glass," Benedict said. He produced a handkerchief from his pocket and lowered himself to sweep up the pieces.

"I was screaming with laughter," Harriet lied. "Mr. Bradbourne told me a most amusing joke."

"Oh?" Elliot lifted a brow as he moved toward the couch. He looked between Harriet and the man who had collected all the broken glass in his cloth. "What was it?"

Benedict peered up at Harriet.

She cleared her throat. "What do you call a noble-woman and a nobleman, just married?"

"What?"

"Cousins." Harriet forced a loud, screamlike laugh from her throat.

23

Harriet crossed through the garden and paused where trimmed hedges gave way to the lawn. Lifting her head, she let the sun slip beneath her bonnet and cast a warm kiss across her cheeks. Benedict felt his own lips curl as she smiled.

It was the kind of day and she the kind of woman that could make a man forget himself.

As Harriet stepped back into motion, the breeze that made the yellow and brown tree leaves chatter amongst themselves also lifted the ribbons on her bonnet and pressed her skirts against her legs. He remembered the night before—the backs of her soft thighs pressing against him, her stunned and impassioned cries—and a rolling heat trickled through his blood.

He moved toward where Harriet now stood on the lawn, beside Eliza Pruett's chair. The younger woman had made use of an easel and paints Lady Cruchely kept on hand for guests. In charcoal, she outlined one of the statues visible from the garden—a cherub reaching toward the sky with a trail of vines curling around one plump leg.

"Lizzie," Harriet was saying, "you are an excellent artist. I vow, that statue does not look so good in reality as it does on your canvas."

Eliza gave a shy shrug. "It is just a hobby I picked up."

"How is it that your hobby is a skill of great talent and mine involves killing potted plants that have in no way merited my wrath?"

"I did not know you had a green thumb, Harriet."

"Green"—Harriet sniffed—"with the blood of those unfortunates who so quickly expire at my hands."

Eliza giggled. Benedict had noticed she made no move to hide her smile when Harriet was around. "You go too far."

"It's true," he said as he drew closer to the women. "There are posters in all the greeneries of London, depicting Miss Mosley's likeness and barring her from buying flowers." He peered at Harriet suspiciously. "I thought I recognized you."

Her attention was not on Benedict, however, but the horse that had been trailing after him. Her brow crinkled with worry.

"What is this, Mr. Bradbourne?" Eliza pointed at the gray with the tip of her paintbrush. "You are going for a ride?"

"No. As part of a wager I made with Miss Mosley, I am obliged to improve her riding skills. That is to say, at least make her steady on the saddle."

"Oh, no, sir." Harriet laughed worriedly. "I would not want to trouble you. The ride we shared was more than enough to pay your debt."

He met her gaze, more than a little apprehensive in the shadow of her hat brim. "I insist."

She sucked in a great breath, filling her cheeks, and then released it.

"You should let him teach you, Harriet," Eliza said. "You never know when you'll have the chance again." The young woman blushed when Benedict offered her a grateful smile.

"All right, then," Harriet said with no small amount of resignation.

"Let's move to the west lawn." Benedict pressed a hand to the flat of her back. "We do not want to trample Miss Pruett."

"I'm afraid"—Harriet eyed the horse that walked alongside them—"my skill with horses might rival that of my gardening."

"Have you ever killed a horse?"

"No," she admitted, "but then this is only my second occasion to be in close contact with one."

He drew the mount to a halt, facing Harriet. "How is it you are afraid of riding, but can dance before a crowd of strangers and stroll through a graveyard without batting an eye?"

"I'm always better while on my feet."

A sudden image of Harriet's reflection in a mirror, standing with her nails digging into his thighs and her eyes squeezed shut, passed through his mind's eye.

He cleared his throat. "Do you remember how to get on?"

"Of course," she said, and lifted her right foot toward the left stirrup. When Benedict was about to correct her, she looked back over her shoulder and winked. She dropped her right and slipped her left foot into the stirrup. Clutching fiercely to the saddle horn, she lifted herself and then wavered; when she was about to fall back to the ground, Benedict unceremoniously caught her bottom in a palm and gave her a boost.

"Scoundrel," she quipped before swinging her leg

over the saddle. She fell forward, flattening herself against the animal's back and wrapping her arms around his muscled neck.

Eliza shouted with laughter. "Even I know that's not how you sit on a horse," she called.

Harriet sat up and with quick, efficient movements set her skirts to rights around her. Only a small portion of her stockings was visible above her boots.

"You know," Benedict said, "there are side saddles for women to use while they are in dresses."

"Madness," Harriet whispered, holding the saddle horn so tightly her knuckles turned white. "I'm certain a man thought of that. Perhaps looking for a way to dispose of his wife and prevent a visit from the authorities."

"I'm beginning to think you read too many books."

"You are not the first," she murmured. "I see the ladies in Hyde Park riding and they all look very distinguished and elegant. I have my doubts that I have the same pose."

"You will in good time," Benedict said. "Now, take the reins."

She frowned at him. "Shouldn't someone more experienced be in charge of them?"

"I'll hold the bridle." He moved to the front of the gray as she gave up the saddle horn for the reins. "You'll do fine, Harriet. I won't let you come to any harm."

"Easy for you to say." Her eyes went round as he drew the horse forward. "You've probably been riding since you were a little boy."

He shook his head. "Actually, I was nineteen."

"That's funny, I'm nineteen." She gave him a dirty look when he laughed.

"Garfield taught me," Benedict continued, noting

with some pleasure that Harriet's eyes had finally returned to their normal size. "Neither I nor Garfield
had any horses, but he had a friend at the track. I am
probably one of the few people who can say they
learned to ride on some of England's fastest thor-
oughbreds." He smiled at the memory. "For the
longest time, I battled with the horses. I kept trying to
lead them into walls and fences. That's when Garfield
said, 'Son, *what you need is a good set of specs.*'"

Harriet smiled down at him as he reached the edge
of the lawn and turned the horse in the opposite direction. "It sounds like your Mr. Ferguson was more
fatherly than friendly."

"He was both." Benedict nodded. "My sisters and I
came to England with little more than the clothes on
our back. Had it not been for Garfield and his wife,
we would have had a rough time of it. Garfield especially worked hard to help me take care of my sisters
and not forget I had growing up to do on my own."
Absently he noted the small path that appeared in the
dense growth of trees surrounding the lawn. He
pointed. "That is the horse path. Would you like to try
it now?"

"If we can walk, certainly."

Benedict chuckled, pulling the gray along. They
moved so slowly, the horse was able to choose thick
tufts of grass from the lawn and chew casually upon
them.

Harriet asked, "How old were you and your sisters
when you began to take care of them, Benedict?"

"I was fifteen and my sisters four."

She made a face. "I am nearly thirty and cannot
keep a petunia alive."

Benedict was grinning when he heard the sound of
hooves beating into brittle leaves, as if not far behind

them charged the Hounds of Hell. He scowled suddenly, bringing the gray to a halt at the flash of movement on the horse path, but Harriet's mount was much too close.

He shouted a warning a heartbeat before the dappled white mare burst from the wood only a hairsbreadth away from Harriet's mount. The gray gave a startled shriek, front hooves coming off the ground to snatch the bridle from Benedict. He heard Harriet gasp as the horse reared and then her breath leave her as she fell to the ground.

Elliot reined in, turning back. "So sorry! I did not know there was anyone out here."

"You should have watched," Benedict snapped as the gray trotted off in the direction of the stables. He ran to where Harriet lay, arms flung out and wild mass of hair free and spread like sun rays around her. She was staring at the sky.

"Harriet!" He knelt beside her, putting a palm to one of her flushed cheeks.

"It is a beautiful day," she said conversationally.

"Are you hurt?" He did not like the urgency in his own tone. He eyed her arms and legs for any signs of breaks.

She shook her head, then her gaze shifted and she met his eye. "Why do these things keep happening to me?" she whispered.

"Miss Mosley, darling, are you in pain?"

Elliot had yet to dismount and Benedict—as the other man drew closer—was certain he was going to crush her.

"No," she said calmly.

Benedict looked up at the other man and something in his gaze made Elliot move back a few paces. "You could have broken her neck." His voice was guttural.

"It was not my intent." Elliot blinked.

"Get the hell out of here."

"Benedict!" Harriet admonished from where she still lay on a blanket of grass.

"I will check on you later, Miss Mosley," Elliot said, and trotted away.

Benedict could feel the muscles in his jaw working, his skin hot with anger, as he slipped his palms beneath Harriet's back and lifted her into a sitting position. "Damned fool," he grated as he worked at untying her bonnet. It hung around her neck by its ribbons.

Harriet looked at him thoughtfully. "Why are you so angry, Benedict?"

"I promised you wouldn't get hurt and you very nearly did." He was still focused on the knot in her bonnet.

She lightly touched the back of his hand, and when he looked up at her, Harriet wore a gentle smile. She looked like some sort of beautiful fairy-tale character who lived in the forest. Her thick hair hung over her shoulders and a few leaves were tangled in the tresses.

"Benedict," she said, "I think your Garfield must have been proud with the man you became."

Their lips were only separated by a few inches and their breaths mingled. He could feel the warmth of Harriet's gaze like a tangible thing.

She blinked, looking around. "We are much exposed here, sir. I should get up before anyone else sees my embarrassing state."

He nodded, suddenly aware that a house full of windows was not far away and somewhere outside were Elliot and Eliza Pruett. Harriet was quite unusual in most aspects, but he would not tread carelessly on her reputation. After Benedict had helped her to her feet, she smacked her skirts and shook the leaves free of her hair.

He offered his arm and they walked together back toward the house.

"You know, Benedict," Harriet said when they were halfway there, "you are an interesting person to be around."

He lifted a brow. "You are the first to ever think that. I'm certain many others think me dull, if not boring."

She looked up at him and said seriously, "They must not know you at all."

Harriet sat at her journal for some thirty or so odd minutes, but could not compose the words to describe what had happened the night before. More often than not, she was gazing out her window as her thoughts ran away with her. She gave up on writing and was pushing her chair under the table when there was a knock at the door.

"Mademoiselle?"

"Come in," she called while slipping her journal into its hiding spot.

"Good afternoon." Jane curtsied. "Sorry to come so late. I'll just do a little dusting and make your—oh!" She looked at Harriet's bed, blankets folded neatly across the mattress. "You do my chores for me, Mademoiselle Harriet."

"I do not mean to," she said awkwardly. "It's habit."

"Not to worry." Jane drew a feather duster from the waist of her apron. "I'll just take care of this, no? Why do you not sit downstairs? I do not want you to have to breathe in the dust."

Harriet smiled, highly doubtful that the meager

dust in the room could affect her. She left the woman to her work, however, pausing just outside her room to look at Benedict's closed door.

"Mr. Bradbourne went to the village," Jane said behind her.

Harriet winced, wondering if her thoughts were so apparent.

"He asked that I tell you he would be back later this afternoon," the maid continued absently.

"Thank you," Harriet said, relieved the other woman could not read her mind. She turned toward the stairs and froze abruptly when she heard Byron Elliot singing. This was accompanied by the sound of his footfalls as he climbed the steps. She could already smell his overpowering hair tonic.

Harriet spun in the opposite direction and fled down the hall. She found the dark shadows at the far end of the corridor and merged with them, keeping a close watch on the stairs.

It was not that she did not like Mr. Elliot, but his constant talk of poetry and great poets, many of whom she'd never bothered to read, had grown wearisome. When they had gone for their walk days before, he had stared at her intently as he recited a poem about kissing moonbeams and heaven. It had begun to make Harriet feel uncomfortable and soon her polite smile felt like a teeth-clenching grimace.

Upon coming into view, Elliot paused to check his cravat, tied loosely in a very precise manner, and used his fingertips to draw a glistening black curl over his wide brow. That taken care of, he moved directly to Harriet's open door.

"Where has Miss Mosley gone now?" Harriet thought she detected a hint of irritation in his voice.

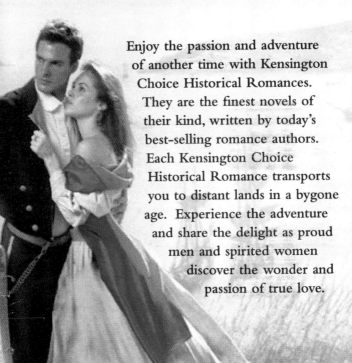

Get 4 FREE Books!

We created our convenient Home Subscription Service so you'll be sure to have the hottest new romances delivered each month right to your doorstep—usually before they are available in book stores. Just to show you how convenient the Zebra Home Subscription Service is, we would like to send you 4 FREE Kensington Choice Historical Romances. The books are worth up to $24.96, but you only pay $1.99 for shipping and handling. There's no obligation to buy additional books—ever!

 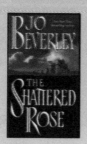  

Save Up To 30% With Home Delivery!

Accept your FREE books and each month we'll deliver 4 brand new titles as soon as they are published. They'll be yours to examine FREE for 10 days. Then if you decide to keep the books, you'll pay the preferred subscriber's price (up to 30% off the cover price!), plus shipping and handling. Remember, you are under no obligation to buy any of these books at any time! If you are not delighted with them, simply return them and owe nothing. But if you enjoy Kensington Choice Historical Romances as much as we think you will, pay the special preferred subscriber rate and save over $8.00 off the cover price!

We have 4 FREE BOOKS for you as your introduction to
KENSINGTON CHOICE!
To get your FREE BOOKS, worth up to $24.96, mail
the card below or call TOLL-FREE 1-800-770-1963.
Visit our website at www.kensingtonbooks.com.

Get 4 FREE Kensington Choice Historical Romances!

▶**YES!** Please send me my 4 FREE KENSINGTON CHOICE HISTORICAL ROMANCES (without obligation to purchase other books). I only pay $1.99 for shipping and handling. Unless you hear from me after I receive my 4 FREE BOOKS, you may send me 4 new novels—as soon as they are published—to preview each month FREE for 10 days. If I am not satisfied, I may return them and owe nothing. Otherwise, I will pay the money-saving preferred subscriber's price (over $8.00 off the cover price), plus shipping and handling. I may return any shipment within 10 days and owe nothing, and I may cancel any time I wish. In any case, the 4 FREE books will be mine to keep.

NAME _____

ADDRESS _____ APT. _____

CITY _____ STATE _____ ZIP _____

TELEPHONE (_____) _____

E-MAIL (OPTIONAL) _____

SIGNATURE _____

(If under 18, parent or guardian must sign)

Offer limited to one per household and not to current subscribers. Terms, offer and prices subject to change. Orders subject to acceptance by Kensington Choice Book Club. Offer Valid in the U.S. only.

KN126A

Iₙ.ₗₗₗₗ.ₗₗ.ₗ.ₗₗ.ₗₗₗ.ₗₗ.ₗₗₗ.ₗₗₗₗ.ₗₗ.ₗₗ.ₗₗ.ₗₗ.ₗₗ

Zebra Book Club
P.O. Box 6314
Dover, DE 19905-6314

"I'd have thought she passed you on the stairs, monsieur. She left only a moment ago."

Elliot frowned and looked farther down the hall. Harriet pressed her back against the wall, squeezing her eyes closed as if that would make her invisible. Then she heard footsteps going back down the stairs and the echo of booted feet to the left of her.

To the left of her was the bend in the hall, where there was only a few feet of walking space before one hit the charred remains of the old staircase.

Harriet slowly turned. She felt the hair on her arms lift. The sound of footfalls grew louder, as if someone was drawing near.

Even as she held her breath, she could feel the change in the air. It was abruptly cold and then the chilled temperature gave way to an almost humid heat. Harriet frowned as she took a step closer to the empty space where a staircase had once been, unable to recall if it had been so hot when she last visited the place. A drop of sweat emerged from her hairline and trickled down the side of her ear. As she wiped it away, the footsteps stopped.

A shudder ran from the tips of her toes to her fingers. She had been preparing herself for another encounter with the man with the dark hair and cold expression, but no one emerged from the dark chasm in the floor. Harriet stepped closer to where the floorboards were burnt open and looked down inside. She could make out nothing in the darkness, but thought a heated wind was coming up through the space.

She pressed a hand to her forehead, wondering what lunacy had possessed her in the promise of adventure and a good story to tell her friends back home. Then she eased herself to her knees, careless of the soot and dust that caked the floor, gripped the edges of the opening and peered down into the black chasm.

She smelled it, nose wrinkling at the acrid stench, a moment before the smoke hit her. It rushed out of the darkness with a sound of heartbroken whispers and burst up through the hole. The great mass of near-black smoke hit Harriet with such intensity she fell backward, spine making contact with the floorboards with bone-jarring force. Harriet's eyes teared but she wiped them away to see, behind that great mass of smoke so thick one could touch it, the poisonous lick of flames.

Gagging on the sour air, Harriet scrambled back away from the fire and to her feet. She heard the distinct crackle of flames devouring wood and spun, screaming as she began to run.

"Fire! Everyone out!"

She pounded with her palm on doors, not knowing who remained in their rooms. She could feel the heat of the fire on her heels, see from the corner of her eye as bright orange flames curled up the walls and around the ceiling.

Lizzie's door swung open and Beatrice appeared. "What is—?"

"Out!" Harriet grabbed the woman's fleshy elbow and yanked her from the doorway. "Come along, Lizzie," Harriet ordered when she saw the younger woman behind her. "The fire is coming fast."

"What fire?" Lizzie said, but Harriet ignored the mad ramblings.

She pushed Lizzie along with her mother, getting them down the corridor as she did not knock, but opened the other doors in the hall to be certain no one else was on the floor. Jane stood in the doorway of Harriet's room and Harriet simply grabbed her wrist and drew her along with the others. She began to worry that the flames had captured the hem of her gown, the heat was so intense behind her. By the time they reached the stairs, Lizzie and her mother were running, Jane saying what sounded like a French prayer, moving down the steps quickly with Harriet close behind.

They stumbled at the foot of the stairs, Beatrice colliding with Byron Elliot. Their shouts and running had brought most of the house to the stairs.

"There's a fire," Harriet said breathlessly.

Latimer marched toward the women, looked from Harriet to the stairs and then began to climb them.

"You cannot go up there." Harriet reached for his sleeve but he shook her off and Lady Cruchely came to put an arm around her.

It was as Latimer disappeared up the stairs that Harriet realized she could no longer smell smoke. Her attention shifted to Lizzie and her mother. The younger woman was smiling gently, and Beatrice stared at Harriet as if she were a lunatic.

Latimer clomped down the stairs, stopping halfway as soon as he could fix his eye on Harriet.

"There is no fire," he said.

24

Eliza Pruett was waiting for Benedict upon his return. At the foot of the stairs, sitting with her hands folded neatly in her lap and back straight, the man hoped she hadn't been there too long, or she might have caused her body serious strain.

"Mr. Bradbourne." She glanced briefly at the wrapped parcels he carried, not waiting until he closed the door to rise. "I'm afraid something has happened to Harriet."

Benedict had put his things on a table and was removing his greatcoat, but froze at the young woman's words. He looked at her closely, trying to read her features for any sign as to what had happened in his absence. As images of arrows and men in sack hoods flashed through his mind, he felt his chest constrict.

"What is it?" His tone was ragged and demanding, one he often used with cutthroats from the London streets. He ignored the sudden widening of Eliza Pruett's eyes. "Is she hurt?"

"Not that I can say, sir. It seems she's had a terrible fright is all. I would like to check on her, but she has shut her chamber door and will not answer when I knock."

Benedict was moving before Eliza finished her sentence, slipping up the stairs around her and taking the steps two at a time. "What frightened her?" he said over his shoulder.

"Fire," Eliza said. She was following, moving up the steps at a mannerly pace. "She thought the manor was on fire. Came pounding on doors and dragging Mother and I from our room and down the stairs to safety. It was most decent of her to think of everyone." Benedict halted at the top of the stairs and looked down to see Eliza shake her head. "But there was no fire."

Benedict scowled.

Eliza flushed pink, looking away.

He went to Harriet's closed door, not pausing before he reached for the handle. "Harriet, it's Benedict. I'm coming in."

The room was a mingling of varied black shades—the furniture and bed a collection of darker shadows in a room cloaked by drawn curtains. The opened door cast a prism of light into the chamber, a lighted path to the bed and the woman who lay on top of it. Harriet winced and rolled to her other side, presenting her back to the door.

In that brief moment before she turned away, Benedict saw her cheeks were pale and her nose red. They were the features of a woman struggling not to cry, and they did not suit Harriet, were not to Benedict's liking. She was a woman accustomed to making jokes, unflappable in the face of overprotective mothers and men with guns. The sight of her upset to the point of losing the characteristics that most defined her squeezed Benedict's heart.

He closed the door behind him, but not before the light illuminated the valise laying open near the bed and the silken gown spilling over its opening. The vise on his heart tightened.

His footsteps were loud to his own ears as he moved around the bed and knelt where he imagined her head to be.

"What happened?" he said.

"I was dreaming," Harriet said. "Must have been walking in my sleep."

"Have you ever sleepwalked before?"

"No. I wasn't even sleeping. But that is what Lady Cruchely believes and I'd rather trust her than consider the alternative."

"Which is?" His eyes had grown accustomed to the gloom and he could make out the shimmer of Harriet's gaze.

"I'm losing my mind."

Benedict frowned. How long had she been lying here worrying over her mental health? "Tell me exactly what happened, Harriet."

She sighed. "I've already told the story again and again."

"Not to me."

She was silent. Benedict waited a moment, then reached for her hand where it lay near her pillow. Her fingers were cold, delicate in his, and he found himself rubbing them between his palms.

"Go on," he said.

"I was hiding at the end of the hall, where we first encountered Lady Cruchely's ghost."

"Hiding from what?"

"Mr. Elliot." Her tone was indifferent. "I thought . . ." Harriet trailed off and he could see her eyelids draw together as if she were scrutinizing him. "I could smell smoke coming up the old staircase and then I saw it. It was fast, making it difficult to breathe. I heard the flames and felt the heat as I ran. It was like no dream I've ever had before, Benedict. It felt very real and frightening." The pillow whispered as she shook her head. "I keep going over it in my mind, trying to convince myself that it wasn't real. I've been trying to pretend it never happened, but I cannot shake the sound of the burning timber or the smell of smoke."

She squeezed Benedict's hand. Her hair had fallen loose from its bindings and fanned out like dark gold upon the pillow, and when she shifted he could smell that same clean scent that had haunted him since their ride. "I'd give anything to make it all go away. Anything to put it out of my mind and think of something else." Her eyes were almost beseeching. "Do you think I'm crazy, Benedict?"

He kissed her. His mouth meeting Harriet's in the darkness as if it had been made to do so. She was startled; he could feel her jerk with surprise, and then her free arm came up around his shoulders and she held him so fiercely he groaned. The fingers of one hand laced with hers, the other pressed into the pillow beside her and Benedict parted Harriet's lips with his. As his tongue traced the curve of her bottom lip and lightly brushed hers, he tasted tea and sweetness not unlike that lovely scent that radiated from her skin.

She pressed up against him, sighing into his mouth, and a great shiver wracked his frame. He hoped their kiss was clearing her thoughts of troubles at least half as much as it was clearing his of all sense.

He hadn't closed the door tight. When Eliza rapped lightly on it, the door swung open and the light from the hall illuminated them. Benedict was sobered quickly by the young woman's gasp.

"Sorry!" Her wide eyes moved between Harriet to Benedict and then to the wrapped packages she held. "You forgot these downstairs and I thought I'd check—" Flustered, she put the parcels on the floor and turned quickly from the room with another murmured apology.

The door closed with an audible snap.

Harriet lifted a hand to her bruised lips and Benedict pushed away from her, rising to his feet.

"Miss Pruett will certainly think less of me now that she knows you've had your way with me."

Harriet's laughter released the vise around his heart.

He fumbled around until he was able to open the curtain nearest the bed, noting with purely male pleasure the color now present in Harriet's cheeks as she sat up in the glow of the descending sun. She grabbed fistfuls of her hair and coiled it at the base of her skull, pinning it there.

She looked to the packages on the floor. "May I ask where you were? I haven't seen you since this morning."

He lifted a brow, testing, "Did you miss my company, Harriet?"

She grinned without hesitation. "I daresay I've never seen fires that were not there when you've been around, Benedict. And as for the strange things I have seen, at least when I'm in your company I have a witness to my not being mad." Her lips pursed as she eyed him head to toe. "Then again, you do wear spectacles."

Benedict chuckled. "I don't think I've ever met a woman like you before, Harriet."

"You'd be surprised how often I hear that."

* * *

Harriet spent a good portion of the evening, while dressing and brushing her hair, worrying about the looks she would receive at dinner. It was hard to face the world when she was certain they thought her either a sleepwalking ninny or a madwoman. The moment she closed her bedchamber door, however, the one across from it opened and Benedict appeared. The man offered her his arm and she wondered, as they entered the dining room, if he had been waiting for her to leave her chamber for the sole purpose of accompanying her downstairs.

The idea warmed her insides.

Sir Randolph greeted them. "Good evening, Harriet. Benedict." And as Benedict held the chair for Harriet, he addressed the younger man, "You went into the village today? How did you find it?"

As the men spoke and she unfolded her napkin on her lap, Harriet could feel an eager stare touch her with purpose. She looked up beneath her brows to the woman who sat opposite her.

Lizzie was smiling with an indecent amount of wickedness. She looked to Benedict briefly before meeting Harriet's gaze.

She did not speak, but mouthed the words, *"I told you so."*

Harriet focused her full attention on the wine being poured, though the edges of her mouth twitched.

" . . . I could not possibly enjoy my afternoon respite. It kept me awake, that terrible draft. It came from down where the corridor ends. Upon investigating, I found a hole—of all things—right in the floorboards!"

"I'm sorry to hear you've been bothered so, Mrs. Pruett. I'd not have put you in that room had any of my previous guests complained of such things," Lady Dorthea was saying.

Beatrice Pruett swallowed a great mouthful of roast pork, dabbing at her mouth. "I'm very sensitive to such things. "

Dorthea smiled with good humor. "We can move your belongings to a different chamber if you like, far from the end of the hall."

"Wonderful." Beatrice smiled, unaware of the piece of parsley stuck between her front teeth.

Lizzie rolled her eyes.

"What is back there, Lady Dorthea?" Sir Randolph focused on the other conversation. "I tried looking down in the chasm, but it's like the blackness eats up the light."

Harriet wondered if others investigating the break in the floor happened to see the man in strange attire climbing up out of the gloom. In light of the afternoon's embarrassment, she did not ask.

"Actually," Lady Cruchely was saying from the head of the table, "as we began rebuilding the manor, we did so in the places least affected by the fire. What we sit in now was considered the rear of the house. Our builder did wonders leveling the space out and working the best with what he had. He changed the side of the manor into the front and used a servant's staircase to build the one we use now. That charred staircase leads down into what had once been the front of the house, the bottom floor proper."

"There the chambers remain?"

"Those that did not collapse when the beams burned"—Dorthea nodded—"yes. We should clean it out, gut it so to speak, but I can't manage to do it. I went down there once, when we first moved, and it is much like it is here."

"If one ignores the smoke damage and soot," Latimer said from where he stood next to her chair. "There are even things that once belonged to my family, items of little worth not scavenged away. I cannot destroy it. It is a link to the past and all that happened there."

Harriet looked at Benedict beside her and was not surprised when she found him looking at her.

They made polite chitchat throughout dinner and were careful not to seem rude in excusing themselves from the table before anyone else. Less than an hour after being told where it led, Benedict and Harriet stood on either side of the ragged opening at the end of their hall. Benedict had produced a lantern and Harriet did not ask from where, but peered over the edge of the hole as he held the light aloft.

"Are you certain we will be all right?" she whispered as if she didn't want to disturb the ghost of a menacing pirate.

"I'll go down first and catch you." Benedict set aside the lantern and shrugged out of his jacket.

"I don't like you being down there alone." Her gaze moved from the darkness to Benedict's broad shoulders pressed into his shirtsleeves. "I should hate it if something happened to you." Something like being murdered in the same manner the ghost murdered his wife years before.

"I'll be fine." When he spoke, Benedict's voice had lowered an octave and Harriet's eyes met his. Their soothing brown shade darkened. He moved the lantern nearer the edge of the opening, tested the soot-stained wood, and then sat at the edge. "If you'd rather wait here—"

"No," Harriet said before he could finish, and for some reason that made him grin.

Without further worry, Benedict dropped down into the darkness.

Harriet dropped to her hands and knees, using one hand to hold the lantern over the hole.

"Pass down the light."

She sighed, and held the lantern farther down until she felt it being captured from below.

"Your turn."

"Are you certain you can catch me, Benedict?" She held the edges of the gaping hole with both hands as she peered down into the chasm. "In case you haven't noticed, I'm rather tall."

"Now that you've mentioned it . . ."

"It would be embarrassing to break my leg and then some sort of harness would have to be fashioned to drag me out of there." She imagined herself sitting alone in the gloom while Benedict went for help, and she shivered.

He lifted the lantern and his features were cast into golden relief. "I will not let you fall," he said.

Harriet shivered again.

"All right then," she said to herself. She turned on her knees until her back was to the hole, and then pushed off from the floor. Her legs dangled down into the opening and she held herself with straightened arms and flat palms.

Warm fingers wrapped around her ankles. "You'll have to drop down."

Harriet took a deep breath and released the floor. She fell neither far nor hard, as arms came up quickly around her middle. She was eased slowly to the ground, her back dragging against Benedict's front.

His hot breath tickled her ear before he stepped away.

Harriet looked longingly at the opening above them, the glowing light from the hall, and then strong fingers laced through hers and tugged.

"Let's go."

25

The dark cavern that had once been the busy front of the great manor smelled of mildew and, more faintly, charred lumber. On the night he and Harriet first found the opening in the hall, Benedict had thought he smelled smoke, but here—where the evidence of the house's demise could not be clearer—he smelled nothing of the sort.

Conditions for investigating the ruins were less than suitable; the lantern did not properly illuminate the length of the corridor and the few open chambers that remained. When he lifted the light above their heads, he could see the ceiling was black with damage, and near the floor there were more black stains low on the wall to show where the fire had probably followed a runner.

Beside him, he heard Harriet sigh.

In the flickering glow of the lantern, Benedict read her features and saw her eyes and dusky mouth cast in relief against her skin. With lips pursed and brow slightly furrowed in concentration, she looked heartrending.

He thought, as her gaze shifted to meet his, she also looked quite beautiful.

"Shall we look in the rooms?" Her voice was hushed as if they were in a tomb.

Which, given the sordid past of the place, they were.

Benedict nodded, leading the way into the first chamber. It was barren save for a few piles of ashes, the remains of furnishings or other household items. There were several windows, but they had been boarded up long ago.

They moved to the next chamber where there was a skeleton of a chair and settee. With the toe of his boot, Benedict nudged a piece of silver in a pile of ash and it rolled away clean—a candleholder. He saw sconces, the wax candles they once held melted to liquid that became one with the cold floor, spaced on the walls around the room.

"This place must have been well used." Harriet said what he had been thinking. After lightly touching the arm of the burned chair, she continued. "You know, Benedict, there was no one who saw Captain Rochester kill his wife or burn down the house . . . What if the blaze and the circumstances that led to it did not happen as everyone believes?"

He lifted a brow. "Did not the servants hear them fighting?"

"Everyone has fights. That isn't necessarily a prelude to murder. What if Warren Rochester loved Annabelle?"

Benedict watched Harriet, little more than a shadow standing outside his lantern. "I've seen love make men do terrible things."

"That isn't love then, is it? I'm no expert on the subject, but I've seen my friends in love and it lifts them up. Even when it falls apart and hearts are broken, it brings sadness, not lunacy. There is a darker emotion, something wicked I imagine, that disguises itself as love and makes those men do terrible things."

Benedict stepped closer, bringing Harriet into the light of the lantern. She was not looking at him, he saw, but staring at the chair without seeing it. There was something troubling in her frown, perhaps because she was so rarely without a smile.

"Are you sure"—he cleared his throat—"you have never forgone your ghost stories for tales of love and romance?"

Harriet blinked, looked at him, and made a face. "Bite your tongue."

He chuckled.

"Come"—Benedict nodded to the door—"there are a few more rooms."

"I know it sounds strange," Harriet said as she dusted her hand against her skirts and trailed him into the chamber opposite the second, "and I really have no reason to believe it. But I do not think Rochester murdered his wife."

Less than a breath after she spoke the words, the door to the third chamber slammed closed behind them. Harriet emitted a small sound of surprise and stepped into Benedict.

He unconsciously put an arm around her middle, but his gaze was fixed on the lantern. The flame inside sputtered wildly and then went out.

For a moment the closed room was filled only with the sound of their breathing, heavy with the tension of their surprise. Then Benedict spoke. "A draft."

"Yes. A draft in a closed-off corridor where the windows are boarded up tight," Harriet's tone was dry and, despite the circumstances, made him laugh.

His smile disappeared when the lantern came silently back to life.

Harriet's lips were parted as she pressed her tongue to the corner of her mouth. She cocked her head to the side, looking from beneath her brows first to the lantern and then to Benedict. She abruptly turned for the door, but froze before taking a step. Benedict could feel his eyes widening as Harriet's did, as together they saw the inside of the room.

"Bloody hell," he said, struck with incredulity.

"It looks as if the fire hardly touched it," Harriet breathed.

Not even in the hearth, which dominated a good portion of the room, were there more ashes than pieces of unburned firewood. The two enormous chairs, arms as wide as tree trunks, were equally untouched. There were pieces of blue cloth, embroidered with large flowers at the center, at the tops of the chairs. Benedict walked closer and found, at the very edge of one corner, a small charred spot. The candle stands rising up from the floor had dried wax pooled at their tops, and the backless couch, pressed against one wall, was in perfect shape. The cushions appeared to be in place still and the velveteen covering, blue and embroidered like that on the chairs, was clean.

Benedict felt his gaze drawn to the small couch when he would turn away and from nowhere thoughts of Harriet on that bench emerged. Not Harriet sitting properly, but lying back with her hair unbound and tawny tresses brushing the stone floor. Benedict imagined her bodice parting to expose the soft curves of her breasts and her eyes darkening with passion as she looked up at him. The skirts of her gown spilled back to expose her perfect ankles, soft calves, knees, and thighs. . . . Thighs she lifted to wrap about his hips.

"It's too hot."

The words shook him from his dreamlike state. He felt his features shift into a scowl as pain and desire coursed through his frame. He turned to Harriet, registering her words and the sudden warmth in the air at the same time.

Her cheeks were flushed where she pressed the backs of her palms against them. She was staring at the couch just as intensely as he had been moments before. When she felt his gaze, Harriet met Benedict's eye and looked away quickly, as if with embarrassment.

Benedict felt sweat collect along his spine, making his shirt stick to his back, and looked to the hearth as if some magic had made the fireplace come to life after almost a hundred years. Harriet pressed a hand to the back of her neck and Benedict saw the hair at her nape was damp and watched a single drop of perspiration trickle out from behind her ear. The moist droplet caressed the delicate line of her jaw then made a faint streak down her neck to the hollow at its base. The drop sparked like a star as it slipped from her neck and moved with mocking slowness down into the valley between her breasts.

He carefully placed the lantern on the floor at his feet.

"Benedict," she said, and her words were as ragged as his breathing. The movement of her breast was erratic as she took quiet, shallow breaths. Harriet's hands shook visibly as she ran her palms down her skirts and he closed the space between them. "Do you feel that?"

"*Yes,*" he hissed, and covered her mouth with his.

Harriet had been on the world for thirty years and had long ago decided she was not like other women—

hadn't the resources to be perfectly reserved and socially adept. It was not in her to tease in important matters and she would have felt like a fool attempting the coy games that many women could so easily play. She was different, honest and forthright, and would never be more thankful for the peace she had made with herself as when she, without hesitation, gave herself up to Benedict and the passion that consumed them both.

The flats of his palms burned as they rode the ridges in her spine and then settled on her bottom, pressing her into the fire of his body. Harriet arched, sighing at the much-needed touch, and Benedict watched her with blazing and hungry eyes. She suddenly recalled stories from her childhood, books about tropical lands inhabited by natives who climbed trees like monkeys, and Harriet felt the urge to shimmy up Benedict's frame in the same fashion in search of whatever delectable fruits he might share. A giggle escaped her, and at the parting of her lips, Benedict's teeth closed over her bottom lip and brought all laughter to a halt.

Her fingers fisted in the material of his coat as he trailed a burning line of kisses from her jaw to the base of her neck and then lathed that sweat-dampened part of her with his tongue.

Benedict's hand pressed flat to her belly and then upward, caressing the swell of one breast before fingers locked in the sleeve of her gown and drew the material down over her shoulder and without pause to the crook of her elbow. There was only a brief heartbeat of time when the damp air touched her and then Benedict's hand found her neck, squeezed gently, his thumb lightly caressing the hollow at the base of her throat, then his hand moved lower. His coarse palm pressed into the flesh he had exposed there and Harriet's fingers slipped under his coat, nails digging into Benedict's shirt as he cupped one soft breast, his thumb finding a nipple and caressing it with the same motion as he had the hollow in her throat.

Harriet's back pressed into the stone wall as Benedict pressed furtive fiery kisses past her throat. Hot breath teased the oversensitized skin of her breasts before the faintest flicker of a tongue, the light scoring of teeth, and Harriet's fingers found Benedict's hair and pulled. She begged in silence for the pleasure she knew was to come, the exquisite release he had shown her before.

A leg pressed between hers, pushing her unresisting thighs apart, then lifting to the aching core of her.

There was a brush of warm air above her stockings as her skirts were being lifted. She could feel their hem tickle her knees, and Benedict was cupping her thighs, lifting her. Without hesitating, Harriet wrapped her legs about his middle, felt the groan rumble deep in his chest as that sensitive part of herself met the frantic throb of his body.

Benedict shuddered. He placed his hands against the stones on either side of her head. As his forehead rested against Harriet's, her lashes lifted and she could see him struggle to regain control of the situation and the raging desire that ate through them both. Harriet smiled, squeezing his shoulders, running her fingertips along the defined muscle of his chest through his sweat-soaked shirt, and a laugh of pure satisfaction escaped her as she felt Benedict tremble and his hips shift, as if of their own volition, to press nearer the satisfaction to be found between her thighs.

He made a savage sound of impatience, an audible sign he had lost the battle with the control he was trying so hard to possess.

Of its own accord, Harriet's lower body pressed into Benedict's, seeking relief from the terrible gnawing ache that pulsed in time to the beat of her heart. It was not an unfamiliar ache. Benedict had brought it to life and then vanquished it most thoroughly a night before.

"Harriet . . ." It was a breathless rasp against her lips before his hand moved between their bodies, lifting her skirts higher and reaching for the buttons on his breeches.

They came together easily, pieces of a puzzle made to fit. Harriet gripped his lean hips tightly, her ankles locking together behind him. Her back was rubbing into the rough stones of the wall but she was numb to anything beyond the feel of Benedict's body in hers. She bit her bottom lip and he clenched his teeth, guttural groans reverberating from his chest.

Harriet could feel the few hairs he missed in shaving before dinner as his cheek rubbed against hers, and then she felt nothing at all. Nothing other than the sudden explosion that erupted low in her belly, flashing like lightning to her limbs from where she and Benedict's bodies were joined. She was absently aware of Benedict's shout. Her nails dug into his shoulders and his dug into the stones behind her.

As she slowly regained conscious thought and control of her senses, Harriet decided—pirate ghost and phantom fire be damned—this was the best holiday she'd ever had.

"Perhaps that was what they fought for," she gasped. Their breathing was shallow and fast, like that of someone who'd run a race.

"It would be worth it," Benedict said against her lips in an unsteady tone that matched hers. He made no move to separate himself from her.

"Have you ever . . . Like this?"

"No. This was"—his gaze lifted to meet hers—"extraordinary."

26

Jane found him chopping wood, far from the house where the sound of their voices couldn't be heard. When she spoke, however, she did so in a whisper.

"You threatened Mademoiselle Harriet?" Not a question, an accusation. It had been days since she'd seen him, days since Bradbourne confronted her about the attack, but her blood boiled.

Jeffrey Hogg hadn't paused in his work when he caught sight of the maid hurrying across the drying grass and into the woods where he stood. At her words, her defiant tone, his ax halted midway between the darkening sky and a felled tree. His head turned slowly and he regarded Jane with an ugly glare he often used to put her in her place. One of his eyes was badly swollen and the skin over the bridge of his nose scabbed over.

Her lashes fluttered slightly and she shifted as if she would—but then did not—step back. She held her ground, chin lifting as she refused to be afraid of the man she had once welcomed into her bed—before she really knew what a callous beast he was.

"Why would you do such a thing to her? She's never harmed you."

"It's no concern of yers what I do, fool woman. Maybe ye're happy serving the rich, putting on costumes, and howling like a lunatic for their entertainment, but I've got bigger plans for me."

"Plans to frighten innocent women? You are nothing more than a bully, Jeffrey Hogg."

She saw him move and made to duck, but not quickly enough to avoid the blow. His open palm connected with the top of her head so hard she stumbled, fell to her knees. As he threw the ax so the blade sank more than an inch deep into the tree, she scrambled backward, shaking her head.

"I won't let you hurt anyone, Jeffrey. I'll tell. That man, her friend, he is—"

He swooped down on her, closing his hands around Jane's throat before she could even gasp for breath.

"Ye'll say nothing, ye bloody whore!" Spittle hit her cheeks with his angry hiss. Jeffrey lifted her from the ground until her legs trembled far above steady footing. "I'll kill ye first. Do ye hear me? I'll kill ye before you ruin this for me."

A pathetic sound of desperation croaked from Jane's constricted throat. She could feel the blood draining from her face, her eyes bulging, and the erratic pounding of her heart against her chest. She squeezed her eyes closed, so her last earthly image would not be of Hogg's features, twisted in rage and madness.

She had never heard a pistol fired before, but knew the sound when it exploded behind her. A moment later she and Jeffrey were falling, she under the weight of his body. Jane gagged, choking for much-needed breath as she uncurled his limp fingers from around her neck. She pushed up at the man's shoulders and uttered a horrified whimper when his head rocked forward limply and his dead eyes stared at her.

With surprising strength she hurled Jeffrey, three times her size, away from her. He rolled to his back a few inches away and she climbed to her feet, shaking and suddenly cold. Her wide, frantic eyes scanned the surrounding brush and behind her she saw a figure in a dark cloak running toward the stables.

She did not pause to think, but began to run in the opposite direction.

"Mr. Bradbourne"—Latimer was standing at the edge of the opening—"your assistance is needed."

Benedict looked at the other man askance, wondering how long he had been waiting for them to emerge. "What is it?" He reached down into the space from which he'd just extracted himself and captured Harriet's hands. When he drew her up into the light he saw she was still flushed from their lovemaking, but he doubted Latimer would notice, or understand why she was so colored.

Harriet looked from the other man to Benedict in question.

"Outside," Latimer said. He glanced briefly, meaningfully, at the woman rising to her feet.

"What's going on?" Harriet asked.

"It might be better if you stayed at the house, Miss Mosley," Latimer said.

Harriet scowled, folding her arms. "I'm going."

Benedict shrugged into his coat. "It would have been best had you not said that, Mr. Latimer."

"I see," the other man said, and led the way down the hall.

Harriet stayed at Benedict's side as they strode from the manor to the patch of woods on its western side, matching his every step with two of hers. He saw the cuttings of firewood, the ax handle standing up from the tree, but she saw the body first. Harriet came to an abrupt stop, her eyes going wide as she dropped her gaze to the decaying leaves at her feet.

Benedict moved to the dead man's side, reading his features frozen in a mask of surprise. "The stableman?"

"Jeffrey." Harriet's voice was faint.

He looked back at her and saw that she stood steady, understandably alarmed but holding her ground. She would not look at the body.

He wore a gray flannel shirt, folded up to expose his pale forearms and his hands curled as if to grasp for life. The material of the shirt was darker across his chest, stained into a large circular shape that ran down beneath one arm. There was a large ragged hole at the center of the circle.

Benedict knelt, gripped the man's broad shoulder, and lifted to look beneath. There was a smaller, less tattered wound opposite the one in Jeffrey's chest.

"Shot in the back."

"Another servant found him," Latimer, who had been silent as Benedict inspected the body, continued, "when he did not return with the firewood."

Benedict nodded, coming to his full height as he surveyed the darkening wood with a shrewd, calculating gaze.

"Harriet."

"Yes?"

He looked at her over one shoulder and tried to make the order gentle. "Go back to the house."

She was stubborn, but not stupid or without understanding. Harriet nodded and turned away. He watched her walk, wondering at how she felt at this journey that had her making love one moment and walking into dead bodies the next. He saw Harriet freeze then, her head tilting slightly as if she peered thoughtfully toward the pink and purple sky, then she spun back around.

"Benedict," she said, not moving closer. "The voice I recognized, the man in the hood." She nodded. "I think it was him."

27

"There seems to be a strange commotion going on. The servants are sneaking about whispering, and you, my lovely ladies, look as if you've seen a ghost."

Harriet looked toward Randolph and then Lady Cruchely. They had been sitting in two chairs opposite one another at the corner of the room, Dorthea clutching the younger woman's hands as if for dear life.

The duchess's laugh was frightening in its lack of humor. "I'm afraid there's been the sort of horror only you can accurately put into words, Sir Randolph."

Randolph looked at Harriet in question, thick mustache twitching.

"A man has been shot," she said.

He looked around the parlor, as if for a body, then stepped farther inside. "You are joking."

"How I wish it were a joke." Dorthea squeezed Harriet's hands tighter.

Trying not to wince, the other woman extricated her fingers from her grip, and gently patted Dorthea's hands. "One of the men who worked in the stables. Benedict is investigating it now."

"Investigating?" A single, snow-white eyebrow lifted.

"I feel awful," Dorthea said. "Truly, I cannot say that I particularly liked the man, but he did not deserve to be murdered in cold blood."

"Mademoiselle?"

A newcomer, the plump cook with whom Harriet had spoken only a few days before, stepped in behind Randolph. She wore a crisp apron and was wringing a towel between fingers white with flour. Harriet did not miss creases of distress about her eyes and mouth.

She and Dorthea shared a brief conversation in fluid French, of which Harriet could only understand a name spoken.

When Millicent left the room, looking close to tears, Harriet frowned.

"Jane?"

"We gathered together the servants shortly after the body was found, to be certain everyone else was safe. She never appeared. Millicent searched for her, but no one has seen Jane since before dinner." Dorthea glanced briefly at Randolph, and then continued in a hushed tone. "She was . . . close to Jeffrey Hogg."

"Perhaps she is the one who shot the man," Randolph offered, and waved his hands defensively at the women's united gasp. "It is not uncalled for when lovers become enemies. Such attacks happen more than you might imagine."

Harriet scowled, but did not go into her long explanation of the true meaning of love as she had with Benedict. "No," she said simply. "Jane would not have hurt a fly, let alone a grown man." She suddenly remembered the bruise she saw on the woman's cheek a day before.

Harriet heard the door opening and the sound of male voices: Latimer and Benedict. She felt a wash of relief as she rose quickly from her chair to meet them in the hall. Benedict must have read something in her expression, because he frowned.

"What is it?"

"Jane is missing."

He looked through the doorway at Lady Cruchely. "For how long?"

"Three hours, perhaps more."

"I'll need to search the estate and grounds."

"Millicent already looked for her," Lady Cruchely said.

Latimer cleared his throat. "I should think the cook would not know what she was looking for in the same manner as Mr. Bradbourne."

"Of course." The duchess sighed at her own ignorance.

"I'll go with you, Benedict," Harriet said, following as he strode to the door.

"No," Benedict said without pause. "You will stay here with Lady Cruchely and Sir Randolph."

Harriet's brows crinkled. "But—"

Benedict rounded on her, his eyes so hard they caused her to take a stunned step backward. "*Damn it, Harriet, you will stay here.* There is certain to be a murderer on the premises even now, and if I have to tie you to a bloody chair, I won't let you stumble upon him by chance."

Latimer slipped through the door ahead of him and then Benedict turned away. The door slammed, with great emphasis, on Harriet's face.

She turned back to where Randolph and Lady Cruchely stood, her tongue growing thick at the back of her mouth. Harriet forced a careless laugh that sounded phony to her own ears and looked away, hoping the others would not see her embarrassment.

"That's the most excitable I've ever seen Brad-bourne," Randolph said in a thoughtful tone that made Harriet look his way. "Hell, I've never seen him anything besides calm and composed." The old man met her eye. "This is your doing, young lady."

"All right," she said, though she hadn't a clue what Randolph was talking about or what had merited the other man's bluntness.

"It's rather darling"—Dorthea found a weak smile—"how he has taken to worrying over you."

For a moment, Harriet almost forgot there had been a man murdered not far away.

Lady Dorthea was noticeably absent from the evening drinks. As if to make up for her employer's nonattendance—or, perhaps to prevent her own thoughts from straying to her missing friend—Millicent brought in a tray of scones heavy with dates, fresh fruits, and buns iced with honey. Also not present in the parlor was Benedict, and as she chewed thoughtfully on a slice of pear, Harriet's attention shifted every now and then to the doorway.

She sat with Lizzie and her mother, feigning ignorance when Beatrice Pruett spoke of the sudden lack of servants available. When Mrs. Pruett nodded to where Latimer sat, looking uncomfortable as he entertained the Chesterfields, and brought up Dorthea's absence, Harriet was quick with a defense.

"Lady Cruchely has attended to her guests' every need since I've been here. I would think the woman deserves some time to herself. Taking care of duchess-type duties, perhaps."

Lizzie grinned. "And what duties would those be, Harriet?"

Harriet's eyes sparkled. "I haven't a clue."

"I'm sure." Beatrice sniffed, somehow able to look down her nose at the younger woman without even looking at her.

The corner of Harriet's lips twitched as Lizzie scowled at her mother. It was evident Mrs. Pruett hadn't forgot Harriet's stint in trousers. At movement from the doorway, Harriet turned her hopeful gaze in that direction.

Sir Randolph managed a look of suffering when her expression changed to one of disappointment. Harriet smiled in apology.

She was less anxious than she had been hours before, when she feared Benedict might find some evidence of Jane's demise. Instead, he reported that the maid's bonnet and coat were missing from their place in a kitchen closet, as was her reticule gone from its place in a cabinet. Harriet put much faith in his belief that a murderer would not allow his prey the time to don a coat and hat as well as a needless purse before he exterminated her. Jane, Benedict had assured her with a relieving amount of certainty, had run away.

Unable to bear the man's absence any longer and eager to know if he had learned more about Hogg's death, Harriet rose. She wished the other women a good evening before returning to the buffet table. A plate in hand, Harriet left the parlor for the stairs and moved purposely to Benedict's room.

"It's Harriet." Hands full, she tried to make use of her slippered toe in a ladylike knock.

Benedict opened the door, shirt partially unbuttoned and spectacles gone.

"I feel guilty," Harriet said.

"Because you have gotten over Hogg's death?"

She blinked, surprised he understood so quickly.

"Don't feel guilty, Harriet. He surely took part in the blackmailing of Lady Cruchely. More importantly, he was the one who threatened you and may have been the bastard who nearly ran you through with an arrow. Hogg is the last person on earth for whom you should mourn. He doesn't deserve it."

She nodded. "I brought you a plate. Were you asleep?"

"No." He held the door while she entered and then closed it. "Changing. And thank you." Benedict took the plate from her and put it on a table nearby.

When he continued to unbutton his shirt, Harriet felt indecently few qualms in sitting on the edge of a chair to watch. Her gaze drifted momentarily from the lean muscle in his shoulders to the black shirt he drew over them and then the brown wrapping paper he had opened atop the bed. She remembered the package he carried on the day of the imaginary fire.

"What are you about, Benedict?" She fixed her attention on him as he tucked the new black shirt into his black breeches.

He looked up at her from beneath his brows. "It is best if you do not know, Harriet."

She scowled at him, lips pursed.

The corner of his mouth twitched at her expression. "If you must know, my dear, I have plans of illegal entry into the home of Miss Edwina Aldercy. Now, I'm afraid, you are an accomplice to my wicked devices."

Harriet felt excitement wash through her. "You are going to steal the journal of Lady Rochester?"

"Not steal, Harriet. Borrow. If all goes well, I will return the damned book tomorrow evening."

Harriet had risen, unconsciously picking up Benedict's discarded shirt and folding it neatly before putting it on the bed. Such things were habit for a woman unaccustomed to servants.

"I want to go with you," she said.

"Absolutely not." Benedict looked over his plate, used bare fingers to tear loose a piece of bread, and popped it into his mouth.

Harriet fisted her hands on her hips. "Benedict, you must let me come. I shan't be a bother."

"Harriet, you've been a bother since I first met you." Benedict did not look up from his plate, did not see the sudden expression of injured surprise flash across Harriet's features. "I came to this house to find the man who attacked my friend and somehow you've gotten me entangled in a blackmailing mystery and now the murder of a house servant." He reached for his spectacles. "I cannot forget what brought me to this blasted house in the first place. Harriet?"

She was aware of the weight in her throat, the chill in her hands as she looked at Benedict. Harriet had backed away on silent feet until her back made contact with the door, and she reached behind her for the handle. She cleared her throat and forced a smile. "I'm sorry, Benedict. I did not mean to make such a nuisance of myself or force you into things you did not want to do."

He moved with the same fluid grace, the same speed he had when they had been accosted on their journey from the Aldercy home. Before she could turn to go, he had a hand on the door above her head, holding it closed. With his free hand he gripped her arm.

She looked at him briefly—they stood nearly nose to nose—and saw his brows were drawn together, his jaw clenched. It was frightening, she thought, that someone had so quickly took up most of her thoughts and feelings.

"You misunderstand me," Benedict said roughly, and Harriet was tempted to believe hers were not the only feelings so quickly touched.

"I did ruin your plans for your investigation," Harriet said. Her tone was not petulant—she had too much self-respect for that—but as she said the words and thought about them, she understood their truth. "You might have had a lot more done by now were it not for my interference with other matters."

"True," Benedict said, and she could sense his smile before she saw it. "But as a diversion, I cannot say I've ever had one more pleasant."

Harriet felt the weight in her throat disappear, her heart scuttling about against her ribs as she saw the gleam in his brown eyes.

"If a man was to have someone interrupt his efforts at any task, he could not ask for a better woman than you to do it."

Harriet grinned and a new weight filled her throat. "That's the nicest thing anyone has said to me, Benedict." She pressed a quick kiss to his mouth.

His smile suddenly disappeared, his eye taking a new sort of gleam, as he slipped one hand to her back and used the other to cup her nape. When he kissed her, it was with a gentle urgency, as if he could not help himself. Harriet, equally helpless, brought her arms around him, holding tight to his strong shoulders as she lightly tested his bottom lip with her teeth.

He growled, shifting them both until she was in the room and he at the door.

"I have to go," he said, drawing away and holding Harriet at arm's length. "Stay here. I'll be able to get in and out of the place faster. If you are with me, I'll be thinking more of you and your safety than the matter at hand."

Harriet, who could not recall anyone ever worrying about her safety, nodded. "I'll wait for you."

Before he was gone, Benedict gave her a last fierce kiss. A kiss that hinted he had never had anyone wait expectantly for his return.

28

Harriet watched from her window as Benedict departed. He sat astride the gray gelding, maneuvering the mount with fluid skill down the drive and onto the road. Dressed as he was, black trousers and coat with his hat pulled down low, Harriet thought he looked like one of those heroes from the romantic tales Augusta so loved. She had read a few of the books and had to admit some were not without merit. Harriet had a particular liking for those in which the hero was imagined to be some sort of scoundrel at the start of the story—a highwayman clad all in black, for instance.

When Benedict had turned the gray in the direction of the Aldercy home and trotted out of sight, she sighed.

"He does so well on that horse," she said to herself, and pretended she hadn't been watching the defined muscle of Benedict's thighs as they gripped the animal's sides.

As if she had been waiting only for the man to depart—which, in fact, she had—Harriet turned from the window and crossed her bedchamber to the door. Pausing only a moment to retrieve a lighted taper, she looked up and down the hall before making her way to the staircase. She did not step down to join the others in the parlor. She moved up toward the attic.

It was not that she wanted to keep secrets, but if he could attend to matters on his own, she could do the same. She doubted Benedict even remembered the house had an attic, so focused was he on the search for a murderer, never mind Lady Dorthea's blackmailer and the new turn of events with Hogg. Harriet also doubted Benedict would have agreed with her plans to inspect the uppermost rooms of the estate without his company.

Most especially following a slaying.

The staircase ended in a door, and when Harriet tried the handle, it moved easily, unlocked, but the door would not budge. She set her taper aside and applied both hands. The aged wood groaned, and when she took her hands away there remained two perfect, hand-shaped, clean spots in the thin layer of dust. Harriet rested her hands on her hips, thinking. Then she remembered what Viktor Channing, Shoop's popular book character, would do when encountering an obstacle such as this.

Harriet turned sideways and slammed her shoulder into the door.

He lips opened on a silent scream as she caught the stair rail in an effort to prevent her collapse. Pain bolted like lightning up her arm and she was afraid for a long moment that she had broke the bones there.

"There's a reason it's called fiction," Harriet said to herself through clenched teeth.

She waited until her pain subsided then took a

deep calming breath. The wheels in her mind turned anew and she recalled one particular chapter in which a woman had trapped herself in a burning room—apparently she hadn't the sense to simply put out the fire. Channing was obliged to rescue her, as so often was the case with the hero and his ladies. He had not used his shoulder to break down the door on that occasion.

Pursing her lips, Harriet pushed at the door again. This time, however, she moved her hands around, looking for the exact spot where the wood was caught. Only a little past the door handle, the wood wouldn't give from the jamb at all.

She stepped to the edge of the landing, took a second to gather all her strength, and then lifted her right foot. She slammed her heel into the wood and before her foot even reached the floor, the door had popped open.

"Ha!" She knelt for her taper and entered the attic as a knight might enter a captured castle.

The first thing she saw, as the combined scent of mold and damp wood filled her nostrils, was the gaping hole of the window she had seen from the lawn many days before. Now that she knew more about the fire that had assaulted the estate, she knew it had had no effect so far up as this. The window did not explode from too much heat, but had been deliberately broken. Perhaps by a passing group of youngsters who shared ghost stories and dared one another to throw stones at the house. After going to the window and looking down at the lawn so far below, Harriet reconsidered. It was hard to imagine anyone throwing so high. A bird could have flown in the window and shattered it, she decided, and faced the interior of the attic again.

The room was vast, mostly filled with pieces of furniture identifiable by their shape beneath tied blankets and haphazardly tossed sheets. It was the materials closest to the shattered window that wore splotches of gray-green mildew. There were old paintings stacked against the wall. Strangers in expensive tunics and gowns stared at Harriet with cold eyes and emotionless faces. She looked away from the images of people who, in all probability, were buried in the graveyard behind the house.

In one corner she spotted a tall candelabrum, three of its six openings holding beeswax tapers. Harriet brushed the cobwebs that connected the branches of tarnished silver and lit the three remaining tapers with hers. She couldn't be sure what was better: the room when she could see little more than gloomy forms, or the attic as it was now, with shadows flickering like live things in the golden light.

She began to wonder if she should return to her chamber and continue her search in the morn or later tonight with Benedict.

Harriet shook off the thought and reminded herself that it was Gus who enlisted her help when she heard strange noises outside the house or in their own attic. In turn, Harriet called for Augusta whenever a particularly vile sort of insect would appear.

Besides, Benedict would ask what she was looking for, and she couldn't answer that. She didn't even know herself.

Harriet began to walk around the room, starting in the darker spots to get them over with and circling into the light. She picked under blankets and sheets to be certain what looked like a chair was a chair, a table a table. She found several leather trunks and some of wood. The first two she opened held folded pieces of cloth, blankets, and batting. The third—a thing of cracked leather with ornate metal corner protectors—she had to open with her fingernails under the tarnished brass latches. The smell of old paper and, oddly enough, perfume wafted out of the trunk as it creaked open. Harriet eyed the dome top, painstakingly lined with silk that had faded to a dull brown, before she peered into the trunk. The box was only partially filled, but at the very top of the haphazard mix of personal items was a hand-sized oil painting of the sort that one might have had made to carry on their person—while on a ship, perhaps. The painting was of a lovely young woman with dark eyes and pale skin, coal-black hair spilling over her shoulders. Unlike the paintings against the wall, the figure in this work wore a tentative smile.

It was the woman Harriet had seen in the graveyard.

She fought an inner battle over whether or not she should pack her bags and go home—it was one thing to believe she was crazy, but quite another to have proof of a ghostly encounter. Harriet's doubt lasted less than a minute before she knelt on the floor beside the trunk.

She carefully lifted the painting to the light and saw that, though she was pale and her eyes soulfully dark, the woman did not appear unhappy or like one trapped in an unbearable marriage. Harriet set the small portrait on the floor and peered again into the trunk. There was a long sword that she withdrew—slipped the blade only a bit from its sheath to allow the metal to shimmer in the candlelight—and then set aside. She had to use two hands to lift a book wrapped in fine linen, which Harriet unwrapped. She set the Bible aside as well. The last item in the trunk was a small jewelry box, long ago emptied. Most likely by Lady Cruchely's great-uncle.

Harriet sat back on her haunches, looking over her plunder and realizing that—in finding it—she really found nothing at all. More disappointed than she thought she would be, she returned the jewelry box and sword and was reaching for the Bible when something small and vaguely disgusting scampered across her hand.

In the second it took her to look, there was suddenly what felt like a million somethings crawling up her arm. Harriet released a horrified cry as she shook free the first cockroach, a monster roughly the size of a ripe plum, and scrambled to her feet. In the same motion she shook her arm and hit at the bugs clambering up as if to seek refuge in the sleeve of her gown. There were only three, really, but they felt like a million and one seemed to hold on for an eternity before Harriet used an index finger and thumb to flick him across the room. She spent roughly five minutes shaking all over, running her hands up and down her arms, across her nape and into her hair, as she continued to feel as if there were dozens of pests crawling all over her. There was a floor-length mirror evident under a sheet behind the trunk. Harriet tugged the sheet free and closely inspected her back and hair and behind her ears for more bugs.

She made a sound of disgust and moved to finish packing the trunk so she could leave before the roaches reorganized their troops. She had inadvertently kicked the Bible while doing her creepy-crawly jig and reached for it and at the same time for the linen in which it had been wrapped. Because she held it by the spine, the book fell open and a few folded pieces of paper fell from the pages and to the floor.

The hair on Harriet's nape rose, and it was not the aftereffects of her cockroach assault.

She set aside the Bible and inspected the folded letters. Each was addressed to Lady Annabelle—on one, however, she was not Rochester, but titled by her surname, Bishop—and each already bore a broken seal. Harriet opened the first, addressed to the lady before marriage.

> *Lady Annabelle,*
> *Thank you for your kindness. I enjoyed visiting your family home. I am much obliged to your brother for bringing me.*
> *I want to see you again.*
> *Forgive my hand. I do not write letters.*
> *Warren Rochester*

Harriet folded the letter closed and returned it to the Bible. She opened the second and immediately identified the writing as not that of the man who scribed the first letter.

> *Dear Lady Rochester,*
> *It is with my deepest sympathy that I send word of your sister's death. She took a terrible fall from one of the new stallions—*

Harriet—recalling her own tumble—quickly refolded the letter and slipped it back into the book. The last, again, was from Rochester.

> *Wife,*
> *I rec'd your letter a few days ago, but all this business with the authorities not permitting our loading of the ship is sorely trying my patience. Kindly tell my*

*devoted brother I wouldn't give him water if he were
dying in the desert. DO NOT give him any more funds,
as he spends it on gambling and things a lady should
not know about. Have Churchill throw him off the
premises as soon as you read this letter.*

*We will be back at sea tomorrow and home within a
few weeks' time, good weather prevailing.*

W.

"All right, then," Harriet told the letter with no
undue sarcasm. Neither letter had helped her at all.
She folded the foolscap and returned it, the Bible,
and the portrait to the trunk.

"Maybe he did kill her." She snapped the lid closed
and lifted her head.

In the mirror directly in front of Harriet, she could
plainly see Annabelle Rochester standing behind her.
Harriet spun and released a startled cry when she saw
nothing, human or otherwise at her back. When she
turned back to the mirror, Lady Annabelle was still
there. She stumbled backward and in the mirror she
saw herself walk through the woman.

A sound not unlike a whimper trembled in Harriet's throat when her back made contact with the
cold wall.

Annabelle's lips parted, but no sound emerged. Instead, a fog formed on the mirror as if it were freezing
and she breathing a hot breath. She lifted a single digit
and in the cloud of condensation, she fingered ON.

Harriet walked away. She doused the tapers in one
breath, grabbed her single light and—heedless of
items she knocked into on the way—she left the attic,
slamming the door closed behind her.

It wasn't until she reached her chamber and
screamed several times into her pillow, that her heart

began to return to its even cadence. A thought suddenly struck her like the spark before an explosion. She sat up abruptly and pushed the hair from her face. She stared at her window a moment before walking to it and then breathing across the glass.

With her fingertip, she wrote as Lady Annabelle had—as if she were Lady Annabelle herself.

Not ON.

"No," Harriet whispered.

He did not knock, as he wanted no undue attention, not the curious stares of other houseguests from around doorjambs, eager to know why Benedict was looking for a woman alone in the middle of the night. The door was not locked and it made nary a creak as he eased it open. He told himself it was to prevent undue attention still when he stepped into the quiet room without being bid enter.

There was a lantern atop a small writing desk that had burned down to an inch of its life. From the shadows of the bed came a rhythmic, not unpleasant sound of snoring. He stepped nearer the bed and found Harriet atop the undisturbed bedclothes. She wore the same sleeveless nightgown she had on the occasion of their first evening meeting, her hair tamed into a thick braid that fell over one shoulder. With her arms flung out to the side, legs bare beneath where the gown had collected at her knees, Harriet betrayed in herself an innocence she hid well when standing taller than most women and making easy quips.

Benedict drew his attention from her slumbering form with some effort, his body tightening and his heart whispering things he'd rather not think about.

His gaze fell upon the leather-bound book atop the table, next to the candle, and a bottle of expensive India ink. With a lack of compunction that did not surprise a man who had been illegally trespassing in another's home an hour before, Benedict opened the book to the first page and read the feminine scrawl that titled the book as *Harriet Mosley's Journal* and explained that it was from her friend Augusta Merryweather who insisted that were it not for Harriet, *"my life would be bereft of laughter."*

Benedict flipped from the dedication to the next page. The new handwriting was surprisingly small and delicate, as if Harriet would not waste her gift with ungainly penmanship.

From the Journal of Harriet R. Mosley
Thank goodness Emily and the others have seen fit to send me on my journey, as I would be quite embarrassed to suddenly meet my demise and have someone, upon finding this book, see my life as a boring state of affairs. I would feel silly writing about my feelings or my daily activities that include talking with my friends, trash novels, and the occasional shot of good brandy. Though we did recently come into the possession of a certain notorious Book for Lovers *that has some very interesting articles and more than its share of naughty illustrations.*

This time tomorrow evening, I should be thoroughly ensconced in a house of haunts. Who knows if I shall hear strange noises in the dark or see bizarre, headless forms in the shadows? Perhaps, if I am lucky . . .

Benedict grinned.
"I must insist that you not steal my journal. Although there are a few interesting tales of mysterious

goings-on and even now a mention of murder, it would be nothing you have not heard, or been witness to, before."

In reading, Benedict had not heard the silence that fell when Harriet ceased snoring. He did not jump when she spoke, not because she did not surprise him, but he had steeled himself against such erratic movements long ago. When he closed the book and looked at Harriet, she lay as she had been—eyes still closed and features absent of any irritation she could have felt at his snooping.

"A boring read," she said to the canopy above. "Really."

"I beg to differ, Harriet. Your writing is not without merit. Perhaps you should try your hand at those trash novels you so enjoy."

Her eyes opened. "Do you think so?"

"Yes," Benedict said honestly.

Harriet smiled then turned her head to look at him. "Did you get Annabelle's diary?"

"Yes."

Her brows drew together as her gaze roamed him from head to toe and he tried to keep his thoughts focused on her words. "All went well? You are safe?"

"I would like to regale you with an exciting tale of attack dogs and the like, but I was in and out easily enough."

"Good." Harriet sat up, unconcerned with her bare shoulders or feet, which, Benedict thought, was understandable, considering how they had spent a portion of their afternoon together.

There was, however, a comfortableness that filled the space around them when he was with Harriet. He could not, in fact, think of a time he had ever felt so

at ease with another human being. Not even with
Garfield, who had been like a father to him.

"Well?" she said, and he realized she had her hands
open expectantly. "You are not going to make me beg
for it?"

Something dark and devilish stirred inside Benedict. He lifted his brows above his spectacles as his
gaze shifted to the soft breasts pressing to the front of
her nightgown and the dusky pink of her lips.

"Benedict?" Harriet's tone showed she had no hint
of his evil turn of thoughts.

He sighed and reached into his inner coat pocket.
He sincerely hoped there would come another time
when he would hear pleas from deep in her throat
and not for a damned diary.

29

"You know," Harriet said an hour later, her tone not void of interest, "as far as diaries go, I would say this one is a bit on the dull side." When she received no response, she looked up from Annabelle Rochester's somewhat slapdash handwriting.

Benedict sat at the writing table, slouched deep into the chair with his fingers linked across his middle. His head was bowed forward and Harriet could not see his eyes through the glare of candlelight across his spectacles.

"Benedict, are you asleep?"

He jerked abruptly, straightening in the chair. "No," he said quickly in a sleep-roughened timbre. "I was thinking."

Harriet grinned, testing. "What were you thinking about?"

He tilted his head and through the now-clear glass of his specs, Harriet saw no trace of drowsiness. "I was remembering that it was you who found out about the diary."

"Yes?"

"So my statement that you were diverting my

investigation was more than incorrect. You discovered the only thing that might be of some help to finding that damned watch."

Harriet smiled, feeling warmth wash through her. She wondered if it was normal to feel so complimented by Benedict's statement. She looked down at the book in her lap and sighed then.

"We do not know that for certain, Benedict. So far, I've only read of the daily happenings of Lady Annabelle's home and family. Her only sister died after a tragic fall from a horse and a local merchant tried to sell her spices that were filtered down with other ground particles. She mentions her husband a few times, even days when they have terrible rows due to his nasty temper, but these are usually followed with—" She looked up at Benedict from beneath her brows, cutting her words short as she flipped to the next page of the diary.

"Followed with what, Harriet?"

She cleared her throat, shrugging as she turned her attention to the diary again. "Instances of their resolving the conflict," she said primly, and Benedict chuckled.

"I see."

As she had been before waking Benedict, Harriet lifted a hand to the book. With her palm facing toward her, she used it to guide her way down the written text. Not reading, she scanned the words in a fast manner and looked for those that might mean something to one reading them so many years after they were printed. She went through a dozen more pages in this manner before her hand froze, her eyes darting back along the lines of text.

"Benedict," she said, easing to the edge of the bed. *"Benedict."*

He moved at the urgency in Harriet's tone, shifting

to the edge of his chair. He rested his elbows on his knees as he leaned forward.

"What is it?"

"Listen." The single word quivered with excitement. Harriet read, *"Warren insists that he requires nothing, that the gift of a son was all he ever wanted of me that was more than myself. I think he will be very surprised when I give him the watch. Though my husband has little time to study such things, the man I have employed to make the timepiece is renowned throughout all of England for his craftsmanship. I think even Warren will appreciate the work of Mr. Savage."*

Harriet looked up to Benedict. "This will help you, will it not?"

"I think so, yes."

Harriet smiled tentatively. "Perhaps I am an even greater help than you first imagined, Benedict." She returned her attention to the book, turned a page, and then frowned. She read Lady Annabelle's words twice over, biting her lip as her brows drew together in thought.

Benedict, who had risen from the chair and began to pace the room as if he could not bear the thought of waiting until morn to find members of the Savage legacy, caught her look of dismay and came to a halt.

"Harriet, are you all right?"

She blinked as if just remembering he was there. "Nothing," she said quickly, and closed the diary. She rose from the bed and held the book out to Benedict. "You'll be needing to take this back then."

He reached not for the book, but for Harriet's wrist and squeezed gently. "What did you read?"

"Nothing, Benedict. Really." She waved a dismissive hand, and when he would not release her she offered only, "Lady Annabelle writes of an argument she and Rochester have, on the next entry."

"It disturbs you, their fighting?" Benedict shook his head. "Harriet, Lady Cruchely told us he killed her. They couldn't have been happy."

"No, it is not the argument that bothers me, Benedict." Her cheeks burned as she admitted, "It is their reconciliation." She looked at him briefly before diverting her attention to the fingers wrapped about her arm. "It happened in Captain Rochester's parlor . . . Many of the . . . details are much like what happened between you and me today."

"Harriet . . ."

She recalled the heat she would feel before the sound of arguing, the solemn stare of the woman in the graveyard. "I have seen and felt many strange things since being here, Benedict. Was what happened, down below in the room that had surely once been the parlor, was that another such occurrence? Was it not even us touching?"

"Harriet, I don't know of what strangeness you speak, and forgive me for being so blunt, but you sound like a lunatic."

Harriet moved quickly through her dismay to feel irritation. She looked up to scowl at the man who stepped nearer to her.

"The actions of people decades before us," he went on, "do not direct our actions. At least not in the manner you are thinking. I made love to you then because I have wanted you since we first met, not because the ghosts of other lovers made me do it."

"But it was the same room . . ."

"To hell with the room, Harriet." Benedict's tone was sharp as he none too gently pulled the diary from her fingers and tossed it atop the writing table. He then drew Harriet closer, cupping her elbows in his palms. "I want you just as badly now as I did then, and we are nowhere near that bloody parlor."

"Oh," Harriet said, finally seeing the fire in his dark eyes.

"Now, if you will kindly rid yourself of that nightgown"—Benedict lifted a brow—"I will show you what I mean is true." He released her then, giving Harriet the opportunity to bid him farewell for the night.

She would never forget the expression on his face when she lifted her nightgown up and over her head. Though sorely tempted to do so, Harriet made no move to cover herself. Clad in only thin muslin drawers that clung to her hips and bottom, she kept her back straight and her chin lifted as Benedict closed the space between them. She focused on his throat, watched the muscles work convulsively there as he lifted a hand.

His fingers were as light as the golden glow from the hearth that kissed her naked shoulders and belly, trailing from her neck to the space between her breasts. Her heart pounded, her breasts rising and falling in time with the sound of Benedict's ragged breathing. Harriet sucked in a gasp when his fingers brushed the skin of her stomach and she saw him smile when she released a small giggle at the tickle of his fingertips. The rough pad of his thumb slipped under the thin lace waistband of her drawers, brushed across the skin of her hips as his palm shifted beneath the garment to cup her bottom. He pressed her to him, making his need evident low against her belly as he used his free hand to caress her nape beneath her braided hair.

"*Harriet.*" He said her name the way a man might call for water in the middle of the desert. His lips brushed her forehead before he pressed a kiss to her closed eyelids.

A violent shiver wracked her frame, and when she parted her lips to wet them with the tip of her tongue, Benedict's mouth closed over hers.

Their lovemaking was decidedly less urgent than that which had consumed them both earlier. Benedict's touch—the stroke of his open palm down her belly, the faint touch of his tongue on the space of skin between her earlobe and collarbone—suggested he was a man who had all the time in the world. More than once—more than twice—Harriet found herself on the verge of crying out with eagerness, shifting her legs with impatience as he only chuckled against her breast and then punished her with the drag of his teeth across her nipple. He held her at the brink of exquisite release so often she thought she would sob with exasperation, and then he moved. Rolling and taking Harriet with him until with one twist of his hips and one adjustment of her knees, she was astride him and he was inside her.

The position was not unfamiliar to her; she had seen it before in a certain notorious book.

Harriet imagined at first she would finally bring an end to the tortuous game Benedict had played with her, but then, looking down at him through hair blanketing them like a cape, she realized she could now have play of her own. She barely moved her hips against him and the hands gently cupping her naked breast slipped around to her back, nails gently scoring her flesh.

Benedict managed to sit up with her still astride him and he pressed a line of feverish kisses down her neck. Harriet's head fell backward and his teeth played across the swells of her breasts much like his nails on her back. His hot breath tormented a nipple he had brought to its peak with a twist of his tongue.

"*Benedict.*" A breathless whimper reached Harriet's ears and she was momentarily surprised that it was her own.

Giving herself a mental shake, pushing at Benedict's muscled shoulders until he fell back against the pillows, she forced herself to wait for the pleasure she knew was inevitable. She saw the muscles work along his neck and the tiny beads of perspiration rise above his upper lip. The latter, Harriet tasted with the tip of her tongue, allowing her mouth to be captured briefly in a fierce, plundering kiss. She moved slowly against Benedict, running her fingernails down his chest until she could feel him shake below and within her.

"Bloody hell, Harriet," he grated through gritted teeth, and the words rumbled through her body from the point where they were joined. "Are you punishing me?"

Harriet laughed like—she was certain—some sort of wanton creature who did enjoy such excruciating pleasure.

Benedict snapped at the sound of her amusement. He muttered a curse that would have made Beatrice Pruett faint dead. As if unable to take it anymore, he took a firm hold of her waist and moved her as he would see fit. His body rocked up to meet hers each time she moved and soon the friction between them was almost too much. Agony. Sweat shone across their bodies, fire burning deep within Harriet before that one moment when they found their release together.

She did not slump against him afterward, though waves of pleasure quivered through her body from where they remained as one. She watched Benedict's features register the same pleasure-pain she felt, saw him settle back to Earth as if he had been hanging from the moon. When his eyes opened, she thought she could lose herself in their dark depths. Then he smiled that smile Harriet was—with a surprisingly little amount of shame—beginning to assume belonged to her.

"Harriet," he said, "you're amazing."

"Thank you." Harriet's smile opened into a grin.

30

The man at the table looked up when Harriet and Benedict entered, his eyes three times their natural size behind a pair of thick spectacles. As if the eyewear were not sufficient, he gripped a magnifying glass in one gnarled fist. In the opposite hand he held a pair of steel tweezers as delicately as one might a robin's egg.

The sign outside the cottage had read SAVAGE WATCH AND CLOCK REPAIR, & SMALL MECHANICS. Upon entering, the visitors were assaulted with what sounded to be more than a dozen ticks and tocks and the heavy clicks associated with larger clocks. There was a bookshelf that bore no books, but timepieces that varied from bronze statues to slate mantle clocks. Toward the front of the shelves on small pieces of velvet, were a few pocket watches—most without chains and one missing a face.

"Looking to be fixed or to buy a tenderly used piece?" The man at the table spoke loudly, accustomed to doing so over the clanking clocks.

"Neither," Benedict said, then introduced Harriet and himself. "We're looking for information."

"On watch repair?" The old man carefully placed

his magnifying glass and tweezers atop the table and rose with more than a quiver or two to his feet.

"On the Savages that originally started the shop."

"Are you related?" Harriet asked.

"Can't say I am." When he straightened fully, the repairman's knees made a sound not unlike those of the clocks. "Fagin Osborne." He held out his hand, and Benedict went forward to shake it before the man had to move. "Nice to meet you." He blinked his owlish eyes. "It must have been almost fifty years since I bought the place from the widow Savage. Kept the name out front. Did you know it used to be famous?"

"Yes," Benedict began, but was quickly silenced by the waving of a hand full of misshapen, arthritic fingers.

"Of course, of course, that's why you're here. What was it you were looking for?"

Harriet looked around them with grim amusement. "A watch in a watch stack."

"You know, I just didn't get the name with this place." Osborne's large gray eyes surveyed the store with pride. "The widow, she was the original owner's daughter. Her husband was good enough to take over for her father when he passed, but when she was left alone she gave it all up to live with his family in the East. She had no use for all the old equipment and pieces, so she included them in the sale."

"We were looking for information on a watch her father crafted," Benedict said, "in all probability, more than fifty years ago."

"Now, is this the watch made for the Captain Rochester?"

Harriet blinked owlishly without the benefit of spectacles.

"The same," Benedict said, his voice exhibiting the same surprise.

"How did you know?" Harriet said.

The skin of his eyelids looked as massive as the folds of an elephant as he again gave his thoughtful squint. "Must have been four months ago that a fellow came in here asking about the same thing."

Harriet could feel the sudden tension in the man whose coat sleeve brushed hers.

"Along with the equipment," Osborne was saying, "the widow left behind workbooks that belonged to her father. He kept all his appointments in the books along with notes for ideas, measurements and such. Me and that fellow must have gone through three whole books before we found the watch he was looking for."

"Do you still have the book or did the man take it?"

Osborne made a face at Harriet. "I wouldn't have given anything that important away. It's history, if you ask me. The fellow did ask for it, though. Offered me money, if you can believe that, when I said no. Like an old man needs the extra pounds to go jaunting across country."

"May we see the book?" Benedict said.

"If it's not too much trouble," Harriet added sweetly, recalling Lady Aldercy's difficulty with sharing.

"'Course, 'course." Osborne shuffled to a rear doorway, leaving Harriet and Benedict waiting.

She looked up at Benedict and saw his jaw was clenched, his gaze fixed on the wall ahead.

"You are getting close," Harriet said softly.

"Not close enough."

Osborne returned with a tome that looked as thick as he was wide. It made a great thud as he put it on the table and began flipping through the pages. Toward the back of the notes of scrawled measurements and designs that had been scratched out and drawn again, he opened the book wide.

"Here it is."

PAID had been written in large letters at the bottom of the page. In the center of the paper was a neat drawing of the watch with arrows and penned instructions to clarify designs. One of the arrows pointed to the back and beside it was written *A.R.'s inscription*.

"So," Osborne said as they looked over the design, "are you after the watch for the same reason this fellow was?"

"He stole the watch and killed the man who had been wearing it," Benedict said. "I am going to find him."

Harriet cleared her throat. "Sir, may we borrow some parchment to copy this drawing before we go?"

Osborne drew his gaze from Benedict with some effort, and then reached for the book. With abrupt precision, he tore the page free from the rest. "Take it," he said.

Harriet sat before Benedict on the gelding they shared, and as he guided the mount she looked at the page Osborne had given them. The pocket watch had been carefully drawn, the delicate shape of its inner workings like art, the cranks and dials so precisely detailed that it was difficult to believe a mortal man had created it.

A.R.'s inscription. Harriet read the words thoughtfully, looking up from the paper. She frowned in the sunlight that pressed down on their path. The trees that bordered the road and the farms behind were not familiar.

"Are we taking a different route back to Lady Cruchely's?"

She could sense more than see Benedict shake his

head. "This is the way to the home of your maid, Jane. Her brother's, that is."

Harriet carefully folded the paper Osborne had given them. "You think Jane may be there now?"

"One can only guess," Benedict said as he drew off the main road and onto a path made of barely crushed grass. In the latter, the thin tread of wagon wheels could be seen. "Latimer said she spends her free time with her brother's family. He and his wife have visited her at the estate on a few occasions."

The home Jane frequented was a thatch-roofed cottage, scarcely large enough to hold a kitchen and separate bedroom. There was an acre or less of cleared land, adorned for the most part with growing vegetables. In a rectangular pen, a milk cow was pressing her head through the fence rails and munching Swedish turnips.

The woman who emerged from the cottage did not see Harriet and Benedict as they dismounted, Benedict tying the reins loosely to the pen. The pale cow looked at the gelding in a warning fashion, as if daring him to touch her turnips. The woman, with a bolt of red cloth tied about her head—made of the leftover material from the making of her form-fitting apron—carried a basket to a line of rope tied from a corner of the house to a tree several yards away. She dropped the basket to the ground at her feet and began attaching a pair of children's bloomers to the line.

She looked back casually at the sound of footsteps, as if she doubted her hearing, then jumped when she saw Benedict and Harriet.

"I didn't hear anyone come up," she said as she pressed a hand to her flat chest. She looked from the road to the horse and back to her unexpected visitors with cornflower-blue eyes.

"I'm sorry if we gave you a fright." Harriet smiled disarmingly. "You must be unaccustomed to visitors so far out in the country."

She nodded, and then said, "If you're lookin' for Eustace, he won't be back for another day."

"Actually, we're looking for a woman named Jane . . ." Harriet's words drifted when she realized she didn't know the maid's complete name.

"Wrigley," Benedict clarified. "Is your husband Eustace Wrigley?"

Though not precisely friendly, the woman's expression had been open and polite until that moment. Her features shifted oddly, the corners of her eyes twitching as she worked to keep her expression neutral.

"Wrigley is our name. I am Emily."

Harriet brightened. "One of my best friends is named Emily."

Emily Wrigley was not impressed. She bent and drew a well-worn baby blanket from the basket. "What do you want Jane for? She doesn't live here. She's a servant at Rochester Hall."

"We know," Benedict said. "We are guests at the house. Miss Mosley here"—Benedict nodded toward Harriet—"has been worried because Jane hasn't been seen or heard from in two days."

"This," Harriet clarified, "after another servant was found dead in the woods."

"I haven't seen Jane since my youngest's birthday," Emily said with a strange absence of surprise at the mention of murder. She was hanging a pair of men's stockings. "She brought her a toy horse."

Harriet and Benedict exchanged a look.

Harriet said, "You have not seen her at all? Nor heard from her?"

Emily Wrigley gave Harriet the look of a cow protecting her turnips. "You think me a liar, miss?"

"No." Harriet shook her head quickly, looking to Benedict for help.

"We were only hoping to find word of Jane," he said. "We wouldn't call you anything, madam."

"Good. You hardly know me." With little concern for the wet garments still inside, she hefted her basket. "If you'll s'cuse me, I've a little one inside that needs tending to."

"Mrs. Wrigley?" Harriet said after her, and when she did not turn, "Emily?"

The woman had reached the cottage without looking back.

"Come along, Harriet." Benedict took her arm. "Perhaps we can find information elsewhere."

Harriet saw Emily come to a dead halt in the cottage doorway as Benedict drew her toward the horse. She watched Jane's sister-in-law turn, still holding her basket of clean, wet clothes.

"Did you say Harriet?"

31

The kitchen was hot, the air stagnant from being closed up as the evenings grew cooler. The coal oven was lit and atop was a great cauldron of a cooking pot that bubbled and created a slightly burned perfume. After they were seated, offered porridge they both politely refused, a small boy emerged from the other room, his dark blond hair flattened on one side and sticking up on the other and a cheek wrinkled with sleep. With his arms linked beneath her bare arms, he carried a baby wearing only her cloth diaper and a toothless grin. Harriet's eyes widened as Emily Wrigley took the baby from the boy, amazed that such a fat little being had been birthed from a bone-thin woman.

"Sit, Jamie. Time for your supper."

The boy, looking less than enthused, climbed into the chair opposite Harriet as his mother worked around the stove, the plump and dimpled baby fixed to her hip.

"So you saw Jane after the shooting," Benedict said. He removed his spectacles to wipe away the fog collecting on the lenses.

"Only for a bit. She told Eustace and I what had happened and we decided it best if she get out of here all together."

"I'm glad to know she is safe." Harriet nodded.

"As far as I know she is at their uncle's place by now. Eustace on his way home, I suspect." She came to the table with some act of physical enchantment, holding the baby, two bowls, and a pair of wooden spoons.

She dropped a bowl of porridge before Jamie and the contents quivered menacingly for a full five seconds afterward. Harriet watched as the boy picked up his spoon and prodded one of the black flecks of burnt oats. He looked up from beneath his brows, sending her a look of such abject misery that she had to cough to hide a laugh.

"She mentioned you." Emily nodded toward Harriet. She was shoveling mouthfuls of the porridge into the space between the baby's grinning gums. "Said she hated leaving you there without a word of warning."

"Does she know of what happened with the shooting?" Benedict asked.

"She was there when it happened. Said that nasty stableman she used to have a thing for was strangling her. Would have killed her too if it weren't for him getting shot in the back, if you ask me."

With some effort, Harriet drew her attention from the boy who had filled a spoon with porridge then turned it upside down. The gelatinous mass oozed slowly to the bowl, a rope of bumpy gray matter.

"Is she all right?"

"Got some bruises around her neck—ain't pretty to look at—and she's talking funny. She'll be fine, though." Her charge had finished her porridge, her eyes growing teary as she watched her mother lay the spoon in the empty bowl.

At the sound of her brother pushing his bowl away, easing it closer to her, she smiled triumphantly. She sank her hand into the goop then slapped a palm full of the porridge into her mouth and across the pink skin that surrounded it.

Harriet winced, looking at the brother, who shrugged.

Benedict said, "She saw the shooter?"

Emily shook her head, heedless of the porridge splattering across her apron as her daughter fed. "She heard the shot, saw the fellow fall to the ground dead, and ran. Never did look back."

"Why did he attack her?" asked Benedict.

"He had done it before," Harriet said. "I saw a bruise on her cheek the day after she and Millicent told me about the diary."

"Told us Hogg had more money all of a sudden. When she asked him about it, he said someone was paying him for information about Lady Dorthea. She thought he was the one who went to frighten you off, and confronted him, told him she was going to tell about what he was up to and he went into a rage."

Harriet looked at Benedict.

"He was supplying the blackmailer from inside Lady Cruchely's own house," he said.

Harriet felt a sudden fear trickle down her spine. Hogg had very likely been the man to shoot at her with the arrow and would have had access to the house when Lady Dorthea and Latimer were absent. Surely he found the time to puncture the floor. The man, who had been sleeping under the same roof as she, had nearly killed her.

He, however, had not gone through with the deed. His cohort, the man employing him for his devious actions, had proven himself to be a killer. Could he be under the same roof as well, plotting as she slept?

Beneath the table, she felt a hand cover her knee. She forced a smile, but could tell by the slight drawing together of his lashes, Benedict was not fooled.

32

Harriet was in her chemise and corset, dressing early for the evening ahead. She thought if she had herself ready to go, she could spend an hour reading and relaxing and not thinking about blackmailers or shootings. Because Jane was gone, poor Millicent was much harried by taking over the role of lady's maid. Her round cheeks were flushed red and her hair damp with sweat as she ran to and fro between Mrs. Pruett's and Lady Chesterfield's chambers, one woman calling to have her drawers aired out and another insisting her hair be curled by hot iron.

Harriet had traveled down the corridor—smiling briefly at Millicent as the larger woman ran down the stairs in search of hair wax—in her chemise and robe. She knocked lightly on the Pruetts' door, pretending not to hear Beatrice complaining about the serving staff.

Lizzie opened the door, looking about as exhausted as Millicent. "She's too loud, I know. I've been trying to calm her." Then she noticed the corset in Harriet's hands.

"I'll tie yours"—Harriet smiled—"if you'll tie mine."

Their own undergarments secured, Eliza and Harriet struggled together to draw closed Beatrice's corset. Harriet gritted her teeth and worriedly eyed the straining seams of the garment.

"Mother, I think you really need a larger—"

"Hush you!" the older woman snapped. "You just need to put a little muscle into it."

"Suck it in then," Lizzie ordered, surprising a laugh from Harriet.

The elder Pruett woman was purple in the face once the corset had been tied.

"I cannot sit down until the blasted thing gives a little. I'll need help with my stockings."

"Run," Lizzie whispered.

Harriet hadn't yet donned her gown shortly after returning to her chamber, when a knock came from her door. Biting her lip with worry over what Lizzie might need help squeezing her mother into next, she opened the door to Byron Elliot.

His eyes went wide, though she wasn't certain why. She was holding her robe together at her neck and there was less of her skin visible than when she was clad in an evening gown.

"Mr. Elliot."

"Byron, please."

"Byron."

He smiled at her and Harriet saw he wore no coat or cravat. His shirt was unbuttoned a little past his neck to expose a forestlike growth of hair.

When he said nothing, she cleared her throat. "May I help you, sir?"

"Yes, Harriet. I was hoping to speak with you in private. Would you mind?"

"Now?" She blinked, curling her stocking toes on the floor.

"It will only take a moment." He gripped the edge of the door. "I promise."

Harriet sighed and stepped back. She sincerely hoped the man hadn't come to share more poetry. She only let the door shut partway before facing Elliot.

"I haven't had a chance to see you, Harriet."

"You saw me at dinner."

"Only for a few minutes. You seem gone more than you are here. With the strange goings-on lately—Lady Cruchely acting out of sorts and Latimer and Mr. Bradbourne lurking around every corner—I worry about you."

"There's no need, sir." Harriet shook her head. "You can see I am quite safe."

He walked slowly around her and, as he drew nearer to the door, she hoped it was a sign he would soon take his leave. "And when you are gone, you are always with that Bradbourne fellow. It makes one wonder at his feelings toward you."

Thoughtful of protecting her reputation and her lover's good name, she said, "We are friends."

"Ah." Elliot halted with his back to the door. "I had known you would not fall for his ploys. Though I sincerely doubt a man like that has anything in the way of charm to offer a woman. You know he is obliged to have a career? He has no title and no wealth of which to speak."

Harriet frowned. She remembered Benedict the night before, pressing feather-light kisses against her knees. His breath had tickled her thighs before he'd dragged her closer and his tongue had done something she dare not mention in polite company. Even the thought of it now made her warm.

"Mr. Bradbourne's personal character more than

makes up for any title or wealth he might or might not have."

Elliot frowned a little, and then shook it off, his smile returning. "You are a very unusual woman, Harriet Mosley."

Harriet gave an inward roll of her eyes. "Yes, I know."

Elliot drew his hands behind his back and used them to push the door closed. There was an audible "click" of the key turning in the lock.

A cold chill ran down Harriet's spine and she scowled. "What are you about, Elliot?"

"Do not play coy, love." He stepped forward, hands dropping to his sides. His fingers squeezed closed and then opened again. "We cannot play this game any longer. It makes my body ache."

"Game?" Harriet stepped backward until her bottom collided with the desk chair.

"Your adoration of my poetry and that intoxicating ensemble of breeches and a man's coat donned to purposefully entice me. . . ."

Harriet blinked. "You are mistaken. I did nothing, purposely or otherwise, to—" her stomach rolled— "entice you."

He lunged. She dove, hopping onto the bed so she could kneel at its center.

Elliot's laughter was a high-pitched giggle. His oily hair had fallen over his eyes and he gazed at Harriet through it, licking his lower lip. He began to climb onto the bed.

Harriet pushed away, felt him catch the hem of her robe, but refused to be held back. She heard the material rending as she hit the floor. She got to her feet quickly, glaring at the man crawling across her mattress.

"This is my only robe," she snapped.

He reached for her and she slapped his hand away.

"Oh?" His eyes took on a new gleam. "You like it like that, eh?"

"I'd like," Harriet said, lifting the ends of her robe to inspect the damage there, "you to get the bloody hell out of my room."

She wasn't certain what happened. One minute she was standing and then she collided with the wardrobe, knocking the items carefully arranged atop it to the floor. Elliot sat on the edge of the bed, hands still extended from when he shoved her.

"I'll like," he said, "to climb between those long legs of yours." He spoke conversationally as he let his hands drop. "I always wanted to try it a bit on the rough side. Would you like me to call you foul names?"

"Damnation," Harriet whispered, and scrambled to her feet. She was just turning for the door when Elliot grabbed her wrist in a surprisingly fast and almost painful gesture. The sound of him slapping her bottom echoed in the room. She peered back at her backside, and then gaped at Elliot.

"You're a very naughty girl," he said, and smacked her again, hard enough to send her stumbling into the corner.

Ghosts, Harriet thought, murderers, and now this. Some things could not be endured—not even to have an excellent story to share with friends. Her gaze fell on the silver candlestick that had fallen when she collided with the wardrobe.

"Come here you naughty bitch and get your licks."

Harriet groaned, knelt, and reached.

There was a knock at the door.

"Give me a moment, minx." Elliot composed himself

in a blink. He straightened his hair as he strolled to the door. "I shall get rid of whoever it is."

She climbed to her feet, fingers fiercely tight across the candlestick.

"Bradbourne!" Elliot was saying. "I'm afraid Miss Mosley cannot come to the door. She is busy at the moment."

Harriet was more than a little embarrassed when Benedict saw her in the corner, breathing heavily and quite prepared to bash a man's skull in. Then Benedict's gaze turned to ice, grim understanding etching his features, and his head slowly turned back to Elliot.

"What?" the other man quipped. "She likes it r—"

Benedict slammed his fist into Elliot's face.

Benedict felt a satisfaction akin to bliss course through his veins at the crunch of Elliot's nose. The man's eyes went wide with surprised shock and pain as he wobbled. He fell ungracefully to the floor, hands cupped to his nose and blood spilling down from his nostrils.

When one of Benedict's sisters was younger, she had returned home early from a social gathering looking much like Harriet. Instead of a robe being torn, it was the sleeve of Sara Elizabeth's dress. Had it not been for Garfield's wife—pulling the girls aside to share a private chat as they became women—and a strategically placed pin in Sarah Elizabeth's hat, something terrible might have occurred. Harriet—Benedict recalled the candlestick gripped in her tight little fist—appeared to have her own method to dissuade unwarranted male attention.

He had found the young dandy who had cornered Sara Elizabeth in the library of a mutual acquaintance and gave him a sound thrashing. Benedict relished the idea of doing the same to the pale and sweating Elliot.

He couldn't imagine what would have happened had he not been in his room to hear the crashing sound from Harriet's chamber.

"You boke by dose!" The man on the floor glared up at him.

Benedict reached down, grabbed Elliot by the front of his shirt with one hand and curled the other into a fist.

From the hall beyond the opened door, Beatrice Pruett screamed. Eliza ran into the chamber, quickly moving toward Harriet.

"Benedict," Harriet said.

He brought his fist up into Elliot's chin and heard the man's teeth snap together. The lecher's eyes rolled for a moment then he was flailing at Benedict with loose fists.

"Benedict, stop!"

He paused to look at Harriet, his fist lifted for a third blow. She had left the corner, was standing nearer the fray with wide, horrified eyes. Benedict took a moment to eye her head to toe, to make sure her robe was the only part of her that had been harmed by Elliot.

From the doorway, they heard Latimer's cool voice. "Bradbourne, be so kind as to not kill the man. Dorthea's house can take no more excitement this week."

"This *year*," Dorthea insisted, clutching the man's arm.

"I don't think Mr. Elliot intended to attack me," Harriet was saying. She looked at the man hanging from Benedict's fist with a thoughtful expression. "He's just incredibly obtuse."

Reining in on his rage, Benedict released the other man who collapsed like a sack of potatoes.

"*By dose,*" Elliot whined.

"We'll have him removed from the house," Lady Cruchely said as Latimer slipped inside the room.

He scowled at the nearly unconscious Elliot. "He can take a coach from the village to London."

"I'm heading that way," Benedict said. He had been planning to return Annabelle Rochester's diary before the evening's entertainment. "I'll see to it Elliot boards safely." He fixed his gaze on Harriet. "Are you hurt?"

"No." She sighed. "Only a bit embarrassed by it all."

Beatrice Pruett sniffed with disdain as Latimer dragged Elliot from the room. Her attention was not on the prone man, but Harriet. "I daresay none of this would have happened if you would learn some decorum, Miss Mosley."

Harriet gasped and Benedict rounded on the old woman, but it was Eliza who spoke.

"Shut up, Mother," she snapped, making her mother turn to her in shock.

"*Eliza!*"

"Don't you even hear the ugliness that comes out of your mouth?" The young woman marched around Harriet, shaking her head.

Dorthea, eyes wide, turned and quickly walked away.

"Harriet is kind and witty and the best sort of friend a woman could have. You, on the other hand, are cruel and judgmental and know less about good manners than a fly on a pile of horse—"

"Eliza!" Beatrice's eyes were wide as saucers, her face becoming an unattractive shade of gray.

"You make it so people can't stand you." Eliza squinted at the older woman. "Even your own daughter." She lifted her chin and stomped past her mother, leaving Harriet's bedchamber for her own.

Beatrice made a strangled croaking sound, looking from Harriet to Benedict as if searching for help. Then, at a decidedly slower pace than her daughter, she trudged down the hall.

Harriet, Benedict saw, was grinning ear to ear. She appeared enthralled with what had just occurred, as if she had already forgotten the events before it. "I'm so proud of Lizzie," she breathed.

33

Harriet opened her bedchamber door and came to an abrupt stop. Had she halted a moment too late, she would have collided with the woman standing in the hall only an inch away. She had given up her too-tight corset for a sleeping gown and ruffled cap.

Beatrice Pruett wore a slightly pained smile. Harriet followed her gaze as the woman peeked out the corner of her eye. Eliza stood only a few feet away, hands folded across her chest and toe tapping.

"Hello, Lizzie."

"Hello, Harriet. Mother has something she would like to say to you."

Harriet's brows lifted.

Beatrice sucked in her cheeks and lifted her chin. "I wanted to apologize for what I said earlier. As a lady, you are most virtuous and refined," she lied.

"Well, I want to apologize for calling you a bitter old prune," Harriet said in the same civil tones.

"You never said that." Beatrice frowned.

"I thought it."

"Thank you, Mother. I'm sure you want to go to bed now." Lizzie dismissed her with a lifted brow.

The older woman moved slowly toward her room. "I still say you should not attend this terrible thing downstairs."

"You are being excessive."

Beatrice said, "I know what I am talking about. The Bible forbids communication with the dead. Forbids it, Eliza."

"This woman Lady Dorthea has invited is little more than an actress playing a part. It is entertainment. Any speaking to the dead, as well as any knocks or thuds we hear after, will like as not be well rehearsed."

"That woman"—Beatrice uttered the last in a dubious tone—"is a gypsy. Lady Dorthea said so herself. Tricksters for the most part, the male of the class will go so far as thievery to make a coin or two. I won't even discuss what the gypsy women will do."

Lizzie gave an exhausted sigh.

Harriet stepped forward. She closed the door behind her and offered the other woman a smile she hoped would convey her sincerest support. "On your way down?"

Lizzie smiled. "Yes. You will join me?"

Harriet nodded, and though it was not her custom to do so, she linked her arm through Eliza's. "I thought she planned on attending the séance?" she whispered from the corner of her mouth.

Lizzie barely moved her mouth as she said, "That was before her corset split at the seams."

Harriet bit her lip and the younger woman had to look away so she would not be tempted to laugh.

"The woman is driving me mad," Lizzie whispered at the head of the staircase.

Harriet made a sympathetic sound.

"My father left us when I was a child. Abandoned us to the care of my grandparents. It was quite a scandal in our little village. I used to tell myself that's what made my mother the way she is. Now, I believe it is because of the way she behaves that my father left."

Harriet carefully watched the younger woman as she shared her tale. Her features were serious, composed in grim certainty.

"Sometimes I consider following him out. My father, I mean. I've looked into joining a convent as a means of escape. I imagine walking away from the house with only the clothes on my back and finding my own way in the world."

Harriet brought them both to a halt at the foot of the stairs. From down the hall they could hear voices and murmured laughter.

"I never had the opportunity to know my mother," Harriet said. "My father was in prison the last few years of his life. He enjoyed the gaming halls a little more than he could afford, and when he could not pay his debts he was locked away. I was left to live with an aunt who saw me as a nuisance and never hesitated to let me know the fact.

"I visited my father once," she confided with the other, a secret only Augusta Merryweather knew. She smiled wryly. "He asked to borrow a few coins. Some of his fellow inmates were making bets on rats they had trained to run. I gave him the coins and never returned."

Lizzie took her hands, shaking her head. "Harriet, I'm sorry. My troubles must seem so trivial—"

"Not at all." Harriet squeezed the younger woman's hands. "I only told you this so you could understand that my upbringing left a lot to be desired. Instead of an overprotective mother, I had a father who took me to all sorts of gambling establishments. It is because of the way he raised me that I am the way I am today. It takes a bit more to really frighten me than your average woman, and I feel comfortable traveling alone to a great old house said to be filled with ghosts. And here I made a friend, whose mother cannot be so awful if she made in her daughter such a wonderful person."

Lizzie turned as pink as her dress, but offered a smile. "She did allow me to come here, despite her qualms with the house."

"Indeed, she did." Harriet nodded and together they moved toward the sound of voices.

Lady Cruchely had established the perfect setting for their evening with the spirits and Benedict expected Harriet would adore the melancholy shadows that made up the parlor. The lanterns had been dimmed with painted glass in shades of purple and red. A round table had been moved to the center of the room and covered with crisp white linen, and at its center was a scrolling candelabrum. The flicker of candlelight could be seen in windows backed by nightfall. Benedict glanced at the clock atop the mantel and saw there were only a few minutes until midnight, the witching hour when the séance was to begin. He had thought he might be late as he had a certain journal to return under the blanket of darkness.

"Bradbourne!" Oscar Randolph looked up from the small group who sat near the fire. "You're just in time to hear our Miss Mosley have her palm read." He moved his great white brows up and down in a sinister attempt. "We shall soon learn what evil lurks in her soul."

Benedict's gaze shifted from Randolph to the woman seated in one of the high-backed chairs closest the hearth, appearing none the worse after the commotion with Elliot.

Lady Dorthea had asked that her guests dress in their dark finest and Harriet had donned a gown of pitch black. It was a simple garment—cinched sleeves just covering her shoulders and a dainty black ribbon tied into a bow beneath her breasts. Her skin was pale against the onyx fabric, her smile white as moonlight when it flashed his way. His gaze met hers from across the room, the darkness of her clothes and surroundings made her wheat-colored eyes all the more brilliant.

"There is no evil in her soul." He hadn't realized his intimate tone, or that he had spoken aloud, until Eliza Pruett turned to stare at him with wide, knowing eyes.

Harriet's smile faltered nervously.

"Yes, well, do carry on, Madame Lyuba," Lady Dorthea said with a wry smile. "I shan't be the only one exposed."

"There is great wealth in Lady Dorthea's future," Randolph told Benedict with a nod.

As Benedict drew closer, he saw Harriet's hand rested palm up atop a pale, plump hand with shimmering black fingernails. Madame Lyuba had hair dark as coal and eyes that shone crystal blue in the firelight. She was a zaftig woman, more than three times the size of Harriet sitting opposite. Her generous frame was garbed in layers of vibrant colored fabric, and earrings so heavy with stones they would have dragged a less substantial woman to the ground, danced above her shoulders.

With a single fingertip, the gypsy traced a line down Harriet's delicate palm.

"You have a smooth lifeline," she said without looking up from Harriet's hand. "You will live to be an old woman. There are joining lines, good friends helping you."

Harriet nodded, and then whispered to the woman, "Do you see any fish?"

Madame Lyuba looked up from beneath her brows. "No fishes."

Harriet made a face and those who stood around her laughed.

Lizzie saw Benedict frown at the joke and explained, "Fish are a sign of wealth and prosperity."

"There *is* a treasure of sorts in your future," said Madame Lyuba. "A prize that you must find."

Harriet smiled at the woman. "Can you just tell me where it is?"

"It does not work that way."

"I was afraid of that."

The gypsy looked down at Harriet's palm with a furrowed brow, then lifted her gaze and pierced the younger woman with eyes like shattered glass. It was as if she read only a part of a story in Harriet's hand and searched for the end of the tale in her eyes.

"You are falling in love"—the gypsy released her palm with great finality—"with someone in this house."

Benedict felt a heavy heat strike the center of his back. Lizzie looked at him and then quickly away before anyone could notice. Harriet did not look at him at all.

The room was uncomfortably silent and Benedict could hear his heart pounding in his chest.

Then Harriet lifted her palm until it nearly touched her nose and sighed. "I wish she saw a fish."

"Let us begin our communion with the spirits."

Harriet was uncertain of the reason, Madame

Lyuba's serious tone perhaps, but a faint shiver worked the length of her spine. They were seated about the round table, its candelabrum replaced with a group of nine candles. The varied lengths of beeswax had been divided evenly amidst those present, the gypsy with eyes that shone like diamonds asking them to think positive and pleasant thoughts as they each held their candle.

Harriet had to try very hard to keep her thoughts from those feelings of embarrassed astonishment that had pervaded her well-being since her palm was read.

She cautiously risked a glance at the man seated next to her because, for once since he had entered the parlor, she could not feel his gaze upon her. Had Benedict known of whom Madame Lyuba spoke? Had he imagined the man who Harriet was falling in love with another in the house? Felt distressed at the idea it might be him or hoped it was?

When his head began to turn in her direction, Harriet quickly looked away. She fixed her attention on the gypsy and told herself the woman might very well be performing an act and at every performance she proclaimed one member of her audience to be soon of good fortune and another falling in love.

"Please," Madame Lyuba was saying, "take the hand of the person on either side of you."

Harriet had both hands sitting atop her lap and before the last of the directions were given, she felt strong fingers lace through hers. She peeked at Benedict and he met her gaze, giving her hand a slight squeeze.

Harriet wrapped her free hand around Lizzie's on her opposite side and focused again on the gypsy. Be she a charlatan or not, her reading of Harriet was more than accurate.

34

It never would have happened, had Lizzie not leaned forward and asked Madame Lyuba, "Can we not have one more?"

This after the clock chimed the passing of the second hour since the woman's arrival. She had spent half the time at the table with eyes squeezed tightly shut as she searched whatever it was psychic palm readers saw in the darkness behind their lashes. In that pose, with head tilted as if listening for mice in the walls, she brought before them three spirits—a pair of mischievous children and an old woman with a terrible ache in her bones. Neither Harriet nor anyone else besides Madame Lyuba saw the ghosts, of course, though she did catch herself searching the corners of the room as the gypsy scolded the young boys for doing something dreadful to a black cat. The cat, Harriet imagined, had been dead for centuries as her tormentors, the gypsy explained, had died while swimming unattended in a now dry ravine, some 200 years ago.

Madame Lyuba served as medium between her audience and the dead, explaining what the deceased were wearing and sharing a few physical characteristics before she started questioning the unseen guests. Her interrogation moved through a series of questions, varying from the age of the deceased when they died to asking the reasons for their state of being. She had assured Harriet and the others before she began the séance, that the dead most often move on after death, to whichever heavenly setting they found most pleasing. There are, however—as she confided in her most serious tone—lost souls who, for whatever reason, never find their way.

The boys for whom Madame Lyuba spoke had said they had neither seen such place nor even a hint of direction as to where their heaven might be.

From the corner of her mouth, Lizzie—whose hand Harriet felt jerk at the mention of the abused black cat—murmured, "Perhaps they were not meant for heaven."

The old woman, as Madame Lyuba explained, had died before her husband. There was no love lost for the widower, it would seem, as he married a neighbor woman only a few weeks after. When the newly married couple suffered a violent death from the plague— the Black Death, as the woman called it—the first wife left whatever peace she had found behind. Too heartbroken at the thought of perhaps running into her beloved husband and his new much-adored wife.

Whereas the story of the mischievous, if not cruel, youths, made Harriet only slightly frightened, the old woman made her sad. Perhaps it was the mournful quality of Madame Lyuba's voice as she recounted the tale or the idea that, even in heaven, heartache could be found. She wondered if she were to suddenly meet her demise, would she wait at the edge of her most peaceful place and search the incoming spirits for one in a likeness of the man seated next to her.

She was pushing the thoughts away, condemning her housemate and best friend, Augusta, for sharing the text of her favorite love stories with her, when Lizzie made her plea for one last encounter before the gypsy took her leave.

The robust woman looked at the clock, not appearing tired in the least despite the passing of the hour, and Harriet took a moment to inspect her fellow audience members' expressions. The medium sat at the head of the table and to her left was Sir Randolph who appeared amused and shot Harriet a wink when he caught her eye. She winked back and turned to the duchess beside him. Lady Dorthea was looking at Latimer and he her, with a kind of smile that made Harriet wonder what their feet were doing under the table. The Lord and Lady Chesterfield, opposite their hosts, were a comparison in contrast. Lord Chesterfield appeared as if he might fall asleep at any moment and his wife as giddy as a child.

When Harriet shifted her attention to the man beside her, he smiled politely. Nothing like the smile that passed between Latimer and Lady Dorthea, Harriet realized with a little disappointment.

"Well, Miss Mosley, how are you enjoying the festivities?" he inquired with no intimacy, as if he were speaking to Lizzie or Randolph.

"It is an interesting way to pass the night," she said with equal politeness.

He released her hand. "I hope this is not the most interesting way you can imagine spending an evening," he said in low tones, lean fingers covering her skirt-blanketed thigh.

Harriet's eyes went wide as she examined his closed

expression. Benedict's features remained neutral, but upon further inspection Harriet saw, behind the lenses of his spectacles, his eyes burned over her.

Her heart began to beat a little faster as disappointment evaporated. The corner of her mouth twitched. "Perhaps. One or two things come to mind."

He squeezed her thigh. "I can think of only one. But it is extraordinary."

Harriet felt heat wash through her and looked away before she smiled a wholly inappropriate grin for dealing with lost souls.

Benedict found her hand and his thumb stroked hers.

Goose bumps rose on her exposed arms and he must have seen for she heard his low chuckle.

"Clear your minds, please," Madame Lyuba said and Harriet could feel the younger woman beside her tense with excitement, "and think of pleasant things."

Harriet heard Benedict chuckle again.

The gypsy closed her eyes and instead of Harriet's flush waning, she felt herself grow warmer still. The nine flames at the center of the table quivered violently.

The parlor door opened and no one stood beyond.

"This is new," Benedict murmured.

Harriet heard Lizzie gasp with excitement as they stared into the empty corridor beyond the doorway. The candles trembled again and this time Harriet felt the breeze that toyed with them. It was not a cool evening wind, stealing in from some open window in the house, but a warm air that was dry and uncomfortable. It brushed her cheeks with familiarity and Harriet frowned.

Madame Lyuba tensed and opened her eyes wide as she did every occasion when a spirit made its presence known. Harriet watched the candlelight flicker in the gypsy's gaze, the woman fixing her attention as they all had on the empty door. Softly at first, as if in a room above or below, Harriet heard the sound of footsteps. She began to shake as the sound grew louder, and she saw Madame Lyuba's stunned gaze shift from the doorway to the table directly across from Harriet.

She was being watched—Harriet could feel it—and the sensation made a sound not unlike a whimper quake in her throat. Her head slowly turned and she pressed her spine into the back of her chair, but could not find the strength to push away from the table.

The table was the only thing separating her from a dead woman.

Annabelle Rochester's eyes were the same unfettered black as they had been on the first occasion Harriet saw her, looking up from the gaping hole above the ballroom. Her skin was alabaster, tinted with a whisper of glowing blue color and her dark unbound hair floated as if she were underwater, as did the wide sleeves of her gown. Her pale blue lips parted and Harriet wanted to squeeze her eyes closed, but could not.

She thought she might burst into tears, her terror was so heartrending—and there was something else. Something that reached to her from the dead woman on the other side of the table. A crippling misery hung in the air with the uncomfortable heat and Harriet had no choice but to breathe it in, and it became icy talons that grabbed hold of her heart.

When the apparition spoke, it was as a faint melodious whisper.

"You will tell them? The truth of what happened here, to me and my beloved?"

Harriet stared, speechless.

"Please."

Annabelle lifted a hand with entreaty and it was not pale as the rest of her, but black and charred. Harriet could see exposed bone and underlying sinew where fire had burned away flesh.

She nodded once, quickly, looking away. Less than a heartbeat passed before the oppressive heat was gone and the candles went out.

"What was that?" Lizzie said, releasing Harriet with surprise.

Benedict shifted as if to get up, but she would not let him go.

"Harriet?" He tugged.

It felt like aeons, with Lord and Lady Chesterfield complaining and Lady Dorthea uttering words of calm reassurance, before the parlor was filled with light. Latimer stood near the newly lit wall sconce and looked everyone over.

"Did you see that?" Lizzie was grinning.

Harriet nodded only slightly.

"The door slammed closed out of nowhere and then the lights! What was it, Madame Lyuba?"

Harriet shifted her attention from Lizzie to the others and realized they had seen nothing of Lady Annabelle as she had. Though there was a strange gleam to the gypsy fortune-teller's eye as she spoke.

"I do not know, Miss Pruett. Sometimes the spirits are not meant for my eyes, but those of another." She looked at Harriet briefly, so only Harriet noticed.

"Harriet," Benedict said again, finally extracting his hand from hers. He looked from her to his palm and she followed his gaze.

His hand was red where she had gripped him and there were tiny grooves made by her nails.

***

Benedict watched Harriet work; she was wringing out the washcloth before sitting beside him and reaching for his hand. She dabbed at the grooves she had made with her nails, her brow furrowing with consternation. The woman holding his hand had squeezed it so fiercely during their last moments with Madame Lyuba, it damn near hurt. It had got his attention, making Benedict look at Harriet in puzzlement. The terrified expression on her face, the sheen of tears in wide eyes staring at a point on the opposite side of the table, made him forget the pain.

"Do you want to tell me," he said, the sound of his voice loud in the empty kitchen, "what it was that frightened you so you nearly took my hand off?"

"I'm sorry, Benedict." Harriet's look of angst intensified and she shook her head. "I did not mean to do this."

"I know, Harriet." He made his tone gentle. "And it doesn't hurt. I would just like to know why you were scared."

She met his gaze briefly, and then looked away. He thought she was not going to answer and was shifting in his chair to be near enough to touch Harriet, when her lips parted.

"I saw something in there, in the parlor with us." She sighed wearily as if she knew by speaking the words aloud she was in for some sort of injury. "I've seen it before."

Benedict's brows drew together. He turned the hand Harriet was ministering to and took hold of hers. Her fingers were cold. "What is it?"

Benedict recognized the man's heavy, thudding

footsteps before he entered the kitchen. Latimer's gaze moved briefly over their joined hands.

"This came for you earlier, Bradbourne. We were unable to find you in the house prior to the parlor games."

Benedict released Harriet to open the folded square of paper. He read aloud the slightly shaky script, "'*Mr. Bradbourne and Miss Mosley, I recalled the name of the gentleman who inquired of the watch. It was Roposh Crandal. Signed, Fagin Osborne.*'"

"Strange," Harriet said. "The name, I mean. Do you know it?"

Benedict shook his head, but said nothing. He was watching Latimer, who hadn't left the room. When the other man caught his look, he took a deep breath and reached into the pocket of his jacket.

"Dorthea found this on her pillow." He held out another piece of paper, unfolded and filled with neat script.

"When?"

"Tonight."

"The same handwriting as on the other letters?"

"The same." Latimer nodded curtly and his unpleasant features went uglier still. "He was in the house with us. The note was not there when she left her room shortly before eleven and she found it upon returning from the parlor."

"I'm not surprised," Benedict said, scanning the note.

"What do you mean?"

"Benedict thinks the blackmailer is in the house, do you not, Benedict?"

He lifted a brow, looking at Harriet from over the edge of the paper. "Have I ever told you how quick-witted you are, Harriet?"

For the first time since the scene in the parlor, she smiled. "Thank you."

"What do you mean," Latimer repeated with a new edge to his voice, "'in the house'?"

"Mr. Hogg lived on the premises and had free entry into the house, did he not? It would not surprise me if there was not another part of the household taking advantage of his place."

"What of the servant who disappeared? She is in on it?"

"Not Jane," Harriet said, shaking her head.

"No," said Benedict, "not Jane, but someone . . . Perhaps not a servant in the house."

Latimer laughed, a bitterly suspicious sound. "You think Lord and Lady Chesterfield capable of murdering a man? Sir Randolph or the Pruett girl, Harriet's friend?"

Benedict shrugged in response.

Harriet said with loyal haste, "It might very well be a past guest, who knows the house and a bit about Lady Cruchely's past."

Benedict shrugged. "They got into the house unnoticed."

"It would not be hard," Latimer said, calming a little. "The servants had either gone home or were in bed for the evening. I was with Dorthea in the parlor, as was everyone else who would have noticed a strange intruder."

"A possibility," Benedict said. "Who was the last to arrive tonight?"

"Besides you?"

"Lizzie," Harriet said, "and myself."

"The Chesterfields were the first to join Dorthea with Madame Lyuba, then Sir Randolph," Latimer finished.

"I want a list of guests Lady Cruchely has entertained

here, and servants—past and present." Benedict laid the last blackmail letter on the table. "In the meantime, do not leave Lady Dorthea alone tonight. It has been several days since the last time the blackmailer made a physical threat."

"You do not," Latimer said as he turned from the room, "have to say it twice."

35

He watched from the shadows as Bradbourne and Mosley moved up the staircase, the man with a single hand pressed proprietarily, familiarly to Harriet's lower back. Their heads were close as they spoke in quiet tones.

No matter. The man in the shadows had been watching them for some time. It had been a priority for him to keep a close eye on the two since he first realized their help had been enlisted to find Lady Cruchely's blackmailer. He, being the blackmailer, could find no danger in Miss Mosley's interest. Bradbourne, however, was another matter entirely.

The blackmailer had done his research or, rather, sent Hogg to research before the other man's demise. Benedict Bradbourne, it seemed, had been a Runner on Bow Street since he was old enough to be accepted into the clan. He was the youngest, to date, to be invited to join the exclusive group of public servants. If the fact he had come to England bearing two sisters and cared for his family at ten and five in a manner some men could not muster in their forties was any indication, his acceptance was well deserved. He had, apparently, more than proved himself in his time working with Bow Street and that worried the blackmailer. Bradbourne had yet to leave a case unfinished, a villain unrepentant, and in order to bring the Runner's glowing track record to a halt, drastic measures might be required.

The blackmailer tilted his head in consideration and tapped the toe of his well-made shoe, recalling the quick and faultless manner the other man had dealt with Hogg when the scoundrel tried to run him down with a horse.

How did one bring a halt to the actions done by a man capable of such calm calculation?

The man in the shadows stilled a moment before his thoughtful gaze returned to the staircase. He focused on neither Bradbourne nor Harriet, but the hand resting on her back. A bit too close to her bottom for propriety standards.

The blackmailer had an idea.

"I've seen ghosts here."

It startled him. Not the content of her words, but the fact she said them. Benedict had thought Harriet asleep. He had not moved or spoken since he woke, only lifted his lashes to gaze in silent appreciation at the woman on the pillow beside his. The light on her closed eyelids had gradually changed from gray and purple, to orange and pink. When the light was golden, kissing her exposed shoulder and lips and making crescent-shaped shadows beneath her eyelashes, he had grudgingly decided she had to leave his bed and make her way to the room across the hall, before anyone saw. Then he decided to give her a few more minutes of sleep and himself more time to appreciate her beauty, so comfortable in the rising sun.

"You're unsettling," Benedict said.

Her features remained lax, as if she still slept. He thought perhaps she was talking in her sleep until she said, "Because I saw ghosts?"

"Because you look asleep when you are not. How long have you been awake?"

"I was not meant for this life. That of a spy or agent for the crown, perhaps . . ." Her lips twitched. "I do form a fine man when given a pair of breeches and a nice hat. It's my height, I think."

He pushed himself up on an elbow to stare at her. Her eyes opened, a luminescent gold encircled with bands of vibrant green. When she made no move to explain, he leaned forward and kissed her—hard—before he could ask any more about things it was best he did not think about.

"I'll like as not ever make it as a spy," she said with only a little regret. "It's rare for women to be employed for espionage and authorities might hesitate before enlisting the skills of a lunatic who sees dead people in old houses."

"When did you see them?"

"I saw one last night." Harriet's smile was gone, her tone serious.

"The commotion at the séance?"

She nodded, the pillow making a whispering sound as her hair brushed it. "That has not been the only time I saw her. It started the day I nearly broke my neck falling through the upstairs hall." She said the words with grim determination, meeting Benedict's eye directly. Searching for a reaction that would bring her words to a halt. "She is Annabelle Rochester, I am certain."

"Is that all?"

She shook her head again. "Warren, once." Harriet sat up, the bedclothes falling down around her hips. As she folded her legs under her, one of the straps on her chemise slipped off her shoulder. The stubble on Benedict's chin had burned the delicate skin there. "I think I heard them before all else. It's happened more than once. I'll be asleep or preparing for bed and my room suddenly becomes uncomfortably warm. Sometimes smoke creeps under my door and I can smell it, the burning. They are shouting at each other, but I cannot make out the words. It sounds like they are in the hallway, at the head of the stairs. I open the door and there is nothing."

Benedict looked at the strap of her chemise for a long moment, then said, "It is possible you are asleep, Harriet. You say you are awoken or it is before you go to sleep. What if you are dreaming that you are awake?"

"I am not asleep, Benedict. I know what I see and I know what I hear. My senses are not failing." She pursed her lips. "It is my mental faculties I cannot attest for."

"Harriet, don't speak of this to anyone."

"You needn't say that. I've told no one but you and I'm starting to doubt my decision to do that," she finished in a wry tone that made him scowl.

"Harriet—"

A soft knock played on the door.

"Did you hear that?" Harriet asked.

Benedict, already off the bed and slipping into his breeches, nodded.

"Good. I thought it might be my sanity knocking."

"My apologies for disturbing you at such an early hour," Lady Cruchely said as soon as Benedict opened the door. The woman looked as if she hadn't slept the night through. Her eyes were circled with dark shadows and the corners of her mouth were pinched.

"We were awake," Benedict said, and winced inwardly. Harriet would likely frown upon his betraying the fact they woke together and the implications that came along with it.

"Good morning," Harriet said, appearing at his side. She smiled, though her gaze showed concern as she eyed the woman on the other side of the doorway.

"Good morning, Harriet." Dorthea smiled in return with a lack of shock that bothered Benedict. "I thought it urgent," she said, "that I bring you the information you requested." She held out several sheets of delicate paper.

"The guest lists and a record of employees?" Benedict was already scanning the names.

Dorthea nodded. "As well as their last known home address. Many of the staff listed is still here. A young maid was wed a year ago and left us to start her family. Then there was Mr. Hogg."

"You'll excuse me." Harriet brushed Benedict's elbow on her way past. "I think I'll freshen up before breakfast."

And, Benedict thought, before anyone else caught her making the short trip between his door and hers. He nodded absently and looked up from the list to speak to Dorthea.

"I don't think we'll find anything useful here. I had my doubts when I asked Mr. Latimer last night. I'm sorry to have wasted your time."

"No waste. I needed to do something to keep my mind off of the nonsense with the blackmailer anyway. I've actually considered rethinking this scheme of bringing him out of hiding. If I were to pay his demands, things would be a lot easier."

Benedict met her gaze. His was the hard practiced stare of a man who was accustomed to making witnesses speak the truth. "You will be at the mercy of a man who has murdered his only cohort in his plan. One who has gone to some effort to make you fear for your own life and almost injured Harriet in doing that."

Saying her name, Benedict's gaze drifted over Lady Cruchely's head, to the door opposite his. Only then did he see Harriet had opened the door, but not stepped inside. Instead, she stood on the threshold of her bedchamber, arms limp at her sides.

"Harriet?" Benedict said, not without concern.

"Someone has been in my room," she said in a casual tone at odds with her words.

Harriet moved willingly to the side when he gave her a gentle nudge, so that he might witness the sight that held her transfixed.

"Bloody hell," he breathed.

Someone had been in her room, left its content in hazardous disarray to leave no doubt of the fact. The blankets had been torn from the bed and piled on the floor in a lump that looked disturbingly like a human body. The wardrobe had been left open, its contents strewn out as if Harriet's clothing had exploded from the chest. One of her pale gloves was now stained with a black puddle made from the bottle of ink tipped atop the writing table. Every candle had been snapped in half and ashes from the fireplace drug to the middle of the floor. Ashen handprints, large like those of a man, were spaced evenly across the windows, as if someone had gone to great lengths to put them there.

"Harriet," Benedict said to the woman still in the doorway, "look for anything that might be missing. A money purse or jewelry."

She blinked at him with wide eyes, a woman clearly unaccustomed to being personally invaded. She regained control quickly, however, and was reaching under the bed for her valise.

"You think a thief did this?" Lady Cruchely worked her fingers together as she stepped into the room. She looked older than she had moments before.

"I doubt it," Benedict said, watching Harriet as she extracted a small reticule from her bag.

"All my money is still here," she said. She rose and reached atop the wardrobe, producing a pair of earrings and a necklace. "My jewelry." She made a face. "Not that it is worth anything. Perhaps the robber was angry with my pitiful stash and decided to smash the place to pieces?"

Benedict was silent, thoughtful as he gazed at the steady drops of thick black ink that fell from the table. "Harriet, you kept notes on our investigation in your journal?"

"Yes." She smiled with quick understanding. "You needn't worry about prying eyes, Benedict. I hid my journal where no one would find it."

He lifted a brow. "Beneath the mattress?"

Harriet could not hide her disappointment before she moved past Benedict and to the writing table. Its contents, save the bottle of ink, had been knocked to the floor. Harriet dropped to her knees, but not to riffle through these discarded items. She reached beneath the table itself and, after a few twists of her wrist, produced the book from where she'd attached it to the underside of the table.

She shook her head at Benedict before confiding in

Dorthea, "Amateur." The duchess, however, smiled only briefly before something across the room caught her attention.

Benedict, tempted to smile at Harriet himself, followed the older woman's gaze. What had started off as a smile turned into a dark and ugly glare. He could see his expression clearly as he moved to the mirror above the hearth, could make out his features between the words that had been painted across the reflective glass in bloodred.

GET OUT OF THIS HOUSE

"That isn't"—Dorthea shook her head behind him—"what I think it is. Is it, Mr. Bradbourne?"

Benedict lightly tested the congealing letters of brilliant red with his fingertips. He rubbed some of the stuff between his thumb and forefinger, eyed the small seeds. "Jam."

"Strawberry or raspberry?" Harriet asked politely. And when he turned his dark glare on her, she winced and confided, "I'm allergic to raspberries."

"Harriet," Lady Cruchely chastised in a motherly, worried manner, "this is serious. Perhaps you should take your leave."

"Indeed, it is serious." Harriet nodded, her expression the least disconcerted of those present. "If our man has gone so far as to threaten me personally, Dorthea, it is because we have made him very uncomfortable. Benedict and I must be getting closer to the blackmailer. That is exactly why we must not take our leave. It would be giving the villain exactly what he wants. Is that not so, Benedict?"

He stared at Harriet, unable to believe the excitement he could feel rising from her like a physical heat. "We will talk about that in private," he said, and for the first time saw her triumphant smile falter. "For the time being, you will not leave my side for any reason, Harriet. If this murderer—and he is a murderer, madam, lest you forget—has some grievance against you, I want him to have no chance to act upon it. I want to be able to see you no matter what."

Harriet made a face. "If I must powder my nose?"

His hands clenched into fists and he said through his teeth, "I will hold the powder."

She blinked at him, stunned.

"What shall I do, Mr. Bradbourne?" Lady Cruchely said, clearly eager to be doing something.

"Find Mr. Latimer. I believe you safer with the man at your side."

"Yes." She managed a smile that conveyed a wealth of love that had not been present in Harriet's expression when Benedict ordered her to his side.

"Together," he went on, "search your rooms for more vandalism, and then be ready for any of your guests who might have tales to share of strange sounds in the halls last night."

"Did you hear nothing?" Lady Cruchely looked between him and Harriet.

Benedict's body tightened. The only thing he could remember hearing during the night was the sweet sound of Harriet's ragged breathing against his ear and then the whimper of his name when she found release.

"No," Harriet said, simply enough.

"We'll check the rest of the house," Benedict said, "and if anything strange turns up we shall find you."

"Strange? In the face of this and everything that has happened so far?" Lady Cruchely held her arms out to encompass the room. She then dropped them to her sides and shook her head. "Anything stranger than this, Mr. Bradbourne, and you can have this bloody house. I am moving back to London."

The duchess left the room with a determined stride and Benedict turned for his battle with Harriet. He was taken aback when he saw her brows were crinkled and she was biting her bottom lip.

She whispered insistently, "I have to powder my nose."

36

"Benedict, really. Is all this necessary?" Harriet scowled when the man seated across from her did not look up from the note he had decided to write his cohorts in London. He had been ignoring her questions and comments since the incident in her bedchamber, as if her words were moot or—to put it bluntly—stupid.

She attempted to direct invisible daggers at the top of the man's head with the power of her eyes. She wished she had the same skill at such things as Emily Paxton, who could make the most impenetrable of men quiver. As it were, Benedict did not look up from his writing. Harriet sighed, folding her hands in her lap and scanning their surroundings. The kitchen, as it were, made a pleasant workroom. It smelled of fresh baked bread and wasn't too warm with the door opened wide as Millicent used a brittle old broom to sweep flour down the walkway and into the grass.

"Harriet," Benedict said finally, and not in the tone of a man terrified by the cold glare directed at him, "I know you think me unreasonable, but you must trust me."

Her brows lifted as she waited for further explanation. When he offered none, she gritted her teeth to hold back her scream of frustration. "You exasperate me sometimes," she said.

That made one of his brows lift.

"What does your message say?" She had tried reading the note upside down, but Benedict wrote in a fashion that curled his arm over the top of the paper. She thought with some irritation that he was doing it purposefully, so she could not read the message, but he answered her question readily enough.

"I am asking a friend to look into Lady Cruchely's past. Or, rather, that of her family."

Harriet shifted, folding her arms atop the battered table. "You think there's a link between her family and all this mess?"

"It is a fact, Harriet, that crimes, more often than not, are perpetrated by individuals who are friends or family members of the victim. At least, that is the case with the more affluent individuals."

Another reason, Harriet thought, to be happy with her somewhat modest lot in life. "I thought all of Lady Cruchely's family were deceased."

"Everyone that *she* knows of," Benedict murmured absently.

Harriet squinted as she felt the wheels in her mind turn, then she leaned in to the table. "She knows very little of her great-uncle and his accomplishments."

"Exactly." Benedict signed his name with a few jerky movements and folded the message.

"I had completely forgotten about that aspect of Dorthea's life."

"I do have my better skills, Harriet." Benedict looked at her from beneath his brows. "Besides being exasperating sometimes."

Harriet lifted a hand to her mouth to hide the twitch of her lips as they threatened to curve upward.

"I want to search the house again," Benedict was saying, "but I don't like the idea of trusting the servants with this message. I'll have to take it to the village myself and have it sent from there."

"While you're gone I can—"

"No."

"But I—"

"No, Harriet. I won't make you take the ride to the village with me, but I will not leave you here to your own devices either."

Harriet crossed her arms indignantly. "Honestly, Benedict. You make it sound as if I'll get myself killed if not under constant watch. Who will be my guard while you are away, sir? Perhaps you will utilize the local militia?"

She did not like the way Benedict seemed to honestly consider her suggestion and, less than fifteen minutes later, the way he smiled at her, prepared for his trip to the village.

Harriet shifted her gaze away from the man who stood before her and shrugged back farther into the settee. From the corner of her eye, she glared at the woman who sat as regally as a queen in her throne in the corner of the parlor.

"You may rest assured, Mr. Bradbourne," Beatrice Pruett said with her nose lifted and her chin barely moving, "Miss Mosley will be safe under our watch."

Less than an hour passed before Beatrice Pruett began to snore. Harriet slowly looked up from the book she hadn't been reading. Beatrice's hands lay palm up atop the chair on either side of her, in her lap the knitting she had been attempting to work on when slumber consumed her. Her chin rested on her chest, distorting her lower face in an unflattering manner, and her eyelids twitched as if she were already so far asleep she was being chased by a nightmare.

Harriet's gaze shifted to Eliza on the settee beside her. The younger woman's eyes slowly moved from her mother to Harriet.

"Have you a plan?" she whispered.

Harriet frowned. She had been so certain she would be forever stuck in the parlor, listening to the elder Pruett woman go on and on about proper behavior when dealing with an unmarried man of Benedict's rank—which, Beatrice explained aloud, was little more than a common laborer when one really looked at it—that she hadn't gone so far as to think of what to do if freed.

"Benedict and I were to search some of the house," Harriet returned. "I could begin alone."

Lizzie worried her bottom lip with consideration. "Mr. Bradbourne did appear quite intent on you not being left alone, Harriet. Is there something going on that I should know about? Are you in danger of some sort?"

Harriet made a face. The mess in her room had startled her, but whoever had gone to such trouble to frighten her had done so in vain. She would not allow a scoundrel who refused to show his face keep her from helping Benedict in their investigation.

She rose from the settee. "I shall be fine."

Lizzie fixed her attention on her mother as she followed Harriet. She held her breath until they left the parlor behind and almost slammed into Harriet's back. She had paused to consider her options.

"Where would it be best that I begin my search?"

"What are you looking for?" Lizzie kept her voice at a whisper.

"Signs of an intruder in this house. A place where he might have entered and exited unnoticed, or waited in the shadows until he was free to roam the halls as we slept."

Lizzie shivered visibly. "Is there such a dark and secluded place in this house?"

Harriet looked at her and nodded.

"I should go with you," Lizzie said. Her countenance, face pale and eyes wide with fear, suggested she wanted to do no such thing. She looked from the dark gaping hole in the floor to Harriet, holding tightly to a lantern that trembled in her grip.

"I appreciate the offer, Lizzie, but I will be all right on my own." Harriet pretended not to notice the other woman's relieved sigh. "You should go be with your mother. She will be quite put out if she wakes and you are not there."

"She will be upset if you are absent, Harriet," Lizzie countered.

"I shouldn't be long at all. Benedict and I have already searched some of the floor, so I only need to finish the whole of it. I'll like as not return before she awakens."

Harriet peered down into the darkness and, for the first time, felt some of her bravado wane. She told herself she had been in the confines of the dark corridor before and handled herself well enough. She would be fine without Benedict at her side.

"You will hand the lantern down?" She looked up at Lizzie and the younger woman nodded somberly. "All right, then. Off I go." Harriet sat on the edge of the hole, her legs dangling into the air below, air that seemed distinctly colder than that above.

She had decided to lower herself through as Benedict had on their first occasion to visit the corridor. Harriet might have been able to do so were it not for the fact she scraped her still-tender elbow along the edge of the torn floorboards. She cried out with surprise as her arms gave out and she fell down into the darkness. She landed on hands and knees, without the fluid grace of the man who had so easily lowered himself down into the opening days before.

"Harriet!" Light floated above her as Lizzie yelled down, "Are you all right?"

"I'm fine, Lizzie." She sat back on her haunches, rubbing grit from her stinging palms. Her gaze shifted to the shadows that closed in where the lantern light faded.

"I might be able to give you a lift up," Lizzie was saying hopefully, "if you've changed your mind."

Harriet climbed to her feet, reaching up for the lantern. "I haven't changed my mind."

"Be careful," Lizzie said as she released the light into the other woman's waiting grip.

Harriet nodded, smiling with a bravery that was quickly fading. Lizzie did not leave the opening above her and, Harriet knew, would not until she was gone. Taking a deep breath and lifting the lantern to shoulder height, she followed the path she and Benedict had treaded together a few days before.

She returned to the rooms they had inspected before, not wanting to miss an obvious clue that another had been haunting the halls. Not, she told herself as she left one barren chamber behind for another, that she knew what she was looking for. Harriet hoped she would know an important find when she saw it.

Harriet hesitated only a moment before entering the parlor she and Benedict had spent a good portion of a morning "investigating." She went only so far as the threshold, standing in the opened doorway as she recalled the door slamming closed on them. Had all the doors in the hall suddenly crashed closed, however, Harriet doubted she would be as disturbed as she was by the contents of the late Captain Rochester's study.

It was not as it had once been, when she and Benedict had crept inside and wondered at the room's undisturbed contents. They were gone now, the things that so clearly linked the present with the past. The chair that had been before the hearth was little more than a pile of soot and rubble and the fireplace itself appeared to have caved in a long time ago.

Harriet, with images of the room clean and undisturbed flashing through her mind, swallowed down a moan of discontent. She backed away quickly from the parlor that had been the ghost of a past place upon her first visit and closed the door with a thud. She took no time to tell herself of tricks of the imagination or to contrive a plausible explanation for why the room was in such demise now. She walked away quickly, to the next chamber, without looking back.

She felt the presence of the window before she saw it. A slightly chilled breeze tickled the delicate shells of her ears and drew her eyes instantly across the space of the only room she and Benedict hadn't investigated. The chamber was not as gloomy as the others. Though it had the same windows tarnished with ancient dust and soot, one stood open just enough to allow a breath of outside air and touch of sunlight.

If, Harriet thought, one wished to come in and out of the house unnoticed, this barren room and the not-traveled corridor that followed would serve well. Her slippers whispered quietly along the floor as she moved to the opened window and peered out through the space that left it agape. A dying rosebush filled most of the area before the window, a place to crouch and hide from passersby outside.

Delighted with the knowledge she had to share with Benedict upon his return, Harriet turned to leave. The opened door caught the corner of her eye and when she turned to inspect it more closely she realized there was a small closet in the corner of the room. She wondered if this had once been a storage room or that belonging to a servant. Harriet set the lantern on the floor and leaned into the closet.

The contents of the space were meager, save a jumble of clothing at the floor. Harriet used the toe of her slipper to shift one of the riding boots aside and frowned at the tweed material pressed into the corner underneath. She knelt to retrieve the cloth, shook it loose and held the rough material to the light.

The holes cut into the sack to allow for a man to see through it were unmistakable.

Harriet gasped at her findings and during the same breath felt the presence behind her. She hadn't the time to blink, let alone turn, before a sharp kick was applied to her lantern. Glass shattered against the wall and Harriet was shoved from behind. She stumbled, catching herself on the inner wall of the closet, as the door slammed closed behind her.

As Harriet shifted around in her cramped confines, she heard footfalls moving calmly away from the closet. She reached for the door handle, already certain she had been trapped.

37

Benedict returned to Rochester Hall later than he had expected to. There was no post office in the village and the innkeeper who served as the meager population's postmaster refused to budge on his habit of sending out letters once a week. He had informed Benedict that the day for the mail to go out had been yesterday and glared at the younger man as if he should know better. He grudgingly told Benedict of a coach driver who could be employed to take letters, but it would cost more than a penny to get the message as far as London.

Benedict had pounded at the coachman's door for a good five minutes or so and was halfway from the cottage to the road when he heard the other call out behind him. As he gave his message to the driver, who appeared none too reliable with bloodshot eyes and unbuttoned breeches, and then pressed coins into his calloused palms, he thought it might be a miracle if the letter made it to London. By the time he returned to the house, he thought he could have taken the message to town himself and returned with more time to spare.

His stomach growled loudly as he entered, but he

quickly forgot his empty stomach as the sound of Beatrice Pruett's screeching filled his ears. *Harriet,* he thought as he made his way to the parlor, *was going to be very upset with him for leaving her in the other woman's company so long.*

"Mama, I do not know where she is," Eliza was insisting as he entered.

Benedict felt his gut twist.

When the two women saw him, Beatrice's chin lifted in self-defense.

"I let my eyes rest for only a few moments, Mr. Bradbourne—"

"You were asleep"—Eliza interrupted her mother—"for more than three hours."

Mrs. Pruett gasped. "Eliza Pruett! To your own mother you speak this way?"

Benedict focused on the younger Pruett woman. "You know where Harriet is."

Eliza sighed. "I promised, Mr. Bradbourne."

Beatrice gasped again. "You said you had no notion where she took herself off too," she accused.

"Where is she?" With great effort, Benedict managed not to grab Eliza and shake her.

Eliza looked at the clock and then Benedict. "In the hidden corridor where the stairs have burned away."

He turned and was at the stairs when the woman called after him.

"It has been three hours, Mr. Bradbourne." Eliza gripped the doorjamb and watched him with anxious eyes. "She assured me she would be back before Mama woke. I've been very worried."

During her first hour of confinement, Harriet frightened herself terribly. Her vivid imagination entertained her with notions of the blackmailer—lest she forget murderer—scouring the dark for something heavy and blunt with which to bash in her skull or a sharp instrument to pierce her ribs. If she had to be killed, she decided, she would much rather it be in the same manner of the unfortunate Mr. Hogg. The speediness of a bullet was even better when one didn't know it was coming.

At the passing of a second hour, she began to conceive of ways she could fight off the villain. She positioned herself so that if the door was opened, she could immediately kick out. Harriet thought if she reached for the murderer's weapon, he would not be expecting it, and she might very well get the upper hand. Toward the end of this hour of plots and scheming, her heart began to even its cadence and she to wonder if the blackmailer would be back.

Sitting on the cold floor, she used her feet to beat at the door. After several hard kicks, when not even the dust covering the wood stirred, she stilled. It grew colder and Harriet used the sack head coverings to blanket her legs. Her back pressed to the wall, knees bent in the cramped space, she let her head rest against the arms she crossed over her knees. She hadn't known she was falling asleep, but awoke surprised and disoriented.

Harriet winced at the pain at the base of her scalp and was lifting a hand there before she realized what had awakened her. Footsteps drew toward the closed door. Harriet frowned because she thought something in their hollow thud was familiar.

Light filtered beneath the door and the handle rattled. She parted her lips to call out, but when she took a breath she detected the scent of burning. Her mouth snapped closed as she focused on the light and then realized it no longer came from beneath the door, but the entire wooden shape was beginning to glow. Not the gold of firelight, but an unnatural chilled blue. Harriet's gaze traveled up the door until she saw the brightest spot of light near its top and her eyes went round as that spot began to take the shape of a face.

Rochester.

His features pressed out from the wood as if the obstruction was not present. From a face as craggy as a mountain, eyes black with misery scanned the wall directly ahead, and then began to lower.

A tremble wracked Harriet's frame and she squeezed her eyes so tightly closed they hurt. She pressed her back into the wall, fingernails scratching along the wooden floorboards, as she sensed the pirate leaning over her.

The door handle rattled again and she could hardly hold back her whimper. She could see the blue light through her eyelids and thought she could feel a dead man's breath on her brow.

The door eased open with a sharp creak that made her bones shudder. A scream rose to her throat.

"Bloody hell."

"Benedict?" Her eyes popped open as she spoke, a query unnecessary as she could clearly see the man holding the lantern. The blue light was gone, as was the pirate.

"What happened?" Benedict was saying. His gaze scanned her from head to toe as he pocketed a small metal pick. "Are you all right?"

Harriet nodded, ignoring the dull ache in her back as she pushed to her feet. She did not step out of the closet.

She cleared her throat. "Is there anyone out there with you, Benedict?"

"No. I've been through every room looking for you." Benedict's brows drew together as he watched her.

"And you saw no one—nothing?"

"No," he said again.

Harriet wished he had seen something out of the ordinary, anything. She was beginning to feel like a woman trapped in some sort of solitary madness. She stepped from her prison of the last few hours. "Let's get out of this place, then."

"Harriet?" He caught her arm in one hand and tried to read her expression.

"Please," Harriet said. "I'll explain everything when we are upstairs."

Whatever he saw in her face, Benedict nodded and followed her from the room.

Harriet came to an abrupt halt when she saw what lurked in their path, blocking their way to the opening above the end of the corridor. Not blue light, or the blackmailer who had trapped her, but fire. Harriet stumbled backward into Benedict.

"What the hell?" he said, and when she looked in his eyes she saw the flames reflected in his spectacles.

He grabbed Harriet again, his hold brutal as he yanked her back the way they had come.

"There's a window," she said as he shoved her back into the chamber.

"I saw," he said, close behind as she ran.

They could hear the flames coming down the corridor. Oddly enough, it sounded like a great ocean wave crossing the shore.

The window was no longer open, and when Harriet shoved at it, it would not move. Her heart bobbed between her throat and stomach. "Stuck," she breathed, incredulous.

Benedict reached around her, banging on the window with his fist. She watched behind them as fire filled the corridor beyond the open door and then encircled the doorjamb, crawling up the walls and moving fluidly along the stone floor that should have conducted no flame.

"Benedict," Harriet whimpered.

He hissed a curse she had never heard before even in her father's gambling halls then swung the lantern in an arc to the window. The lantern glass shattered and rained down to the floor. The windowpane remained solid.

"Benedict."

The fire arced the floor around their feet.

Benedict moved fluidly, pressing Harriet into the cold wall and pressing his chest and stomach against her. His arms covered her, his hands wrapping around her shoulders as his head bowed over hers.

A sob broke from her throat when she realized what he was doing. She gripped his lapels, pressed her forehead to the space below his neck.

She whispered, "Benedict, I love you, I think."

"Harriet," he said, and she thought her name uttered in that thick brogue might be the nicest thing she could possibly hear before she died.

Then the sound of fire was gone. The crack of timber abruptly disappeared. The sudden silence hurt Harriet's ears. They remained still long enough that they would not be fooled, not turn and be surprised by the vicious burn of their death.

Benedict shifted. His head lifted as did Harriet's and she peeked over his shoulder.

Much like the blue light and pirate, the fire had disappeared as if it had never been there.

The laugh that parted Harriet's lips sounded demented to her own ears.

When Benedict, eyes wide and mouth agape, looked at her, she said, "I think I should like to go home now."

38

Several hours had passed since they bid each other good night, Benedict feeling as if he was leaving things unsaid, Harriet unnaturally quiet and pensive. He had hoped the knock was hers, and when he'd climbed from his sleepless bed and had opened the door, she'd looked as if she had slept as much as he had. Harriet was wrapped in her well-worn dressing gown—torn in one spot thanks to Mr. Elliot, her hair twisted into two braids that hung over her shoulders.

She eyed the hallway before meeting his gaze and offering a sheepish smile. "I know it is unseemly to ask," she whispered, "but may I sleep with you tonight?"

He cleared his throat and attempted to make her smile genuine. "Do you plan on tormenting me with your womanly charms?"

Harriet stared at him. "No."

He scowled. "Go back to your own damned chamber."

He closed the door on her face, intending to wait a full minute but barely lasting half that time. When he opened the door again, she was no longer closed in on herself. Her arms hung limp with surprise and there was an amused gleam in her eye.

"I suppose you can stay," Benedict said.

She moved past him, smelling faintly of soap and—he decided with some consideration—brandy.

"Please make sure the door is locked," she said, and shrugged out of her dressing gown. She laid it neatly at the foot of the bed, and then climbed beneath the blankets. At the sound of the lock sliding into place, she whispered, "Thank you."

Benedict had used up his few inklings of humor to make the joke at the door. He silently went to the side of the bed opposite Harriet and lay down. The silence that filled the room was not uncomfortable. In fact, Benedict found himself teased by brief images of forever climbing into bed beside Harriet. Her braids slowly turning gray and lines appearing around her mouth from so much smiling during her younger years. His whiskers going white and his back sore from working. Benedict had never in his life thought such things and supposed Garfield Ferguson was hovering somewhere overhead with lopsided angel wings and a knowing grin.

She shifted beside him, the bed creaking as she rolled onto her side with her back to him. He was not offended. On the occasions they had shared a bed before, she had always fallen asleep on her side.

When her breath did not automatically become even with sleep, he said to the ceiling, "You've been acting strange since I found you this afternoon. How can I make you feel better?"

He heard the movement on her pillow, rather than saw her shake her head. "At first I was afraid, but I'm fairly certain I now wallow in self-pity."

He lifted a brow and she answered as if she had seen it.

"It really isn't fair. I've never harmed a soul in my life. At least, not that I'm aware. I have no idea who the blackmailer is or his links to this house, but now I think he is trying to kill me." She took a deep breath. "And then there is the mess with Mr. Elliot and my first experience in so-called sleepwalking. I think, when I was not looking one day, a herd of black cats crossed my path."

Benedict shifted so he too was on his side, gazing at the uneven part that separated her hair. He put a palm on Harriet's back, feeling the delicate bones there and remembering how she appeared, cramped into the closet where he'd found her. He had to loosen his gritted teeth before speaking. "It's understandable, your being upset. I fully imagined you would leave before nightfall after all that happened today. I forget sometimes"—he smiled despite himself—"what kind of woman you are."

She made a scoffing sound. "What sort of woman is that?"

"A force to be reckoned with." He sobered. "Harriet, if this bastard was actually trying to harm you, he had ample opportunity to have done it by now. I think he has no plans to do you injury. I think he wants to scare you off." His hand moved to her bare shoulder and squeezed. "You do not have to be afraid. Not with me here. I would die before I let you come to harm."

The single taper he had left lit was fading and his spectacles sat on the table beside it, but when Harriet shifted to look over her shoulder at him, he could see the color that reappeared in her cheeks and feel the warmth of her smile.

She pressed a loud kiss to his mouth before snuggling

down, shifting a few times until her back was against his chest and her bottom cupped in his thighs. Soft fingers gripped his wrist and pulled until his arm was wrapped around her like a blanket. It was only moments before the breath fanning his palm was even with sleep.

Wrapped around her so comfortably, his heart beginning to thrum at the same time as hers, he remembered the words she had said hours before when the apparition of fire had closed in on them both. He shifted until his head was on her pillow, his lips almost touching her hair and his nostrils filled with her intoxicating scent.

"Harriet," he breathed, "I think I love you too."

Morning came with darkness akin to night. Thunder awoke Harriet and when her lashes lifted she gazed through the closed windowpanes into a dreary, gray dawn. She climbed from beneath Benedict's arm—lead heavy in sleep—and slid into her slippers, watching as clouds so thick and dark they looked as if they could be touched shifted tumultuously over the treetops. Gusts of wind pressed to the window raindrops that had been falling hard and fast from the sky.

Harriet shifted her attention to Benedict who slept silently. He did not snore nor shift about unnervingly in his slumber, and Harriet imagined she might sleep easy with him forever. Perhaps she even slept better than when she was alone, and he appeared to do fine with her open mouth snoring and—she winced as she wiped residual moisture from the corner of her lips—occasional drooling.

The sudden thought crept into her mind like some cruel and ugly thing. Without rhyme or warning a nasty part of herself reminded Harriet that this would be their last evening together. This time tomorrow, she would be loading her things into a carriage to leave Lady Cruchely's estate.

Harriet pushed her worries aside and refused to acknowledge the sudden sadness that crept up toward her heart. Nor would she allow herself to entertain the idea that, because Benedict lived in London as she did, this place might not be the end of their acquaintance.

She turned away from the man who was surprisingly handsome in his sleep, a characteristic heightened by the fact the bedclothes had collected around his hips to make the sculpture of sinew in his arms and across his chest plainly visible.

Harriet eased backward into the corridor between their rooms, closing the door quietly after her. She realized she had not checked the hall for others; at the same time she sensed another presence not far away.

Harriet winced and looked to her left, and when she found the hall clear there, shifted her attention to the right.

Her hands went cold and her breathing stilled in her chest. The pirate's broad back was to her; he stood facing the staircase and showed no sign he knew Harriet was there. Hands beginning to shake, gaze fixed on the material of the dead man's vest, Harriet stepped backward toward her chamber door. She was terrified, but could not bring herself to return to Benedict's room to find him awake and curious about her frazzled state.

As she moved, she saw Warren Rochester was not alone. His long-expired wife stood before him, a pale forearm in his fist. Harriet was relieved to see the appendage pale, but not the charred remains she had witnessed during the séance. Annabelle's hair blanketed her face and shoulders like a hood and the flush of color in her cheeks and at the tip of her nose, the evidence of tears in her eyes, made her appear anything but a ghost.

Harriet reached behind her, fingers fumbling against her door as she searched for the knob, and Annabelle fell.

"Warren," she said, and her voice was like music, devoid of hatred or surprise.

"No!" Rochester shouted, and Harriet could feel the word to the roots of her teeth.

Harriet ran, not into her bedchamber, but to the head of the stairs. Her nails dug into the wood of the rail as she peered down into the shadowed foyer below. Warren was no longer on the stairs, but on the floor. He held his wife's limp body in his arms, rocking her to him until her head shifted from its unnatural angle to lie on his shoulder. The flames came to life around them, a ring of fire that played golden light across the woman's unblinking eyes.

Warren looked up from Annabelle, his cheeks wet with tears and his features twisted into a mask of agony. When he met Harriet's stare, she clutched a fist to her mouth to hold back a scream.

"Good morning, dear lady!"

A squeak escaped her at the touch of fingertips on her back. She spun around, bringing her spine against the wall as she faced a fresh and alert Randolph.

He looked instantly worried, holding his weathered hands, palm up, toward her. "Terribly sorry, Harriet. I did not intend to frighten you so."

She looked from the corner of her eye and was not surprised when she saw no fire eating away at the foyer and the dead pair gone. She swallowed hard and forced her hand to her side. She tried to smile, though feared the movements made her look like a lunatic and quickly shook her head.

"I did not hear you behind me."

"I was on my way down for tea." He relaxed. His freshly groomed mustache twitched with his words. "It seems like a day that begins in this manner requires a nice hot cup. Shall I ask for a cup for you as well, my dear? It will be ready when you are dressed."

Heat stole into her cheeks as she remembered she was in her chemise, her dressing gown forgotten in Benedict's chamber. She nodded, wrapping her arms around her middle. "Please. I'll just freshen up."

"Excellent." Randolph moved down the stairs without any idea of what Harriet had just seen, and she let herself into her room wishing she had seen nothing at all.

When Benedict awoke, he was more disappointed than surprised to find the mattress empty beside him. The fact there was a young man in a rain-dampened coat lounging comfortably in the chair next to the door impressed him.

"Was the door locked?"

"The door to the house, no." The man, only a few years younger than he, beamed with pride. "The door to your room, yes."

"Should I be impressed?"

Garfield Ferguson II sighed with disappointment. "Not really. The lock was not a good one. Not difficult to work." Not only did young Ferguson gain his father's knack with picking locks, many of his features were reticent of the man now deceased. His hair was brilliant orange and his eyes green. At twenty years he was already developing the large arms and rounded belly that characterized his father.

"You brought the information yourself?" Benedict pushed out of bed and reached for his clothing.

Ferguson nodded toward a sheet of folded foolscap on the table beside Benedict's spectacles. "A list of names. The Rochesters kept excellent records of births and whatnot, as those who have some noble lineage in them are prone to do."

As Benedict slipped on his specs and reached for the paper, the other man cleared his throat. When he again spoke, his accent was more pronounced. Benedict had noticed as the eldest Ferguson entered adulthood, he worked his accent for his own gains—when making a joke or around a particularly attractive woman.

"Is this yours, Benedict? I ask"—his words trembled with repressed laughter—"because it looks as if it may be a bit snug around the shoulders."

Benedict frowned, turning.

"The ruffles"—Ferguson grinned—"are quite fetching."

He was holding Harriet's delicate dressing gown. As Benedict watched, he lifted the soft material to his face and breathed in. "She smells nice, Benedict. What's her name?"

"Harriet," he said without hesitation. "Now put that down before you ruin it."

Ferguson shrugged and carefully returned the gown to the end of the bed, patting out the wrinkles. "The girls have been worrying about you." Ferguson had only brothers. He spoke of Benedict's two sisters. "And Mother," he added. "Normally she would have had a fit what with me leaving London out of the blue, but when she heard I was coming to see you . . ." Ferguson

let the rest trail off. "I was a little worried myself, Benedict. No one wants you to cause yourself harm trying
to find Da's murderer. He wouldn't have wanted it
either. He put Mother and I to shame with his worries
over you."

"He was concerned about his own family as well,
Garfield," Benedict said quickly.

Ferguson waved that off. "None of us had departed
Scotland at fifteen with little more than the clothes on
our back and two sisters barely out of diapers to see
after. He loved you and he wouldn't have wanted you
to put your life on hold for him, especially in his
dying."

"You may rest assured I have found little to go on in
the matter of your father. I am helping Lady Cruchely
with some events troubling her."

Ferguson nodded and his seriousness evaporated.
His gaze fixing on Harriet's gown again, he smiled.
"You seem different. It is because of this fine-smelling
Harriet?"

Benedict focused on the paper he had unfolded,
not answering.

"Da had been trying for a long time to get you to
find a good girl and settle down." Ferguson chuckled.
"I'm glad to see he finally managed at least part of the
task."

Benedict was squinting, not totally in an effort to
ignore the younger man. "Is this English? I cannot
read a damned thing you've written."

Ferguson climbed out of his chair, grumbling his
ire. "I have fine penmanship."

Benedict gave him the paper.

"It says," Ferguson began, squinting himself a time
or two, "there were two Rochesters. Warren and his
younger brother, Arlo, and both men had one son

before their deaths. The youngest Rochester, incidentally, died from being shot in the back of his head while leaving a gaming hall."

Benedict lifted a brow. "They all seem to have met bad ends."

Ferguson made a sound of agreement and continued. "Lady Cruchely's father, William Rochester, was the son of Annabelle. Lady Cruchely is the last heir on that side of the family. Arlo Rochester sired an illegitimate son whom his mother felt obliged to take into her nest, though she refused to give the child the family name. His name was Randolph, the last of their clan." Ferguson drew the sheet of paper closer to his nose. "His full name is . . ."

The hair rose on Benedict's nape and he said, "Oscar."

Ferguson blinked up at him. "How did you know?"

Benedict did not answer. He was already running from the room.

39

Benedict went to the dining room first, focusing on Eliza who watched him with worried interest.

"You are looking for Harriet?"

"Yes. Where is she?"

"She went for a walk when the rain cleared. She was afraid it would start again and wanted a chance to get fresh air." Lizzie looked from Benedict to the man who accompanied him, curious.

"What is going on here?" her mother demanded from the table.

"Which way?" Benedict said.

"Through the gardens." Lizzie pointed.

When he turned to leave, Ferguson caught his arm. "Trouble?"

"Maybe." He nodded to the two women. "Stay with them, will you?"

Ferguson focused on Lizzie and said, voice thick with accent, "My pleasure."

Lizzie flushed nervously, but spoke to Benedict. "You mustn't cause yourself undue alarm, Mr. Bradbourne. Harriet did not go alone. Sir Randolph accompanied her."

* * *

The air smelled of rain, the leaves on the trees and bushes weighted down and dripping. She and Randolph kept to the path that led from the estate, the stones glossy beneath their feet. The sky remained gray, thunder warning them from far away that the storm was not over. It was not cold, but there was a slight chill with every breeze. Harriet was glad she had worn a long-sleeved gown and tugged lightly at the cuffs, drawing them closer to her wrists.

"You're cold?" Randolph caught her movements with the twitch of a furry eyebrow. He began to unbutton his jacket. "Take this."

"No, no." Harriet waved the gesture away. "I am fine," she assured him when he looked at her skeptically.

He eased back into his jacket and offered an elbow. "You had best hold tight, dear lady. I should hate to have you fall on the slippery stones." After a moment of shared silence, Randolph said, "I've been working on a new story."

"While on holiday?" Harriet appreciated his dedication. She had to hold in check the part of her that wanted to demand to know if her favorite character was returning to solve more tragic mysteries.

"Of all the parts of the human anatomy, the brain never shuts down." Randolph tapped his temple. "That is where Viktor Channing lives."

Harriet smiled. "For the longest time, Viktor was the only man I ever loved."

Randolph looked at her, and for the first time Harriet realized he had to lift his chin to meet her eye. "Not since coming to Rochester Hall, Harriet?"

She flushed and focused on a bright orange

gerbera that had been bent close to the ground under the rain.

"I thought you might allow me to ask you a few questions, for this new story?"

Harriet blinked. "Me?"

"Apparently"—Randolph rolled his eyes—"my female characters have something to be desired."

"Character." Harriet nodded. When she saw Randolph squint his eyes at her, she bit her bottom lip.

"That is what my publisher said."

Harriet shrugged and offered quickly, "The women play a small role in the stories, however."

Randolph sighed. "Well, I have been toying with the idea of bringing in a female to assist Mr. Channing in his ghost hunting. Unfortunately, I could never conceive of a woman with the particular traits that would serve the job well."

Harriet nodded thoughtfully.

"Then"—Randolph's thick mustache twisted with a grin—"I met such a woman in the flesh."

"Who?" She pointed to her chest. "Me?"

"Let's have a seat, shall we?" Ushering her to a low cement bench off the path, he removed his jacket and laid it atop the damp stone so she would have a dry place to sit, then reached into his waistcoat. He produced a small pad of paper and the weathered stub of a pencil. He sat beside Harriet. "Now tell me, dear, how is it that when frightful things happen, there comes to be an excited gleam in your eye?"

Harriet stared at him. "I cannot say. Perhaps it is in my upbringing?"

"Your parents taught you to never be afraid of anything?"

"No, I wouldn't say that." Harriet shrugged. "My father took me to a lot of places that were scary and I became accustomed to them." She looked at Randolph from the corner of her eye. "Also he introduced me to trash novels which acclimated me to things that go bump in the night."

Randolph nodded, licked the tip of his pencil, and scribbled something on the paper. "Is it in this manner that you became so intelligent?"

Harriet grinned. She cleared her throat. "I lived with my aunt and uncle for a time and they sent me to school. I thought they would be proud of me if I did well and worked hard."

"Were they?"

Harriet's nose wrinkled. "My cousin wasn't as quick as I with learning new things and that made them angry with me."

"He was a boy, your cousin?"

"And three years older than I."

Randolph chuckled. He tapped his chin with the pencil, thinking. "How can I make it so my heroine is of the means to do as she wishes, with no family supporting her financially?"

Harriet's brows lifted. "She could own a bookshop."

"Excellent idea, Harriet. Perhaps you should be writing your own stories."

"You know," she said, "you're not the first person to say that." When she looked up from Randolph's writing to his face, however, the man was not looking at the paper or at her.

His features were closed suddenly and in his eyes she thought she saw something shrewd and disappointed. Harriet followed Randolph's gaze and realized there was a man standing on the path not far away.

"Benedict, good morning." Her smile was lopsided and it took some effort to create it. His features were hard, his eyes a cold glare behind his spectacles. The hands at his sides were clenched into fists.

When he spoke, it was in even tones, harsher than he'd ever spoken to her before, "Harriet, come here. Now."

"Benedict?"

Randolph sighed beside her. "I was afraid of this when I saw that young man creeping up the stairs this morning."

"Harriet." Benedict took a step nearer.

"No," Randolph said roughly.

Harriet winced when the older man took her wrist in a painful grip.

"Get the hell away from her, Randolph."

Randolph set aside his pencil and paper and reached again into his waistcoat. His finger was around the trigger of the pistol, but he laid it on his lap, facing the greenery.

"Please, Bradbourne, do not make me have to point it at her."

Harriet's heart rose to her throat as she moved her attention between both men. "What is going on?" she insisted of no one in particular.

"He is the blackmailer, Harriet." Benedict stood still, his gaze fixed on the gun.

She gasped, looked at Randolph who nodded. The skin above his white mustache turned pink. "Terribly sorry, dear. I was hoping it would not come to this." He focused on Benedict. "I'll ask you to stay where you are, Bradbourne. We'll stand up slowly and then you will lead the way to the opened window in the secret corridor." When a muscle in Benedict's jaw clenched, Randolph shook his head. "No need for drastic measures. I have no plans to harm either of you."

Through his teeth, Benedict said, "You nearly killed Harriet on more than one occasion."

Randolph shook his head. "No, no. That was the deplorable Mr. Hogg, I assure you. Had I known the sort of man he was, I'd not have enlisted his help. I only noticed he was greedy at first." He looked at Harriet. "The fact that he was extremely stupid, I missed." He made a shooing gesture with the pistol, as he held tight to Harriet. "Move along, Mr. Bradbourne. You know where the window is. I saw you inspect it after you rescued Harriet from the closet."

He nudged Harriet into motion once Benedict began to move, scooping his jacket up over his arm to hide the gun. "I did push you into the closet, dear, I will admit. I also made the mess in your bedchamber. It was very hard to tear apart the room without making a single noise. Fortunately you and Mr. Bradbourne were . . . occupied elsewhere."

She looked at him in question and his features shifted into an apologetic frown.

"I was trying to scare you away, Harriet. You proved very stubborn with the warning in your chamber, so I thought I might get Bradbourne to insist upon your leaving with the closet fiasco. I misjudged his desire to keep you with him, however.

"Incidentally, I didn't mean for you to be in that closet as long as you were, dear. I hadn't thought it would take so long for Bradbourne to return from the village."

Benedict looked back over his shoulder and scowled.

They had reached the window at the rear of the house. It was opened and there was a stranger standing near with his arms folded across his weighty chest.

"Mr. Quinn." Randolph nodded toward the man. "I

wish I had found this gent before Hogg. It would have saved me a lot of grief. He is greedy, but nowhere near as stupid."

Benedict glared at the other man. "He delivered my message to London."

"Made the trip in record time." Quinn grinned.

40

"Not too tight, Mr. Quinn. I do not wish them to suffer permanent damage."

Benedict glared at the old man who kept the pistol aimed at his heart. They had been moved to the old study, the room where he had first made love to Harriet. As Randolph had held Harriet close to his side and his pistol, Quinn put two chairs back to back and left the room. He returned moments later with heavy rope.

Benedict's fingers brushed Harriet's as their wrists were bound together to the chairs behind them. He caught her chilled hand and squeezed briefly. She had been silent through most of their capture.

Once the knots had been pulled tight and Quinn stepped away, Randolph gave the other man the pistol. He unfolded his jacket and laid it gently across Harriet's lap.

"I don't want you to catch a chill down here in the dark," he said.

Benedict felt a muscle clench inside him. "Why don't you get the hell away from her, Randolph? She's undoubtedly troubled that her favorite author and friend has turned out to be a thief and a murderer."

Randolph stepped back from them both, his features a mask of sorrow. "Harriet, you must understand. I did what I had to do. It was bad enough when I realized I was sharing the same house with a Bow Street Runner, and then you, my new friend, turned out to be quite the investigator. Individually, I might have been able to elude Mr. Bradbourne and yourself. Together, however, you are a force to be reckoned with."

"Thank you," Harriet said faintly.

Randolph smiled. "You'll be safe here as my business is completed upstairs."

"You will not harm Lady Cruchely?" Worry touched Harriet's words and Benedict felt his gut clench. She was concerned more about the other woman than herself.

"I think not." Randolph combed his mustache with his fingers. "I sincerely hope Mr. Latimer does not do something foolhardy and cause himself suffering. I will tell someone you are down here before we leave, so you are not trapped for an uncomfortable length of time."

"You are mad," Benedict said.

Randolph looked at him and his smile disappeared. "No. I am only a man claiming what is rightfully his. Now"—he turned to Quinn—"if Mr. Bradbourne here tries anything, you must bring it to a stop at once. His looks are quite deceiving and I have no doubt he will cause the both of us personal harm if he has the chance."

"You are correct," Benedict said.

"Under no circumstance," Randolph continued, "is my greatest supporter to come to any harm." He began to leave the room.

"What if she tries something?" Quinn said, eyeing Harriet suspiciously.

"She will not, or Mr. Bradbourne will be shot."

Benedict felt Harriet jerk. When Randolph disappeared down the hall, she sighed.

Her tone was miserable when she spoke so softly, Benedict was certain she was talking to herself. "He was never interested in my ideas at all."

Mr. Quinn checked the ropes binding them to the chairs, and then moved to the doorway. He put the pistol in the waist of his breeches and drew a pipe from his coat. He sat on the ground, back propped on the outside wall, as he lit the tobacco and drew in a lungful of the pipe.

Once the other man was comfortably seated, Benedict began to move. He drew his leg against the side of the chair and struggled with his hands until he managed to add some slack to the rope. His fingers strained to the edges of his left boot. With some maneuvering of his leg and pushing his fingers as far as they could go, he touched the dagger.

"Benedict?" Harriet whispered.

"Shh," he breathed, drawing the blade free and moving it against his palm to work on the rope. "I'll have us free shortly."

"Sorry there, bloke," Quinn said. He stood over them, pipe at the corner of his mouth, pistol lifted butt first. "You heard the old man."

The gun came down hard and fast and everything went dark.

Harriet cried out, both for Benedict's sake and her own. There was a dull thud of the pistol making contact with his skull and then a sharp pain when his head snapped back and hit hers. She heard something clatter to the floor and watched Quinn kick Benedict's dagger against the far wall.

He put his face in front of hers, snapped fingers before her nose.

She blinked sluggishly as his thumb doubled then became one again.

"Sorry, love," the hired-man said, then returned to his sitting position just outside the doorway.

Her head rocked forward as she squeezed her eyes shut and forced down the dizziness that thrummed through her. Benedict had gone limp, creating extra pressure on the rope that bound them. Harriet cautiously opened her eyes, waiting as the floor stopped rocking back and forth beneath her.

"Benedict?" she said.

No response.

Harriet swallowed, fighting the tears that rose to her throat. She squeezed his hands, but he remained unmoving. She sensed Mr. Quinn's return and quickly released Benedict's hands, keeping her head low in case the other man thought there something diabolical in her movements. Minutes that felt like hours passed, Harriet with her head bowed and her captor unmoving.

Her neck began to hurt and she silently cursed the stranger who was trying, she was certain now, to intimidate her with unvoiced threats. When she could bear his oppressive attention looming over her no more, Harriet gritted her teeth. She took a great breath and lifted her chin, intent on facing down the brute that had hurt Benedict.

It was not Quinn that loomed over Harriet, however. The ghost of Warren Rochester looked just as real as the other man seated at the doorway. Harriet's gaze rolled up over his thigh-high boots, the brilliant red band tied about his middle. Her eyes peered at his face from beneath crumpled brows and she could inspect little of his hard features before their eyes met and his held hers in a cold, emotionless grip.

A ragged breath escaped Harriet and the pirate reached for her.

It was not an unpleasant dream, the fog into which he fell upon being knocked unconscious. He was bound to a chair and his arms hurt dully, but his attention was not on that pain, but the agony erupting in his lower body. He was not alone in the misty abyss. Harriet stood only a few feet away, clad in her nightgown and her hair twisted into thick golden braids. She must have washed the gown, because the material had shrunk. The bodice was taut across her breasts, the soft cloth clinging to her thighs.

Despite the ache in his arms, Benedict smiled.

As if the curve of his lips were a cue, Harriet walked toward him. Her movements were fluid and her own smile coy to the point of being wicked. She rested her open palms on his shoulders, lifted a leg to straddle his lap, and sat atop his aching loins.

He groaned and she pressed a light kiss to his chin, stroked his shoulders with her fingertips and then the sides of his neck. Her fingers sank into his hair, and when he leaned forward to kiss her she shifted to press her lips to his ear.

"Benedict," she breathed, and her voice reached to the core of him. She was wrapping her fingers in his hair.

His arms quivered, muscles straining to hold her.

"Benedict . . ." she whispered again, this time a plea.

He groaned, clenching his teeth, gladly prepared to die to give her whatever it was she wanted.

The pain was sharp, intense, as she gave his hair a violent yank.

His eyes opened wide and the mist was gone. A soft palm came up to cover his mouth. Harriet was not on his lap, but her lips were still touching his ear.

"I'm sorry," she whispered, pained. "I couldn't think of another way to wake you quietly."

His eyes rolled to meet hers and she slowly dropped her hand. He blinked, suddenly comprehending the fact she was not bound to the chair with him and, actually, he was no longer bound himself. His arms hung limp at his sides and he grimaced as he lifted them to his lap.

"What the hell happened?" he whispered.

Harriet's gaze had fixed itself to the doorway. "Mr. Quinn hit you."

"I know that." Benedict scowled as he looked around the room. "How did you manage to get free?"

Harriet would not meet his eye. "That is not important right now." She pressed his dagger into his palm. "How do we get out of here without being shot?"

He squinted at Harriet, and then gave his head a shake. The action made a dull, thudding pain come to life where he had been hit. His gaze moved to the door where he could make out Quinn's legs sticking out across the floor.

41

Harriet winced as Benedict pressed her into the empty hearth. It might not have been uncomfortable for an average-sized woman, but she had to hunker her shoulders and turn her head at an odd angle.

"Don't move," Benedict said.

She scowled at him. As if it would take less than a lever to pry her out of the cramped space.

Something in her dirty look made him smile, and when he pressed a brief, fierce kiss to her mouth, she forgot her moment's discomfort. His boots surprisingly silent on the floor, Benedict moved across the room. He picked up one of the chairs from the center of the chamber and followed the wall until he was standing on the opposite side of the stone where Quinn had propped himself.

Benedict moved fluidly, lifting the chair above his head then hurling it as if it were a child's ball.

Harriet winced at the crash of splintering wood against the far wall. She heard Quinn uttering a few good words and opened her eyes in time to see him appear in the doorway, gun barrel preceding him.

From his place beside the doorway, Benedict

captured the other man's wrist and gave it a vicious turn that sent the pistol clattering to the floor. Benedict did not pause in his motions. At the same time he kicked the weapon aside, he jerked Quinn's arm behind his back. The other man gave only a moment's struggle before Benedict slammed his full weight into his back. Quinn hit the wall hard, his head snapping forward and making contact with a distinct thud.

"Sorry, bloke," Benedict said, and let the man fall, unconscious, to the floor.

Harriet climbed out of her hiding place as Benedict used the rope that had kept them affixed to the chairs to tie Quinn's wrists and ankles together. She watched the efficient movements of his hands with some wonder as he worked the rope and appendages without causing the unaware man further injury.

"Do you do such things very often, Benedict?"

He looked up at her as he drew taut one last knot. "You'd be surprised."

Harriet scowled at him until after he picked up the fallen pistol and gave her his full attention.

"All this time you might have entertained me with such tales. Instead you let me suffer the stories of Beatrice Pruett and how she almost met the queen."

He stepped nearer, placing his free hand low on Harriet's back. His breathing was only slightly altered by his exertions. "Perhaps I had hopes for years to come when I could regale you with my stories."

Oblivious of the man bound and silent on the floor and quickly forgetting she herself had been tied to a chair only minutes before, Harriet smiled.

"Let's get out of here and find Randolph." Benedict caught her elbow and guided her to where they knew there was an opening to the floor above.

Harriet felt sudden concern press at her. "Lizzie and her mother, the Chesterfields—"

"Do not worry, Harriet. Randolph is after none of them." Benedict paused only briefly when they reached the opening. He pressed the pistol between his back and his breeches, and then in an amazingly agile move he jumped up and caught the broken floorboard. He drew himself up and then, after a moment when Harriet assumed he was eyeing his surroundings, he reached down for her. "He only felt the need to deal with you and I because we were a threat."

Harriet asked as she was being lifted up to the next floor, "Why is he doing this, Benedict?"

"I cannot say I know all the facts, love, but I imagine it has a lot to do with old-fashioned jealousy and greed. Oscar Randolph is, for all intents and purposes, Lady Cruchely's cousin. He must think himself entitled to the family resources."

Harriet shook her head, running to keep up with Benedict's even stride as they found his bedchamber. "That is wrong for so many reasons, Benedict."

"I know that and you know that, Harriet." Benedict pressed his palms against the wardrobe, arms straight and muscles straining until the massive piece of furniture slid a good three feet across the floor. "Now we must convince Randolph."

Harriet watched at he used his fingernails to pry loose one of the floorboards. He set the flat of wood aside and produced from the hideaway his own pistol. He placed Quinn's gun inside the opening before replacing the floorboard.

"Benedict," Harriet said, not without appreciation, "your hiding place is so much better than mine."

"Not bad"—he grinned—"for an amateur."

She was contemplating a witty retort when a strange

popping sound echoed overhead. She looked up as if she might be able to peer through the floorboards to the floor above.

"Gunfire," Benedict said.

Harriet's chin slowly lowered and she stared at him with wide eyes.

"Will you stay here?"

She slowly shook her head.

They heard Dorthea first, her voice at a near-hysterical shriek. *"How could you?"*

"I warned him twice," Sir Randolph said, his tone at odds with the woman's. "Very politely, I might add."

"You've killed him!"

"It's only a flesh wound, madam. Please contain yourself."

Harriet tried to keep her footfalls as even and silent as Benedict's. The man was a good three feet ahead of her, and though he held her hand, she was tempted to believe it was more to keep her away than safe. She did not complain, however. As a rule, she did not argue with men who carried pistols.

Benedict drew them both closer to the wall as they closed in on the opened door to Lady Cruchely's bed-chamber. As he peered into the room, Harriet lifted herself to her toes and peeked over his shoulder.

She saw Latimer first, seated on the edge of a chair. His head was bowed, but Harriet could make out the shine of his gritted white teeth. His right arm hung limp at his side, and he held tight to it above the elbow with his free hand. His shirtsleeve was red with blood.

Harriet lifted a hand to her mouth to stifle a gasp, her gaze shifting to the terrified Dorthea and then

Randolph, who shifted his gun from the woman to Latimer at even intervals.

"I've told you more than twice." Lady Cruchely's voice turned to that of exasperated rage. "I have nothing left to give you. My husband squandered away everything I had."

Harriet could see Randolph understood, watched his features as he grappled with the truth. Suddenly she felt sorry for the man.

"Randolph!" Benedict spoke in a loud voice that made the hair rise on her nape. It must be a voice he practiced regularly on the streets of London. "I'm coming in. I want you to put your gun down."

Harriet grabbed fiercely to Benedict's free hand, not wanting to let him go to suffer as Latimer.

Randolph fixed his pistol on the doorway where the younger man stood. He was beginning to look tired and frustrated. "Benedict! What the hell happened to Quinn?"

"Put down the gun," Benedict returned.

Randolph sighed, shaking his head. "Do not make me shoot you, too. I sorely loathe to do it."

"You can't. You've already used your only shot on Mr. Latimer."

Harriet's grip on Benedict's hand slackened.

Randolph lifted his pistol nearer his nose and frowned. "So you're right." He tossed the weapon into an empty chair.

Benedict moved fluidly into the room. His pistol remained fixed on Randolph—the old man casually lifting his hands into the air—as he approached Latimer.

"Are you all right?"

Latimer looked at the other man. "I am getting too old for this business."

"Ah, Harriet, my dear fan." Randolph sighed when Harriet entered, his features a mask of self-deprecation. "I hate for you to see me this way."

"Just who do you think you are, sir?" Lady Cruchely had wrapped her arms around her lover and was scowling at Randolph, her cheeks pink with anger. "I invite you into my home and you treat me this way? How could you?"

Harriet's brows drew together, something drawing at the back of her mind.

"I deserve my place in the family and all that it entails."

"Sir Randolph," Benedict explained as he put the other man's gun in the waistband of his breeches, "is your cousin, Lady Dorthea. He thinks himself the right to a portion of your wealth."

"Randolph, I cannot even begin to tell you how wrong you are." Latimer managed a chuckle.

"Benedict," Harriet said.

"You are perhaps wealthier from those horrid novels you write," Lady Cruchely was saying, "than I am from running this house."

Randolph made a face. "The books bring in surprisingly little."

"Benedict," Harriet said again, a cold sinking sensation drawing at her heart.

He frowned at her pallor. "What is it, Harriet? You do not look well."

Her throat closed up for a moment and she swallowed heavily, looking from the old man who had been so kind to her, despite the brushes with death Harriet incurred from Mr. Hogg. She thought with some sorrow about how it felt to have gained nothing in one's upbringing. Randolph seemed to have less than even she, who had been given a decent education and an inherited knack with cards.

Then she looked at Benedict, who had been searching for the one who killed his best friend.

Harriet sighed. "Mr. Osborne's note said the one who had made inquiries about the watch was named Roposh Crandal." She recalled thinking about the strangeness of the name and something else tugging at the back of her mind.

"What about it?"

"It is another anagram, I think." She glanced at Randolph who looked both understanding and worried. "The same letters as in Randal C. Shoop and Oscar Randolph."

Her attention returned to Benedict in time to see understanding register. His features went hard, ugly with undiluted hatred. He turned on Randolph. *"Ferguson,"* he said.

"No. Wait." The older man stumbled and fell back into a chair.

"You killed him." Benedict lifted his pistol.

"No!" Harriet cried.

"No!" shouted Randolph in the same horrified tone. "Hogg is the only man I ever harmed physically. He was a risk and had been one since I sent him to London."

Benedict had wrapped his finger about the trigger of his pistol and Harriet went to him, heart pounding in her ears as she grabbed his elbow. "Please. Let's listen to what he has to say."

The old man spoke quickly, frantically. "I did go to the watchmaker and ask about the Rochester timepiece. I've been collecting things, you see, since I first began to make money off my books. Items that once belonged to my family and had been sold away. I wanted to find the watch and I sent Hogg to London. He was to send me word, give me the details of the piece. Then I was going to make an offer to Ferguson. I wanted to buy the damned thing! Hogg was a lunatic and was going to steal the watch, but Ferguson put up a fight. Hogg said he pulled out his dagger when the old man wouldn't back down."

Randolph looked away from Benedict, to Harriet with wide beseeching eyes. "You must believe me. I never intended for Ferguson to come to harm. I killed Hogg because of what he had done to your friend and because I was certain he was going to kill that poor maid."

"Had you never interfered," Benedict said through clenched teeth, "Ferguson would still be alive."

Harriet squeezed his elbow tighter. "But would he want you to do this, Benedict? Would your friend Mr. Ferguson want you to shoot another man who only led to his demise by a fluke?"

She did not know who the man was in the doorway, had not even realized he was there—with Lizzie gripping tightly to his arm—until he spoke. His green eyes were earnest and, she thought, filled with tears. "No. He would want no man's death on Benedict's conscience. Especially not his own."

42

Latimer had been shot a time or two before, as he himself explained it. He offered no further comment and nobody asked the bear of a man to elaborate. Dorthea used a pair of gilded scissors to cut a straight line from the cuff of his fine shirt to the shoulder and pressed her lips together when the material fell open to expose a raw wound and blood-stained skin beneath.

"Only a flesh wound, love." Latimer smiled for her, showing all his uneven teeth.

Lady Cruchely scowled at him. "You should have sat still. You're not as young as you once were."

"I'd hoped to get better with age like wine, my dear."

Dorthea cupped his jaw in her palms, her dark look fading with only a small fight. "Foolish man," she whispered, pale eyes alight with love.

Harriet cleared her throat, wondering if the pair had forgotten she had been left behind with them. "Can I get you anything, Mr. Latimer?"

The man dragged his gaze from Dorthea's. "I could use some whiskey. It's in the cabinet there."

"Now is no time for a drink," Dorthea said. "We must send for a surgeon."

"I'm not so far gone as that." He nodded his thanks to Harriet as she came to his chair, bottle and snifter in hand. "And it is a perfect time for a drink, not that I'll be needing one."

Harriet halted midpour to look at Latimer. He reached for the bottle.

Without pause and only a slight wince, he poured a measured quantity of the liquor down his arm. He splashed a good portion into his wound until it was flushed clean. The wound, as Latimer had assured them, was not so deep as to require stitches.

Dorthea was pressing a fine linen handkerchief to the cleaned abrasion when Benedict appeared in the doorway.

"They are on their way?" Lady Cruchely said.

Benedict nodded. "Garfield still had his phaeton out front. He is using it to take Sir Randolph back to the authorities in London."

"What will happen to him?" Harriet said.

He focused on her, weary in the midday sunlight. "There may be a trial. Prison, I am certain. Even if he is not directly responsible for Ferguson's death, he did kill Hogg and he was behind an extortion plot."

Harriet nodded and wondered if it was wrong to feel sorry for the old man. She sighed and in one gulp drank down the whiskey she had poured for Latimer.

"If you'll excuse me," she said as she carefully set down the snifter, "I'll check on Mrs. Pruett."

The elder Pruett woman had been overcome with the excitement of the day. Though she had not been shot, hadn't even been in the room where the shooting took place, she was certain she would suffer a fit of the vapors. She was coming up the stairs to Lady

Cruchely's chambers as young Ferguson and Benedict moved down with their charge. On sight of Sir Randolph, she stumbled back into the wall and waved a pale hand over her face.

Harriet had not missed Lizzie's exasperated roll of the eyes as she guided her mother away. What sort of fit, Harriet had wondered, would the woman have had were she to have seen Benedict and Garfield carry the unconscious Quinn from the basement?

She thought she could hear Beatrice Pruett's pitiful moans as she reached the second floor of the house. The Pruetts had been moved to an empty room nearer the staircase, far from the one where the mother had insisted she felt a chilled breeze from the abandoned stairwell.

Harriet paused—fist lifted to knock on the Pruetts' door—and slowly turned her head to peer down the hall. The dark shadows at the end of the corridor were silent. No faded shouting was audible around the corner. She treaded quietly to the dark corner and stared down into the gloom beyond the opening in the floor. A strange and sudden sadness gripped like a fist around her heart, and though she hadn't done so in many years, she thought she might cry.

She rested a hand on the charred wall and whispered, "I'm sorry I could not help."

She screamed when an icy hand closed over her shoulder.

Eliza Pruett screamed back, hands shaking in a warding off gesture, as Harriet spun to face her.

"*Sorry.* Sorry." Lizzie shook her head vehemently. "I did not mean to scare you."

"I'm not scared," Harriet squeaked, and lifted a palm to press to the violent thrum of her heart.

Lizzie looked behind Harriet. "I thought I heard you talking to someone." She eyed the other in question.

Harriet cleared her throat, cheeks burning, and shrugged. "God. Talking to God. He's everywhere, you know."

"Indeed." Lizzie lifted a brow in return.

"How is your mother?" Harriet thought her change of subject was fluid, if not unnoticed by her friend.

"Fine. Cognizant enough to insist I find out what all the commotion was upstairs. I think, once I find out, I'll make her suffer a bit before I share the details." She linked her arm through Harriet's as they moved back up the hall. "Tell me, what did happen with Sir Randolph? I could not believe it when I saw him being led away."

Harriet let out a long breath. "It so happens Randolph was not exactly what he appeared to be. He was related to Lady Cruchely in some fashion and believed himself entitled to a portion of her wealth. He was blackmailing her to obtain it."

Lizzie gasped. "I had no idea!"

"Nor did I," Harriet said.

The younger woman squeezed her arm. "How unfortunate for you, Harriet. I know you enjoyed Sir Randolph's friendship and he always seemed so taken with you."

"When I was a bit younger, I had another admirer. He delivered packages for the shopkeeper near my home. Once my uncle found him rummaging through our garbage, one of my torn stockings tied about his neck." Harriet pursed her lips. "What does that say about me, that a blackmailing author and refuse scavenger would admire my person?"

"I don't know." Lizzie made a face. "One does best

to remember only Mr. Bradbourne, who seems to feel more than admiration toward you."

Harriet could think of no reply to that, staring at the tips of her slippers. They had reached Lizzie's chamber, but she made no move to open the door.

She smiled at Harriet. "You both make your homes in London, do you not?"

"Yes."

"But you did not know one another before coming here?"

"No."

"I imagine," Lizzie said meaningfully, "Mr. Bradbourne will make a point of keeping your friendship alive when you both return home. I shall probably read a wedding announcement in the *Post*."

Now it was Harriet's turn to make a face. It hadn't even occurred to her to imagine such things. For the longest time, she had entertained herself with the idea of she and her friends growing into old spinsters together, enjoying tawdry affairs and peculiar adventures along the way. Her dear friend Abigail Wolcott had attempted such an affair with a manservant, who later turned out to be a marquis and then her husband. Augusta Merryweather, with whom Harriet shared her home, was already engaged to wed her Mr. Darcy.

"Has Mr. Bradbourne spoken of what will happen when you leave the estate?"

Harriet was pulled from her thoughts, suddenly realizing that they would be leaving the next day. She shook her head.

"If I enjoyed a good wager, I would bet you a coin or two that the man has every intention of continuing your acquaintance. It is more than evident he appreciates your company and, I vow, I have never seen a man as respectful of a woman's thoughts and opinions."

"I cannot say he appreciates my thoughts entirely." She held up a hand, spacing her thumb and index finger an inch apart. "I'm afraid he thinks me a bit deranged."

"You most certainly are not deranged, Harriet Mosley."

Through the door they heard Beatrice Pruett moan. "Eliza, is that you? I'm feeling weak." Then in a much less frail voice, "Did you find out anything about the shot we heard?"

"You'd be surprised," Lizzie said, "how much I know about the mentally unsound."

43

The mystery of the blackmailer solved, Benedict found himself struggling with a plausible excuse to approach Harriet. As they shared a somber dinner with the house—a meal that might have been more pleasant were it not for Mrs. Pruett constantly bringing up the matter of Oscar Randolph—he watched his Harriet. She ate with effortless grace, tried to change the topic of conversation once or twice, and said things to Eliza Pruett from the corner of her mouth that made the younger woman lift her linen napkin to hide her grin.

It had been easy before, when he could approach her with some pretext of investigating a rumor or hunting diaries. Since the capture of Randolph, Benedict found himself recalling he had never been particularly comfortable making conversation with women. Even his sisters had always made a point to complain he never understood them.

As they retired to the parlor for drinks, he tried edging closer and debated topics of conversation. He had nearly settled on a discussion of books when he remembered what had recently occurred to her favorite author.

It was absurd, really, his inner struggle. Especially considering in the hours before dawn he had roused to find his hand cupping her soft breast and his knee snuggled comfortably between her thighs.

Like a sudden flash in the dark, he remembered her gift with cards and thought he might challenge her to another game. He could make a bet he would not lose. Perhaps offering to take Harriet on a ride tomorrow if she won. He had been about to push off from the wall where he leaned to make his mentally rehearsed move, when Harriet rose from her settee and wished everyone a pleasant evening. Offering him only a brief, noncommittal smile, she moved past and from the room.

To preserve her good name, Benedict did not permit himself to immediately follow her from the room. He shared a glass of scotch with Latimer, had a brief conversation with the younger Pruett woman in which he tried to focus on her questions about his career. When he finally excused himself, Eliza wore a secretive, knowing smile.

On his way from the room, he pocketed a deck of playing cards that had been left out for use. He had spent too long coming up with his scheme, he could not give it up now. Like a youth stepping out to ask his first young lady to dance, Benedict tugged at his jacket and ran his palms down his waistcoat. Halfway up the stairs, he removed his specs, polished them, and told himself he really was acting foolish. Crazy to be nervous when about to encounter a woman he had been undressed with—pleasantly so—on more than one occasion. The thought had him grinning as he lifted a hand to knock at her chamber door.

The door opened before his knuckles made contact with wood.

"Benedict," Harriet greeted, looking from his raised fist to his face. "Come to blows, have we?"

"I was about to knock." He thought it might have been an obvious, if not stupid, thing to say. She made it even more difficult for him with her appearance.

Prepared for bed, she was in her night rail and barefoot. The golden highlights in her hair had been bound into two loose braids, one very much lopsided, hanging over her shoulders. Her nose and cheeks were pink, and from the scent of flower petals that hung over her, freshly scrubbed.

He realized he wasn't saying anything, was only staring at Harriet and thinking he would very much like to do nothing more than that for the rest of his life, when she saved him.

"I had remembered," she said, "that man with the pistol clobbered you in the head. Are you injured, sir?"

"I hadn't even thought about it." He lifted a hand, feeling for any sore spots. He found it not far from his temple and winced.

"Why don't you come in and let me have a look." Harriet stepped back from the door.

"Benedict," Harriet said, brows drawing together a little, "why are you grinning like that?"

He looked at her from the corner of his eye as he closed the door behind them. The odd grin disappeared, though the clenching of Benedict's jaw suggested it was taking considerable effort on his behalf.

"Benedict?"

"Truth told, Harriet, I spent most of the evening scheming to place myself in your company. I had not imagined you would invite me in."

She pursed her lips, and then pointed to a chair.

"Sit," she ordered, carrying over a taper. He obeyed her order silently and allowed Harriet to manhandle him, cupping the base of his head to tilt him forward so she might have a better look at his scalp.

She made a sound, the vexed clucking of a mother hen, but her fingers were gently sifting through the thick hair above his brow. "There is blood, Benedict. A knot and a small cut. Does it not hurt?"

"A dull ache, nothing more," he said to her breasts.

Harriet sighed. It was annoying, she thought as she went to the ceramic washbowl and dipped a folded cloth into the water inside, that the man could capture a blackmailer and go about his day without a concern for his own person.

The words parted her lips before she knew she would say them, wringing lukewarm water from the cloth before turning to face him. "Who takes care of you when I am not around?"

"No one." His eyes were amused behind the gleaming lenses of his spectacles. "I imagine no one thinks I need the care. I do well for myself."

Harriet shook her head as she returned to him. "Everyone needs someone to love them." She gave a silent gasp at the feelings her words betrayed. She saw Benedict go rigid, the laughing gleam disappearing from his eyes, and Harriet quickly focused on applying the damp cloth to his bruised skull.

His hands moved, coming up to rest gently on her hips as she ministered to his wound. His thumbs stroked her sides and she bit her bottom lip.

"Did I have to scheme," he said to the floor as she tilted his head downward, "to share your company, Harriet?"

"No," she said. She smiled a bit, imagining no one had ever put considerable thought into being close to her. Well, perhaps the strange gent with her stocking tied about his neck . . .

"You only had to knock," she said. "I would have let you in."

Benedict's head lifted and she clutched the washcloth in both hands against her.

"I wanted to speak to you about something important."

"Sir Randolph?"

"You and I."

"Oh? What is it we need to discuss?"

"Leaving this place, returning home to London." His fingers shifted to her waist and gave a gentle squeeze. "I have been entertaining myself with plans of you and I there. Making a home together."

Harriet stared at him and he fixed his gaze again, unseeing, on her breast. "You perhaps think our companionship a fluke brought about by the strange circumstances of the blackmailer and the adventure that came with it. I thought we could spend some time together once we returned to Town, so you might learn that what we have is no momentary thing—as I have already come to understand." He cleared his throat. "It would give me time to court you, Harriet, without the excitement of arrows in darkened graveyards and men in hoods. I have never done such a thing before, but I imagine if I applied myself I would do well." He chuckled dryly. "I have captured a band of thugs who once terrorized the streets of London, and hunted down a man who brutalized several prostitutes on the west side. I should hope with a little effort I could convince the woman I care about to marry me."

Harriet carried the washcloth back to the basin, Benedict rising to his feet behind her. She smiled with her back to him and then took in a great sobering breath.

"Benedict," she began as she turned, "do you think me a madwoman?"

He lifted a brow above the rims of his specs. "You mean you must be mad to marry a Bow Street Runner with as little to offer as a small town house and a modest income?"

She scowled at him for bringing up such nonsense as income. She tugged at the sleeves of her night rail, barely reaching her wrists. "I mean, I have on more than one occasion seen the specters of long-dead individuals roaming this estate, not to mention the graveyard."

"And?" His expression was thoughtful, his brows drawing together as he rested his hands on his hips.

Harriet stared at him. "And nothing, I suppose. You do not believe me."

Sensing the seriousness lurking behind Harriet's glib words, he scratched his head and winced when he hit the space she had so carefully cleaned. "Harriet, I believe you saw something. A trick of the light, perhaps, or furniture in shadows that reminded you of the stories we heard of Lady Annabelle and Rochester."

"I saw a pirate." She lifted her chin, well aware she was goading him into something beyond his calm, measured tones. "On one occasion, he was so close I could smell the sea on his dead skin. His good wife reached out to me with a badly burned hand, pleading for help that I could never give."

"Harriet, what are you trying to do to me?" He scowled.

She stared at him, shook her head. "I want you to admit you do not believe me."

He was immobile, his chest not even moving with his breaths. A muscle ticked in his jaw and his deep brown eyes were hard. It was, she thought, the face of a hardened man who could capture bands of thugs and men who brutalized women.

He said, "I do not believe in ghosts."

Harriet nodded, took in a great breath and, when it left in a shuddering sob, squeezed her hands into fists.

"Harriet." Benedict reached for her, arms wrapping around her shoulders familiarly.

She buried herself against him easily and the comfort in his hold made her release another sob. He squeezed her tighter.

"But you saw the fire," she said against him, tears dampening his shirt. "You saw it. I know you did."

He sighed. They were nearly the same height when Harriet wore no shoes; his words brushed her cheek. "You don't know, Harriet, but unusual events, excitement, can make people see things strangely. I've seen it in my work. Everyone says the highwayman who robbed the carriage at gunpoint was wearing a black shirt, black pants, and black boots, when we know he wore brown boots."

She was exasperated and embarrassed with herself. "Benedict, I've no idea what you're talking about."

He gripped her arms tightly, pushing her away so he could look in her eyes. "What would you have me do? I will not lie to you. I care about you too much to pretend I believe in something I do not."

Harriet looked down at her bare feet between his boots, took a deep breath, nodded. She lifted her hands to wipe at her damp cheeks, gratefully accepting the handkerchief Benedict pressed into her fingers.

She faced him and Benedict's expression suggested he found her forced smile less than convincing.

"You're right. I would not want you to lie." She

sighed, puffing out her cheeks as she did so, and stepped away from him. "It's been a long day, Benedict. If you'll excuse me I think I should like to go to sleep now." She opened the bedchamber door and stood aside so he could exit. "You should get some rest yourself and be careful with your wound."

He watched her a long moment, and when she said nothing more, he slipped past her and out into the hall. "Harriet . . ." He turned to face her.

She smiled at him, pressed a kiss to his mouth, and against his cheek she said, "I do love you, Benedict."

Before he could reach for her, she closed the door. Forehead resting on the cold wood, palms pressed to the door on either side of her as if she feared to move them would be only to open the door again, Harriet felt her heart break into a million pieces inside her.

The day dawned as a contrast to the one before. The pink-and-gray sky was already bright with the promise of sun when Benedict awoke. He rose as a man on a mission might. He had fallen asleep pondering the strange goings-on with Harriet and awoke knowing he had to make things right or, at least, be certain everything was going to be okay.

Dressed and freshly shaved, he did not leave his room for the stairs or the promise of breakfast down below, but strode to the closed door opposite his.

"You only had to knock," she had said. *"I would have let you in."*

He knocked and the door swung open quietly. He knew something was wrong before he stepped inside, before his sharp gaze honed in on the neatly made bed and the wardrobe, open and empty. He pushed the chair at the writing table aside and dropped to his knees, looking beneath the desk to find the underbelly free of her journal.

His heart pounded savagely in his ears as he strode from the chamber, down the stairs to where he nearly collided with Lady Cruchely in the hall.

"Miss Mosley is gone," he said.

"Yes." Her tone was of forced brightness. It was evident that she was attempting to hide surprise that the woman's lover did not know she had gone. "She left early. Already had one of my drivers waiting for her in a carriage out front when Latimer and I came down."

"Mr. Bradbourne?"

Benedict hadn't realized young Eliza had closed in behind Dorthea, her footfalls as silent as a woman on tiptoes. She had a small piece of foolscap folded between her hands. She held it to Benedict.

"Harriet asked me to give this to you."

"Ah," Lady Cruchely said. She nodded and smiled. "This must be directions as to where and when she will meet up with you in London." Her tone bore a certainty that did not reach her eyes.

Benedict took Harriet's note to his room. Sat in the chair across from the bed they had shared more than once and stared out the window for a long time, the single sheet of paper weighing heavily on his knee. Teeth pressed together, heart in throat he opened the note.

Dear Benedict,

Please forgive me for departing so suddenly and without speaking to you in person. I knew I would not be able to do it, say good-bye that is, if I had to look into your eyes as I did it. It is hard enough knowing you still sleep only a floor above this parlor.

I can understand why you do not believe my ghost stories. You must understand, however, that I have very little in this world. Most of my clothes have been handed down. I share a home with my best friend for which I do not have to pay, as her kind parents will not take a penny from me. I am obliged to find employment in a small bookshop.

My word, such as it is, is all that I truly have in this world that has been and always will be mine alone. I always mean what I say and I have never backed down from a spoken promise. The idea of spending my life with a man who cannot accept me at my word weighs down on my heart far too much to allow it to happen.

Though I am sad that losing a friend brought you here, I'm so glad you came and we have had the opportunity to share this time together.

Love always,
Harriet

44

Oscar Randolph wore his customary smile as he was led to the wagon, large brutes with batons hanging from their belts on either side of him. His features were untroubled and there was a jaunty twist at the ends of his mustache. Were it not for the shackles, one might think him a man on an evening stroll. He watched the first snowflake of winter teeter slowly down from the night sky, only looking away when the wagon was opened and a uniformed man stepped down.

Randolph's smile froze, and for a moment he lost the composure that had governed him throughout his sentencing. He might not have recognized Bradbourne looking so severe in his black uniform coat, his features hard and cold, did he not see the man wear the same expression on the foggy day the damnable Mr. Hogg had threatened Harriet and then tried to ride Benedict down.

Randolph winced, recalling the blood that stained Hogg's hood after a single blow from Bradbourne. "Come to bash my skull in?" he inquired with all the politeness he could muster.

"Don't think I haven't considered it." Moonlight gleamed across the other man's spectacles and made his eyes unreadable.

The two guards all but lifted Randolph into the wagon and latched his shackles to a ring in the floor. The great mountains of men lumbered away with murmured discussion of where they would stop for a pint on their way home.

Bradbourne closed the door, rapped on the roof three times before settling in the hard bench across from Randolph. The wagon rocked into motion, yet the younger man remained still as stone.

"I know you hate me, Bradbourne," Randolph said after they shared an uncomfortable silence for some time. "I do not blame you. I must admit, the fact pains me more than the idea of being locked away. You are a good man and the men you hate must be of the foulest sort."

Bradbourne was silent, his features unreadable in the meager light of a hanging lantern.

Randolph leaned back into the wall. "Does she hate me too, my dear Miss Mosley?" When Bradbourne did not respond, he continued. "Will you tell her that I never meant any harm toward her person or anyone for that matter?"

"Tell that to the man you shot in the back." Benedict was blunt.

The old man ignored the gibe. "I very much appreciated her company and I would offer no fallacies to my dearest fan. You will tell her, Bradbourne?"

Bradbourne shifted and Randolph saw his jaw clench. The silence stretched so long he was sure the Runner would say nothing, then: "She never wants to see me again."

Randolph's shout of laughter made his companion wince. "She's madly in love with you!"

"Harriet"—the name came roughly from his throat—"made it very clear she would not spend another moment of her life with me."

"And you'll let it go at that?" Randolph laughed again. "You know, I had thought that if I had a son I would want him to be like you. Now I must reconsider. No son of mine would allow something so dreadfully dull occur, especially in his romantic life."

Bradbourne scowled at him. "What would you have me do—blackmail her into being with me?"

"That would be better than doing nothing at all." He shook his head. "True, our dear Harriet is an original, but she *is* still a woman. All women want to be wooed and made to feel important."

"I told her I would court—"

Randolph roared at the roof. "*You told her you would*—God save her from such excitement!" He abruptly leaned forward on his bench, his expression serious. "Look here, Bradbourne. Harriet loves you. She practically told me so while we were at Rochester. And if your reaction toward her then and your sour disposition now is any indication, you love her as well." The wagon was drawing to a halt, but Randolph showed no sign he was aware they were closing in on the prison that would be his home for the rest of his life. "When things like this happen, you do not offer to court a lady and you bloody well do not simply accept her excuses not to see you again. You go after her and you make her yours forever." He sniffed with dignity. "A man doesn't have to write love sonnets to know that."

A new guard, built much the same as the men who

shuffled Randolph to the wagon, threw open the door of the conveyance and prepared to remove him.

"Shall I take the prisoner, sir?" he asked Bradbourne.

"Not yet." Now Benedict leaned forward. "He has something I want." When the old man blinked in puzzlement, he grinned. "I never said I wasn't going to go after her, Randolph. I just needed to find something before I did it."

From the Journal of Harriet R. Mosley

After much consideration, I have decided to renege on those things I wrote a few nights ago. I very much do not wish the Rochester estate had burned to the ground a hundred years ago, taking with it any notion that I would ever present myself there so many years later. I do not wish Sir Oscar Randolph had never existed, and this includes his writing which—despite his felonious actions—I am compelled to love still, and those acts of blackmail that came to involve Mr. Benedict Bradbourne.

As to the latter, I do not wish I never met the man. I love Benedict. He might very well have been and continue to be the only man I ever love. One day I may grow to appreciate the fact that we shared a few exciting days together. In the meantime, I will have to deal with the fact there is a pain in my chest like a thousand needles being pressed down by a great, suffocating weight.

Harriet had heard the downstairs door open and close as she began to write in her journal and suspected that it was Mr. Maxwell Darcy paying a call on Augusta as he did on a daily basis. She was surprised, a few minutes later, when there was a light rapping at her chamber door.

She considered pretending to be asleep, though afternoon sunlight filled her room.

"Harriet," a voice not Augusta's said. "I know you are awake. I am coming in." The door opened silently and a woman with calm bay-colored eyes stood in the threshold. It was the same woman who had watched over her appropriation of the notorious *Book for Lovers* more than a month before.

"Hello, Abby, you look well. Marriage suits you, it seems."

The other woman's lovely nose wrinkled. "Calvin and I have been fighting. He insists I order him about as if he were a servant."

"He *was* your servant," Harriet pointed out.

"I think"—Abby nodded—"it might have been better had we remained on an employer-employee relationship."

Harriet thought about Abby's husband, a marquis whom she had met under the guise that he was a butler. Calvin Garrett was lean and muscular and handsome in a manner that had made Harriet wish, for the first time in her life, she had enough funds to warrant a servant.

She grinned. "Including the romantic benefits, of course."

"Of course." Abby grinned in return before sobering. "Augusta and I are going to a café Emily recommended near the park. You will come with us, yes?"

Harriet made a face. "I do not think I—"

Abigail patiently lifted a hand to stop her mid-excuse. "You have been holed up in your chamber since your return. Everyone is worried about you, most of all Augusta who guards your privacy so fiercely I had to argue with her to come up these stairs." Abby shook her head. "I know what heartache feels like, but you cannot allow yourself to be miserable forever."

It would, Harriet thought, have been easier to argue with a woman who had not been in a terrible carriage accident that left her with a brutally misaligned leg and abandoned by the man she loved.

The street and walkways were busy, on the verge of being crowded. Women shopped, carrying stacked boxes or being followed by maids carrying boxes, and men strode briskly from their places of employment with their hats affixed neatly atop their heads and an occasional issue of the *Post* folded under an arm.

As soon as they were able, the three women quickly maneuvered themselves from Park Lane to the calmer pathways of the park. Harriet walked between her friends, relieved that they had finally ceased with their worried looks and careful pats on her back. She thought on the next occasion she returned from a holiday— if there ever was another occasion—and Augusta asked how well she enjoyed herself, it would be best if she did not promptly burst into tears.

"I daresay," Abigail murmured under her breath, "that is the first woman I've seen taller than you, Harriet."

"Indeed it is," Augusta agreed, awestruck.

Harriet made a face, following the direction of the women's gazes. "You needn't sound so surprised that such a beast exists."

Augusta giggled.

Harriet frowned, watching as the stranger in the wide-brimmed bonnet and pink shawl moved down the path that would connect with theirs only a few feet ahead. The gown fit the other awkwardly, even worse than Harriet's gowns fit her. When one side of the shawl slipped down, it was to expose a cap sleeve not only too short, but too tight. The material of the burgundy gown strained at the seams as the stranger who approached shifted the shawl back in place. Harriet's eyes went wide as she caught a glimpse of a surprisingly large bicep.

"That is a man," she hissed so only her companions could hear.

"What?" Augusta was incredulous, and as the stranger whose gender was in question moved into the grass—in a very gentlemanly manner—as they passed, the three women craned their necks watching him. He returned their stares without concern, a silken reticule dangling from one gloved hand.

They faced forward again in unison, more than the corner of one mouth twitching.

"That was a man," Augusta said.

"Or the strangest woman I've ever seen," Harriet said.

"Not with a beard growing in." Abigail, normally calm and composed, trembled with repressed laughter. "I saw a bearded woman once at a carnival when I was a little girl."

"Nice. Now I'll be checking my face in the mirror each night and borrowing Calvin's razor."

"What do you suppose"—Augusta looked back over her shoulder—"he was about, dressing like that?"

"Perhaps he enjoys it."

Harriet gave a delicate snort. "I do not like to wear stockings, and I have to. I cannot imagine anyone dragging them on daily for the pleasure of it."

She, like Augusta, turned slightly to look back at the strange fellow. At the same moment two young men clad in dark attire came at the man from the opposite direction. One of the men slammed the would-be lady in the chest and the other tore the reticule from his gloved fingers.

Augusta gasped beside her as Harriet spun around, both surprising Abigail who hadn't noticed the attack.

"Halt!" the gown-clad man shouted in a masculine timbre.

The youth who had hit him was noticeably taken aback and, using surprise to his advantage, the man grabbed him. The other young man, still holding the purse, ducked around the two and took off at a run in the women's direction.

"Bloody hell," Harriet said as he ran right for Abby, who would not bounce back as easily as the large man from a physical blow. Without thinking, she shifted to stand before her friend.

She held her breath, bracing for the oncoming blow of the running man, when movement caught the corner of her eye. From a dense growth of foliage another man appeared, not dressed in a gown but a black uniform. He ran fast, and before the thief collided with Harriet, the uniformed man slammed into him with his full weight.

Augusta let out a brief shout as the two tumbled past her, brushing her skirts. The younger man—now that Harriet saw him closely, she thought he might be all of seventeen years—was struggling as soon as they hit the ground. It took a single blow of his captor's fist to knock him unconscious.

Harriet's heart started pounding in her ears before the uniformed man turned to them, even before he reached into his coat pocket to retrieve his spectacles.

45

"Benedict."

At the surprised whisper, he was sorely torn between grabbing the woman and covering her face with a thousand kisses or simply giving her a sound shake. With the single enunciation of the word, he recalled every instant she said it before, and his muscles tightened as memories of her crying his name while wrapping her thighs tightly about his hips and digging her nails into his back flooded his senses. Well aware he had the advantage—he had seen Harriet and her companions when they entered the park and might very well have been the cause of one of the pickpocket's escape had he not refocused on his task in time—Benedict gave her a moment to stare and come to grips with the fact they were again face-to-face. Perhaps she thought she would never see him again. There again, he had the advantage, as he knew full well he would not so easily let her leave him.

He wondered if her heart pounded as his and if she struggled to breathe. His gaze drifted to her bodice.

"You must be Mr. Benedict Bradbourne." A throat was cleared.

Benedict drew his gaze from the ragged rise and fall of Harriet's breasts, unconcerned with how his stare might appear.

One of the women accompanying Harriet stepped forward and held out her hand. She did so elegantly, without the awkwardness that might be expected of a woman with a brace on one leg. "Harriet has told us a great deal about you."

"Has she?" He lifted a brow as he took the woman's hand, bowing. He took some solace in Harriet speaking of him.

The woman nodded, her lovely eyes gleaming with polite interest. "You saved her from a terrible fall. I am Abigail Garrett"—she turned a palm to the woman opposite Harriet—"and this is Augusta Merryweather."

The latter smiled, but remained silent as her eyes moved from Harriet to Benedict and back again.

"We are in your debt, sir," Lady Garrett was saying as if she did not stand next to a friend shocked into silence and across from a man who had to force his gaze away from said friend.

"The pleasure was mine," Benedict said, and his eyes moved to Harriet's mouth.

Her lips parted on a breath.

"Bradbourne!" Douglass called behind him, and when he looked back, Benedict saw the other man had already climbed out of his wife's gown and shoved it in his bonnet. "Ready to take these blokes to jail, are you?"

Benedict nodded quickly and turned back to the three women before Harriet could manage controlling the flitting expression of heartache that crumpled her brows and made her eyes fill.

Benedict's jaw clenched. "Excuse me."

"It was nice to meet you, Mr. Bradbourne," Augusta Merryweather said.

"Miss Merryweather, Lady Garrett. Harriet." When he said the last, he smiled and held out his hand to the silent woman. It surprised her, his reach, and she automatically let her hand slip into his. Her gloveless fingers were chilled and soft against his as he gave them a gentle squeeze.

"I . . ." Her voice faltered and she paused to take a deep breath. The smile that she forced across her lips was a sad semblance to that which she had shared with him on so many occasions before. "I'm glad to see you are doing well, Benedict."

He couldn't help it; he stepped forward to close the space that separated them. Cheek pressed to her temple, he breathed against her ear, "I'm not doing as well as it might seem."

He turned away quickly, before he could embarrass them both by saying—or doing—anything more. He did not miss the trembling of lashes around green-brown eyes or the way Miss Augusta Merryweather gave a broad, excited grin.

The two young women walked arm in arm. They came around the corner in bright splashes of sky-blue and pale magenta and each wore exactly the same bonnet, save for the bows that matched their respective gowns. They paused a brief moment, consulting with the small scrap of paper one of the women held, and peered at the numbers on the charming town houses before their gleaming half boots snapped on.

Harriet glanced up briefly from her flowerpots and pail of fresh dirt for a moment, hearing the click of heels on the sidewalk. She wasted only a few moments

on being self-conscious as she surveyed the prome-
nading duo and their elegant style. Harriet wore a
kerchief around her head in the manner of a scullery
maid, donned to keep the hair out of her face as she
worked. She used the back of one gloved hand on her
cheeks to be certain dirt hadn't found its way there,
before focusing again on the pot resting against her
knees.

"Poor little flower," Harriet said sorrowfully to the
brown and rotten thing that vaguely resembled a
gnarled snake-creature. "You never had a chance."

Without ceremony, she dumped the dead flower—
which she told Abby she would never keep alive when
the woman had given it to her a month before—into
her pail of soil. She used a small spade to mix the dirt
and then began to shovel it again into the pot. With a
sigh, she turned her attention on the vibrant green
and spiky plant Abby had given her during her visit a
day before.

"This aloe plant," Abigail had said, "is the one plant
you cannot kill, Harriet Mosley. I know it."

Harriet, as she carefully picked up the small collection of plump leaves and wiggled them into the
refilled pot, had her doubts.

Two shadows fell across her in unison and she
looked up, shielding her face with an open glove.

"Lovely plant," said the woman with hair more red
than brown.

"Beautiful," the woman with hair more brown than
red concurred.

"It won't make it a week," Harriet said. She looked
between the two women who, despite their hair, had
matching brown eyes. "Are you lost?"

"I don't think so." One woman looked at the num-
bered stencils set above the door.

"We are looking for a lady by the name of Harriet Mosley," said the other.

"That's no lady," Harriet said, dusting her hands together as she climbed to her feet. "That's me."

The two women looked at each other, sharing some secret eye communication before smiling even brighter.

Harriet tugged off her gardening gloves—pretending not to notice how stained they were and quite hideous compared to the others' clean white gloves—and considered the other two women. They were pretty in a warm earthy way and, perhaps because of their matching appearance, a bit strange.

"Please, allow us to introduce ourselves," said the woman who was more brown than red. "My name is Olivia Starker and this is Sara Elizabeth Starker."

"We are two sisters who married two brothers," Sara Elizabeth said.

"I see." Harriet didn't really. "Have we met?"

"We've only heard about you"—Olivia inclined her head—"from our brother."

Sara Elizabeth explained, "Before we were wed, our names were Bradbourne, like Benedict."

Harriet stared at the sisters.

When she remained silent, Sara Elizabeth continued. "We very much wanted to meet the lady who had captured his heart."

Harriet stared at them. "Is this some sort of joke?"

"No," Olivia said, "but to hear Ben tell it, you are quite amusing to be around, Miss Mosley."

"Ben?" Harriet felt her discomfort swell as the pair watched her expectantly, as if waiting for her to perform some sort of humorous trick.

The sisters exchanged another quiet look and then Sara Elizabeth said, "The way my brother speaks of you, we could easily imagine the sort of woman you were and anticipate your becoming a part of our family. Such"—she inclined her head—"as it is."

"Do you hate Benedict, Miss Mosley?" Olivia baldly inquired.

"No." Harriet was surprised into speaking before thinking. "Quite the opposite."

The sisters nodded with identical satisfaction.

With a surprisingly small amount of shame to be discussing her personal affairs with two near-strangers, Harriet pointed at her chest. "Does he hate me?"

The matching smiles turned into a grin that was not unlike that of the brother who raised them. Olivia shook her head as Sara Elizabeth said, "He would not have asked us to come here and make certain you are well, did he hate you."

46

"I must admit," Harriet said, "I thought they were a bit odd."

Augusta looked up from her sewing, a tongue pressed delicately to the corner of her mouth for a moment. "Were they twins? Twins sometimes alarm people. Remember the Patchouli sisters? They always finished each other's sentences and shared secretive looks. They were shuddersome."

"No. I cannot say they were twins." She closed the journal in which she had been writing. "I suppose it was because they were so earnest in wanting to meet me."

"Because you were the one who captured their brother's heart, so they said."

Harriet looked over her shoulder at the woman. "I did not tell you that."

"I was listening at my window." Augusta shrugged without shame.

Pushing away from the writing table, Harriet paused. Her fingers wrapped tightly around the seat of her chair and she said, "Augusta?"

"Yes?"

"I miss him."

"Of course you do. He has captured your heart just as you captured his."

Instead of rising, Harriet shifted in her chair, sitting sideways and resting an arm on the back so she could see the other clearly. "I don't know what to do."

"We could have you arrested." Augusta snapped a piece of thread with a pair of silver scissors.

"He didn't believe me. Probably thinks I'm a lunatic."

Augusta looked up at her from beneath lowered brows. "And you say he wanted to spend the rest of his life with you still? He accepted you as you were. It was you who did not accept Bradbourne as he was—a non-believer, so to speak."

Harriet rested her forehead against her arm, squeezing her eyes shut.

"It is hard, I imagine," her best friend went on, "seeing the things he must see in his work. He probably encounters a great many ghouls in living form and has a difficult time believing in things he cannot touch or see himself. Though his sisters did not spell it out, it sounds as if they shared a rough beginning and Bradbourne had to grow up quickly to care for them. I doubt he had time to share ghost stories by firelight."

"I'm an idiot," Harriet said.

"No. But in my favorite books, women who have never been in love before tend to have a hard time of it once they succumb."

A knock sounded from the door not far from the parlor.

"I'll get it." Harriet pushed up from her chair, ignoring the sympathetic expression her best friend wore. She was aware of Augusta folding her sewing and following after.

Harriet opened the front door.

"Good evening," Benedict said.

Harriet slammed the door closed.

She spun around, pressing her back against the door as her heart bounded from the pit of her stomach to her throat. Her wide, alarmed eyes met Augusta's.

"What should I do?"

"Pray you haven't broken his nose." Augusta grinned from ear to ear.

"Not funny." Harriet's eyes frantically searched her surroundings. "Hold the door."

"Why?" The other woman was curious, but moved quickly to replace Harriet's bracing back with her own.

"I'll go out the parlor window." Harriet headed in that direction.

"But you just said—"

"Harriet," Benedict said through the door. He was not shouting, but somehow his voice permeated the wood. "Open this door or I will be obliged to break it in."

Harriet winced, coming to a halt and facing the entryway again. "You best do as he says, Augusta. He has surprisingly fine muscles for a man with spectacles."

Augusta nodded happily and swung the door open. "Good day, Mr. Bradbourne," she said as if the past minute hadn't occurred. "It is a pleasure to see you again."

"Miss Merryweather." He removed his hat and let his gaze travel to the woman standing farther inside.

"Sorry about that, Benedict." She forced a dry laugh. "A breeze took the door from my hand."

He lifted a brow and was silent, as if to bring attention to the still air.

"Were you in the neighborhood?" Harriet forged on.

"No. I live on the other side of town," Benedict said. "I came to see you."

Augusta cleared her throat. "If you both will excuse me, I'll put on some tea." She passed Harriet, giving her friend a meaningful look, before disappearing through the kitchen door.

Benedict still stood on the other side of the front door, eyebrow still raised.

Harriet stared, painfully aware of how much she had longed for his strong, calm features.

"Harriet."

"Yes?"

"Won't you invite me in?" He removed a small box from his jacket pocket. "I've brought you a present."

"You've a very nice home," Benedict said, and meant it.

The town house Harriet shared with Augusta Merryweather was a place of cluttered comfort. There was a wall lined with bookshelves, half of the books stories and poems of a romantic nature, the other half horrid novels of ghosts and goblins. He sat across from Harriet in a high-backed chair that had a patch on one arm. Harriet sat with back rod straight despite the fact her settee was lined with very soft-looking pillows.

Augusta appeared from the kitchen bearing a tray and two delicate teacups. She made no move to hide the suggestive smile she directed at her housemate and disappeared quickly after dispersing the tea.

"If you have anything personal to say, you'd best keep it to yourself as Gus will be listening at the door," Harriet informed him politely.

"I can leave if you prefer," Augusta called through the door.

"There is nothing I came to say to you that I would regret being heard by another," Benedict returned evenly.

He could have sworn he heard a delighted gasp from the other room.

"How have you been?" Harriet inquired courteously after a sip of tea.

"Abysmal," he said evenly, "for want of you."

She surprised him when she said, "I've missed you too, Benedict."

His eyes locked with hers of a lovely green and brown hue. Benedict rose, took Harriet's cup, and set it and his on a table before sitting down beside her. She shifted to face him.

"I'm afraid I was very silly when I left you. It's not your fault you do not believe—"

He placed his palm over her mouth. Her eyes crossed looking down at his fingers and he held back a laugh and the urge to take her in his arms. He dropped one hand as he produced her present with the other.

"Before you say anything, I want you to open your gift. It is a late birthday present."

She appeared puzzled, but nodded, carefully untying the ribbon Benedict had asked one of his sisters to knot for him. Box open, clear understanding flashed in Harriet's eyes as she extracted the watch from the box. The gold metal had darkened with age, the delicate scrollwork worn down from too much handling.

"You should not give this to me. It belonged to your best friend."

He said, "It does still."

Harriet looked up at him.

"Look at this." He forced himself to ignore the urge

to hold her and flicked the watch open with the brush of a thumb. "Can you read it?"

Harriet's brows crinkled as she tilted the watch into light coming in from the window.

"*To my beloved Warren,*" Benedict said. "*Yours always, Annabelle.*"

Harriet's smile was a beautiful thing, brighter than the sunlight streaming in across her features. "I was right."

"You were right. Whatever happened in that house so long ago, I don't believe Rochester killed his wife. If he was so cruel, I doubt she would have gone to such lengths to sneak about the village to get him a gift."

"Yes." Harriet nodded.

"But how did you know?"

She looked at him askance and Benedict took a deep breath.

"I've been thinking about it for as long as we've been apart. How did you come to know there had been no murders in that house and, more importantly, how did you get yourself out of those bonds Quinn tied about us? We could hardly move, certainly not enough to untie the rope. It only makes sense that something strange has been going on."

"Benedict, you do not have to."

"I know, but I do believe you, Harriet." He smiled at her. "Then again, a man in love would believe the sky green and the grass blue if the object of his desire insisted it was so."

Harriet cupped his face, looking at him with love that made him curse the time that had passed before he found her, and covered his mouth with hers. His fingers slid deep into her thick hair as his mouth parted and it was as if the days they spent apart had never occurred.

When he drew away, Harriet's lips were red and damp and her eyes luminous.

"I've missed you, Benedict. So much that I decided it didn't matter if you thought I was crazy, as long as we were together."

"Oh." Benedict tried and failed to keep his tone serious. "I still believe you're a madwoman at heart."

Harriet made a face. "And what does that say of you, being loved by a woman such as me?"

His features sobered. "I'm one of the happiest men in the world."

Harriet looked as if she would cry until she heard the delighted, if very unladylike, shout from the other room.

Epilogue

They had nearly completed their journey on the
road to Rochester Hall when Benedict nonchalantly
reached for the *Post*, lying on the seat across from
them. He opened the paper with more noise than was
necessary and cleared his throat.

"'The eagerly anticipated novel of infamous story-
teller Randal C. Shoop entered bookstores early yesterday morn. The crowds rushing to buy the book
were the largest on record for a Shoop novel. One can
only guess the reason being the author's recent incar-
ceration after having been convicted of extortion and
murder under his real name, Oscar Randolph.'"

Harriet had been close to sleep, her head resting
against Benedict's shoulder and warm beams of sunlight resting along her cheeks from the window. She
opened her eyes, peering out at the passing land-
scape, stark tree limbs and a carpet of white snow.

"Benedict, I know of the new book and have no
interest. You needn't—"

"'Devotees appear less than concerned as to how
the imprisoned writer found the means to continue
his craft,'" Benedict continued to read, as if she

hadn't spoken. "'Readers of this latest novel proclaim it, as a matter of fact, to be his best yet. Many believe this is due to the fact private detective Viktor Channing may have met his match in an intelligent and amusing heroine. Mary Elise Roth is a pleasant change from the damsels in distress who normally grace Shoop's pages. She is independent, quirky, and tends to wear clothing that never fits quite right. This writer will not go so far as to betray the ending of the novel, but Mary Elise is sure to capture the reader's heart as fully as she does Channing's.'"

Benedict lowered the paper; a single brow lifted as he looked down at the woman snuggled against his side.

The carriage was drawing to a halt, packed snow giving way to stone as they closed in on the estate.

"He was not toying with me when he asked my opinion," Harriet said.

"Indeed, he was not." Benedict inclined his head. "Even I caught the switch of letters from your name to Mary Elise Roth."

Harriet grinned.

The carriage came to a stop and Benedict leaned forward to lift the edges of her wool scarf to her chin before opening the door. His boot heels crunched in the crisp snow as he turned and offered a hand.

"Perhaps," he said as she took his arm, "as you permitted him to use you as a muse, Sir Randolph will be so kind as to suggest you to his publisher once your book is finished."

Harriet's cheeks warmed despite the chill in the air. "Benedict, really, I've only worked on a few pages. It might not be worth publishing."

"I certainly enjoyed the few pages I read."

Harriet ignored his grin as he so slyly referred to the

night before, when they shared her much-too-small bed. She had rested her naked, exhausted frame mostly atop Benedict as he read in the candlelight.

The door to the estate opened before they could reach it. Dorthea and Latimer had left for the Season, but Millicent was kind enough to take their coats and pass on a lantern before they moved up the stairs.

When they reached the charred opening that had once been another set of stairs, Harriet was clutching the pocket watch Benedict had given her in one fist. She looked at him, "You are certain you do not mind?"

He squeezed her hand. "It is yours, Harriet, to do with as you wish. I still think I should go with you."

She shook her head. "I need to be alone." When he scowled, she kissed his mouth. "Do not worry. I shan't be gone long."

"See to it you are not," Benedict said, "or I will come down for you."

Harriet slipped the watch into her sleeve as Benedict gripped her hands to lower her into the dark chasm. When her feet touched the stone below, she reached up for the lantern. She could still make out Benedict's features above.

"Be careful," he said.

It was colder down here than in the house. Harriet walked quickly down the corridor, counting doors until she reached the remains of the study Lady Annabelle and her husband frequented. Setting the lantern on the dust-carpeted floor, Harriet surveyed the shadowed room and drew the watch from her sleeve.

"I'm trying to write a book," she said, wincing at the loudness of her voice. "It's about you. I have found some records at the museum and a few from private collectors. Lady Cruchely has been so kind as to loan me your letters and I'll use these to gather information about your lives." She felt very much like a lunatic, talking to the empty space. Taking a deep breath, she finished quickly, "I will make it clear there was no murder here."

Harriet focused on a crack in the wall, perhaps made by the settling of burned wood and the expanding of stone from the heat. She slipped the watch inside, pushing it as far as her fingers would allow.

"I thought you might want this back," she whispered.

Harriet returned to Benedict and he made quick work of lifting her out of the darkness. They thanked Millicent again for her kindness before taking their leave. Their carriage still waited in the drive, but as they walked toward it, Harriet gripped Benedict's arm tighter, slapping his coat sleeve with her free hand.

"Benedict." She dug her feet in the snow, looking up over her shoulder. "Benedict, look."

He followed the direction of her pointing to the window in the far right corner of the house. Workers had filled the opening with glass since they had left, and because the day was overcast, one could see through the windowpane.

They were there for a heartbeat, the man in the wide-sleeved shirt and the lovely woman who appeared to be clutching something—a watch perhaps—to her heart. Then they were gone.

"Benedict," Harriet said as he put an arm about her shoulders and urged her toward the carriage. "Benedict, did you see that?"

"No." He did not meet her wide-eyed stare. "And you didn't either."

* * *

From the Journal of Harriet R. Bradbourne

I visited Oscar Randolph today and cannot say he looks like a man suffering at the hands of the authorities. Benedict knows a gentleman employed at the prison and I was thus permitted to join Randolph in his room with no supervision. He has only a cot, table, and chamber pot in the small cell. But there are several quills, bottles of ink, as well as some fine paper.

He said he had read the announcement in the Post *and was very happy for Benedict and I, then asked when little Benedicts and Harriets would be about. I told him of my writing and he sounded genuinely interested. Before I left, he gave me a small sheet of paper with the name of the gentleman who handles his writing affairs on it.*

Other than that news, there is little else to write of. I am settling well in Benedict's home and growing accustomed to the frequent gatherings with his sisters and the Ferguson family. It is quite strange to switch from having a few loyal friends and no family to speak of, to a place such as this.

Benedict has made no comment as to my continued employment of sorts at the bookshop and will even accompany me on the days he does not work. All my friends love him; even Emily calls him by his first name.

I must admit, when I invited Lizzie to live with us after her letter sharing the final battle she had with her mother, I thought I was doing her a good turn. She is fast becoming a much necessary member of our household, however. Once she was obliged to suffer my terrible cooking one night too many, she began to cook the evening meals, and breakfast on the weekends. She spends most of the day cleaning the house and when we try to give her money for her hard work, she uses it to purchase food or household items. By the new gowns and expensive jewelry she wears, I am guessing she finds her own kind of financial success elsewhere. She has begun to stay out very late at night since I taught her how to play cards.

Benedict has been so kind to ask some of his fellow Runners to keep an eye on her when able, and young Garfield Ferguson II has become a sort of admirer.

I'm afraid Benedict comes home on occasions few and far between to share with me some exciting event at his work. Many times the criminals he encounters are little more than pickpockets and drunks, and though I try hard not to look disappointed when he shares with me no tales of exotic mystery, he can read my mind and laughs all the same.

Lizzie has been telling me about a castle in Scotland that is supposedly haunted by a medieval madman and a flame-haired banshee. I will bring up the idea of travel tonight after dinner and will like as not have to coax Benedict a bit. Unless, of course, I wait until much later than dinner when he is most contented and agreeable to my desires. I will have to be careful not to give in to my more urgent needs before speaking of the castle. Benedict makes it very difficult sometimes, and on more than one occasion I have been forced to pull a pillow over my face, so Lizzie could not hear my screams. I think he knows this and enjoys it to an awful extent.

For a man with spectacles, he really is quite a scoundrel.